Praise for

GAME ON

"Readers looking for a new author to try out will enjoy this emotional, sensuous, well-written story set around football. Her pairing of football bad boy Shane Devlin with serious, business-minded Carly March makes for an entertaining read." —*Night Owl Reviews*

"Solheim's gift for creating empathetic characters and heartbreakingly plausible scenarios keeps the narrative moving on at a fast clip, leading to a heart-pounding finale that sets up the planned sequels." —*Publishers Weekly*

"Tracy Solheim's book resounds with sharp, witty dialogue and a plot that has many unexpected twists and turns while remaining so grounded that I got lost in the story." —*Dark Faerie Tales*

Foolish Games

TRACY SOLHEIM

BERKLEY SENSATION, NEW YORK

THE BERKLEY PUBLISHING GROUP
Published by the Penguin Group
Penguin Group (USA) LLC
375 Hudson Street, New York, New York 10014

USA • Canada • UK • Ireland • Australia • New Zealand • India • South Africa • China

penguin.com

A Penguin Random House Company

FOOLISH GAMES

A Berkley Sensation Book / published by arrangement with Sun Home Productions, LLC

This one is for my own William Anthony.
Thanks, Dad,
for gifting me with your love of reading.
I miss you every day.

ACKNOWLEDGMENTS

As always, I am grateful to the wonderful people who continue to support me in making my dreams come true.

Cindy Hwang, thank you again for your suggestions and guidance that made this book the best it could be. Kristine, Courtney, Amy, and the rest of the staff at Berkley, who lent their talents to crafting and promoting this book, thank you. It is a pleasure to work with you all.

Thank you to my agent, Melissa Jeglinski, for always being there to talk me down, no matter what the issue.

Writing can be a solitary business, so I am thankful for the author friends I've made along the way. In particular, Christy, Susan, Laura A., Laura B., and the ladies of Women Unplugged and Romancing the Jock.

Thanks to the women of Talking Volumes Book Club, the gym rats, the barn moms, the band moms, and my Epiphany People, for running interference when real life intersected with deadlines.

Melanie Lanham, thank you for being my beta reader. Somebody's got to do it, right?

Thanks, also, to Mary Mullenbach for answering your phone the many times I call with crazy questions about grammar and word choice.

Jackie Pierce, thank you for your dogged promotion of my career.

Kim McNamara and the wonderful staff at Read It Again Books, thanks for supporting a local author.

Finally, thanks to my family, near and far, for believing in me.

And to the three family members who endure the most torture during this process—Greg, Austin, and Meredith—I couldn't do this without you. I love you.

One

Paternity.

The word reverberated inside Will Connelly's head, pummeling his temples until they began to throb. He clenched his jaw firmly in place, at the same time willing his knuckles to release their death grip on the leather chair. It was an effort to appear unfazed despite the fact the supposed purpose of the meeting had taken a 180-degree turn. If ever there was a time for Will to put on his game face, this was it.

The U.S. senator sitting across the conference table was sadly mistaken if he thought he was a match for Will's trademark inscrutable stare. There was a reason he was known as William the Conqueror throughout the NFL: Will Connelly tore through offenses relentlessly, all the while wearing a stoic expression that caused many an opponent to declare that the Pro Bowl linebacker had ice water running through his veins.

The men seated on either side of him, however, weren't as practiced at remaining cool. Both shifted uneasily in their chairs.

"Come again?" Roscoe Mathis, Will's agent, wasn't one to sit patiently while someone railroaded his client.

The senator's smug grin didn't waver, his gaze fixed on Will. "I said that Mr. Connelly might want to rethink his position as the national spokesman against deadbeat dads. He's been named the father in a rather . . . extraordinary paternity request."

"Now just wait one minute, Senator," said Hank Osbourne, the general manager for the Baltimore Blaze and Will's other companion. Hank was often referred to as the Wizard of Oz around the league because of his ability to quickly turn a team into a contender; his demeanor was normally as cool as Will's. But his tone implied his temper was on a short leash today. "You march us up to Capitol Hill, supposedly to ask questions about an alleged bounty scheme your committee is wasting taxpayer dollars investigating, and then you accuse my player with some cockamamie paternity suit? What kind of game are you playing here?"

The senator lunged forward in his seat. "Correction, Mr. Osbourne. I didn't invite you or Mr. Mathis here for this meeting. This business involves a personal matter between him"—he shot a finger at Will—"and me."

"Your summons was rather vague," Roscoe said. "We assumed it involved this witch hunt into Coach Zevalos's career."

Will's body tensed at the mention of Paul Zevalos, his former coach at Yale. After college, the coach took a defensive coordinator position in the NFL, bringing Will along as an undrafted rookie. Without Zevalos championing him, Will might never have seen a professional gridiron, much less become one of the league's most elite players. And now the world expected him to turn on his former coach.

Like hell he would.

Senator Stephen Marchione sank back into his padded leather chair. Somewhere near forty years old, the well-respected politician likely didn't have a daughter old enough to interest Will. And married women were off-limits in his book. Will relaxed slightly, confident that a mistake had been made. Extremely careful in his personal life and monogamous with the women he dated, he took precautions to prevent children. He had to. No child should be subjected to the childhood he'd endured.

A ripple of unease crawled up his spine, however, as he remembered a sensual encounter the night of his best friend's wedding. But that had been nearly a year ago. If the woman had conceived a child, she'd have made her claim long before today. Besides, the woman was Italian or French, the designer of the bride's wedding gown. It was unlikely she and the senator would cross paths. Reassured, he pretended aloofness by adjusting the cuff of his suit jacket as he waited for Marchione to continue.

The senator pinched the bridge of his nose and sighed. "You're right. Congress shouldn't be wasting time and money investigating professional sports. That's for the leagues to police. But I'm in the minority, and this is politics. Connelly, you don't want to testify against your old coach and I can impede the committee from forcing you to do so. For the time being. In return, I need you to do something for me." He eyed the men seated beside Will. "Something I think both of us would like to keep private."

For the first time since entering the ornate conference room, Will spoke. "They stay." He wasn't sure what the senator was up to, but he wanted his agent and his boss as witnesses in case something went awry.

"Suit yourself." Marchione pulled a file folder out from the portfolio in front of him.

"Hold on." Roscoe pointed to a white-haired gentleman in a dark suit seated behind the senator. He was the only person to accompany Marchione to the meeting. "We'd like some assurances from your staff that whatever this is about, it'll remain private."

"That's Mr. Clem," the senator said. "He represents the child."

The room was silent for a moment while the men processed that statement. Will's temple throbbed harder as he realized another kid had been born a bastard. *Just like him.*

The senator's face was chagrined as he slid a photo across the table. Will's breath hitched as he caught sight of the alluring woman in the picture. Laughing, bright amber eyes dancing, she stood among several brides who towered over her curvy, petite frame.

Apparently, the senator did know the bridal gown designer.

Will silently contemplated the photo as his pulse ratcheted up several notches.

"I take it you recognize my little sister." The senator's voice sounded almost apologetic. "She designs under her mother's maiden name, J. Valencia. But her real name is Julianne Marchione."

He could feel the eyes of all the men in the room on him. Will was embarrassed to admit he and his mystery lover hadn't exchanged names. Hell, they'd barely spoken at all. His palms began to sweat as he pondered the ramifications of his one and only one-night stand. In the world of professional sports, men and women hooked up all the time, no strings attached. But not Will. He'd borne the shame of being the consequence of a one-night stand all his life. "Your sister didn't offer her name, Senator," he bit out. "In fact, she gave the impression she spoke little English."

Marchione winced as he leaned back against his chair. "Julianne is multilingual. But since she's as American as I am, she's perfectly fluent in English." He sighed. "She has a bit of a flair for the dramatic sometimes."

Will pushed back from the table and stalked to the picture window behind him, turning his back to the men in the room as he wrestled with his composure. The spring sunshine illuminated the Capitol against a bright blue sky, but he didn't notice the postcard picture in front of him. His brain was scrambling to make sense of the meeting.

"Does that flair for the dramatic include seducing a multimillion-dollar athlete to be her baby daddy?" Roscoe earned his enormous salary with that one question.

"My sister is a lot of things, but she is not promiscuous!"

Roscoe gave a snort. "Forgive me, Senator, but in this

business, women aren't always what they seem. Not even little sisters."

Will leaned his forehead against the warm glass of the window while Roscoe and the senator argued behind him. He dared not join in because in his heart, he wanted to believe the woman—*Julianne*—hadn't been a conniving seductress. Everything about that night lingered in his memory as a mystical, erotic fantasy. One he relived often in his thoughts, each time wondering if the encounter had been real or imagined.

He didn't have to wonder anymore.

The wedding reception had been over for several hours. A summer storm pummeled the coastline of Sea Island, casting the resort into an eerie darkness despite the fact it was still early evening. Will remembered an overwhelming feeling of restlessness. Being back among his childhood friends always made him that way. Despite their friendship and the acceptance of their families, Will always felt like an outsider. His best friend, Chase, had married his longtime sweetheart that morning. Will's other friend, Gavin, was off somewhere with his fiancée. And, once again, Will was alone.

He'd left his room to fill his ice bucket when he saw her wandering the hall, still dressed in the knockout red dress that had every man at the wedding doing a double take. She'd tried to remain unobtrusive throughout the event, but she was hard not to notice with her curves and that luscious mouth. She stopped a few doors from him, fumbling with her key card. Her door wouldn't open and she mumbled something in Italian. Will wondered if she'd been drinking more than just the club soda he'd heard her order all day.

"Here, let me try." He'd been raised in the South, after all.

Startled, she nearly dropped the key card. Will caught her hand and a jolt of electricity shot up his arm. At the time, he attributed it to the storm churning overhead. He tried the card unsuccessfully.

"You must have put it too close to your cell phone in your purse." He carefully handed the card back to her. "These things demagnetize easily. They can fix it at the front desk."

A savage bolt of lightning suddenly lit up the floor-length window behind Will, illuminating her face. She wasn't drunk, she was terrified.

"Hey." He gently took her elbow. "Why don't I walk with you downstairs to get this fixed?"

She said something that was a jumble of English and Italian, but he had no trouble picking up the gist: She hated storms. Just as they turned toward the elevator, another crack of lightning hit, knocking out the power, and the hallway was enveloped in blackness. She let out a little squeak and dug her fingernails into Will's arm.

"Change of plans." He maneuvered her back toward his room, where the door was propped open by the security lock. The blue glare from his laptop screen provided enough light to guide her over to the king-sized bed. As he eased her down, her eyes locked onto the storm outside the window. Lightning streaked across the dark sky. Will crouched in front of her, gently laying a hand against her cheek. "Shhh," he said, trying to reassure her. "It's gonna be okay."

Her stare darted between him and the storm raging on the beach, fear still paralyzing her face as she fingered a cross around her neck. There was no hope for it. Will lay down on the bed and gathered her in his arms, gently stroking her back.

At this point, things got hazy.

He wasn't sure who kissed who first, but when their lips met, something ignited within them both. She tasted of coffee and smelled of tropical flowers and he couldn't seem to get enough of her. Their clothes melted away, giving Will's hands and lips access to warm, soft skin. When he entered her that first time, she welcomed him, wrapping her legs around his hips and bringing him to near-perfect ecstasy.

The thunder and lightning were winding down the second time they made love, her fingers and mouth torturing his body before he found his release. The third time he took her, the storm had dissipated outside but continued to rage on between them as the electricity he'd felt in the hallway reached a fevered pitch. Will had never felt such an intense connection with any other woman.

Until she called out another man's name while climaxing. And then the condom broke.

When he woke the next morning, she was gone, the battered beach the only evidence of the previous night's storm. Will's psyche was as ravaged as the shoreline. His mystery lover had checked out of the hotel and disappeared without a word. As it turned out, she might have taken a lot more from him than a little piece of his ego.

Will took a deep breath and grabbed at his tie to loosen the stranglehold it had around his neck. He needed air. Roscoe and Hank were standing when Will turned to join them.

"You can't leave!" Mr. Clem threw his body in front of the double doors. "That boy needs you!"

Will felt his chest constrict. *A son. I might have a son.*

"Mr. Clem." Roscoe's voice sounded miles away as the world spun around Will. "We're not acknowledging anything without a paternity test."

"We don't have time for that!" Mr. Clem slammed his fist against the door as his face turned scarlet.

The senator slapped both hands on the table in frustration. "She doesn't want you to acknowledge the baby! She doesn't want a red cent from you. You never even have to see him."

Rage swarmed through Will as he rocked back on his heels. What the hell was going on? Who was this woman? If the boy was his, there was no way Will wasn't going to acknowledge him! Much less be a part of his life. A very big part.

Hank stepped in front of the senator, getting right in his face. "I'm going to ask you this one more time, Senator. What kind of game are you playing?"

"It's not a game. My sister never wanted Will to know about him. Her plan was to raise him herself. In Italy. But things have changed. Julianne needs your help." The senator's voice sounded like a plea.

Will barely heard Mr. Clem over the roaring in his ears. "She doesn't want your money!" The man practically wailed. "She wants your blood!"

Two

The monitors in the neonatal ICU beeped incessantly. Their sound, combined with little sleep and even less food, worked to numb Julianne Marchione into a zombielike state. She tried to refocus her thoughts and concentrate on the words her business manager, Sebastian Flanders, was saying, but her mind kept wandering to the incubator containing her four-week-old son, Owen. Her arms ached to hold him, but the disease poisoning his blood kept her baby confined to the NICU, tubes and wires marring his tiny arms and legs.

"Jules, sweetheart." Sebastian's British accent permeated the thick fog that surrounded her brain. "You don't have to do this right now. You shouldn't be making such rash decisions in the state you're in, love."

She gave her head a little shake and gazed over at the man across from her. The handsome black Englishman with the laughing coffee eyes had put as much blood, sweat, and tears into her career these past ten years as she had. His eyes weren't laughing today, though. They were fearful and apprehensive. Worst of all, Julianne saw pity reflected there.

They were seated at a round table in one of the private vestibules Children's Hospital provided for the families of its NICU patients. The small, windowless area was not quite a room; a curtained partition made up the fourth wall. Aside from the table and four chairs, the only other furniture was a sofa, too small and too hard to sleep on, and a television. She found it hard to conceive that anyone could watch TV while their child was so ill.

"I don't have a choice." Julianne's voice was hoarse. Her hand trembled as she picked up a pen and let it hover over the documents spread out on the table. "I don't have medical insurance. At least not the kind that will cover all of Owen's expenses. Selling JV Designs ensures me enough cash that"—her voice began to shake—"if Owen doesn't get a blood transfusion his body will accept, I can afford whatever treatment I need him to have to keep him alive." She didn't want to contemplate the alternative.

"Julianne," Sebastian coaxed. "There's still time. The father will come, love. And the doctor said there's a seventy percent chance he'll be a match. If that's the case, Owen will beat this and go on to give you gray hairs before you're forty. You don't need to sell. It's going to work out." He covered one of her hands with his and squeezed.

"I have to do this." Julianne was resolute. She no longer had the confidence Sebastian possessed. Owen was already being punished enough for the mistakes she'd made and the lies she'd told. It was only fair that she suffer, too.

Sebastian's voice was anguished. "They're going to take your designs and mass-market them."

Julianne smiled grimly as her eyes met Sebastian's. They both knew she hadn't sketched a single design in nearly six months. She'd begged off commissions as soon as she'd found out about the baby. Even if her pregnancy hadn't been difficult from the start, the guilt Julianne suffered had completely drained her creative juices. There was no telling when she'd get them back—if ever.

"Last I checked, Princess Kate bought clothes off the rack," Julianne quipped.

"Carly, help me out here!" Sebastian pleaded to the woman seated on the sofa behind her.

Julianne didn't have to turn around to feel the wave of disappointment emanating from her closest friend, Carly March Devlin. The two had met when both were students in boarding school nearly sixteen years ago. Theirs was a friendship deeper than sisterhood, born out of the shared experience of each losing their mother at a young age. But Julianne's lies and omissions these past several months had damaged their friendship. This morning's confession just might have pushed the relationship past the stage of irreparable.

She heard Carly rise from the sofa and closed her eyes to hold back the tears as her friend approached.

"Sebastian is right." Carly gently massaged Julianne's shoulders. "You're not thinking clearly right now. You're exhausted and worried about Owen. Now's not the time to be thinking about selling your company. Instead, you need to concentrate on taking care of yourself so you can take care of Owen." Carly hesitated. "Once Will gets here, he'll help you through this."

Julianne's shoulders sagged underneath the enormous weight of shame she carried. *Will Connelly.* What must it feel like to suddenly find out you have a child? Would he be furious? And what would he think of her?

She didn't have any answers because she knew so little about her son's father. Embarrassment washed over her as she thought of the meeting taking place in her half brother's office. She hoped Stephen wasn't too hard on him. Will, like Owen, was innocent in all of this. Not that her brother saw it that way. He was more concerned with the ramifications to his political career. The senator wanted Julianne and her illegitimate son out of the country and away from any reporters who'd yet to snoop out the story.

Carly's words also grated against Julianne's fragile confidence. She spoke as if Will would arrive on a white horse and snap his fingers, and miracles would happen. As if his blood would be a match. As if the man rumored to be as cold as ice would forgive her for not telling him he had a son. Of course, Carly knew Will better than she did, which made revealing Owen's paternity all the more difficult.

Julianne had never meant to put her friend in such a position. Mortified by her fling at a client's wedding with a man she barely knew, she kept it a secret from Carly. After the shock of discovering her pregnancy, she vowed to keep the baby and raise it herself. She had a successful business and the means to support a child comfortably. Avoiding Carly had been easy while her friend was preoccupied forging a relationship with her new husband, Shane, and his young brother, Troy. To make the deception work, Julianne remained in Italy, away from the prying eyes and a multitude of questions.

In the end, though, Julianne couldn't keep her secret any longer. Her son was born with advanced hemolytic disease, a dangerous blood disorder treatable with a transfusion. In most cases, blood from the standard blood bank was compatible. But Owen wasn't one of those babies; he needed blood from a parent. Julianne prayed she'd be able to cure her son without having to reveal the father's identity, but her prayers went unanswered. Owen's body rejected her blood transfusion. To save his life, she had to admit that her fling wasn't with a stranger, but with a man who happened to play football with her best friend's husband.

"And you shouldn't worry about the money," Carly said as she slid into the seat next to her. "Will is worth millions. He can certainly pay for whatever treatments Owen needs to get better."

Something snapped inside Julianne. She didn't want Will Connelly to pay for her son's medical care. Owen was *her* baby . . . her family. After her mother's sudden death, her father had abandoned her to a boarding school before remarrying and beginning a new life. One that didn't include any reminders of Julianne's late mother. Twelve years her senior, Stephen had a family of his own, leaving Julianne in a sort of purgatory between her two remaining family members. But she would always have Owen to love. And to love her back. Sharing him was not an option. Forcing the pen into her hand, she scrawled her signature on the contract.

"Well done, Carly. That was ever so much help." Sebastian's sarcasm shattered the awkward silence that followed the scratching of the pen on paper.

Julianne slid the contract across the table to him as Carly sat stunned, gaping at her.

"With that I think I'll walk across the street and fetch some of that inferior tea they serve at Starbucks." Anger and disappointment radiated off his body. He shoved the contract into his computer bag. "I'll need some fortification before I have to call Nigel and tell him we won't be spending our month in Tuscany this year, because your wedding gowns will now be made in China."

Sebastian stood abruptly and Julianne could tell it was costing him to hold the rest of his comments in check, but she was grateful he did. Her body and mind felt battle weary, and she wasn't sure how much more she could take.

"May I bring you ladies a tea?" Even furious, Sebastian was a well-mannered Brit.

Carly shook her head. She'd closed her mouth, her lips now pursed in an angry line.

"A skim latte for me, please." Julianne's voice shook slightly. She was a little leery at being left in the room with Carly, and she figured she'd need the caffeine after whatever was to come.

Sebastian stalked out of the room, and it was a few moments before Carly spoke. "I don't know who you are anymore."

Julianne leaped from the chair and began to pace the small room. "Well, a lot of things have happened to me lately. Maybe I've changed."

"All these years, you've been pretending, then?" Carly had always been the quieter of the two women and less confrontational, but she'd found her voice today. "Since you were fourteen, you've been planning your career as a fashion designer. You left art school after one semester to follow that dream. Five years later, you were established as one of the youngest bridal gown designers in the business. Your gowns have been worn by rock stars and princesses. And you just give it all up?"

"I'd do anything to save my son!"

"Oh no you don't!" Carly charged up from her chair. "This isn't about saving your son! If the doctors are right, Will Connelly's blood will save Owen. And he has enough money to pay the bills, too. This is about something else. I only hope it has nothing to do with Nicky."

"It's not about Nicky!" Julianne felt as if she'd been punched in the abdomen, her breath was so difficult to catch.

"Then tell me what it *is* about! Don't shut me out anymore. Tell me why you kept this all such a secret from everyone. *From me.*"

Julianne spun around to face her friend. "I can't tell you!"

"Why not?" Carly cried.

"Because if I tell you everything, you'll hate me!" The words were out of Julianne's mouth before she could stop them.

They stood in silence, the infernal monitors beeping in the background as the sounds of hospital personnel going about their business echoed beyond the curtained wall.

"Julianne Marchione," Carly finally said, pulling her friend into her arms. "I could never hate you."

They made their way to the sofa, where Carly settled Julianne's head on her shoulder. "Start at the beginning. I'm tired of guessing at this story," Carly said, stroking her friend's hair.

"I'm so ashamed and afraid you'll hate me once you hear everything," Julianne whispered.

"I promise I won't hate you, but I can't help you if I don't understand how all this happened."

Julianne sighed. "It was at Chase Jordan's wedding. I wanted you to come with me, remember?"

"I *will* hate you if you pin this on me," Carly cautioned.

Julianne let herself relax a little. "I'd had a migraine all week, so I was taking my medicine."

"The one that makes your birth control ineffective. I

think we covered this when you first told me you were pregnant. For the record, you were six months pregnant when you finally confessed, but we'll let that pass for now. Go on."

Guilt once again clamped onto Julianne's belly. "Well, the pills make me kind of woozy, too. I was careful not to drink, but for some reason the medicine seemed more potent than usual. I found out later I'd been prescribed a higher dosage than I normally took, but the pill looked just like my regular one. Anyway, after the wedding there was a bad storm."

Carly's hand stilled on Julianne's head. "Oh! And you were on Sea Island, right on the beach."

"Yeah. With an excellent view of the churning ocean."

"Oh, wow. That must have brought back some bad memories for you. I'm so sorry." Carly hugged her a bit closer.

Julianne shivered as memories of a tragic night on the ocean flashed through her mind. "I ran into Will in the hallway. I recognized him as one of the groomsmen, but I didn't know who he was at the time. The storm was raging and I couldn't get my key to work in the door. And then the lights went out. He took me to his room. He was going to get me a new key. I was a little . . . out of it with fear and everything. Will was trying to make me feel better, to reassure me. He held me. And then, one thing led to another . . ."

Carly stiffened beside her. "Look at me. He didn't force you, did he? Because if he did, I'll kill him. I don't care if he is built like a truck. I know people who are bigger than him."

Julianne smiled at her friend, relieved at finally having someone to share her story with. "No, from what I can remember, the kissing—and everything else—was mutual."

"You don't remember?"

"Well . . . I mean . . . not everything really. But I know I was a willing partner."

Only part of Julianne's statement was true. Despite the fog of her medication, she remembered every hot moment she'd spent in Will Connelly's arms. She'd relived them often enough alone in her bed at night. That evening on Sea Island, he'd been compassionate and kind, so unexpected from a man who made his living tackling and crushing other men.

His hands, huge and strong, had been tender and gentle on her frenzied body. He'd tasted like bourbon and smelled like a day at the beach, if that were even possible. Julianne succumbed to the touch of his mouth and hands without any resistance.

Right up until the most embarrassing portion of the evening: when she'd called out Nicky DiMarco's name as she climaxed. Her stomach roiled and her face burned as that moment replayed in her mind yet again. Burying her face in her hands, she tried to rationalize it for the millionth time.

She and Nicky had spent the better part of their young lives in each other's company while their fathers had served in the diplomatic corps together. In many ways, Nicky was the only link she had left to her mother—the only one who shared her profound loss. After all, he'd been in the car accident with Julianne and her mother that tragic night. Since that time, Nicky had been one of the few constants in her life. Always there for her if she needed him.

For years, Julianne had considered Nicky to be her soul mate, the man she fantasized about spending her life with. But as she entered adulthood, she realized that type of relationship with him was impossible. That didn't stop her from measuring all other men against the ideal fantasy she'd created in her mind, however.

One night spent with Will Connelly surpassed all the fantasies she'd ever had about Nicky and more, though. *So much more*. It was the only reason Julianne could come up with for calling out Nicky's name. That—and even more shameful—she hadn't known her lover's name.

The fact remained, Will Connelly had been the perfect lover. But she didn't want her friend to know just how vulnerable she was to him. *To his body*.

"A word of advice here," Carly said. "When you two talk about this, and you two need to talk about everything, don't mention that you don't remember having sex with him. He's a professional athlete and if his ego's anything like my husband's, he won't take it very well."

They were quiet for a few minutes before Julianne forced

herself to ask the question she most wanted the answer to. "What's he like?"

"Will? Oh gosh, I don't know if anyone really knows the real Will Connelly. He keeps to himself. Definitely the strong, silent type. Very cerebral. He went to an Ivy League school, Yale, I think. I know that management and the guys on the team really respect him both as a player and a person."

Julianne pulled out of Carly's embrace and began to pace the room again. "But what about his personal life?"

Carly sighed. "I don't know a lot about that. Like I said, he's very private. He was involved with an actress from a crime drama that's on cable, but I don't think it was serious."

"She said in several interviews they were very serious."

"Aha! So you at least took the trouble to find out his name and keep tabs on him. Good to know." Carly sounded relieved. "I wouldn't worry about what some actress said. They all try to use a relationship with an athlete to get publicity . . . wait . . ." Carly stood and turned Julianne so they were face to face. "Is that why you never said anything to him about the baby? You thought he was involved with someone?"

"That was a big part of it. The birth control failed and I got pregnant. I didn't want to mess up a relationship that might have been important to him because I wanted to keep the baby. I have the money to support a child, and I'm not the type of woman who wants to brag about her kid's famous father just for publicity's sake. Besides, the whole idea of having that conversation with a total stranger was humiliating. I just thought we'd all be better off if no one knew who Owen's father was."

"Well, you're going to have to have that conversation now. And everyone is going to know Will is Owen's father."

When Julianne didn't say anything, Carly reached out and grabbed her shoulders. "Oh no, Julianne." Her voice was laced with disappointment. "You don't seriously think Will is going to come in here, give his son a few pints of blood, and then walk out of your lives? Is that what you want? To take Owen back to Italy where you can hide out until you figure out what to do with your life? Pretending Will doesn't exist?"

Carly's tone implied she was disgusted again, the fragile truce they'd been working on these past few minutes gone. "There is something you should know about Will. He didn't grow up with a father in his life. I don't know the whole story, but I do know he is very passionate about a father doing right by his children."

Pulling out of Carly's hands, Julianne crossed her arms defiantly. "We don't know that for sure. Maybe he doesn't want kids right now. Maybe he'll be just fine with us going back to Italy and going on with our life without him!"

The color drained from Carly's face, her eyes focused owlishly behind Julianne. Taking a slow peek over her shoulder, she saw the object of their discussion standing in front of the curtain. His posture was equally defiant. Julianne licked her lips and wondered how a man so massive could move so quietly. As she turned, she took in his Gucci loafers and an Armani business suit that made him look like he preferred lobbying politicians to crushing opposing players. Her gaze wandered up from his strong, square jaw to meet angry green eyes.

"Don't count on it," he said before disappearing behind the curtain again.

Three

Mr. Clem prattled on about something, but Will wasn't listening. Instead, he tried to rein in his temper. The woman was insane if she thought he'd let her take his son to live in another country. She was certifiable if she believed he'd give up his paternal rights to any child of his.

If in fact he was the boy's father.

That pertinent bit of lab work still had yet to be resolved. His DNA had been collected as soon as he and his entourage had arrived at the hospital, but according to Mr. Clem, the results could take up to twenty-four hours in spite of the fact the hospital had put a rush on them.

That technicality didn't deter the hospital ombudsman one bit, however. Mr. Clem was prepared to rip off Will's jacket and begin transfusing blood immediately. The man's enthusiasm for his job was a bit over the top, but Will was glad the baby had someone in this world protecting him. Someone other than his lunatic mother.

She burst through the curtain in much the same manner as he ruptured offensive lines, with a ferocious look on her face. Not that she was necessarily intimidating. Standing

nearly a foot shorter than his six-foot-three-inch frame, she'd
have to stand on her toes just to reach his shoulder. He knew
from experience she weighed next to nothing. Pregnancy
hadn't exactly fattened her up. In fact, she looked nothing
like the woman he'd encountered that long-ago stormy night.

Gone was the hot dress she'd worn to tantalize the men
at the wedding. Today, she was dressed in an ivory turtleneck,
the outline of the cross necklace she wore visible beneath
it. Her black yoga pants fit snugly over generous hips, but
they were frayed slightly at the bottom. Not exactly the haute
couture she was supposedly famous for creating. Tortoise-
shell glasses couldn't hide her red-rimmed eyes or the dark
smudges beneath them. Her wild mahogany hair pulled tight
in a high ponytail accentuated the gauntness of her face.
The only part of her that hadn't changed were her lips: still
pink and full where she'd obviously been gnawing on them,
much like the night they'd made love.

She opened her mouth to speak, but Will raised the palm
of his hand to silence her and she stilled, her eyes wide. If
she spoke, he wasn't certain he'd be able to control his anger.
He'd worked all his life to suppress the rage he often felt,
channeling his pent-up aggression into football while per-
fecting his stoicism so no one saw the intense ire that boiled
beneath his surface. The crazy nymph in front of him just
might shatter his carefully crafted façade. When he thought
about her scheme, his fingers itched to wrap themselves
around her neck and throttle her.

Or pull her in for a kiss.

And that pissed him off even more. He was disgusted at
the part of him that still wanted her. She leveled angry eyes
at him as she crossed her arms under her breasts. Those had
definitely benefited from pregnancy, not that they were bad
before. Will had to take a reflexive step back as a bead of
sweat trickled down his back.

Mr. Clem stepped in between them, momentarily defusing the situation. "Miss Marchione, we won't be able to
perform the transfusion immediately, unfortunately." He
shot a furious glance at Will.

Julianne's hands dropped to her sides as Carly Devlin emerged to support her with an arm behind her back. He wasn't sure why the wife of the Blaze's quarterback was here, but he'd figure out that mystery later. Right now, he needed answers to the many questions Mr. Clem hadn't been able to answer during his hurried explanation of the blood disorder Julianne Marchione's baby had been born with. Until he got them, there was no point in arranging a transfusion.

"I don't understand." Julianne sounded deflated as her eyes darted to Mr. Clem's face.

"It's pretty simple, really." Sarcasm dripped from Roscoe's voice as he spoke from somewhere behind Will. "Until we know definitively who this baby's daddy is, no one is sticking another needle in my client."

"Roscoe!" Carly admonished her husband's agent and best friend.

"We don't have time for this!" Julianne's eyes were slits in her face." My baby needs a transfusion as soon as possible, and you're his father." She flung a hand at Will.

He arched an eyebrow at her, not relishing the fact that he wasn't enjoying her discomfort more. "Not until the lab says so."

"Will!" Carly turned her censure onto him.

Julianne shrugged out of Carly's embrace and stepped to within inches of Will. His body's visceral reaction annoyed him. "Of course you're his father! My God! If I were going to make up an imaginary father for my son, do you think I would pick *you*?" She finished up with a few mumblings in Italian.

"Julianne!" Carly was practically calling roll in their little drama.

Will absorbed the pain of her words and internalized them without flinching. Of course she thought he wasn't good enough. No one ever thought Will Connelly was good enough for anything. No matter how he tried to improve himself, he'd still be the poor, fatherless kid from the trailer park whose mother drove a school bus and cleaned houses for a living.

But this woman had another thing coming if she thought she could walk all over him. Nobody did that anymore.

"Perhaps we'd best take this discussion inside." An urbane-looking black man appeared at Will's shoulder, carrying an armful of coffee and scones. His British accent made the statement sound like a question. The expression on his face, however, made it clear it was not.

"Sebastian's right." The senator herded their party behind the curtain. "Let's take this to a more private location if that's even possible." He pulled his sister down beside him on the small sofa. Hank Osbourne offered a chair to Carly before taking another for himself. Roscoe turned one of the remaining chairs around and sat straddling it, his arms draped over the back. The Brit, Sebastian, offered the final chair to Will, but he declined. Instead, he propped a shoulder against the wall closest to the curtain and tucked his hands beneath his armpits in a defensive position. Mr. Clem stood, fidgeting from one foot to the other.

Sebastian handed Julianne a paper coffee cup before opening a box of scones and placing it on the table. Steam rose from his own cup as he pulled the lid off and took a sip.

"Ahh. Everything looks better after a bracing swallow of tea." His tone dripped with civility, though his eyes were anything but civil as they met Will's. "Now, what's this I heard about you not believing you're Owen's father?"

Will twitched slightly. The boy had a name. *Owen.* He remained silent as the Brit took another sip of tea.

"Of course, you're the boy's father. Otherwise, why would Julianne involve you?" Sebastian's imperious tone was beginning to grate on Will's nerves.

"That's exactly what I tried to tell him!" Julianne sprang from the sofa before her brother pulled her back down.

"And you"—Sebastian turned to point an accusing finger at her—"need to settle down and learn to be more gracious. I'm sure this whole situation was quite a shock to Mr. Connelly this morning. He needs time to adjust without you caterwauling at him." He turned back to Will. "As much as

I can appreciate your discomfiture, time, unfortunately, is something we don't have right now."

"Which is what I've been telling him all morning!" Mr. Clem's shrill voice could have made a statue cringe.

Will remained motionless as he carefully dissected the scene before him. Julianne shifted on the sofa, her eyes focused on her hands in her lap. Swallowing hard, she wiped away a tear that ran down her cheek. It was costing her a great deal to have to ask for his help. She was apparently so ashamed at having Will as the father of her child that she intended to keep the baby's paternity a secret. And that part made him furious. But was he angry enough to let an infant suffer?

"Will." Carly's voice startled him. He hadn't noticed her rise from her chair to stand beside him. "I've known Julianne practically all my life. She may have made some irrational decisions these past few months." Her voice hitched a little before she continued. "But she wouldn't lie about this. Owen needs this transfusion and you're the only one who can give it to him. I know this has been quite a shock and your pride might be a little stung right now, but you have to think of Owen first. After he's better, then you and Julianne can work this all out."

Before Will could respond, a nurse poked her head into the room. "Miss Marchione, Dr. Ling says you can have fifteen minutes to visit with your son now."

Julianne was striding for the hallway before the nurse had even finished her sentence. Will followed quickly behind her. He hadn't intended to move at all, but his feet seemed to have a mind of their own. They entered a small anteroom just outside the NICU suite. Julianne was hurriedly dressing herself in a yellow paper gown and booties. She moved to wash her hands and hesitated as she noticed him behind her. Turning quickly so he wasn't able to read her eyes, she handed him a gown and some booties. "See if you can make these fit."

The gown she wore swallowed up her petite body, while he was forced to remove his suit jacket so his wouldn't split down the back. She sat on the bench and slipped booties over her tiny ballet flats. Will's booties barely stretched over his loafers, but at least he was able to leave his shoes on.

"You need to soap up thoroughly," she said, demonstrating at the sink, "and rinse for a full sixty seconds."

She waited quietly while Will sanitized his hands. They both then proceeded into the NICU, the door hissing as it sealed shut behind them. The suite was quieter than Will expected, the monitors more muted than out by the nurse's station. Instead, James Taylor sang a lullaby softly over the intercom. Will's eyes took a moment to adjust to the low lighting as Julianne quickly made her way through the maze of incubators to one in the far corner. He followed closely, realizing he didn't even know which of the infants belonged to her.

A woman dressed in hospital scrubs adorned with bears scooped up a baby, expertly wrapping him in a warm blanket so that the tubes and cords he was still hooked up to wouldn't get tangled. Julianne took the baby from her, a serene smile enveloping her face. Curious now, he stepped nearer to get a better glimpse. Would he even look like Will?

It took a moment for Julianne to register that Will was still with her. When she did, her eyes flared briefly with fear before guilt took its place. She chewed on her bottom lip as she gathered Owen closer to her, a mother instinctively protecting her child. But if Owen was his, she'd soon learn there would be no way to keep Will from his son. He reached over to pull the blanket away from the baby's cheek, but Julianne quickly turned and gestured toward the glider next to the incubator.

"Sit," she commanded, surprising the hell out of him.

Not wanting her to change her mind, he squeezed his large frame into the chair. She hesitated a moment before slowly lowering the baby into his arms. Grasping his left hand, she showed him how to cradle the baby's neck. Will's breath hitched as he looked into the face of the small bundle in his hands. Owen wasn't much bigger than a football, swaddled as tightly as he was in the blanket. The silly cap on his head covered up what little hair he had. Will was surprised to see it was blond, like his own. All morning he'd been picturing a baby with his mother's coloring. The baby's eyes were closed, and disappointment flickered through Will. He wanted to see them, to see into them.

Julianne crouched down in front of the pair, pain etched on her face as another tear slipped from her eye. "Owen," she said softly. "This is your daddy. He's come to make you better."

Will's heart nearly stopped when, at the sound of her voice, Owen squinted with one blue eye as he worked a hand free of the blanket to give a pump of his right fist, before he worked the hand to his mouth. At that moment, Will knew there would be no more waiting on a paternity test. He prayed his blood would be a compatible match because he'd give this baby every drop of blood in his body to see him survive.

Owen was his son. He'd figure out what to do about Julianne later. For now, getting his baby well was the top priority.

Four

The procedure took less than six hours. Without hesitation, Will neatly rolled up his shirt sleeve and stretched out on a gurney in a sterile room beside the NICU. Casually crossing his ankles, he didn't even flinch when the nurse inserted a needle into his arm. Restless, Julianne had paced the room while Will stoically watched the blood flow from his body into the collection bag. Twice Julianne attempted to speak to him, but both times he'd held up a large paw to silence her. He'd been doing that all day, much to Julianne's aggravation.

Not that he didn't have every right to be angry with her, he did. But Julianne was a talker. The anxiety she felt for Owen made her more chatty than usual. If she could just clear the air with Will rather than be subjected to the silent treatment, she'd feel better. Less guilty. She'd explain everything. Well, maybe not everything. Because if she explained everything, she'd have to say she was sorry. And even though she was very sorry, she wasn't about to give him more power over her and Owen. Instead, she bit her lip. It was better than staring at the palm of his hand in her face.

When they'd extracted and processed what looked to Julianne like a ridiculously large amount of blood, the nurse brought Owen and his incubator into the room. Unlike his father, the baby was not as easygoing during the transfusion process. Owen howled as Dr. Ling and the nurses poked his tiny arms and feet with needles. Julianne stood to the side, tears streaming down her face, wishing she could somehow absorb her son's pain. It was only after the procedure was over that she realized Will stood beside her the entire time, his annoyingly patronizing hand rubbing her back as she cried.

All that was left now was the waiting. Dr. Ling had explained that it would take a couple of hours before she knew if Owen's body would accept the antibodies in Will's blood, but the doctor was optimistic the procedure would be successful. In nearly all cases, one of the parents' blood proteins was a match. Julianne felt that familiar stab of pain that her blood hadn't been good enough to save her child. Once again, she'd had to rely on someone else.

She'd lost all track of actual time. The last shift change was several hours ago, so she assumed it was late evening, although it was hard to tell inside the hospital. Sebastian was at dinner with friends. Carly had left, too. She'd gone home to her new family. The knife twisted in Julianne's gut again. Owen was supposed to be *her* family. And if the blood disorder didn't take him from her, the behemoth pretending to sleep on the sofa would certainly try.

She glanced over at Will stretched out on the love seat, his long legs protruding into the center of the room. Either he was a very heavy sleeper or the champ at playing possum because he hadn't so much as moved since he'd closed his eyes an hour ago. Both hands lay across his midsection, and his muscled abdomen rose slightly as he breathed. He looked less forbidding with his eyes closed, his long lashes resting against his cheeks. In this state, he seemed almost approachable. More human. When he was awake, Will resembled a Norse god, his intense eyes, square jaw, and massive shoulders intimidating. All that was missing was the horned helmet.

His jacket and tie lay folded neatly on the back of one of

the chairs. Childishly, she wanted to walk over and rumple them up to see how he'd react. He'd been annoyingly cool and unflappable all day, in complete control as if he'd come from his Viking ship to rescue her. Except he hadn't come to save her; he'd come for their son. Given the opportunity, she figured he'd toss her overboard without a backward glance.

Dr. Ling pushed through the curtain, her rubber-soled shoes squeaking on the tile floor. Will's eyes shot open.

"Good news!" Dr. Ling smiled widely at them both. "Owen's body is thriving with the new blood cells. In fact, he's even generating blood proteins of his own already, which tells us he's going to make a complete recovery."

Julianne's hands were shaking as she pressed a finger to the cross beneath her shirt and whispered a prayer. Tears were streaming down her face as she reached out and hugged Dr. Ling. "Thank you! Thank you so much for saving Owen."

"Don't thank me." The doctor laughed. "It was his dad's blood that did the trick." She pulled a sheet of paper out of the metal chart case she carried. "And this makes it official. The DNA test is positive. You're Owen's father."

Will's face was impassive as Dr. Ling handed him the results. Without looking at it, he folded the paper up and placed it in his shirt pocket. "How long until he can be released?"

The question sent a shiver of unease up her spine.

"He'll need to stay in the NICU for several more days, just to be sure his body functions return to normal. Once he has the all-clear from the various specialists, then he can go home." The doctor looked at each of them, clearly wondering who would be taking Owen home. "I'll leave you two to sort everything out. I'll stay a few more hours to keep an eye on things, and I'll update you after his morning blood work."

Dr. Ling seemed unfazed by the unorthodox relationship between her patient's parents. Of course, she worked in a hospital, so it was likely she'd seen all sorts of awkward family situations. Nonetheless, Julianne was still embarrassed. She looked over at Will, who had buttoned his cuffs and was pulling on his suit jacket. When his hands were occupied draping his tie over his shoulders, she jumped on the chance to speak.

"Thank you." The words fell soft and hollow, almost as if she'd dropped them down a well. Clearly, they were inadequate, but she couldn't think of anything else to say. "Thanks for saving my son."

He paused with the tie in midair behind his neck. "What did you say?"

Julianne swallowed. The look in his eyes made her want to run, but she stood her ground. She deserved his derision and his anger. Owen had been through so much and now he was going to live, thanks to the man towering in front of her. She owed him his pound of flesh. She just hoped she'd still be standing when he was done with her.

Will dropped the tie and stalked toward her. Julianne pushed her shoulders up, determined to force her body, and her soul, to withstand whatever he planned to dish out.

"Owen is not *your* son." He tapped his chest where the paternity test results were tucked away. "This little piece of paper says I have just as much right to him as you do. He's *my* son, too."

This was the part where he whipped out his Viking sword and ripped out her heart. Blinking back tears, she forced her question through dry lips. "How exactly are you going to exert those rights?"

"Princess, we've just teed up the ball for the kickoff. This game has barely started. But the first thing *we* will be doing is getting Owen's birth certificate amended so my name is on there."

"Your name *is* on it!" *Sort of.*

Will arched an eyebrow at her as he pulled his iPhone from his pocket. He scrolled through it before reading aloud. "Owen Connelly Marchione. Nice touch with the middle name." The insincerity of his tone belied his words. "Mother, Julianne Valerie Marchione. Father, unknown."

Obviously his agent had been busy while Will was giving blood. Julianne stared at him. There were no words she could offer. No explanation that he'd accept for not listing him as Owen's father. At least none that she could justify.

"No child of mine is growing up a bastard!" His shout reverberated off the walls in the small room. Julianne cringed as she imagined that the entire hospital heard him.

"Okay," she whispered. There was no other answer she could give. She'd never meant to deny either Will or Owen. She just hadn't thought the whole thing through. But explaining that to him right now seemed like a moot point.

He raked his hand through his hair, mussing up his perfect appearance. "Get your things. I'll take you home."

"My home is in Italy." Technically, she had a place in New York, but it belonged to the company she no longer owned, so she didn't feel she had to mention it.

"Fine, I'll take you to your brother's place. I assume he lives here in D.C.?"

He did, but she wasn't going there, either. "I'm not leaving Owen." She crossed her arms in front of her. If he wanted her to leave her son, he'd have to drag her out. Julianne shivered as she mentally pictured him doing just that.

Will blew out a breath as if he were counting to ten. "You need to get some rest and you won't get that here. We've got a lot of things to work out, and I'd appreciate it if you came to the discussion with a clear head."

"I don't need you to take care of me." She was being churlish, she knew, but it irked her that he thought he could control her life now that he knew he was Owen's father.

"What you need, Princess, is a keeper!"

Before Julianne could open her mouth to protest, Carly and Shane Devlin stepped in front of the partition.

"Connelly." Shane's hand wrapped around Will's bicep, pulling him back from Julianne. "Keep it down unless you want to read about this on TMZ tomorrow."

Will jerked out of Shane's grasp, shooting him a malicious glare.

"Don't get all pissy with me." Shane went nose to nose with Will. "I didn't know anything about this until a couple of hours ago."

Will looked over at Carly, who just gave him an empathetic shrug, which irritated not only Julianne, but Shane as
well. "My wife didn't know you were the father, either. Not
until this morning. So watch yourself with her or you'll
answer to me."

When Will's eyes met Julianne's, she held his stare for a
moment. Something flashed in them that she couldn't make
out—anguish, she thought—before they were hard emeralds
again.

"Make sure she gets some rest, will you, Carly?" Then
he disappeared through the curtain, his long stride echoing
down the corridor.

Julianne wanted to chase him down. She wanted to rail
at him, to scratch his eyes out. Anything to wipe that smug
look off his face.

But most of all, she yearned for him to hold her, just as
he'd held her that night at the wedding. The past several
months of pregnancy and duplicity, coupled with Owen's
brush with death, had exhausted her. Guilt was weighing
her down and she wanted someone to help carry her burden.
Not since her mother died in that awful accident on the sea
had anyone been able to provide Julianne with comfort the
way Will Connelly had the night they'd spent together.

And now he hated her.

Julianne shook herself. Thinking about Will would only
make her crazy. She'd deal with him and whatever plans he
had tomorrow. Right now she needed to concentrate on
Owen. Her baby was going to live! Joy and relief surged
through her body as she collapsed onto the sofa. Carly gathered Julianne in her arms as she sat down beside her.

"Owen is going to live," Julianne said through her tears.
"My baby is going to be okay."

"I know." Carly rubbed Julianne's back. "Will's blood
was all Owen needed."

Julianne felt the now-familiar hitch of anguish and anger
at the mention of Will saving Owen. But she pushed it deep
down. The fact remained that despite the way she'd duped
the man, he'd stepped in and saved Owen with only her word

that he was the father. She owed him much more than just her gratitude.

Julianne wiped her face with her hands. "I know. And I'm going to make it right with him, Carly. Whatever it takes, I'll do it." She got up to get a drink of water, completely missing the troubled look that passed between Shane and Carly.

Five

Sleep eluded Will that night. Every time he closed his eyes he saw Julianne, dressed like a temptress in that skintight red dress, her hair flowing behind her as she laughed at him while she pushed Owen in a stroller across the turf in the Blaze stadium. No matter how hard he tried to catch them, they kept getting farther and farther away. The senator's voice blared across the PA system repeating over and over again: "She never wanted you to know about the baby. She's going to raise him by herself in Italy. You'll never have to see him." Will's cleats sank like cement into the grass at the fifty-yard line as he helplessly watched her flounce out of the stadium, Owen in tow.

He woke up drenched in sweat and in need of a cold shower, for multiple reasons. It was hard to separate the erotic fantasy Julianne presented from the duplicitous woman she was. The fact that his body still reacted to her made him madder than hell. He would never be able to trust her. She had every intention of denying him the right to raise his son. The sooner he got Owen's paternity sorted out legally, the better. Especially if it meant less contact with his son's mother.

Thirty minutes later, Will made his way downstairs to his kitchen for some much-needed coffee. As he peered over the metal railing leading down from his bedroom to the high-ceilinged living area of his loft apartment, he spied a pair of yellow running shoes hanging off the side of the sectional sofa. Unfortunately, they were still attached to the muscular legs of Blaze tight end Brody Janik. Will swore as he stomped down the stairs.

The Today Show blared from the sixty-inch plasma TV hanging above a gas fireplace. Will maneuvered through a storm of dust motes floating across the oak plank floor in front of the large industrial windows. He wasn't in the mood to deal with the ineffectiveness of his cleaning service, much less the six-foot-three, two-hundred-ten-pound pretty boy sprawled out on his sofa.

"That Natalie Morales is hot. Think she's married?" Brody thought every woman was hot. And hot *for* him, which, given his cover-boy good looks and athletic super-stardom, was probably true.

Will shoved Brody's sneakered feet off the sofa and picked up a bottle of orange juice that was leaning precariously against the ottoman. "Show a little respect, Janik. This isn't a frat house."

"Jeez, Grandma." Brody pulled himself up to a seated position before standing and following Will into the state-of-the-art galley kitchen. "You treat this place like a museum just because it's been featured in *Architectural Digest*."

He doubted Brody, who'd grown up in a wealthy Boston suburb, could appreciate the sense of accomplishment Will took in living in a place he actually owned. It had nothing to do with his loft's appearance in national magazines. That was his buddy Gavin's doing. Gavin, a successful architect, had helped to design and restore the bank of warehouse lofts in the trendy Federal Hill area of Baltimore, where Will now lived. For Will, the eighteen-hundred-square-foot loft represented a form of security he'd never felt growing up inside a drafty trailer parked in hurricane alley.

Standing in the galley kitchen decorated in varying

shades of gray, Will surveyed his home. The kitchen featured concrete counters, stainless steel appliances, a glass-tile backsplash, and glass-front mahogany cabinets. The two-story living area and the large upstairs master bedroom gave the illusion of an abundance of space, but he was just one person living there. Where would he put Owen? And the kid's crazy mother, if it came to that? There weren't any parks or playgrounds nearby. Boys needed a place to run and throw balls. Owen couldn't do that in Fed Hill.

He loaded a canister into the Keurig machine and contemplated his housing dilemma as Brody straddled one of the two bar stools, hooking his heels on the bottom rung. "I brought you some doughnuts."

Will watched as Brody crammed half a chocolate doughnut in his mouth, sprinkles raining down on the counter like confetti. "Seriously, how do you eat such crap and still run the forty in four point six seconds?"

"Great genes." At least that was what it sounded like around the doughnut.

Shaking his head, Will grabbed a piece of wheat bread and the peanut butter out of the pantry. When he was growing up, peanut butter made up two meals a day most weeks. He swore when he had money he'd never touch the stuff again. But when he was stressed, his body seemed to crave the familiar taste. After slapping the peanut butter on the bread, he pulled his cup of coffee out of the machine and took a tentative sip. He was reminded of Sebastian and his tea the day before, and he felt the squeezing begin at his temples again. "How'd you get in here, Brody?"

"You gave me a key, remember?" He tossed a key chain with a miniature bobblehead Blaze football player onto the counter.

"For *emergencies*." Will picked it up; the player was wearing number forty-eight, Will's number. He shook his head as he pocketed the key. "Like when that crazy porn star was stalking you."

"She wasn't a porn star. She made independent films."

Will took a bite of his sandwich and arched an eyebrow at Brody. "Don't give me the story you tell your mother."

Brody crashed at Will's apartment only when one of his four older sisters visited, which was often. They were constantly trying to fix him up with their friends, often forcing the tight end to seek refuge in space containing less estrogen. Why he crossed the line of scrimmage and picked Will, a defensive player, to be his mentor was still a mystery. Despite Will's attempts to shake him, Brody had latched onto him during his rookie season and hadn't let go.

Brody guzzled the rest of his orange juice. Will sensed the tight end was stalling. Unlike most of the world, Will never underestimated the man seated in front of him. Brody took great pains to portray himself as the immature jock who thought nothing of using his good looks and perfect smile to get ahead in the world. But behind those lazy blue eyes was a shrewd twenty-five-year-old who wasn't always successful at hiding his brain beneath his brawn. Even his clothes, cargo shorts and neatly ironed T-shirt, looked haphazardly thrown together, but Will knew that a consultant, probably one of his sisters, had likely pulled the pieces into an outfit. Brody also was aware of his place in the hierarchy of the team. Despite being a marquee player, he would never show up unannounced at a more senior player's home without a very good reason.

"There's been talk in the clubhouse." Brody flipped the bottle cap between his long fingers, but his eyes never left Will's face. Despite the fact it was the off-season, many of the Blaze players remained in town for Organized Team Activities, which consisted of optional twice-weekly conditioning sessions. The OTAs not only helped the players stay in shape, but they kept the esprit de corps among the team.

"There's always talk. I imagine there's more gossiping done in an NFL clubhouse than in a ladies' room."

"Yeah, well, everyone's getting a little antsy about this investigation into your old coach and whether some of the dirt will rub off onto our team."

Will took another swallow of coffee. One good thing

about the previous day's baby ambush—he'd completely forgotten about the witch hunt surrounding his former coach. Several players had filed lawsuits against coaches in the league alleging injuries they received were the result of players receiving cash payments for inflicting punishing hits. Coaches had instituted a bounty scheme to remove certain players from the game, these players claimed. And the coach named at the top of the list: Paul Zevalos, Will's former head coach. As could be expected, Congress couldn't pass up a chance to get involved in something other than the tedium of running the country, and Senate committees were already investigating the matter. Will nearly snorted in disgust.

"You were down in D.C. on Capitol Hill yesterday, Connelly. All day. That's pretty serious."

It had been serious, but not for the reasons his teammates thought. The story was going to get out soon, today probably, and Will needed to get things finalized. "Tell the boys not to worry. The stink from the Zevalos investigation will never reach Baltimore because there's nothing there."

"A senator asking questions usually means there's something to the story."

Will drained the coffee from his mug before rinsing it out and loading it into the dishwasher. He pulled a sanitized wipe out of a carton and cleaned up the crumbs from his sandwich and Brody's sprinkles. "The meeting wasn't about Zevalos."

Walking toward the door, Will picked up his wallet and keys from a basket on a table in the entryway. Brody trailed after him. "Then what was the meeting about?"

"A baby." Will pulled the bobblehead key chain out of his pocket. "*My* baby." He watched as Brody's jaw dropped before Will tossed him the key. "Here. Keep these. You can use the loft whenever you want. It seems I'm gonna need a bigger place."

Owen looked much better than he had the day before. His skin was pinker and his breathing less labored.

The baby had even treated Will to his one-eyed stare when he'd held him earlier. Dr. Ling pronounced Owen totally cured, and Will felt an overwhelming sense of pride at having been able to save his baby's life. The feeling was so surreal, he couldn't quite wrap his head around it. Winning the Super Bowl a few months ago hadn't felt this good.

He was still riding that crest of emotion when he sat down with Julianne later that morning. They'd ventured out to one of the courtyards outside the hospital to talk undisturbed. Will stared at her as she reclined in a deck chair, eyes closed, the spring sun shining down on her face. Perhaps she'd gotten some sleep last night or maybe it was the relief that Owen was going to be okay, but she looked less weary today. *Less fragile.* She was dressed more like the fashion icon that she was with tight gray pants, clunky black boots, and a pink V-neck sweater that tied in a bow at one side. Her hair was done up in a messy knot and she'd forsaken the glasses for contacts. Inky black lashes fanned out against her cheeks and her lips were glossed to a high sheen. Will shifted in his chair as he reminded himself that the sultry woman in front of him was the same one who'd tried to steal his child.

"So I guess this is when we get down to the nitty-gritty," she said without preamble, eyes still closed.

"It's a conversation long overdue, don't you think?"

She opened one eye and squinted at him much as Owen had done earlier. Somehow, the look was a lot sexier on her. Releasing a breathy sigh, she sat up and leaned her elbows on the table, giving him an excellent view of the silver cross and the breasts it was dangling between. "Look, this situation is awkward enough. Can we start fresh today and figure out how to make this work with Owen's best interest in mind?"

Will arched an eyebrow at her. "You want me to just forget you tried to hide my son from me?"

Julianne sat back in the chair, wrapping her arms around her. "No, but I want you to move on from there because, at the time, I thought I was making the best choices for myself and the baby."

His jaw was clenched so tight, he was surprised he could

get any words out. "But the hell with me, right? I'm just some dumb jock who could give a rat's ass about how many kids I father, is that it?"

"No!" She grabbed the cross around her neck and began to fiddle with it. "I didn't even know you! When I found out I was pregnant, I was shocked, but I wasn't going to give him up. I had the money to support a child."

"I wouldn't have made you give him up! And you should have stuck around the morning after to at least exchange names, given that the condom broke."

"Oh." She bit her lip. "I thought it was just my migraine medicine that made my birth control ineffective. I don't remember the condom breaking."

"It was at a pretty pivotal part of the evening, Princess."

"My medicine makes me a little woozy, so I don't really remember the evening that much."

"You don't remember?" *Jesus! The best sex of his life and she'd been stoned?*

She didn't meet his eyes, giving him a little shrug instead. Will felt like his head was going to explode. He closed his eyes and tried in vain to sort out his feelings. Her story was plausible, but he still didn't trust her. He didn't *want* to trust her. Well, at least most of his body didn't want to.

"Now do you see why we should just start from today and move forward?" She posed the question softly. "Our lives are going to be forever entwined with Owen's. It would be a lot easier if we could at least get along. For his sake."

Will rubbed his hands down his face. "You're not taking him to Italy." He'd compromise if he had to, but not on that. "You'll have to tell your clients you're working from the U.S. until we can arrange something."

"Not a problem. I've . . . I've put my work on hold for now. I need to concentrate on Owen." Her statement surprised him. When he'd Googled her the night before, Will had discovered that Julianne was a rising star in the very competitive design industry. She'd been right when she said she could easily support a child, but what effect would a prolonged absence have on her career? Begrudgingly, he had to admire her devotion to Owen; he only wished that dedication to do what was best for her son had included allowing his father in his life long before the baby's illness forced her to.

"Owen is just a tiny baby," she said. "He needs his mother right now. I can get a place here in D.C. or closer to you in Baltimore. You can see him every day. But I can't be separated from him. Not after I almost lost him."

Will leaned back in his chair and closed his eyes. He had no intention of keeping her from Owen. She was right, the baby needed her. Hell, he didn't even know how to feed him, much less change a diaper. But in three months he'd be back playing football, and that meant he'd have little time to care for Owen. He needed to bond with him now, to let his son know he wasn't a fatherless kid who'd be looked on disdainfully by everyone else. Like Julianne, he didn't want to be apart from his baby right now.

Julianne's tone became more urgent at his silence. "Please, I'll agree to joint custody; we'll live wherever you want us to. I'll do whatever you want, Will." The last part came out as a strangled whisper.

He opened his eyes and considered her for a moment. "My place in Baltimore is small and in the heart of the city. The only other home I own is in coastal North Carolina. I planned to spend a couple of weeks or so there during the summer, but I can go now. It's a big house and the sunshine and sea air will be good for Owen."

"We'd all live in the same house? Near the ocean?"

Jesus, was she already backpedaling? "A minute ago you said you'd do anything, live anywhere. Was that just lip service, Princess?"

"I meant it! It's just that babies cry and don't sleep through the night. Caring for a baby is twenty-four-seven. You need to be sure you know what you're getting into. You might want some space."

"I have three months until training camp begins and the season starts up again. Right now I have nothing but time on my hands." Not exactly true—he had obligations during the off-season—but he wasn't going to let her martyr herself by putting her career on hold and have it bite him in the ass later on. "You're not the only one who wants to bond with Owen. And, like I said, it's a big house. Plenty of room for you, Owen, and me." He didn't bother mentioning his mother lived there, too.

Damn, he'd forgotten to call his mother. He needed to before she heard about this from somewhere else.

Annabeth Connelly insisted on living in the small town where she'd grown up on the poor side of the tracks, the same place she'd raised Will. If she ever felt the same contempt for the townspeople who'd treated them with such disdain, she never showed it. Will spent as little time there as possible, going back only when Chase or Gavin were in town. But Gavin was living there indefinitely, sorting out his father's business after his death of a heart attack, and Will found himself in Chances Inlet more frequently lately.

"Okay." Julianne wasn't successful in hiding the reluctance in her voice. But to her credit, she brooked no argument. "As soon as Dr. Ling says Owen can be released, we'll go to your home."

Will could only imagine what a homecoming it would be. The locals didn't have a problem sucking up to him now that he was a famous, rich football player. But he could already hear the whispers once he arrived with his bastard son and his baby mama in tow. They'd say he'd turned out just as they expected, except, perhaps, wealthier. He suppressed a shudder just thinking about his childhood spent longing for a normal family dynamic of two parents who were married to each other.

Hell, he wondered, *does that dynamic even exist anymore?*

Long ago, he'd made a promise to himself that any child of his would have that one thing he wanted most of all: legitimacy. Despite his best efforts, he'd failed his son. *Not that it was too late.* He rubbed a hand over his forehead, trying to scrub that ridiculous thought from his mind as he glanced over at the woman who'd borne him a son. Julianne was babbling on about all the things they'd need for the baby, her previous trepidation suddenly diminished by thoughts of shopping. In that respect, she was just like any other woman. He held a hand up to quiet her. "Just give me a list. I'll have it taken care of before we get there."

Her eyes narrowed and she bit her lip to stop herself from complaining. "Fine," she said. "I assume we'll work out a long-term agreement when we get there?"

"You already agreed to do whatever I want." He leaned the chair back on its back legs and tried to remind himself not to flirt with her. She was the enemy. Instead, he forced his best William the Conqueror stare on his face. It worked to intimidate rookies all the time.

A flush spread over her cheeks. "Only with regard to Owen."

"Since Owen is the only one I care about, we shouldn't have a problem." Something flashed in her eyes before she reined it in. It was killing her that he had the upper hand, but she didn't dare challenge him.

Suddenly her face lit up as she sprang from her chair. "Nicky!" she cried. Will felt his jewels shrivel up at the sound. The last time she'd cried out that name, he'd been buried deep inside her on a hotel room bed.

Six

Julianne breathed in the familiar scent of Nicholas DiMarco as she hugged him tightly. "I knew you'd come," she whispered against his neck. His hands gently patted her back. *Nice hands. Normal hands.* Nothing like the oversized mitts Will was always holding up in front of her face.

Nicky gently gripped her shoulders and took a step back. "Of course I came, Jules. I had to make sure my best girl and her baby were okay. Carly shared the wonderful news that Owen is getting better by the hour. All of our prayers have been answered."

She looked over Nicky's shoulder at Carly, who was giving Will another of those empathetic shrugs. The gesture annoyed her. Carly never understood Julianne's relationship with Nicky. Her best friend couldn't seem to grasp that Nicky was more than a childhood crush—in spite of any lasting sexual fantasies. Sure, Julianne had spent much of her life dreaming about Nicky as her soul mate, but she was well aware that his devotion lay elsewhere. That's what made him so safe.

Brushing her hands over his shoulders, Julianne adjusted

the clerical collar on his starched black shirt. "Oh, Nicky, it's so wonderful! My baby is going to be okay!"

Will cleared his throat loudly behind her. Wincing, she grabbed Nicky's hand and turned to face him. The inscrutable behemoth linebacker from yesterday was back, looking none too happy that she'd referred to Owen as *her* baby. "Nicky, this is Will Connelly . . . Owen's father." The humiliation of the situation seemed to be choking her, and she struggled with the introduction she'd never envisioned making. "Will, this is Nicky. Father Nicholas DiMarco, Vatican Emissary to the Holy See."

Nicky dropped her hand to reach for Will's. She held her breath as Will's hand seemed to swallow the priest's more gentle one, nearly crushing it in his grip. "We're all so glad you're finally in the picture, Will."

Julianne tried not to cringe. Years of diplomatic training and that was what came out of Nicky's mouth? She could feel Will's stare piercing through her, but she didn't dare look at him. Fear and shame that Will might say something about that night kept her eyes focused on the fountain in the center of the courtyard. Anywhere but on either man's face. "I would've liked to have been part of *the picture* much sooner, Father, but your *best girl* seemed to have other ideas." The tone of his voice indicated that whatever accord they'd reached a few minutes ago might be slipping away, and Julianne felt helpless to stop it. He had every right to be angry and, once again, guilt churned through her stomach.

Nicky laughed. "Ah, yes, our Julianne is passionate in her stubbornness, isn't she?" He wrapped an arm around her shoulders as he proceeded to regale Will with a story from their childhood, a time when she refused to reveal where she'd hidden something or other, but Julianne wasn't listening. Apparently Will wasn't, either, because she still felt his eyes boring into her.

Hitching a quick breath, Julianne scrambled to figure a way out of this awkward encounter. Her world was completely tilted on its axis. Owen was recovering. Carly hadn't deserted her and now Nicky was here to lend his support. She should be ecstatic that everything had fallen into place. Instead, she felt light-headed and confused. And Will stood three feet from her like a ticking time bomb ready to explode. She just hoped that when he did, she could contain the damage.

"But all's well that ends well," Nicky was saying. "It's her penchant for drama that makes her a fabulous designer, and her passionate nature will make her a devoted mother, so you needn't worry. She'll be a fierce advocate for her son's well-being."

If Julianne had eaten anything at all today, Nicky would probably be wearing it on his shoes right now.

"I hope you've forgiven her for her lies of omission, Will."

"We've come to an understanding."

She finally chanced a look at Will. His square jaw stuck out slightly and his eyes were like emeralds, hard as stone and glinting at her.

"In fact," he went on to say, that glare never leaving her face, "you're just in time. Since you're such a good friend of the family, I'm sure you'd like to perform our marriage ceremony."

Ka boom!

Stunned, Julianne tried to force a protest past the lump in her throat, but all that came out was a gasping sound. Carly and Nicky were both speaking, but she couldn't make out what they were saying as she struggled to breathe. *Married?* No way had she agreed to that!

Will's hand was tapping her back as she choked on her angry rebuttal. She gasped again and Will scooped her up in his arms. He carried her over to a bench, where he sat down with her in his lap, his palm still kneading between her shoulders as he calmly told her to breathe.

Breathe? What she really wanted to do was kick him, only she was too busy choking.

Carly knelt before her, a bottle of water in her hand. "Take small sips. Slowly."

The water helped to unlock the muscles in Julianne's throat and enabled her to take several gulping breaths. As her breathing returned to normal, she relaxed into the crook of Will's arm. He continued to rub her back. The instinct to sink into his caress was overwhelming and Julianne began to wonder if he'd cast some spell over her, just like the night at Chase Jordan's wedding.

Wedding!

She blinked back the tears that had formed in her eyes while she'd been gasping for air and stiffened her spine. Will's fingers tightened their grip on her back, as if they sensed she'd returned to full mental capacity.

Slowly, she turned her head and shot a death glare over her shoulder at him. "I'm sorry, I thought you said we were getting married?"

The muscles in his face remained impassive, but triumph briefly flared in his eyes. "I did. And we are. As soon as it can be arranged. It comes under the provision of *anything I want*, according to our little agreement."

Julianne's stomach lurched again and she felt her pulse ricocheting at the base of her neck. This man was infuriating! She dug her elbow to his belly only to be met with the definition of *Abs of Steel*. The pressure on her back became more firm.

Don't even think about it, his eyes warned her.

"Jules?"

She looked ahead at Carly. Her friend's face was full of anguish as she glanced between Julianne and Will. "Is this true? You agreed to this?"

"We were just working out the details before you two arrived," Will lied. Julianne was too angry to find the words to refute him.

"This is wonderful news! Of course I'll preside over a ceremony. But you understand, we won't be able to have it in a church."

Nicky's words shook her to the core. She was getting married. To someone she didn't love. Even worse, to someone who didn't love her. Yet Nicky sounded . . . happy.

"Julianne, sweetie." Carly's voice permeated the storm of emotions fogging up her brain. "Is this what you want?"

"It's what's happening." Will's tone was final.

"Shut up, Will." Carly had obviously learned a thing or two being married to a football player because her tone was just as lethal as Will's. She took one of Julianne's hands in her own. "I'm talking to Jules."

Frequently throughout these past two days, Julianne thought her friend had been on Will's side. But when she'd needed her most, Carly was there. With her. She swallowed to keep the tears at bay, relieved to know she could still count on her friend. But Carly's question weighed heavy in her heart. It didn't matter what Julianne wanted; her wants had been sacrificed when she'd committed the egregious sin against Will by trying to deny him his son. The guilt of that offense was eating her alive. Julianne owed Will and apparently, he'd found his pound of flesh. If she was going to agree to this—and she still wasn't sure she could—she'd do so for the sake of her son, another innocent victim in all of her deceit.

That didn't mean she was giving in to Will without a fight. Her son's father might be holding all the cards right now, but she had some ground rules she intended to lay down before any wedding—even a fake one to pacify Will's enormous ego—took place.

She squeezed Carly's hand. "I'm good. Would you both mind going to check on Owen while we finish"—she wanted to say *negotiating*, but she didn't want Carly to worry—"working out the logistics?"

Carly hesitated a minute before standing and releasing her hand. Nicky stood, too, giving Julianne a gentle squeeze on the shoulder. "This is for the best. You'll see." Neither his words nor his gesture pacified her. Instead they left her feeling as if he were placating her. Again.

Julianne attempted to jump off Will's lap, but he held her there. "Wait until they've gone inside before you start spitting nails at me," he breathed into her ear.

As soon as Carly and Nicky entered the hospital, she wrenched herself free of his grasp and scrambled for the chair Nicky had vacated, rushing to get her point across before he could raise a hand to stop her. "First things first, this is a marriage in name only." She wrapped her arms around her as a cool breeze blew through the courtyard. Her body instantly missed the warm heat of Will's, and she shivered involuntarily. "There'll be no touching like that again."

Will's mouth tightened into a straight line before he spoke. "True that, Princess. From now on, even the Heimlich maneuver is off-limits. Like I said before, my only interest in this relationship is one with my son."

His words were a vicious reality check. Julianne tried to get a handle on the roller coaster of emotions she felt about Will. One minute she hated him. The next, her body was shuddering over the loss of contact with his. She needed to keep her wits about her. To set up barriers to ensure she survived any and all close encounters with him.

"I'm not doing your laundry or cooking your food. I'll take care of Owen and myself. You can spend as much time with him as you want, but I'm not pretending we're one big happy family."

She thought she heard him grind his teeth. "I don't care what happens inside the house, but when we are out in the town, no one knows this is a sham."

"Oh, come on! They'll all know it's a sham when Owen and I pop up out of nowhere."

"I don't care! My son will *not* go through what I did as a child living in that town!"

Julianne felt a moment of fear. Where was he taking them? What would Owen be exposed to?

She felt a measure of distress, too, for the man sitting next to her. He'd obviously had a tough childhood growing up without a father. One that left scars. She didn't want that for her son. Maybe he was right to want her to pretend. *But marriage?*

Sighing, she rested her head in her hand. "Will, this is crazy. I know you're angry with me for . . . lots of things." It wasn't hard to admit she was guilty on so many levels. And she empathized with his desire for Owen to live a respectable life, but she suspected her calling out Nicky's name while they were making love was the trigger for this unorthodox marriage proposal. "But a marriage just doesn't make any sense."

He arched an eyebrow at her. "Actually, it makes perfect sense. It's the only scenario that gives Owen exactly what he needs." His tone turned lethal. "Unless you and the priest had other plans? Shall I call him back out here to discuss it?"

Julianne lunged from the bench to grab at Will as he started to rise. "Absolutely not!" She couldn't let Nicky ever know what she'd done. It was mortifying enough that Will knew.

His next words were ruthless. "I'm taking Owen to North Carolina as soon as he's able. If you want to come with us, you'll come as my wife. The other option is you get back on the bus to crazy town and wait for a custody battle that will air *all* your dirty laundry."

Julianne's whole body trembled. She'd brought this mess on herself with her behavior and lies. If Will's intent was to punish her, he'd hit the bull's-eye.

But Owen was hers and she wouldn't give him up no matter how hard Will bullied her. He'd said it was only three months until the season started. By then, Owen would be completely recovered, and that was all that was important. She could do anything for the sake of her son. Even spend a few months married to a Neanderthal.

"For crying out loud, we don't know anything about one another," she whispered.

"So do a Google search on me." He stood up, towering over her. She couldn't see his face with the sun shining behind his head, but she felt the derision rolling off him landing like heavy rain in her lap. "Roscoe can draw up a prenup and send it over tonight. We can have a civil ceremony as soon as I get a license. I'll make the arrangements. Don't bother with one of your gowns, though. This isn't going to be a party."

Later that evening, Julianne sat on the hard sofa in the waiting area, her bare feet tucked beneath her.

Sebastian, Nicky, and Stephen were seated around the table, debating the prenup forms Will had sent over. His lawyers had worked quickly. Still, they'd have to wait forty-eight hours for a marriage license, even with her brother pulling strings.

"It's a pretty straightforward agreement," Sebastian explained to her brother. "When they dissolve the marriage, both leave with the monies they came in with. Until then, Will provides for Owen's everyday care while Julianne provides for her own expenses. He's establishing a trust for Owen for his education and so forth. As prenups go, it's really standard."

"I really don't like the way you keep saying *when* they dissolve their marriage. You're dooming it to failure before it even begins." Nicky had been singing the same tune all day.

Sebastian refrained from commenting. Like Carly, he'd never been a big fan of Nicky. Besides, they all knew the marriage was a farce and destined to end in divorce. She and Will just hadn't gotten around to discussing that part of their ridiculous plan.

"*I* really don't like the way no one told me she'd sold the company." Stephen had not taken that news very well.

"It is . . . was . . . my company. I didn't need your approval to sell it." Julianne was getting tired of this whole discussion.

Stephen turned in his chair to face her directly. "Julianne, after you pay everyone off, you won't have that much left to live on. A couple of years, tops. Then what are you going to do?"

"I'll worry about that later. Right now, I just need to take care of Owen."

"That's my point! Seriously, Julianne, you have such a Scarlett O'Hara complex." Stephen pinched the bridge of his nose. "Will's agreed to take care of Owen, but how are you planning to take care of yourself if you don't have any money? Are you willing to start another design business from scratch?"

Julianne doubted she would design again at all, since she hadn't been able to sketch anything worth producing in nearly a year. If she told Stephen that, he'd have a coronary. "I have Mom's paintings. I could sell them if I needed to."

Stephen's face grew redder, if that were possible. "Your mom's paintings? Are you kidding me?"

She never understood Stephen's attitude about her mother's art creations. "Nicky and I think they could sell for quite a lot."

"You and Nicky? You two are the only ones who'd buy them!" Her brother's voice was so loud, she was surprised security hadn't come to investigate.

"Daria's oil paintings are fantastic and incredibly unique. A knowledgeable collector might pay a great deal for them." Finally, Nicky said something that made sense.

Stephen directed a frosty look at the priest. "You would say that." He turned back to Sebastian. "As long as Owen is taken care of under this agreement, you can let her sign it. My sister is going to do what she wants. She always has." He stood to leave.

"As long as your nephew becomes legitimate, you mean!" She and Stephen had never been close, but his contempt was more than she could emotionally handle tonight. "Heaven forbid my life interferes with your campaign!"

"For God's sake, Julianne!" Stephen's rant had Nicky clearing his throat. "This isn't about me. It's never about me. You're my sister and I want to see you protected. Taken care of. Except you won't let anybody do that for you. You make it impossible. I only hope Will Connelly knows what he's getting himself into." He pushed out a heavy breath before he leaned down to kiss her on the forehead. "Are you coming back to the town house tonight? Faith and the kids are there. They wanted to be here for your wedding."

Julianne's stomach clenched. She didn't want Stephen's family at the wedding. Truth be told, she didn't want anyone to witness the ceremony. Especially her niece and nephew, who were too young to understand it wasn't real. But Stephen was her half brother, one who obviously had finally decided to take his role seriously. So she kept her protests to herself. She was all in now, and there was no stopping.

She shook her head. "I'll probably get there after everyone's asleep. I want to feed Owen again tonight."

He looked like he wanted to say more. Instead he nodded at Sebastian and Nicky and headed out the door.

Just as she had the day before, Julianne put a shaking hand to paper and signed the prenuptial agreement. It was the first step; in a few days, she'd be married to Will Connelly.

Seven

It should have been a simple thing, getting married.
Theirs was to be a marriage based strictly on a business
arrangement, a perfunctory step to legitimize Owen. When
the words had shot out of his mouth at the hospital the other
day, the idea made perfect sense. They could rusticate in
North Carolina and no one in town would dare question
Owen's legitimacy. Problem solved. All that was needed
was a license and the brief utterance of a few select pro
forma words to make the whole thing legal. No flowers, no
music, no cake, no *wedding* and all the inane crap that went
with one. Easy.

Instead, the process took two full days to pull off. Two
days in which everyone had equal opportunity to throw their
two cents at Will. Starting with his mother.

"Are you sure about this, Will?"

The question, posed in his mother's soft, unassuming
Southern drawl, had begun to burn a hole in the side of his
head, he'd heard it so many times in the past forty-eight
hours. Teammates, his coach, Hank, Roscoe, and now his

mother were all questioning his sanity with the same five-word refrain.

Was he sure about marrying Julianne Marchione? *Hell no!* But since she was his son's mother, it was a necessary step.

"I'd think this would make you happy, Mom. Finally, there will be a marriage in the Connelly family."

He hadn't meant for his words to wound, but his mother's mouth tightened ever so slightly as she clasped and unclasped her fingers in her lap. With a sigh, Will sank down on the leather sofa beside her, taking one of her hands in his. They were holed up in the study of Hank Osbourne's house. Maryland's marriage license requirements were the least restrictive in the D.C. area, so the ceremony would take place in front of a judge who happened to be one of Hank's golfing buddies. Best of all, they'd be away from the glaring eyes of the media.

Despite Will's attempts to keep things simple, Julianne's brother seemed determined to turn the nuptials into a three-ring circus, repeatedly asking Will if he wanted to invite any special guests. Will was used to people who wanted to rub shoulders with famous jocks, but he wasn't going to invite any of his friends to witness a pretend wedding. That would only make a joke of their own marriages. He certainly wasn't going to ask his teammates to participate in this farce. And he couldn't ask Coach Zevalos, the one man who'd been like a father to him all those years ago, not while the senator's name was linked to the mob of media and senate committee staff trying to bring him down. Instead, his mom would stand up as his only witness.

"What I'm sure about is this is the best thing for Owen." He brushed a strand of soft brown hair off her cheek. Attractively dressed in a shimmery peach dress that wrapped around her narrow waist, his mother looked younger than her age of forty-six. But then, she'd always been pretty, oftentimes the object of many leers and taunts from the teenage boys she'd transported to school during her days as a bus driver. If she knew how many times he'd fought over the suggestive remarks other boys had made about her, she never said.

Whereas Will was brawny and muscular, she was small-boned and delicate. The only similarity between mother and son: emerald green eyes. Today, Annabeth's glistened with unshed tears.

"Lots of professional athletes father children with women they're not married to. It's not like you'd be a pariah. Sadly, I think it's actually become socially acceptable."

"Not for me," Will growled. "I can't believe you're even suggesting it."

His mother patted their joined hands. "I'm not. Truly, I'm proud of you for taking responsibility for this. But you don't know this woman. Not really. How can you trust her enough to marry her?"

"I *don't* trust her. It's like that saying, keep your friends close and your enemies closer. And I don't need to trust her fully because it's not that kind of marriage. I only have three months before I have to be in training camp and then the season starts. I can't waste that time arguing over who'll have custody on which days. I want to bond with my son instead, which means we need to live together in the same house. Being married shields Owen from the negative stigma you know he'll face."

"He's a baby! Do you think he really cares?"

"I care." Of all people, his mother should have understood that. Will was annoyed that he had to defend his decision to his mother. "We've both signed a prenup, which will make the process easier when we separate after the season starts."

"My heavens, you make it all sound so romantic."

"This from the mother who used to tell me that fairy tales were for books and movies, but not real life." It was one of the things Will most admired about his mother; she was pragmatic and determined to roll with whatever life threw at her.

She wiped away a tear. "I only said that because you were

constantly dreaming our life would suddenly turn into an episode of *Dawson's Creek* or a Disney movie where a football coach would arrive in town and announce he's your long-lost father."

"It wasn't always a football coach. I would have been happy with the Matrix." Or any man who would give his mother back her youth and rescue them from the poverty that had constantly nipped at their heels.

She leaned her head on his shoulder. "I just want you to have a chance at a relationship. A real marriage. It's too late for me, but I'd hoped for something better for you."

Will placed a finger beneath his mother's chin, lifting it so they were eye to eye. "Hey, who says it's too late for you? You could have a relationship. A marriage, too. You just need to get out of that stupid town and live a little."

It was a familiar argument. Thanks to the outrageous salary Will earned to play a game, his mother could finally afford not to work and to enjoy life. Instead, she continued to dig into her hometown, choosing to live there and manage her grandmother's antiques store. Maintaining the weathered hundred-year-old building that housed the store cost more than his mother brought in each year, but she refused to give it up. Her unwillingness to venture out of Chances Inlet frustrated Will.

His mother shook her head. "I know you don't believe it, but I'm happy. My life is comfortable and familiar. I'm too set in my ways to want to start over somewhere else, much less *with* someone else. Besides, I'm not going anywhere while my grandson is in town."

Will kissed her on the forehead. "We'll both be able to forge a relationship with Owen. It's not just the two of us anymore."

"And his mother? How does she fit into our new family dynamic?"

His gut clenched at the thought of Julianne. He'd been avoiding her these past few days, catching glimpses of her at the hospital when he visited Owen. The conflicting emotions that rolled through his body every time he saw her made him nuts. On the one hand, he wanted to hate her for attempting to shut him out of Owen's life, but whatever attraction that hummed between them still pulled at him every time he laid eyes on her. He only hoped he hadn't made a mistake by insisting they spend the next three months in close quarters. For once, he was grateful his mother had remained in Chances Inlet; she'd be effective at running interference.

"Julianne will always be a part of Owen's life," he said. "We all need to try to get along, for his sake. Beyond that, she isn't a part of this family."

"In a few minutes, she will be."

"That's just a legal technicality, Mom." He stood, gently tugging his mother to her feet beside him. "It's only temporary."

Her eyes were still sad as she adjusted his tie. "Not exactly what one wants to hear from the groom on his wedding day, but under the circumstances it'll have to do. I guess I raised us both right, didn't I?"

Will smiled down at his mother as she uttered one of her favorite sayings. She'd been a child herself when he was born, living with her grandmother. Both he and his mother had grown up together. "Yeah, Mom. You did."

Just like that, Julianne was married. No wedding Mass. No wedding gown. She hadn't even worn a dress. Not because Will had made the comment about her not wearing one—he was about to find out she was not giving in to him on everything—but because if she dressed like a bride, then this whole mess would seem genuine. The less she thought of their marriage as being real, the more apt she was to get through the next few months. So she'd donned a Calvin Klein silk blouse and pants, both cream colored; her mother's pearls; and a pair of pearl earrings borrowed from Carly. Her sister-in-law, Faith, wanted to put flowers in Julianne's hair, but she'd worn it long instead. The simpler the better.

What she hadn't counted on was a wedding ring. That

little detail was causing her to hyperventilate. When Will slid it onto her finger during the ceremony, she nearly fainted. But no ring was presented for her to place on his finger. And that made her angry.

"So let me get this straight, Will asked you to pick out a wedding band for me and you said nothing to me about it?" She paced the long kitchen in Hank's house while Carly sat quietly at the kitchen table.

"I was doing you a favor, Jules. Will's a guy. A linebacker. God knows what he would have picked out."

"It doesn't matter what he would have picked out! I don't want to wear a ring. Don't you get it? This isn't a real marriage. This"—she waved her hand in front of Carly's face—"makes it real!"

Carly grabbed her hand and guided her down into a chair beside her. "Here's a little news flash: This marriage is real. Legally, anyway."

Julianne slumped in the chair, deflated. "I'm such a hypocrite. I just promised to love a man I barely know for as long as we both shall live. What was I thinking?"

"You were thinking of Owen. And I told you that you didn't have to go through with this marriage. Something could have been worked out, but you are bent on punishing yourself."

Except punishing herself was the only way she could alleviate the guilt she felt. Shaking herself, she quickly pulled on what her brother referred to as her Scarlett O'Hara persona.

"No, I just need to stop feeling sorry for myself. This marriage is the best scenario for Owen right now. A mother has to sacrifice for her children. You'll see when your baby comes."

Carly placed a hand on her belly as her jaw dropped open.

"That move right there," Julianne pointed to Carly's hand caressing her stomach. "It's a dead giveaway. Not to mention the dopey look your husband has on his face every time he's passed the nursery this past week."

"Jules, I . . . we . . . well, we haven't said anything to

anyone yet. It didn't seem right given what you were going through," Carly whispered.

Julianne forced a smile on her face. "Don't be silly. If you'd waited six months to tell me, I would have deserved it. But don't hide your joy because my life is messed up. You and Shane did things the right way. Be happy. I'm happy for you." And she was. But if she were telling the truth, she'd admit to also being a tiny bit jealous.

Carly pulled her in for a hug. "You're doing the right thing, too. I know you'll find your happiness. Maybe even where you least expect it."

Julianne broke their embrace and stood to pace the kitchen again. "Carly, don't start dreaming. There's not going to be a happily ever after with this marriage. The only thing Will and I have in common is Owen. It would take a lot more than migraine pills for me to fall back into bed with him."

"Well, that's reassuring." Will's voice was laced with acrimony as he spoke behind her. "Nice to know I won't need to padlock my door at night."

Julianne spun on her heels to face him. She'd avoided looking at him all morning, which only made their marriage ceremony more awkward. If the judge noticed she'd recited her vows to the lapel of Will's beautifully tailored charcoal suit, he didn't acknowledge it. Likely he'd been paid well not to mention details of their wedding to anyone.

But she couldn't avoid meeting his gaze any longer. She had to steady herself on her high heels when she did. Will was breathtakingly stunning in his anger. That stubborn jaw called out to her to run her fingers, or her tongue, along his skin to relax his mouth. Julianne clenched her fingers on the edge of the table in order to keep her balance. Or keep them by her side, she wasn't exactly sure. Animosity was reflected in his green eyes along with that something that seemed to call out to her body. Something she couldn't define, but that almost had her stepping toward him before Carly jumped between them.

"Hey!" Carly held out a hand in front of Will and

Julianne. "You both just promised to love one another. It doesn't have to be love in the physical sense, but you could try being nice to one another."

"I *am* nice, Carly. So nice, in fact, that I came in here to check and see if my . . . *wife* is okay. She looked a little peaked out there earlier."

Julianne actually quivered at his menacing tone. "I'm fine," she lied.

His eyes never wavered from Julianne's face. "Could you give us a minute, Carly?"

Carly was clearly debating the wisdom of leaving the two of them alone, so Julianne gave her a reassuring nod.

"I'll just be in the other room. With Shane," her friend said, as if the threat of her husband would deter Will from harming her.

"It's okay, Carly. I've got something I need to discuss with my *husband*."

"God, you two deserve each other," Carly mumbled as she stalked out of the kitchen.

Will insolently leaned a hip against the counter as he crossed massive arms against his chest. "Eight minutes into married life and you've already got a problem, Princess? Why am I not surprised."

He'd been counting the minutes they'd been married? It would have been romantic had her husband been anyone else. Julianne took two steps forward, standing inches from Will as she waved her left hand in his face. "This is my problem!"

Will didn't flinch. "You don't like it? Your best friend picked it out. Complain to her."

She felt her face flush with anger. "It's not about the actual ring, you idiot! I won't like any ring because I'm not going to wear one for a marriage that isn't real."

He stepped away from the counter, pulling himself to his full height, and Julianne had to tilt her head back to look at him. "Listen carefully, Princess. There are only two rules in this little farce of a marriage: One, no touching. And two, you'll behave like a devoted wife and mother in public.

Unfortunately, I can't trust you to carry out rule number two, so the ring stays put."

Julianne's head was spinning. "Can't trust me? Haven't I done everything you've asked so far?" She fully intended to honor his request to act the dutiful wife and mother while in his hometown. But only when and *if* she ventured out of the house into town.

"Only because you haven't had a choice. For all I knew these last few minutes while your business manager and your BFF the priest have been chatting me up, you were making a break for it. So no, I don't trust you!"

She let out an exasperated huff. This man was seriously paranoid. She didn't have the financial resources to make a run for it right now, even if her conscience would let her. But he didn't need to know that. It would just give him something else to hold over her. So she tried another tactic.

"Fine." She placed her hands on her hips. "If I have to wear one, so do you. We don't want to give people mixed messages, after all."

"Nice try, Princess. But I'm not the one playing a part. Everyone has already figured out you trapped me into this marriage. Now you have to sell it that you're devoted to me and trying to make it right."

Julianne shook with fury. Will wasn't just paranoid, he was crazy! "Hold on a second, buster. You have seriously been wearing your helmet too tight because that is *not* how it went down. Yes, I got pregnant, but that wasn't entirely my fault. *You* were the one who forced *me* into marriage. Not the other way around!"

She hadn't realized she'd stepped in closer until Will's eyes lowered to the finger she had jabbed into his chest. Julianne felt his rapid heartbeat as he slowly lifted his gaze. Before she could react, he snared her wrist in his big hand and was dragging her around the corner and into a powder room. He slammed the door, locking it, before pressing her against the wall. Grasping both her wrists in one of his hands, he yanked them up between them, while he used his other hand to pin her hip to the wall.

She was locked in a small room with a man twice her size and capable of shattering her wrists with a single squeeze. Still, Julianne wasn't afraid. Not of Will Connelly, anyway. She was, however, terrified of herself and her body's reaction to his closeness. Arousal blazed sharply through her as her hips pressed against his hand in an effort get closer to him. Eyes closed, he appeared to be counting silently to himself, but she could still feel his heart beating as if he'd just sacked the quarterback. If he took her now, her body would sing with joy instead of protesting. Worse, he likely knew it.

She had to defuse the situation before she did something stupid. Like lean into him and start kissing him everywhere. Taunting him was not the brightest idea Julianne had, though.

"You're breaking rule number one. No touching." It might have been more convincing had she not sounded so breathless.

Will's eyes snapped open. She pressed her head back against the wall, trying to put more distance between them. The anger once there had morphed into something else: hunger. Sweat pooled along her back, making her silk blouse stick to her body. If he hadn't been holding her, she might have slid down the wall; her legs were like jelly. One side of his mouth rose up in what probably passed for a smile on William the Conqueror.

"You started it." His lips moved in for a kiss and Julianne closed her eyes. "Again," he whispered, his mouth bypassing hers and moving to within millimeters of her left ear.

Julianne tried to pretend she wasn't disappointed he hadn't kissed her. "Wh-what do you mean, *again*?" She stammered, her eyes still closed.

His breath was warm on her neck. Hot, actually. "That night, on Sea Island, you started it then, too. Remember?"

Her eyes were wide now. "I . . ." To finish the statement would be to let him know she did remember. And she wouldn't, *couldn't* give him that leverage over her. But she hadn't started it. He had. Julianne recalled it vividly. Too vividly. She felt his eyes watching her.

"I don't remember," she lied again as she squeezed her eyes shut.

He was silent for a moment, his lips still within striking distance. "Too bad," he finally said as the thumb anchoring her to the wall began to make lazy circles on her hip. "Because it was incredible."

Heat pooled between her legs as she relived in vibrant color behind closed eyelids exactly how incredible that night had been.

"You were . . . very passionate," Will taunted. "I can't believe you don't remember wrapping your legs around me. Wrapping your fingers around me. And that tongue, very wicked."

She bit her lip to stifle a moan. His tongue had been wicked, too. Julianne wasn't sure if she should pray for the earth to open up and swallow her or a repeat performance.

"It really is too bad," he breathed before abruptly pulling away and opening the door. "Because that's the only time it's gonna happen for us, Princess."

He strode out of the powder room as Julianne struggled to breathe, the wall propping her weak limbs up. She swiped a tear off her face, and her shiny wedding band glistened with the moisture. Carly was right: Julianne was punishing herself. Three months sharing a house with Will and not being able to act on her desire for him wouldn't just be punishment, it would be torture.

Eight

Annabeth Connelly stole into Hank Osbourne's study and quietly blew her nose. She needed a few minutes to compose herself. As if the shock of finding out she was a grandmother hadn't been enough, the scene she'd just inadvertently overheard when she'd tried to use the powder room a few minutes ago had scattered her already frazzled nerves. Despite her son's claims to the contrary, there was more to his marriage to Julianne Marchione than providing a blanket of legitimacy for their son. There was passion. Rousing passion, judging from the sound of it.

"Fake marriage, my ass," she muttered. Will and Julianne were a ticking time bomb, and Annabeth wasn't sure she wanted to be around when they exploded. *What must it be like to be so attracted to another person?* Annabeth sat down on the leather sofa, releasing a heavy sigh. She'd never know the answer to that. Her experiment in the free love her flower children parents preached about had landed her pregnant and alone at sixteen. She'd been paying the price ever since. Passion just wasn't part of the picture for a single mom struggling to raise a son and herself at the same time. Not for Annabeth, anyway.

"Um, can I get you something? Or someone?"

Annabeth shot to her feet and turned toward the darkened corner of the study. A teenage girl dressed in a kitschy peasant dress and cowboy boots emerged from the shadows. Feathers dangled from her pink hair as the bangle bracelets lining her arms jingled merrily with each step. Another teen appeared beside her, a tall boy, dressed in baggy jeans hanging low enough to give Annabeth, and everyone else, a view of the plaid boxers he wore beneath them. His face was hidden beneath a baseball cap and a hoodie advertising some clothing store, which he'd pulled up over his head to give him that thug look kids seemed to think was cool. Annabeth found it unnerving as she backed toward the door.

"Oh, please, don't leave on our account. We didn't mean to startle you. My dad would kill me if he thought we'd run you out of here." A pained expression crossed over the girl's face.

"Your dad?" Annabeth asked. She tried to recall what she knew about Hank Osbourne. Apparently he was just as mysterious as the Wizard of Oz he was nicknamed after, because she couldn't remember if the man was even married. Most likely, he was since he was a successful, handsome man. It was hard to imagine him not being snatched up by some woman.

"Um, yeah. I'm Sophie. Sophie Osbourne. I live here. Well, not all the time. Mostly I live in Philadelphia with my mom. And Kevin, my stepfather. And the twins, Mark and Matt. They're eight."

Annabeth relaxed a little as Sophie talked, the girl's earnestness taking the edge off her sudden appearance. She still wasn't sure about the tall boy, though. "What about him? Does he live here, too?"

"Um, oh gosh! No! This is Walker. He drove me down." Sophie turned to the boy and smacked him on the shoulder. "Take off your hat in the house, Walker, and say hello."

Walker pushed off his hood and removed the ball cap. "Yo," he said, revealing a mouth full of braces.

Annabeth couldn't help but smile, remembering those awkward days when Will struggled with growing into his body. Walker obviously still had a while to go in the man-child stage.

"So, um, are you okay? Um . . . ma'am, can I get you something?" Sophie walked over to the box of tissues on the desk and carried them over to Annabeth. "You seem a little upset."

Annabeth tried not to cringe at being called ma'am. Sophie was apparently affected enough by Annabeth's distress when she'd entered the study to offer comfort. It was sweet, especially when most teens would probably have laughed.

"I'm better, thank you." Annabeth gave them a reassuring smile.

Sophie answered with a huge grin of her own. "Oh, good. This is supposed to be a happy occasion, right? I mean, it's a wedding! How cool. Are you a friend of the bride or the groom?"

"The groom. I'm Annabeth Connelly."

"Wow! Are you Will's sister?" Sophie asked, her excitement bubbling over.

Annabeth was used to the question, but it still embarrassed her to answer it. "No, I'm his mother."

"Man, you're pretty hot to be a mom of a guy that old." Walker's voice was filled with so much awe, Annabeth nearly laughed.

"Wow," Sophie said. "Like, he must be *thirty*. And you're so . . . young."

"It's because I was sixteen when I had Will." Annabeth watched as her words registered with both teenagers. Walker immediately took a big step back from Sophie, and Annabeth had to bite back another smile. She never passed up an opportunity to use the scared-straight approach to make a point against teen pregnancy. Someone should at least learn from her mistake.

"Oh." Sophie twisted her hands in front of her. "Well, you should be happy, right? Will is getting married and you have a new grandson. It should be a nice ceremony, even if they are doing it in my dad's family room. *So unromantic.* I hope he thought about flowers and stuff. He isn't always tuned in to what needs to be done at a social event. My mom says it's because he's socially inept. Too military minded, whatever that means. But all guys are kinda like that, you know?"

Annabeth didn't think Hank was socially inept. Every time they'd met over the past four years, he'd been the opposite, actually; more gallant, a perfect gentleman. In fact, she'd been guilty of comparing other men to Hank and finding them lacking. Friends said she was too picky, when she'd only been adhering to a standard set forth by a man who would likely only be an acquaintance in her life.

She hated to burst Sophie's bubble. "Actually, there weren't any flowers or music. It wasn't that kind of ceremony."

Sophie's jaw dropped. "What? They already had the ceremony? I missed it?" She turned to Walker, her eyes slits in her pretty face. "I told you not to stop at IHOP! Now I've missed the wedding."

Walker took another step back. "Whoa, chill. I was hungry. Anyways, you can still show your earrings to the designer. She's probably had a few glasses of bubbly, which means she'll be easier to convince to buy your jewelry. After a few drinks, my mom will let me do whatever. How do you think I got the car for the weekend?"

"I'm afraid that won't work, either. No champagne." All in all, the ceremony was pretty bare bones. Annabeth had hoped for at least a photo to preserve the occasion for Owen when he was older—they were doing this for him, after all—but she'd dismissed that idea after glimpsing her son's tortured face when he'd stormed out of the powder room earlier. "And if you're looking for Julianne, she's already left. She wanted to get back to the hospital to see Owen." The bride's face hadn't been much better when she'd exited.

Sophie plopped down on the sofa with an emotional sigh,

mirroring Annabeth's actions from moments before. "Wow. I'm gonna get grounded for sure, and all for nothing. My one chance to get a top designer to see my jewelry, and I blew it."

Walker sat down on top of the coffee table in front of her. "No, I blew it, Soph. I'm really sorry. We shoulda just stopped at a drive-through or something."

Annabeth handed Sophie the box of tissues as she sat down beside her. "Your parents don't know you're here?"

"Well, obviously my dad was gonna find out, but it would have been worth the punishment if I could get Julianne Marchione to use my necklaces or earrings in one of her photo shoots. I didn't even know my dad knew her until my mom was blabbing to all her friends that one of the players on the Blaze had knocked up a famous fashion designer." She looked up at Annabeth sheepishly. "Sorry. I mean, well, about the knocked-up part."

"Nothing to be sorry about. That's exactly what happened." Annabeth reached up to finger one of the earrings dangling from Sophie's ear. "Did you make this? It's stunning."

The earring, a cascade of wire-wrapped clusters of purple amethyst briolettes topped with moss aquamarine stones, shimmered in the room's low light. As the owner of an antiques shop, Annabeth had developed an eye for distinctive and original jewelry, and Sophie's creation was unique and very fashionable. Not to mention marketable.

The girl reached up and withdrew the earring from her ear and handed it to Annabeth for a closer look. "Yeah, I have a matching necklace for them, too."

"Soph is a whiz at making jewelry," Walker chimed in, admiration in his voice. "You should see what she can do with a soldering iron. And those thingies she makes with the leather, they're—"

"Walker, I don't think Annabeth cares about my jewelry." Sophie snatched back the earring and began putting it back in.

"Actually, I do." Annabeth looked over at the girl's

stunned face, her hand poised with the earring halfway in her earlobe.

"You do?"

"I own a small antiques store in a very trendy summer resort town. My customers love one-of-a-kind jewelry like yours. I'm sure it would sell quite easily."

Sophie's face lit up, nearly matching the soft pink of her hair. "Really, Annabeth? Oh my gosh, that's so mad!"

"But"—Annabeth held up a finger as Walker and Sophie were fist-pumping one another—"only if you tell me why you need the money. If you're using it to buy drugs, the deal is off."

"Hey!" Walker cried.

"Drugs? No way," Sophie protested. "I'm so not into that!"

"Yet you'd risk getting grounded to sell some jewelry. Why?" Annabeth had worked with enough teenagers to know things weren't always what they seemed. Her gut was telling her Sophie was sincere. She hoped her gut was right.

"I'm perpetually grounded. I have a D in physics, so I'll likely spend my summer trapped at home watching the twins while my mom plays tennis at the club and weekends at the shore with her book club." Sophie leaned back against the sofa cushions and crossed her arms in disgust. "My friend Lizzie moved to L.A. last year and I want to go visit her. My dad keeps saying he'll take me, but since there's no professional football team in Los Angeles, that isn't likely to happen. So I wanna buy my own ticket. Lizzie says I'd like California. I wouldn't stand out so much there. I just want to meet people like me, you know?"

"The kids at our school are all rich, WASPy tight-asses," Walker added. "They don't appreciate Sophie's artistic genius."

Annabeth's heart squeezed tightly in her chest at Walker's words. She could easily relate. At fifteen, she'd been thrust into a small-town school in the heart of the Bible Belt weeks after her free-spirited hippie parents had been killed in a car accident. Her parents didn't believe in the institution of marriage or school or anything else, instead roaming the country wherever the wind blew them. Needless to say, the transition to normal life was a bumpy one for Annabeth, and acceptance was difficult to achieve. Of course, showing up to school pregnant at sixteen hadn't helped.

"Here." She pulled a business card out of her clutch and handed it to Sophie. "I'll be in the store tomorrow afternoon. Why don't you call me then and we can chat about what you have and work out the details of getting your product to the shop."

Sophie hurled herself into Annabeth's arms. "Oh, Annabeth, I love you!"

"Sophie Claire!"

The three of them jumped to their feet at the sound of Hank's voice.

"Dad!" Sophie squeaked.

"What are you doing here?" Hank demanded.

Sophie clenched her fingers in her skirt. "Um . . ."

Hank ignored his daughter. "And more importantly, how did you *get* here?"

"Yo." Clearly, Walker didn't possess innate self-preservation skills, or he'd have kept quiet.

Fisting his hands at his hips beneath his unbuttoned suit jacket, Hank glared at Walker behind his wire-framed glasses. Not quite as tall as Will, Hank still wasn't a small man. She could see well-defined pectoral muscles beneath his crisp dress shirt. A small abrasion, likely from his razor, marred his rugged jaw, but it didn't detract from his handsomeness. His nostrils flared briefly when his steely blue eyes came to rest on her. Annabeth had to lock her knees at the fierceness of his gaze.

"You got in a car with *him*?" He sliced a finger through the air at Walker. "On the highway with Mr. T-bone-his-mother's-car-the-day-he-gets-his-license? What were you thinking?"

"It wasn't like that! That old geezer didn't look where he was going when he pulled out. It wasn't my fault."

"Daddy, Mom exaggerated that whole thing just so you would back her up when—"

"Enough!" Hank bellowed.

The room was silent as Hank took a few calming breaths, one hand massaging the back of his neck. Annabeth really didn't want to overstep her bounds, but she didn't feel right leaving the kids defenseless, either.

"Walker, why don't you go to the kitchen and help yourself to a piece of the cake I brought. Someone should enjoy it," she said, ruefully.

Right on cue, Walker's stomach growled. He looked from Sophie to her father. Sophie rolled her eyes at him before nodding at him to go. Hank leveled another fierce glare at Annabeth as Sophie sidled up closer to her. Annabeth answered his gaze with a raised eyebrow. If he wanted her to leave, he'd have to ask her.

Hank sighed. "Does your mother know you're here?"

"Not exactly." Defeat rang in Sophie's voice.

He pulled his cell out of his pocket. "For crying out loud, she's probably worried sick."

"I doubt it." Sophie dropped back onto the sofa. "She and Kevin took the twins to Hershey Park today."

"And not you?"

"I'm grounded. My physics grade is still in the toilet."

"So you came here instead of studying because . . . ?" Hank prodded his daughter.

"'Cause I wanted to spend time with my father." She picked at the chipped blue nail polish on her thumb, avoiding her father's face.

Hank slammed his phone on the desk. "Bull!"

Sophie leaped up from her seat. "Of course not! Why would you want to spend time with me, anyway? I came to meet Julianne Marchione. To show her my jewelry and see if she might want to use some with her gowns. Not that you'd understand!"

"Jewelry? What jewelry?"

Annabeth's heart nearly broke at the crestfallen look on

Sophie's face. "God, Dad, don't you even listen when I talk to you? Mom and Kevin have the twins always distracting them, but you don't even have that as an excuse. Nobody hears a word I say."

Sophie headed for the door, but her father blocked her way. "Hold up. I do hear what you say. I just assumed the jewelry you make is for your friends. Not to make money." He ran a finger over the sparkling earring Annabeth had held earlier. "Is this yours? It's beautiful."

Hank's tender tone with his daughter stilled Annabeth's breathing. She'd always wanted a father to listen to her at her darkest hour. How her life might have been different had she had one. Except then she might not have had Will. And that thought choked her up even more.

"I should go check on the guests," she said, making her way past them.

"No!" Sophie cried. "Please don't go, Annabeth. Dad, Annabeth is going to sell my jewelry in her store. We were just talking about it."

"Is that so?" Hank's measuring glance focused in on Annabeth. She licked her lips.

"It is, right, Annabeth?" Sophie sounded nervous, as if her father would force Annabeth to retract her offer.

"Yes, we have a deal." She smiled at Sophie before turning her gaze on Hank, daring him to contradict her.

He contemplated them both before speaking. "On one condition."

"Daaaad!" Sophie wailed.

"That physics grade has to go up a letter grade before you can work on any new jewelry. If it does, you can spend all summer working in her store for all I care."

"Really? Can I, Annabeth?" Sophie's eyes beamed.

Annabeth looked at the girl's father, who raised his own eyebrow in challenge.

"Sure," she heard herself saying. "I can always use the help during the summer."

"Ohmigod! This is so sweet!" Sophie hugged her dad

before wrapping her arms around Annabeth. "I'm sooo glad I came today. Meeting you is the best thing that ever happened to me!" She flounced out the door to find Walker.

They both stood there in silence staring at the door. Feeling the need to flee with Sophie, Annabeth retrieved her clutch from the sofa.

"Mrs. Connelly." Hank's nearness startled her.

She looked up to find him watching her carefully. "It's Miss. I've only ever been a Miss."

Hank lifted a hand in agitation and rubbed the back of his neck again. She'd rattled him. *Good.*

"Yes. *Miss.* I apologize."

He paused for a moment to study her face. Annabeth felt heat flare in her cheeks. He was looking at her differently. Like a man who was interested in her. She'd seen that look many times before. Unfortunately, like the men before him, he wouldn't find her interesting once he got past her good looks.

Hank seemed to shake himself. "Thank you. For backing me up there. She's a little . . . impetuous, but she's a great kid. You shouldn't worry about having her underfoot all summer, though. Physics doesn't come that easily to her. She's not very theoretical."

Annabeth took exception to his remark. Unexpected motherhood had stalled her own education, and she had only a high school GED. Her son never lorded his Ivy League degree over her head, but she knew she was definitely inferior to him academically. Obviously, Hank Osbourne, with his multiple college degrees, felt the same way about his own daughter.

"Shame on you! You should encourage your daughter to succeed. I truly hope she surprises you. And when she does, I'll be delighted to have her work for me."

He didn't recoil from the bite of her words. Instead, his lips curved into a wolfish grin. "I do, too, Miss Connelly. In fact, I may pay for her tutor to come every night before the final exam in two weeks so she does well on it."

Annabeth tried to stalk past him, but he stopped her at the door.

"Aren't you curious about why I want her to succeed?" he breathed into her ear.

She turned her neck to meet his gaze, but said nothing.

He pulled the door open. "Because then I'll have an excuse to spend my weekends in Chances Inlet with its extraordinary . . . scenery," he murmured as she stepped over the threshold into the foyer.

Annabeth didn't dare look back. She was torn—on the one hand, hoping Sophie would surprise her father, but on the other, wary of having Hank Osbourne pursuing her. Hank was a part of her son's world, not hers. He'd quickly realize that fact when he arrived in Chances Inlet.

Nine

The small jet landed smoothly on the runway nestled between the berm and sand. Will had wasted no time getting them to North Carolina once Dr. Ling had discharged Owen that morning, swiftly whisking them off to Reagan National Airport, where a private plane waited. He'd arrived at the hospital with a state-of-the-art infant carrier, insisting their son be properly strapped in his seat the entire time they were in the air. Julianne was relieved that Owen slept peacefully during the forty-minute flight because, had he been fussy, there was no way she was leaving him in that car seat. Her arrogant, domineering husband could bluster all he wanted.

It had been two days since their marriage and that encounter in the powder room. She'd managed to keep her interactions with Will brief and always in front of witnesses. Once on the plane, however, he was difficult to avoid. He took up most of the cabin, lounging in one of the wide chairs across from Julianne and Owen. It was the first time she'd seen him dressed casually, wearing jeans, sneakers, and a tan golf shirt that brought out the green in his eyes. Not that she saw much of them since he'd spent the trip perusing his iPad while Julianne feigned sleep.

"I made an appointment with a pediatrician in Wilmington next week for Owen's well-baby visit," he announced, apparently fully aware she wasn't sleeping. "I interviewed him yesterday. He comes highly recommended."

Julianne cracked an eyelid open. Will was watching her, waiting for a reaction, that cool defiant look on his face. His presumptiveness was really starting to rub her raw. Dr. Ling had already referred her to a pediatrician located in Chances Inlet, a former medical professor of hers at Duke, now in private practice in the small town. Julianne had the woman's name tucked in her purse.

"I've already taken care of it," she said, closing her eyes again. Not exactly true, but she planned on taking care of it once they landed.

She heard Will snap the case of his tablet closed. "Really? Because you weren't even taking notes when Dr. Ling was discharging him. Do you even have a vague idea of the number of checkups and inoculations Owen needs in the next several months? Or do you plan to parent the same way you live your life, by the seat of your pants?"

Julianne was thankful her seat belt was still securely snapped around her waist; otherwise, she might have flown out of the chair and throttled him. Her eyes were wide open now, and she could only imagine what he saw reflected in them. Not that he registered any reaction. His opinion of her stung, however. She wasn't the flaky artist her brother constantly made her out to be. But she didn't live her life encumbered by rigid rules prescribed by society, either.

"I didn't need to take notes, because you, Mr. Ivy-League-brownnoser, were doing such a great job at it. And yes, I know exactly the protocol for well-baby visits. I had several months of pregnancy to memorize it." She reached down to pull on a sock Owen had kicked off in his sleep. "Our deal was that I'd be the dutiful wife in public, but you aren't dictating how I mother my son."

Will's jaw clenched at her slip, but Julianne reminded

herself she was trying to get along. She flailed a hand in the air before he could correct her with some acerbic rebuttal.

"Pardon me. When *our* son"—she was gratified she didn't choke on the word— "has an ear infection or a fever, I'm not hauling him off to a doctor forty minutes away when I can push him in a stroller to a well-qualified, *well-liked* physician two blocks down the street."

Will hesitated, concern briefly flickering in his eyes, before opening his iPad once again. "I have an article on homeopathic remedies for ear infections."

She slumped back against the seat. Undoubtedly he had entire research manuals on childcare loaded onto his tablet. He was apparently trying to debunk the dumb-jock myth single-handedly.

"You aren't going to be able to develop a game plan for your son. He's a living, breathing entity and things are going to happen, as we've already discovered. We're going through with this ruse so you can bond with Owen. If you're stressed about every little thing, he'll sense it."

His only reaction was a brief tightening of his fingers on his iPad. "I'm organized and efficient. Having a plan leads to *less* stress."

Julianne rolled her eyes. "Right! You're wound so tightly . . ."

Will tossed his iPad onto the chair beside him. Julianne's breath caught in her throat as he stretched forward in his seat, his mouth hard. She should have known better than to bait him, but she was tired of his domineering manner and, well, she was just plain tired. And alone. And, truth be told, a little bit scared. In theory, marrying Will and returning to the small town where he grew up sounded doable. But now that she was actually living it, without the protective cocoon of her friends—Sebastian, Carly, and even Nicky—she wasn't sure how she was going to pull it off. The ever-present sexual tension simmering between her and Will certainly didn't help.

"If I'm stressed, Princess, it's because I find myself having to totally restructure my off-season with a kid I didn't know I had and a wife I don't want."

The force of his words sent her pressing further against the seat back. Of course he didn't want her as his wife. It hurt to know that here was another man who didn't envision her as a permanent part of his life. She turned her gaze to the window so as not to let him see how he could wound her. He already had enough power over her.

The pilot's voice came over the intercom, shattering their stony silence.

"Hey, Will, we're five minutes from wheels down, so make sure everything is secure back there, will ya?"

Will was quiet for a moment before switching on the intercom and answering. "Thanks, Ron."

The ocean stretched out beneath the wing of the plane, and Julianne's stomach did a flip-flop. She knew Chances Inlet was a small town located at the junction of the Cape Fear River and the Atlantic Ocean, but she hoped Will's house was at least a few blocks inland. She didn't do well near the sea, not since it had taken her mother from her.

"He's still strapped in?" Will asked.

She forced herself not to roll her eyes again as she peeked over at Owen, still sleeping peacefully, a bubble of spit dancing on his pursed lips. Her heart melted as she looked at her beautiful son. Gratitude for Will's contribution to Owen's creation and saving his life dulled a little of the animosity she currently felt for him. She pulled the blanket up over the blue onesie decorated with Clifford the Big Red Dog, and suddenly a vision of a lace christening gown danced before her eyes. She blinked, but the gown remained fixed on her brain. Relief flickered through her limbs. *Perhaps her gift wasn't gone, after all.* It was the first time in months she'd conjured up a design, and her fingers itched to sketch it. But just then, the plane's wheels hit the runway with a bump and Owen woke up howling.

Will took care of unloading their luggage while Julianne fed and changed the baby. When she emerged on the tarmac twenty minutes later, it was to find Will leaning against a gleaming SUV, chatting up a leggy blonde dressed in jean shorts and a white tank top. She was perched barefoot on the hood like a life-sized hood ornament. The girl—she couldn't have been more than twenty—looked like she was posing for a new-car ad, the wind blowing back her hair as her perfect pink mouth smiled seductively at Will.

"Oooh!" she squealed as she slid off the car and made a beeline toward Owen. "Is this your baby?"

Julianne just barely resisted the urge to pull the carrier holding her son up to shoulder height just to watch the girl fall flat on her face.

"He's sooo cute," she cooed as she looked up at Julianne. "Hi! I'm Brandi. With an *i*."

"Of course you are," Julianne couldn't resist saying. Brandi-with-an-*i* probably dotted her *i* with a heart. Julianne hated the stab of self-doubt that coursed through her stomach. She'd taken care with how she'd dressed today, but next to the athletic, tan Brandi-doll, Julianne looked like the doughy, pasty white mom she'd become.

Brandi turned to Will, who stood on the tarmac, hands on hips, coolly observing the exchange. "Will, you naughty boy! Did you tell your wife about us?" She winked at Julianne. "His mama used to babysit me. Will would let me sit on his lap on the school bus every day. He never lets me sit on his lap anymore." Brandi's pout was impressive.

Julianne had difficulty feeling sorry for her, figuring there weren't many laps she was denied. "That's because he's married." It felt good coming out of her mouth, if for only this one time.

"Oh my gosh, I know, a baby *and* a wife! I was shocked when I saw it on Twitter the other day. You're very sneaky, Will, keeping us all in the dark about your secret love life."

The wind ruffled Will's hair, but that did nothing to diminish his Norse god–like good looks standing there, a stern expression on his face as if he owned the airfield. "There were quite a few people in the dark, Brandi."

Julianne felt the rest of his sentence in the heat of his stare. *Including me* hung in the air between them despite the fact that he didn't utter another word.

Owen grunted in the carrier, his face scrunched up and red as his lunch worked its way through his little body.

"Is there a changing table in the restroom?" she asked Brandi.

"Sure. There's even one in the men's room. Just go on in and make a left at the snack bar. Will and I can catch up while we wait for you."

That was so not happening. "Actually, *darling*, it's your turn." Julianne presented Will with the diaper bag. As usual, his face was inscrutable as he took the baby carrier from her hand.

"Oh, wow, you change diapers, too, Will? You *are* the doting dad, aren't you?" Brandi exclaimed as she led them through the small terminal to the snack bar. "I'll just get you both a drink for the ride into town."

"Nicely executed," Will growled in her ear as he passed by her side.

Julianne grinned. "You're welcome. The goal is to make you look like a hero in front of your hometown, isn't it?"

Will just grunted at her as he used his back to push open the door of the men's room. Julianne took a step in to follow him before he stopped her. "Where the hell do you think you're going?"

"I'm not seriously going to make you do this on your own." Julianne glanced over her shoulder to make sure Brandi had disappeared into the snack bar. "He's likely got a landfill in his diaper by the smell of it, and you've never changed a baby before, have you?"

"I studied a few videos on YouTube. I'll manage."

"Ohmigod! You have got to be kidding me!" It was all she could do to contain her incredulous laughter.

Will obviously wasn't kidding because he slammed the door in Julianne's face.

His son had pretty impressive range. Julianne was right, his diaper smelled worse than a locker room after the offensive line had pigged out on Mexican food. But Will was proud he made it through without losing his lunch. He'd just finished getting Owen cleaned when his son proceeded to piss all over him.

"Argh! You little bugger!"

Owen pumped his legs as he sucked on his hands, his eyes wide at the sound of Will's voice. Will grinned at his son, any anger he might have felt washed away by the precious look on Owen's face. He felt his own face break out into a smile, something he didn't often do as he realized he'd forgive his son anything.

Will cleaned him up a second time, thankful that Julianne had a well-packed diaper bag. His earlier remark about her parenting by the seat of her pants was a little harsh, but he resented her relaxed, casual demeanor on the plane.

It took nearly ten minutes to get Owen changed; Julianne had impatiently knocked twice already by the time Will emerged from the restroom, his shirt draped over his shoulder. Julianne's eyes went from concern to merriment at the sight of his T-shirt-clad chest.

"Apparently, you didn't watch that YouTube video that closely," she teased, eyes dancing.

"I didn't count on a sneak attack."

"You must not have been a Boy Scout. You weren't prepared."

Will tossed the diaper bag at her as she laughed openly at him.

"I hope the damage was minimal."

"I'll live. I've been hit by worse."

"Oh, that's right, you're a big fearless football player. A little pee certainly won't bring you down."

They reached the car, a new Volvo SUV with the highest safety rating. He'd bought it sight unseen, so that Owen would be protected in case of an accident. Will snapped the baby carrier into its base in the backseat as Julianne climbed in beside him.

"Is this one of the perks of being a big-name jock—you get a new car every few months?"

It was for a lot of athletes, but most of the new cars Will received for endorsements or awards he gave to charity. He could drive only one at a time, after all. Will ignored her question as he slid into the driver's seat and started the car. "Make sure he's fastened securely." He glanced in the rearview mirror in time to see Julianne roll her eyes at him. Again.

"Yes, Dad," she murmured as she whispered something in Italian to Owen and laughed.

Owen cooed back at her, and Will felt a twinge of jealousy that his son was interacting with Julianne and not him. *Or was it that she was giggling with Owen and not Will?* "The car is yours to use while we're in town."

Julianne was silent for a moment. "I guess that means our trust issues have evolved significantly if you're allowing me to drive your car."

"I'm trusting you with the car, just not the car seat. That, I'm keeping in my office."

She laughed again, but this time it sounded more patronizing than the laugh she shared with Owen. "Great. The first place I'm going is the jewelry store to buy you a wedding band so the Brandis of this town don't embarrass themselves by throwing themselves at you."

Will turned off the state highway onto the main drag of Chances Inlet as he bit back his second smile of the day. Could it be she was actually jealous of little Brandi Hamilton? More likely she just didn't like being the only one who was designated off-limits. Either way, he had to admire her tenacity. "I believe we've already covered this, Princess; I'm not wearing a ring."

"This marriage may not be real, but I won't have you humiliating me by skirting your way through town while I play the dutiful wife. I never planned to embarrass you with my pregnancy. I would have kept it a secret to protect Owen. And you," she finished softly.

For the first time in nearly a week, Will didn't want to explode when he thought of Julianne keeping Owen from him. Whatever lunatic idea she'd based her actions on, it wasn't out of malice. He understood that now. Of course, he still thought she was flighty and a bit of a fruit loop, but deliberately mean? Not so much.

He stopped at a traffic light and met her eyes in the mirror. "Relax. If I embarrass you, I embarrass Owen, and that's never going to happen."

She didn't say a word; instead she turned sad eyes to the window, and Will felt like a bully. As they made their way toward the ocean, the familiar tree-lined streets grew more congested with tourists making their way down toward the antiques shops and restaurants lining the lanes adjacent to the piers. They passed the town hall and the large welcome sign.

"*Chances Inlet, the home to second chances,*" she read aloud. "Well, isn't that ironic."

"It's bullshit, is what it is. A tale for tourists so they think the place is quaint. Folks in this town don't give second chances." Will maneuvered through the traffic of cars and tourists on foot to turn right onto a tree-lined street.

"If you're so bitter about the way these people treated you when you were growing up, why do you still have a house here?"

"It's not my house, it's my mother's. I offered to buy her a home of her own when I got my first pro contract, and this is where she insisted on living." He pulled into a secluded entry gate and continued up the sand driveway.

"Wait, we're living at your mother's house?" Julianne's voice didn't sound as chagrined as he would have liked it to sound. "With your mother?"

"Yes." He parked the car in front of a detached garage that featured a covered walkway leading to the side entrance of the house.

"Excellent," she said cheerily as Will realized he'd misplayed the mom card. Julianne actually seemed happy to have his mother chaperoning, despite the fact that his mother was definitely on his team.

"Aside from our brief introduction, I didn't get a chance to talk to her the other day at the wedding," she went on.

"Living here will give her the opportunity to get to know Owen better, too. He has only one grandmother to spoil him rotten." Her voice was wistful as she climbed out of the car.

Will reached in and grabbed the baby carrier. He'd never thought to ask about Julianne's parents. "Your mother is no longer living?"

"No."

When she didn't offer up any more information, Will pressed on. "And your dad?"

"Alive and well. He's still with the State Department. He's the ambassador to New Zealand. His current wife always wanted to live there, apparently." She grabbed the diaper bag and headed up to the covered walkway.

Will sensed the distance in her voice. From her demeanor, he could tell she wasn't close to her father. He got the impression she and her brother weren't close, either. But she had devoted friends. Carly had tears in her eyes when they'd left the hospital earlier that day, promising to visit in a few weeks when her husband's young brother got out of school. Her business manager, Sebastian, had already taken off for London, but not before making sure Will knew the consequences for hurting Julianne in any way. Will had to respect the man's resolve, even if he didn't feel the least bit threatened.

The priest, Nicky, was another story. Clearly, he and Julianne shared more than just a friendship; Will needed only to replay the scene of their encounter last summer as evidence of that. But Nicky seemed happy, almost relieved, that Julianne had married Will. And yet Julianne still clung to the priest like a lifeline. Will's threat to divulge her little outburst from the hotel that night had been the thing that cinched her agreement to their fake marriage. The whole relationship didn't add up. What worried Will more was that he even cared.

"Oh. My. God!"

Will stepped up onto the covered walkway next to where Julianne stood looking out at the magnificent vista the house overlooked.

"Incredible, isn't it?" he asked. Waves from the Atlantic Ocean slapped against the barricade fifty yards from the verandah of the two-story home. A long wooden pier stretched over the dunes to the beach beyond. Boats bounced farther out to sea as a lighthouse kept watch from its perch down the peninsula. "My mother always dreamed of having a house on the ocean. This view is one of the reasons she'll never leave here."

"This isn't *on* the ocean," Julianne breathed, her voice panicked. "This is *in* the ocean."

Thanks to his quick reflexes, Will managed to wrap his free hand around Julianne just as her face went white and her eyes rolled back in her head.

Ten

Julianne leaned her head against the cool granite countertop, her eyes closed tightly in an effort to keep the room from spinning. Owen was beginning to fuss and she didn't have time for a nervous breakdown.

"Has she eaten anything at all today?" Annabeth's voice sounded as if she were under water. Not a good sign.

"I have no idea." Will's voice was clearer; she could easily make out the sound of his disgust. And closer, she could feel the heat radiating off his body from where he stood beside her. "Here, drink this."

Julianne cracked open an eyelid. A tall glass of orange juice sat on the counter. It would be easy to reach for it and drink it, but her arms felt like cement. She hadn't eaten more than a banana today, but it wasn't the lack of food that was causing her faintness, it was the familiar panic attack she felt whenever she got near an ocean. Of course, she'd never actually fainted before this. Annabeth might be right, Julianne would be better able to handle the situation on a full stomach.

Owen began his catlike wailing, his *I'm hungry* cry, and

Julianne's body moved instinctively off the bar stool she was perched on. Will grabbed her immediately.

"Oh, no you don't," he ordered, pushing her back down and placing the glass in her hand. "Drink this. Mom and I can take care of Owen."

Annabeth had already scooped Owen out of the car carrier and was carrying him around the warm great room adjacent to the kitchen. As Julianne's mind began to clear, she took in the room's stunning décor. High ceilings and floor-length windows took advantage of the view. The furniture was light wood, upholstered in seafoam green. Ceiling fans whirred softly overhead. The far wall was lined with bookcases with a small fireplace tucked among them. The room was flawlessly accessorized, every knickknack placed properly for display. Everything was so perfect the room looked like a magazine spread.

Will put together a bottle for Owen and handed it to his mother, who sank down on a leather bench overlooking a well-appointed screen porch that could have been featured in a gardening catalog.

"Drink," Will commanded, refocusing her attention.

The orange juice was cool and tangy. Julianne felt her head clear a little more with each sip. Of course, that meant Will's menacing form came into focus as he belligerently stood in front of her.

"So what drug is it this time?" he asked quietly, presumably so his mother wouldn't overhear.

"Excuse me?" Julianne sputtered.

"You heard me. Last time it was migraine medicine that made you loopy. You don't look like you have a headache, so what's today's excuse, Princess?"

Julianne slowly stood. Unfortunately, she gave up the advantage of being at eye level once she left the bar stool, but she wasn't going to take his accusations sitting down.

"I. Don't. Take. Drugs." She spun on her heel and marched into the kitchen. The preponderance of culinary equipment nearly took her breath away, defusing the heat of her anger a bit. Everything about the room was state of the art. The appliances gleamed like new. Pots and pans hung above the massive eight-burner range looking as if they were shined daily. The spices in the elaborate spice drawer were filled to exactly the same level and were placed in alphabetical order. This kitchen was a chef's fantasy. Like the rest of the rooms in the house, it looked unused—almost like a movie set.

Will prowled up behind her. "Something laid you out back there. I swear if I find out you're using, you'll never see Owen again."

As threats go, Will's had teeth. She shivered slightly at the thought of him taking her son away. But Julianne had the truth on her side. *At least the truth about not taking drugs.* She pulled a bag of peanut butter crackers out of the diaper bag, willing her hand not to tremble. "I just had a baby. I've spent the last five weeks in a hospital eating and sleeping only when I had to. I'm hungry. That's all."

Will donned his William the Conqueror expression, which probably intimidated plenty of quarterbacks but had little effect on Julianne.

"I'm happy to pee in a cup for you. You just say the word."

He didn't so much as blink, and Julianne slid past him as she shoved a cracker into her mouth. Annabeth was humming softly while Owen sucked forcefully on his bottle.

"Your home is lovely." Except for the fact that the ocean churned right outside the front door, but Julianne figured her mother-in-law considered that her home's best advantage and not a curse, so she didn't mention it.

"Thank you, but I can't take the credit for decorating it. Will arranged for it."

"That kitchen is to die for. You must love cooking."

Annabeth laughed softly. "I rarely cook. And when I do, not in that kitchen. I have a small guest house on the other side of the garage. It has the best view."

"So you don't actually live in the house?" Julianne was starting to feel queasy again.

"No, the main house is Will's. He uses it to entertain when he's in town."

*More like he uses it to thumb his nose at the locals who'd
dissed him as kid*, she thought. Julianne was starting to put
together a more detailed picture of Owen's father. Sure, his
mother wanted to remain in town, but Will wasn't going to
let her live in anything short of a spectacular show home.

"There are plenty of take-out menus by the phone in the
kitchen. Everyone is happy to deliver," Annabeth said quietly so not as to disturb Owen, whose eyes were slowly
drifting shut. Of course they delivered. Will probably
counted on everyone in town wanting a look at his fabulous
bachelor pad.

"Actually, I love to cook. It relaxes me." Julianne strolled
back into the kitchen. "I'm pretty sure I could happily whip
up a few meals here." She pulled open a few cabinets to
check for supplies.

"I thought you said you weren't doing any cooking while
we were here?" Will asked, as he trailed her around the
kitchen as if to ensure she didn't pilfer anything.

Julianne whirled on him, effectively stopping him in his
tracks. "I said I wasn't going to cook for *you*."

Will opened his mouth to speak just as Annabeth walked
into the kitchen, a sleeping Owen in her arms.

"He's asleep." Annabeth smiled wistfully as she gazed
down on her grandson. "I forgot how beautiful they are when
they sleep."

"Remember that when he's screaming at two A.M."
Gently, Julianne took the baby from her. "Did you have a
chance to get a crib, Will?"

Annabeth nearly snorted. "Oh, I'd say. Owen probably
has the most well-furnished nursery in North Carolina."

If it was anything like the rest of the house, Julianne
could well imagine. She followed Will up a flight of stairs.

"There's a second set of stairs leading up from the foyer,"
Will explained as they came to a large landing. A leather
chair and ottoman sat in front of a picture window, compris-
ing a cozy reading nook, complete with baskets of magazines and a cashmere throw blanket. The entire house
looked like it had swallowed a Pottery Barn catalog. "The

back of the house is the master suite. You and Owen will be up front. The two guest rooms share a bath."

Julianne did some quick reconnaissance; if her bearings were correct, the master suite would face the ocean. With luck, her and Owen's rooms would overlook green terra firma. Will opened the door to the nursery, and Julianne had to bite back a gasp. Not only had Will gotten the crib, but he'd bought every piece of furniture and accessory on the two-page spread she'd given him as a guide. The room looked like it had taken five weeks to put together as opposed to five days.

"How . . . how did you do this?" Julianne whispered as she laid Owen in the crib, covering him with a flannel blanket one of the nurses in the hospital had made for him.

Will shrugged his shoulders as if to say, *I'm rich, famous, and a good-looking athlete, need I say more?* She understood the situation quite well because, up until a few months ago, she was one of those people who kowtowed to that clientele.

She walked over to the window to draw the shade, relief gripping her as she peered out to see grass and two live oak trees below. Will picked up the monitor and headed through a spacious bathroom into another bedroom. Julianne followed. The room featured a dormer window with another comfortable chair and ottoman. Julianne felt herself relaxing further as she envisioned feeding Owen in the cozy spot each afternoon. If she had to marry a stranger and spend three months living with him, she could do a lot worse. This home was perfect, providing she could avoid the front yard.

Antiques in complementing warm woods were situated throughout the room. A queen-sized iron bed took up the rest of the space, an eclectic mix of throw pillows making it look comfortable and inviting. Julianne suddenly realized how tired she was. *Nap when the baby naps*, the nurses had advised her. A perfect idea. Unfortunately, there was two hundred pounds of NFL badass standing between her and forty winks.

"These are the toys I ordered." Will pointed to a box near

the closet. "They are all rated as the top toys for enhancing an infant's learning ability."

Julianne flopped down backward on the bed. "Oh God! You can't be serious? Owen is just over a month old and you're already buying him toys? You have some serious daddy issues."

Will nudged her foot with his sneaker as he stepped closer to the bed. "What's that supposed to mean?"

"You know exactly what it means." Julianne pushed herself up off the bed; she didn't like the way her body reacted to him looming over her. "You grew up poor, without a father, in a town that supposedly treated you badly for it. Now you do whatever it takes to flaunt how you've made something of yourself, with new cars"—she spread her hands out wide—"this house, and, apparently, whatever Owen needs, whether he wants it or not."

"There's nothing wrong with wanting the best for my son." Will stepped closer, his eyes hard.

"No, there isn't." Julianne trod carefully. "Owen will love you for who you are. You don't have to prove anything to him with toys or a fancy nursery. He's the one person in this world who doesn't care about your crappy past."

"You know what?" Will moved in closer so that only inches separated their bodies now. "You weren't lying before; you aren't on drugs. You're just *bat-shit crazy*!"

"Shh!" Julianne pointed to the nursery.

"Oh no, Princess, you had your turn at psychoanalyzing me, now I get my shot. You gave yourself away when you looked at the window back there. You've got a bad case of thalassophobia."

"Thala . . . lasso . . . what?"

"Fear of the ocean!"

Julianne tried to laugh, but it came out sounding brittle. "Wow, no wonder your head is so big; you've got a lot of useless knowledge up there if you can pull that word out. Really, when your football career dries up, you should seriously consider a stint on *Jeopardy*."

"Oh, no. The more I consider this theory, the more it makes sense. You fainted when you looked out front—"

"I was hungry!"

"—and you were pretty out of it on Sea Island, where there's an ocean right outside the hotel. It's all starting to come together."

"You really should consider wearing a helmet when you go out on the football field."

Will snarled at her. "Oh yeah, that's right. You don't remember that evening on Sea Island."

"That part really jacks up your ego, doesn't it? There's actually a woman who exists who can't remember having sex with the great William the Conqueror." Julianne knew she was taking a risk taunting him, but she'd rather he kiss her than delve into her fears.

He grabbed her arms and pulled her against his body. "Admit it, you're afraid of the sea," he demanded.

"Save your brute strength for another patient, Dr. Phil, because you're way off base here."

He seemed to be warring with something in his mind, and Julianne suddenly realized how vulnerable she was. "Will," she breathed.

Will's lips moved closer. "Say it, or I'll make you say it."

Julianne tried to pull back. She wasn't frightened of Will, just scared of where they both might end up if this continued.

"Don't." She shook her head. "Please!"

"William!"

Annabeth's voice cut through the heated air in the room. Will shook himself before quickly releasing Julianne. She took a step back, rubbing her arms as she did so.

Will's face was once again unreadable. Annabeth's, on the other hand, was horrified.

Julianne needed to get away from these people before she fainted again. Will wasn't the type to let it go, though, so she decided to just come clean. It wasn't a state secret, anyway.

"I'm not afraid of the ocean," she hissed. "My mother drowned at sea. It makes me uncomfortable to be near one, that's all. I'm not afraid of anything. Especially not you!"

She stepped through the bathroom into the nursery, closing and locking the door behind her.

Eleven

Will woke to the sound of a baby crying. It took him a moment to get his bearings. He glanced at the clock:
2:46

Owen had eaten a little before midnight, not that Will had been allowed to feed him. His mother, who was supposed to be on his side, kicked him out of the house right after interrupting them in Julianne's bedroom.

"You will not bully that woman," she'd said, pinching his ear between her fingers, much as she'd done when he was five. He was ashamed to say it still hurt. "You don't have to trust her. You don't have to even like her, but you *will* be civil to her."

She'd shoved him out the back door, telling him to go find Gavin and not to come back until he'd cooled off. What his mother didn't realize was that with Julianne living under the same roof, it was impossible for him to cool off. He'd accused her of being crazy, but really, it was Will who was nuts. Julianne made him that way. He felt guilty about the way he'd treated her earlier, but it was either bully her or toss her over his shoulder and give her an instant replay of their night on Sea Island—one she *wouldn't* forget. The fact that she didn't seem remotely interested frustrated him even more.

Owen was wailing now, and Will could hear Julianne shushing him in the kitchen. Sliding out of bed, he grabbed for a T-shirt to pull on with his gym shorts. He padded down the stairs in bare feet, arriving in the semidark kitchen just as Julianne dropped the plastic bottle on the floor. She unleashed an Italian curse.

Will almost swore himself at the scene before him. Julianne was wearing a long, flowing, sleeveless nightgown, the under-counter lighting leaving nothing to the imagination as to what was—or wasn't—beneath. Like his, her feet were bare, except her toenails were adorned with bright pink polish. Her hair was wild, curling around her shoulders, Owen's fist clenching a good chunk of it.

"Oww!" she cried as she tried to retrieve the bottle without dropping him. "Let go!"

Owen only screamed louder. Will bent down and grabbed the bottle, popping it into Owen's mouth so he'd stop crying. The baby took a few gusty breaths before latching onto the nipple and guzzling. Julianne tried to pry her hair loose from Owen's grip, but he seemed reluctant to let go of his mother. Will passed her the bottle and tried to work the baby's fingers free.

"He's got strong hands. He'll make a great defensive player one day," Will joked so as not to fixate on the silkiness of Julianne's hair as he gently pulled it out of Owen's now-relaxed hand.

"Thanks."

The quiet of the house settled over them, the humming refrigerator and Owen's suckling the only sounds in the night. Will was a bit shaken by the intimacy of the moment. He and Julianne stood, their bare feet nearly touching, with only their son between their bodies. Owen, who would forever link them together, closed his eyes in bliss as he drained the bottle. Will brushed a thumb over the baby's head, and Owen propped open an eye at him before closing it again.

Will looked up into Julianne's eyes. They were red rimmed and swollen behind her smudged glasses. *Had he done that to her?*

Guilt weighed on him as he pulled a chair out from the kitchen table. "You're dead on your feet. Sit."

Julianne slid into the chair with a sigh, her body giving a little shake as she shifted Owen to a more comfortable position. Will went into the great room to grab a blanket off the sofa. Julianne's eyes were drifting shut as he wrapped it around her shoulders. He poured her a glass of water and pulled a lemon bar from the container Gavin's mom had given him earlier, placing the snack on a paper towel.

"When was the last time you ate or drank anything?" he asked as he set the water and lemon bar on the table beside her.

She glanced up, her eyes struggling to focus.

Will pulled another chair forward with his foot as he reached for Owen. "Gimme. You eat."

Julianne didn't resist, carefully transferring the baby into his arms. She picked at a piece of the lemon bar. "All you had to do was ask; you don't need to bribe me to hold your son."

"You'll thank me when you taste it."

She arched an eyebrow at him before popping the morsel into her mouth. Her eyes slid shut as she swallowed. "Mmmm. Where did you get this?" She tore off a larger piece and put it in her mouth.

"My other mother made them."

Julianne wrapped the blanket around her more tightly. "You have more than one mother?"

"Uh-huh." He pulled the bottle from Owen's mouth and lifted him over his shoulder, gently rubbing his back. "Growing up, I practically lived at my friend Gavin's house. There are five kids in the McAlister family, so one more wasn't a stretch for them. My mom worked a lot. It was a place to go when no one was home. Mrs. McAlister, Patricia, is dying to get her hands on this little guy." Owen burped, and Will returned him to the cradle of his arms, gently prodding the bottle back into his mouth. The baby's eyes rolled back in his head as he began to suckle again. "I told her to give you a few days first to get acclimated before she descends on us."

"Hey, if she has more of these, she can come over at seven in the morning."

Will stared down at Owen so Julianne wouldn't see the smile on his face.

"So you *do* have fond memories of growing up in this town."

He did have some, but they were mostly of the few people in Chances Inlet who'd accepted him unconditionally, like the McAlister family and his friend Chase Jordan's family. They were often his refuge from his world at the Seaside Vista Trailer Park. Unfortunately, the Jordans had only been summer and weekend residents, the rest of the time living in Charlotte. Still, neither family treated Will as some charity case like the rest of the town did. He was often the special project of the town's do-gooders, and he hated that he couldn't do without their largesse because he and his mother needed it to survive.

"We don't have to stay here. If it bothers you too much to live near the ocean, we can go someplace else. I just need to be within an hour's flight to Baltimore for mini-camps, but we could work something out."

Julianne had pulled her feet up, her chin tucked to her knees and the blanket wrapped securely around her. She turned toward the sound of the ocean ebbing against the dock. "No," she finally said, her eyes meeting his. "You have something you need to prove here, misguided as I may think it is. And this is your hometown, so it'll be Owen's, too. He'll grow up here at least part of the year with you. And with your mom. I need to get a grip on my emotions and stop letting them rule my life. Besides, it's only temporary. For me at least."

Will had to admire Julianne's determination. It seemed there was nothing she wouldn't do for Owen: live by an ocean that constantly brought on panic attacks, put her career on hold, or marry a man she didn't love. He was relieved that she seemed resigned to the fact that Owen would live with each of them separately and that they'd make it work. For his part, Will would make concessions, too—keeping his raging libido in check, for a start. Like she said, their situation was only temporary.

"Enjoy the rest of your day," Annabeth called to the mother and daughter who'd just purchased matching batik scarves. The door chimes jangled as they left the store. She recorded the sale on her iPad, making sure to include Janel's commission. Annabeth sold the scarves to tourists for her friend who operated a mission on the island of St. Martin. Women and children at the mission made the scarves, dresses, and bracelets, carefully dyeing the fabric themselves. The money raised helped to fund education initiatives for the children.

Annabeth loved that she could use her grandmother's shop to help other women in need. Her son clearly didn't understand the situation at all. Will insisted she no longer work. He wanted her to travel or run some charity for him. Or go to college. Annabeth had no intention of doing any of those things. She was happy in Chances Inlet, a town where she knew who she was, what she was. Will wanted her to be someone else. Someone he could be proud of. Annabeth sighed. She'd raised a smart, successful son. Why couldn't that be enough? Her cell phone rang, interrupting the downward spiral of her thoughts.

"Annabeth Connelly," she answered.

"Ah, *Miz* Connelly. Mystery solved."

It took her only a second to identify the voice as belonging to Hank Osbourne. It had been a week since their encounter at Will and Julianne's wedding. His parting words still played out in her head nightly, though.

"And what mystery might that be, Mr. Osbourne?"

"Hank."

Hank. She liked that his name was ordinary, not

complicated, unsophisticated. Unfortunately, Hank Osbourne the man was none of those things. Eventually, he'd find out that she was.

"Hank," she breathed. "What mystery can I solve for you?"

He was silent for a moment. "Well, Annabeth, that's a loaded question. One I hope we can address in the near future." His challenge was issued in a seductive purr, one that caused her to visibly tremble. Thankfully, there weren't any customers in the store to notice.

Hank cleared his throat. "Today's mystery involves Sophie and her texting. Elizabeth noticed she'd been texting this number a lot and, as usual, rather than confront Sophie about it, she has me deal with it."

"Elizabeth?"

Hank sighed. "Sophie's mother. My ex-wife."

"Ahh. She likes to make you the bad guy?"

"Not always, no. She and Sophie are going through a bit of a phase where she doesn't want to intrude too much in Sophie's privacy. It keeps the peace in their household."

"But at what cost to your relationship with Sophie?" It was really none of Annabeth's business, but she liked Sophie. She also didn't want to admit that she hated that Hank's ex-wife used him in such a way.

Hank chuckled. "Don't worry. I get my turn at good cop enough. So, do you mind telling me why she's texting you so often? You aren't by chance a physicist, are you?"

It was Annabeth's turn to laugh. "Not a chance. I admire her for even attempting the class." She fingered the earrings dangling on the display by the register. "She's been sending me photos of her jewelry. And I've been sending her texts of encouragement."

The phone got so quiet, she thought he'd hung up on her until finally he spoke, his voice husky. "You are a very kind woman, Annabeth Connelly."

She pulled the phone away so she could clear her throat. "Well, it isn't easy finding reliable help these days. I need her to succeed."

"I do, too." He covered the phone so he could speak with someone else.

"Well," she said. "If that's all you need . . ."

"No! Don't hang up! I'm sorry. Despite it being the off-season, things are a little crazy around here. How are things down there? With the newlyweds? They haven't killed one another yet, have they? I'd hate to have to go out and find another All-Pro linebacker with training camp only a couple of months away."

Annabeth smiled. "They're both still alive. Just sleep deprived. They're finding out it's a lot harder taking care of a newborn without the help of a medical staff."

"And the baby, he's better, right?"

"Oh, yes. My grandson is perfect."

Hank was quiet on the phone again as Annabeth realized her mistake.

"I forgot about that," he finally said. "You're Owen's grandmother."

Yes, she wanted to scream, *I'm a grandmother! I'm also an undereducated, socially inept woman who you'd eventually find lacking after sleeping with me.* It was better Hank find out now, before she succumbed to his flirting and eventually ended up where she always did with men: with her heart broken.

"He's a lucky kid."

She didn't like the predatory way that sounded, and suddenly she was wishing poor Sophie didn't raise her physics grade just so she didn't have to see Hank Osbourne again. It made her feel awful.

"I should be going. I've got customers," she lied.

"Oh, sure. Just one more thing. Will's doing okay with all this scrutiny of his former college coach, isn't he? Things are starting to get a little ugly. Names are going to come out. I just need Will to keep us informed if any issues arise so the front office can keep ahead of it."

Annabeth paused in restacking the scarves. She was grateful Will had been given the opportunity to get into Yale and play on their football team. It had been his escape from

Chances Inlet, a town Will hated. Coach Zevalos had liter-
ally provided her son a one-way ticket out. But the man
wasn't a saint. He'd been just like all the other men who'd
paraded through town, assuming Annabeth would be grateful enough to do whatever he asked.

   "That's something you should speak with Will about.
Please tell Sophie I said hello. Good-bye, Mr. Osbourne."
She hung up before she heard his response.

Twelve

"**Sources close to the investigation indicate that** more names will be released in connection with the alleged Bountygate masterminded by former Yale and New Jersey Generals coach Paul Zevalos. According to these unnamed sources, while defensive coordinator with the Generals, Zevalos maintained a secret fund to pay his players rewards if they inflicted an injury on an opponent. Twelve players have filed suit against the Generals, the NFL, and Zevalos, alleging they were injured as part of that scheme. A Senate committee has also been convened to look into how the league has handled the investigation and the ensuing lawsuits from the players injured. That's *SportsCenter* in a minute. Now, back to Major League Baseball."

"Jeez, this bounty hunt is getting pretty intense," Gavin said before taking a swallow of his beer.

He and Will were sitting in Will's study watching the Atlanta Braves pummel the Mets. Owen was scarfing down another bottle; his son was perpetually hungry.

"It's nothing."

"Really?" Gavin asked. "Because it sounds like they've

got a lot of nothing to warrant an NFL investigation. Not to mention one in the Senate."

"What a waste of taxpayer dollars." Will shifted a fussy Owen to his shoulder to try to get him to burp.

"You know Zevalos pretty well, and you were with the Generals for a training camp and preseason. You mean to tell me this is all a bunch of bullshit?"

Owen cried a little harder, refusing the bottle when Will tried to give it to him.

"Come on, Owen, give Daddy a break here." Will stood and walked around the room, grateful that Owen's tears provided a quick distraction from the subject. Gavin was perceptive, and Will didn't want to have this conversation with his best friend right now. "What's the matter, little man, huh?"

Apparently, Gavin realized Will was done with the subject of his former coach because he let out a resigned sigh. "Maybe you should get Julianne."

"No, she's trying to nap. He's had us both up multiple times these past few nights. She needs a rest."

"Well, well, not just a doting father, but a doting husband."

"Shut up, Gavin," Will said over Owen's screams. *Doting husband* was a stretch, but he did have a newfound respect for Julianne. That first night home had been a paradigm shift for both of them. Since then, they'd settled into an easy camaraderie, each of them taking turns caring for Owen. It also helped that he avoided touching her and looking at her for extended periods of time. "You have younger siblings and a niece; what should I do here?"

"I don't know nothin' 'bout burping no babies." Gavin took another swallow of beer.

Will swore at his friend.

"Hey, not in front of the baby." Gavin laughed.

The door leading into the house from the verandah burst open, and Will expected to see a wild-eyed, frantic Julianne. Instead, Brody Janik stood on the threshold.

"Dude, are you sticking pins in that baby?" Brody shoved

his sunglasses onto his head as he waltzed into the room, infuriatingly cool, impeccably dressed, a wrapped gift in his hand.

Will stood with a screaming baby in his own hands, spit-up decorating his Yale T-shirt, and a two-day growth of beard on his face. He was used to Brody's unexpected appearances, but today his jarring perfection pissed him off. "What the hell are you doing here?"

"You've been married a week and I haven't given you a wedding gift," Brody said as he gingerly tossed the gift onto the sofa. "Apparently, I got here in the nick of time. Let me have that baby."

Will pulled Owen in closer to his body. It only made the baby scream louder.

Brody held his hands out. "Dude, I can fix this. Trust me."

The last thing Will wanted was Brody Janik in his house, much less holding his kid.

"Give him the damn baby!" Gavin yelled over Owen's cries.

Reluctantly, Will handed his son to Brody, who sat down on the sofa and immediately plopped Owen facedown over his knees. He firmly rubbed the baby's back, then patted, followed by more rubbing. After a few minutes, Owen released a belch that would make a locker room blush, his crying subsiding almost immediately.

"Damn!" Gavin raised his beer in salute. "Where'd you learn to do that?"

"Two nephews and a niece." Brody rolled a delirious Owen up into his arms and gently rocked him. "Hey, little dude. Lucky for you that you don't have your daddy's ugly mug."

Will ran his fingers through his hair, relieved that Owen had calmed down. "Thanks. Now tell me again why you're here. And skip the crap about a gift because you know it wasn't that kind of wedding."

Brody looked shrewdly at Gavin before turning back to gaze at a sleeping Owen. "Your wife. I'm here to see her."

Something in Will's gut clenched, but he kept his

expression cool. He didn't like the way Brody looked at Gavin, as if he didn't want to reveal the real reason for his sudden appearance. "What could you possibly want with my wife?" The words came out in more of a growl than he would have liked. Let Brody think what he wanted.

"I need a wedding gown."

Gavin chuckled. "You're a pretty boy, Brody, but I never pictured you in a wedding gown."

"Funny." Brody shot a lazy grin at Gavin. "You didn't tell me your wife was a wedding gown designer to the stars, Will."

"I don't recall telling you anything about her at all, Brody."

"Yeah, well my sister Tricia is getting married and she's desperate for a gown designed by JV Designs. Tricia's been calling the London office for several months, but they keep saying the designer is not taking any new commissions. When the story leaked that you two were married, I've been bombarded by all the women in my family to ask your wife personally if she'll do this."

What a load of crap. Brody never bowed to pressure from his sisters. He generally just made himself scarce, which might explain his appearance in North Carolina, but Will didn't think so. More likely, there was more chatter in the locker room about Bountygate and Coach Zevalos's involvement. Media and players were beginning to connect the dots and—if ESPN could be believed—names were being whispered. Brody was a smart kid and could connect the dots faster than most.

The tight end was also under the misguided delusion that he was Will's self-appointed wingman and could somehow help. But Will kept his own counsel. He didn't need anybody's help. Especially not Brody's. All he wanted was his teammate out of his house before he started prattling to Gavin about the situation. His best friend was already asking too many questions.

"I'll be sure to ask her." Will scooped Owen up from Brody's arms and placed the baby into the portable crib in the corner of the room. "Thanks for the help with the baby. I'll call you and let you know what Julianne says."

Brody casually stood. One thing about the kid, he wasn't slow; he got the hint the first time.

"Yeah, sure. Thanks." He strolled toward the door leading out to the verandah. "I'm actually in town for a few days." He gave Will a pointed look. "Deep-sea fishing and stuff. I'm staying at your mother's B and B, Gavin. Maybe I'll see you around there."

"No doubt," Gavin said as Brody walked out the door.

Will sat in the chair Brody had just vacated and grabbed his beer, taking a long pull at the bottle. Brody's gift was still on the seat beside him.

"I forgot all about it being your one-week anniversary. I wonder what the gift for that is?" Gavin mused.

Will said nothing, staring at the television screen as the Braves turned a double play to end the inning.

"You'd probably be off the hook with sex, seeing as most couples would still be on their honeymoon," Gavin continued. "Too bad you two aren't having sex. It would really take the pressure off a gift."

Will tossed a football at his friend's head. Laughing, Gavin ducked, catching the ball with the ease borne of having been on the receiving end of football passes most of his life. But Will wasn't laughing. He'd managed to avoid thinking about sex with his wife, who wasn't really his wife, for the past several days. Now he couldn't get the thought out of his mind again. Not only that, but he also had to worry about Brody Janik. What was he really doing in town? More importantly, whose side was he on?

"I'm really not taking on any new clients right now."
Julianne stared into the annoyingly handsome face of Brody Janik. If Will was a Viking god, this man was all Hollywood glamour boy: sparkling blue eyes, perfect teeth, and a ripped body that he wore with ease. Brody was one of those dangerous men who looked like sin and knew it. What his perfect physique didn't get him, his charm likely did. Julianne normally loathed men like him, but it was not

hard to make an exception for Brody. Something about him was irresistibly likable.

"Did I mention her future husband is a veteran?"

Julianne sighed. He had mentioned that fact, several times. Brody's sister was marrying a young doctor who'd served as a military reservist on the USS *Comfort* for eight months. While that didn't actually qualify as combat duty, he was performing a service for those men and women who had seen combat and paid a price for it. It was a nice emotional touch, and Brody used it to his advantage.

They were sitting in the bright kitchen, Julianne sipping coffee while Brody guzzled a mineral water. He'd arrived at the house twenty minutes after Will had left for his daily workout at the gym in town. Dressed in running shorts, a sweaty Baltimore Orioles T-shirt, and a well-worn baseball cap from a Boston bar, he'd seemed only mildly chagrined at having missed Will. Instead, he made himself at home in the kitchen, insisting that he'd come to see her anyway.

Owen chortled from the other room. He was lying on a quilt on the floor, swatting at a mobile held over his head by a colorful stand that straddled his body. Will was right; their son's dexterity was awe-inspiring.

Brody pulled his iPhone from his pocket. "Here, let me show you a picture of them. You'll see that Tricia deserves a special gown."

She tried to protest, but it was too late. An image of an adoring couple flashed on the screen before she could stop him.

"They make a beautiful couple," Julianne remarked. "And lucky for your sister, several of my gowns will be affordably mass-produced later this year and she can get one then."

Information about the sale of JV Designs had not been made public yet, but she needed to shake Brody loose. Aside from the quick image of the christening gown on the plane, she hadn't had an additional epiphany since. What was once as easy as closing her eyes and seeing a design was now a gift locked away in the far recesses of her brain. She had only three months to unlock her muse and begin making money again.

"She doesn't want a store-bought gown. She wants an original. And money isn't the problem. I'm paying." Brody reached over and grabbed her hand, gently squeezing it. "Whatever it costs. Just please say you'll do it."

Julianne wanted to cry. She was touched by the sweet gesture of Brody buying his sister a wedding gown, but she couldn't design one for him. It was impossible.

"Get your paws off my wife!"

She jumped out of her chair, pulling her hand out of Brody's as Owen let out a startled shriek. Will stormed into the kitchen, making a beeline for Brody.

"Dude, is that all the time you defensive types spend working out? No wonder we keep getting scored on." Brody leaned on the back two legs of his chair, clearly unfazed by the menacing wall of muscle descending on him. Of course, she figured he wouldn't be in the NFL if he couldn't stare down a linebacker.

"I swear, Janik, I've had enough of that pretty mouth of yours," Will snarled.

"Stop it!" Julianne picked up a crying Owen. "You're scaring the baby."

She watched as Will took a moment to physically dial back his temper, but when he finally looked over at Julianne, his face was a grim line. Stuffing a pacifier in the baby's mouth, she stepped between the two sparring mountains of testosterone. "Brody just wants me to design his sister a gown."

"I told you I'd talk to her about it, Brody."

"Obviously you haven't, because it's been three days since I mentioned it to you and she didn't know a thing about it." Brody's shine was wearing off; he was starting to annoy Julianne with his taunting of Will.

"It doesn't matter! I'm not making the gown!" She practically had to shout to get the two men to hear her.

Brody slammed the chair down and stood. "Don't let him tell you what to do! You can do it if you really want to."

Will was chest to chest with him in an instant. "Don't you dare talk to her like that!"

Owen started crying again, the pacifier dropping to the ground.

"No!" Julianne cried. "I can't! I *can't* design gowns anymore!"

She turned on her heel and bolted up the stairs, a screaming Owen on her shoulder.

Thirteen

"Jesus! You made her cry. I ought to knock your teeth down your throat!" Will had never wanted to hit another man as badly as he wanted to flatten Brody at that moment.

His teammate took a lifesaving step back. "Well, you were the one yelling. The poor woman probably has post-partum depression or something, and here you are bullying her not to design a stupid wedding gown."

Will counted to ten. It was a skill that had served him well all his life. "Why are you really here? It isn't about some wedding gown. Spit it out, Brody."

"My sister actually does want a dress." Brody put his hands up as Will advanced on him. "But I'll tell her it's a no-go. I really came down to give you some stuff that's been left for you at the training facility. You've had several anonymous packages dropped off since you left. Hank thought you might want to see them right away."

Will rubbed the back of his neck. "So some woman's mailing me her panties again. Just throw them in the trash."

Brody shuffled his feet. "They're not from a fan. Unless

someone in the NFL is sending you panties. The packages have come from the players' union."

That got Will's attention. Whoever was sending him packages anonymously was somehow involved in the NFL. *Which could only mean one thing.*

"Have you opened them?" Will tried to keep his tone cool.

Brody crossed his arms defiantly. "Seriously, dude? I'm your friend. I brought the packages to you because I didn't want them lying around for someone else to find. There's a lot of shit going around right now, and you're definitely six degrees of Kevin Bacon away from it. We're still a team, and I know you play with integrity every game. Whatever happened in the past is best kept in the past. Unfortunately, not everyone sees it that way."

Will blew out a breath. Brody was right; people wouldn't be happy until someone was the scapegoat. His loyalties lay with the Blaze, but his former coach had given him so much. He was walking a tightrope and his balance was getting more precarious. Whatever was in those packages needed to be addressed. But first, he needed to make sure Julianne was all right.

"I'll meet you back at the inn after I've showered." Will turned up the stairs before Brody's voice stopped him.

"Tell her I'm sorry," Brody called after him. "I didn't mean to upset her."

"Get going," Will said, climbing the rest of the stairs.

The door to the nursery was closed. He knocked softly before walking in. Julianne stood in the center of the room, the morning sunlight streaming in the windows. Her hair was pulled into a side braid hanging over the shoulder of her pink cardigan. Capri jeans and pink ballet slippers completed her outfit, somehow making her look more vulnerable. Owen sat in the bouncy seat, intently watching the shadows of the oak tree branches dance on the wall.

Will closed the door behind him, leaning up against it. "Sorry about that. He said he was going deep-sea fishing this morning, so I thought I had time to prepare you."

She sank down to the floor in front of Owen and played with his bare toes. "It's okay. I'm sorry that I couldn't help him."

"Brody's lived a charmed life. He's spoiled and not used to being told no. He'll get over it. Don't feel like you had to do this because he's a teammate."

"But I *want* to do it for him. For his sister," she whispered.

This was why Will hated getting involved with women. He never understood what they were saying. Hadn't she said she didn't want to design Brody's sister's dress not two minutes ago? He crouched down on his haunches in front of her.

"Help me out here. You said downstairs that you wouldn't make the gown."

Julianne sprang to her feet, nearly knocking him over in the process. "No! I said I *couldn't* make the gown."

He counted to ten before realizing he wasn't any further along understanding the minds of women. Maybe Brody was right and she did have postpartum depression. His teammate had older sisters, after all, so he might recognize the signs. Julianne had her back to him, sorting Owen's socks into a pile. Will gently turned her to face him.

"I'm not following here, Princess. Can you maybe explain it to me?"

She bit her lip and looked wistfully out the window. "I haven't been able to design since I got pregnant."

He was even more confused now. What did one thing have to do with the other?

"Why not?"

Definitely not the brightest question. She turned to him, her eyes all squinty and peevish now. "Well, Dr. Phil, if I knew the answer to that, don't you think I'd fix it?"

Maybe it was hormones? He didn't know he'd asked the question aloud until she pushed away from him.

"Ohmigosh, that's all your super-sized brain can come up with? *Maybe it's hormones?*"

Will put his hands up. "Okay, it's probably not hormones,

but I'm sure it's only temporary. A gift like that just doesn't disappear when you have a baby. It'll come back. You'll see."

Julianne had that vulnerable look about her again, and Will had to stop himself from gathering her in his arms. That move always got them in trouble.

"It's been nearly a year." Julianne's voice was soft and sad. "What if it doesn't?"

"It will," he reassured her. "In the meantime, you have other designers on your staff who can carry your company along, right?"

She slowly shook her head. "No, I am . . . was . . . the only designer at JV Designs."

The word *was* hung ominously in the air. Julianne wouldn't look at him, so he bent his head in front of her face. "Was?"

Julianne blinked slowly before nodding. "I sold my company."

"Why?" he asked, although he wasn't sure he wanted to know the answer.

"To pay Owen's medical bills," she whispered.

"Ahhh, for the love of . . ." Will couldn't finish the sentence, he was so angry. He'd wondered why there wasn't a bill when Owen was discharged from the hospital, but he figured it went through insurance first. Did she not have medical insurance? Somehow, he wasn't surprised.

"And before you start accusing me of being bat crazy again, I had to do it. It wouldn't have been fair making you pay for Owen when you didn't want him in the first place."

"It's bat-*shit* crazy, and I don't think even the bats are as crazy as you!" He backed her against the wall. "I told you I was going to pay for half of Owen's care. But do you listen? No! This is why smart people like me plan ahead instead of that whole seat-of-the-pants thing you've got going. I was right that first day, you need a keeper. Obviously the senator and your business manager can't keep you under control. I guess it's up to me."

Julianne's eyes were slits again. "As if you can!"

Her challenge hung in the air for a moment before he descended on her. "Stop telling me I don't want my son."

He wanted to strangle her, but only a psychopath would do that to his child's mother with their kid in the room. So he opted for kissing her instead. And it was an incredible kiss. Like a man who'd gone without food or water for days, he devoured her.

Best of all, she was kissing him back. With a sigh, her lips parted right away, giving him access to her soft mouth. Their tongues played as her hands slipped under his T-shirt and her nails stroked down his back. Will groaned as his fingers kneaded her hips, pulling them closer to meet with his hard body. His mouth left hers to explore her jaw, raining kisses there before visiting the sweet spot on her neck.

"I swear, you've cast a spell on me," he whispered in her ear before finding her lips once again.

His tongue explored her sweet, hot mouth in a soul-searching kiss. The sensation of tasting her again blazed into something raw and needy inside him. Small sounds of pleasure bubbled from her throat as she kissed him with a matching urgent need. Will stepped between her thighs, backing her toward the wall, one hand grazing a breast as the other cupped her bottom. He felt her gasp as her body became aware of his arousal.

"Will," she breathed. "Please!"

Unfortunately it wasn't the *please* he was looking for, because she was pushing him away.

"I . . . we can't do this."

His lips cruised her neck and he felt her tremble. "Why not? We are married."

"Except this isn't a real marriage." Her voice was starting to sound a little clearer and a lot more in control. Not a good sign. "I'm not good at casual sex."

He stepped back, not releasing her totally, and lifted an eyebrow at her. She leaned her head back against the wall, her neck pink where the stubble from his beard had marked her. Will stifled a groan, knowing he might have already lost this set of downs.

"That night doesn't count. I was doped on medicine and I don't remember it."

"So you keep saying."

She traced a finger over his biceps. "This is only temporary. It's complicated enough with Owen, but this . . . this would only make it messier. I'm not good with messy."

"Bull! You're very good at messy. My house looks like a hurricane breezed through it since you've lived here." As compliments go, it wasn't Will's best effort.

She was squinty eyed again. Will swore as he dropped his hands. He wasn't sure what possessed him to say what he said next.

"Saving yourself for the priest, I see."

Her hand made contact with his face and Will didn't try to stop her. He'd deserved it. She deserved an apology. Instead he turned on his heel and left the room for a much-needed shower. A *cold* shower.

Fourteen

Brody was holding court in the crowded tea room of the Tide Me Over Inn, rehashing a call gone wrong in this year's playoffs. The guests were sympathetic to his indignation about getting called for offensive interference, particularly the three young Frenchwomen who most likely hadn't a clue what he was talking about. Will shook his head and began to step into the large parlor before a hand grabbed his arm.

"Don't you dare take him from that room. He's good for business."

Will smiled down into the face of Patricia McAlister, the inn's owner and Gavin's mother. Her fiery red hair had faded into a more serene champagne color after some fifty-odd years, but her smiling eyes were blue as ever.

"Hey, you've got your own professional athlete in the family. Make him entertain your guests," Will teased.

Patricia's eyes dimmed. "The baseball season has just begun. He's too busy. Besides, Ryan doesn't come home anymore. Except maybe for weddings and funerals."

Will mentally kicked himself for upsetting the woman who'd been a second mother to him. Apparently the estrangement between Ryan and his family was as bad as it ever was, especially after the death of his father a few years back. Patricia still grieved the sudden loss of her husband deeply; the rift with her son didn't help matters.

He pulled her in for a hug, brushing a kiss over the top of her head. "He loves you. He just doesn't like being in this town."

"Spoken like one who feels the same way."

"It goes without saying that I love you." Will neatly side-stepped the second part of her statement. Like his mother, Patricia believed Chances Inlet was her destiny, the place where she'd get *her* second chance. Will and the McAlister boys all thought the myth was a bunch of crap, hightailing it out of town as fast as they could to find their destiny someplace else. Somewhere they could be someone else.

"I can't let you in there," Patricia insisted. "Not with those French exchange students in heat and you without a ring on. Really, Will, would it hurt you to wear a wedding band?"

When news of their wedding broke, Julianne's brother had spun an elaborate tale of lost love to the media. Most people believed the marriage was real. But those closest to Will—Patricia and Gavin and a few select others—knew the truth. Both his mother and Patricia were as irritated as Julianne that he would not wear a ring. Not that it mattered to him. If Will ever put on a wedding band, it would be because he loved a woman enough to commit his life to her. His feelings for Julianne were a mix of lust, mistrust, and exasperation. Nothing close to love. And any commitment they might have was scheduled to end in a few months.

"Only if he wore it through his nose," Brody interrupted, slipping from his admirers and joining them in the hallway.

Patricia laughed. "That I'd like to see!"

Will shot Brody a menacing look, but as usual, the tight end wasn't fazed.

"Go pick on your other sons. Brody and I have work to do." He turned to the ornate, curved staircase in the inn's grand foyer, and Brody followed.

"Boys!" Patricia called to them as they climbed the stairs.

Her tone was one Will had heard a thousand times in his lifetime, usually as he and the McAlister boys were off to their attic play space. "No roughhousing. This is a hotel, and I have guests."

Brody winked at her. "Message received. If I want to clean his clock, I'll take him to the gym."

"As if that would ever happen," Will mumbled.

Brody charged up the stairs, Will at his heels, and entered a large suite at the head of the stairs. Patricia had named the rooms after cities and towns in Scotland, decorating them with the colors of the clans who live there. Brody was in the Inverness room, a sunny suite with a king-sized four-poster bed and panoramic views of the Atlantic Ocean just across the street from the inn.

Will moved to the center of the room as Brody closed and locked the door behind them.

"You can't be too careful," Brody said in answer to Will's raised eyebrow. He opened the top drawer of the antique tallboy and pulled out a large envelope and two smaller ones, tossing them on the round table between two overstuffed chairs. Brody slouched in one of the chairs, one of his long legs dangling over the side. He grabbed the remote and dialed up *SportsCenter* on the television.

Will carefully picked up the envelopes.

"Dude, they're perfectly safe. I had them checked out before I touched them."

Will hadn't considered that the letters wouldn't be safe, but he felt a sheen of sweat break out on his back at Brody's words. "Paranoid much?"

"Hey, one never knows. Besides, it gave me an excuse to call this FBI agent I know. You should see what she can do with a pair of handcuffs." Brody winked at him.

He shook his head and sank down into the chair across from Brody, tearing open the first envelope.

"Hey!" Brody sat up in his chair. "You gonna open those here?"

"I thought you said they were safe," Will said as he pulled the contents from the largest envelope.

"Dude, they are. That doesn't mean I want to know what's in them! I don't want to be incriminated in this mess. You know, guilt by association?"

"Relax. I haven't done anything wrong, so . . ." Will stared at a photo of him putting a punishing hit on Denver quarterback Mark Callahan. It was the play that cemented Will's position in the NFL, the one that earned him a starting position. It had also ended Callahan's career with a separated shoulder that never recovered despite two surgeries.

"Damn," Brody said from over Will's shoulder. "That was some hit."

"It was a clean hit."

"I'm guessing someone doesn't think so."

Will threw the photo onto the table and picked up one of the smaller envelopes. In it was a small wooden emblem, a seven-pointed star surrounded by a wreath, a symbol of the Aurelian Society, one of the secret societies at Yale University and an organization Will was a member of.

"Is that some voodoo good-luck charm?" Brody asked.

Will slid the piece into the pocket of his jeans. It wasn't a good-luck charm. It was a message. One about honor and duty to the university to which he owed so much. One about keeping his mouth shut.

He didn't want to open the last envelope, but he couldn't wuss out in front of Brody. Will slid his finger through the seal and pulled out a single piece of paper. It contained one handwritten line:

SNITCHES DON'T LAST LONG IN THIS LEAGUE.

"Dude, you might want to think about getting a lawyer."

Despite her resolve to stay hidden while she was living there with Will, the picturesque town of Chances Inlet—decked out in red, white, and blue bunting and American flags to commemorate the upcoming Memorial Day holiday—captivated Julianne. From the way Will had described his hometown, she'd expected the people there to be cold, perhaps even hostile. They were anything but, constantly regaling her with stories of Will's escapades as a boy. The tales they told were more Norman Rockwell than Will's abbreviated version of his childhood.

Meandering to the town square after her postpartum check-up with an OB-GYN Dr. Ling had recommended, Julianne sat on a blanket beneath one of the huge live oak trees lining the quaint park in the town's center that featured an actual Civil War cannon. Children scrambled on top of the cannon as their parents snapped pictures. The ocean roared somewhere in the distance, but the noise didn't diminish the peacefulness she felt. Owen slept quietly in his stroller, a Blaze baseball cap shielding his face.

The pencil had started moving slowly on the page at first. What started out as doodles was slowly turning into a stunning wedding gown. Julianne dared not breathe. It had been so long, she didn't want to jinx it even by smiling. The lines of the dress were elegant, fit for the wife of a military doctor. She hoped she could hold on to the image until she'd completed the sketch.

Her iPhone buzzed on the blanket beside her, her brother's face popping up on the screen. *Crap!* Just like that, the image of the dress vanished from her head.

Tossing the pencil into the grass, she picked up the phone. "What do you want?"

"My, such a pleasant greeting." Her brother's voice was its usual smug sound. "Can't a brother check up on his sister once in a while?"

"You've called me every day since I got here. I don't think you've called this many times in a year. Ever."

"I just want to make sure everything is okay with you and the baby."

"Owen. Your nephew's name is Owen."

Stephen let out an exasperated sigh. "Julianne, I know my nephew's name. I know your name. I even know your husband's name. How is William the Conqueror treating you, by the way?"

Stephen's calls were the same every day. He asked about Owen, then how Will was treating her, as if he were suspicious that Will might be abusing her. He never asked about her, though. Of course, he never had before. Why should now be any different? She wondered what her pompous brother would say if she told him Will was beating her. Or subjecting her to humiliating sexual encounters. She blushed just thinking about the kiss they'd shared two days ago.

Instead, she answered as she did each day. "He's treating us fine, Stephen." Which was sort of true; Will was treating Owen fine. Julianne, however, was being treated with the chilly reserve Will was famous for. Ever since their encounter in the nursery, they'd gone back to being distant housemates, alternating caring for Owen. It was better this way, she kept telling herself. Easier to make the break when they had to.

Besides, Will's accusation about her and Nicky hurt more than she wanted to admit. People were forever making false assumptions about their relationship. Julianne never spent much effort refuting them because she truly did love Nicky. He was the one constant in her life, the one person who'd always been there for her, especially when she needed him the most. She didn't think her heart was big enough to love another person. Until she'd had Owen.

But Julianne was a realist. Nicky loved her, she knew, just not enough. He loved another more. At first, she'd been devastated by his decision to become a priest. As the years passed, she rationalized his choice by being thankful that at least he would never love another woman more than he loved her.

"He's bonding with Owen, then? Actually helping take care of him?" her brother asked.

An image of Owen sleeping on Will's chest popped into her head. Will had taken to getting up in the predawn hours with the baby, Julianne taking the middle-of-the-night shift. When Owen hadn't been in his crib this morning, she'd panicked, racing down to Will's study to find the baby nestled atop Will's slumbering body, his big hand securely cradling

their son. The scene was so tender it brought tears to Julianne's eyes. She'd quietly retreated to the kitchen, trying to
figure out why she was crying. The purpose of their stay in
Chances Inlet had been for father and son to establish a bond.
Julianne wasn't sure why she'd felt so left out.

"Yeah, they're bonding, Stephen. If anything changes,
I'll let you know."

"Julianne!" her brother called before she could hang up.
"Wait! I need to ask you something."

"I haven't figured out what I'm going to do with my life,
if that's what's keeping you up at night. But don't worry, I
won't embarrass you by sleeping on street corners."

Stephen sighed. "You and Owen are always welcome at
my house. And I have no doubt you'll figure something out.
You're a brilliant designer."

Julianne nearly pinched herself. Her brother had barely
acknowledged her career in fashion. A positive compliment
from him was a shock.

"What I really want to know is what Will thinks about
this whole mess with his former coach," Stephen continued.
"Has he said anything about it?"

Will hadn't mentioned a problem with his coach, but then
they'd hardly exchanged more than polite conversation these
past few days. "What mess with his former coach?"

"It's all over the sports media."

Julianne rolled her eyes. She was more *Project Runway*
and *Chopped* than ESPN, a fact her brother should know.

"It looks like he may be implicated in a bounty scheme
where players are paid to hurt opposing players," Stephen
went on to say.

"Will? Or his coach?" Julianne asked.

Stephen took a long moment to answer. "Well, it could
be both of them if the rumors are correct. Will is known for
some pretty . . . *aggressive* play."

Something within Stephen's tone sent a chill down Julianne's spine. The image of Will deliberately hurting someone else just didn't fit. Sure, he was arrogant and bullheaded,

but he was gentle with Owen and he'd been kind to her that night on Sea Island. Of course, did she really know the real Will Connelly? Could she trust him with her son?

Julianne quickly stood and folded up the blanket, shoving it and the forgotten sketch in the back of the stroller. "Well, Will must not be too worried about it. He hasn't said a word about his coach or this scheme you're talking about, and we talk about everything," she lied. "I've got to go feed the baby now, Stephen. Thanks for the call."

"Look, Julianne, things could get a little ugly. They'll try to make him out to be a monster. If you need me, just call, okay?"

The more salacious her brother sounded, the more suspicious she got. She gave him a quick good-bye before hanging up. Clearly, he didn't want his political career tainted by scandal brought on by his brother-in-law. He didn't really care about the safety of his sister and his nephew. But Julianne wasn't being fair. To Will, anyway. She'd never once felt threatened by him despite his strength and size. And she'd never seen him mistreat Owen. There had to be an explanation.

Julianne pushed the stroller toward the line of shops housed in refurbished warehouses lining the Cape Fear River. Clearly, she needed to talk to someone who'd know what was going on. She punched up Carly's contact on her iPhone, but it went straight to voice mail. Not bothering to leave a message, she hung up and contemplated who else she could get information from. Annabeth? But Will's mother was as aloof as her son, blending into the woodwork whenever she was in the house. Julianne still didn't have a good read on her mother-in-law, and it seemed like the woman wanted to keep it that way.

The beat of a loud bass interrupted Julianne's thoughts. She looked through the large picture window beside her and there stood Brody Janik, looking like he was posing for a deodorant ad inside the Ship's Iron Gym. Brandi, the one-woman welcoming committee of Chances Inlet, was adoringly admiring his form as he hefted a dumbbell.

Brody was Will's teammate, which meant they probably

had some sort of locker room code about not snitching on the other, but if she kept her questions vague enough, she might be able to find out what exactly was going on and how it impacted Will. Believing it was worth a shot, she maneuvered the stroller into the lobby of the gym. The music was loud and Julianne worried it might wake Owen. She'd stay only a minute, she decided, pulling the blanket over his ears.

Being the wife of a celebrity had its perks. The college-aged kid at the desk let her in without having to produce proof of membership. He even asked if she'd need daycare for "the little guy." *Not without earplugs*, she wanted to say. Instead, she shook her head and asked if he wouldn't mind fetching Brody for her, gesturing to the sleeping baby in the stroller.

Brody was by her side instantly, wiping his concerned face with a towel. "Hey, what's up?" He peeked at Owen, still asleep. "Do you need me to get Will?"

"Will's here?"

Darn! Darn! Darn. Of course Will was here. He was a stickler for his routine and he always worked out this time of the morning. Suddenly, she felt ridiculous letting her brother's comments get to her.

Will wasn't a monster. He played an aggressive game, and sometimes people got hurt. Off the field, he was cool and composed. She only had to conjure up the picture of his big hand on Owen's back this morning as the two slept to know Will was gentle and protective. That same hand had rubbed her back during Owen's transfusion. Not to mention how he had comforted her during the storm that night of the wedding. She took a deep, calming breath. Her brother was being ridiculous; she and Owen were perfectly safe sharing a house with Will.

Brody cocked his head, his look quizzical. "Julianne?"

She had to think fast. Wistfully, she remembered the half-finished sketch in the stroller. Julianne wasn't sure if she could finish the design, but she felt like the final image was just beyond her fingertips and she needed something to help her reach it.

"No, I don't need Will. I was wondering if you wouldn't mind texting me the photo of your sister and her fiancé? I—I might have some ideas about a gown."

"It's okay, Julianne," he said softly, his tone laced with empathy. "I have four older sisters. Two of them have kids. After each pregnancy, it took them a while to return to being . . . themselves again." He put a hand on her shoulder and gently squeezed. "Don't push yourself. My sister understands."

She felt the tears threatening. Her emotions were in such a tangle this morning. Maybe he was right and this was some sort of postpartum depression. But if she was going to get back to being herself—Julianne Marchione, fashion designer to the rich and famous—she needed to finish this design.

Something about the compassion on Brody's face made her admit her deep secret. "I haven't been able to sketch much of anything for a while, but I started something this morning and I'd like to see if I can finish it. It might not even be something your sister wants, but . . ."

Brody grinned at her, his cover-boy smile lighting up his face. "Atta girl! I won't say anything to Tricia unless you tell me to. You just take your time." He pulled his phone out of his pocket. "What's your number?"

Julianne gave it to him, and within seconds her phone beeped in response. The emotional roller coaster she was riding was on the upswing, because she felt more optimistic than she had in a long time. Until, of course, her husband's voice boomed behind her.

"Are you crazy? Owen will go deaf in this place! What's he doing in here?"

If Brody was all-American gorgeous, Will was pure Norse gladiator. Despite the fact that both men were nearly the same height, Will's presence loomed larger in the room, more commanding. His hair stood up on end from where he'd run sweaty fingers through it during his workout, and his perspiration-soaked shirt stuck to this body, outlining his well-muscled chest. He was the picture of a virile, conquering male. One who was also angry.

Julianne felt something stir inside her, something other than fear. It was more like desire. And relief that her instincts were not wrong about Will. If he were all the things her brother said he was, he wouldn't be hovering over his sleeping son, worried about his exposure to loud noise.

"Seriously, dude, that kid will be able to play in any stadium if he can withstand this kind of noise." Brody's voice was filled with awe as he glanced into the stroller.

Will answered him with his patented glare. A crowd had started to gather, and Julianne wanted to avoid another argument like the one they'd had in the kitchen the other day.

"There you are," she said, improvising as she went. "I just came to see if you would be home for lunch today."

The befuddled look on Will's face was amusing. True to her word, she hadn't cooked a thing for anyone but herself since arriving in town. Any leftovers had suspiciously disappeared during the night, but she let that go since it was his kitchen.

Julianne took a step closer, whispering through her pasted-on smile. "Be nice, I'm playing the dutiful wife here." Slowly, so everyone could glimpse her shiny, fake wedding band, she reached up and ran a hand over his well-defined pectoral muscle. Will's body went rigid beneath her touch, but his eyes were blazing. She sucked in a breath, drawing her trembling hand back and placing it on the handle of the stroller to steady herself.

"I'll see you at home then," she called out as she hurriedly pushed the stroller out of the gym, not risking a glance back at her husband.

Fifteen

"**Oh my gosh! This place is cooler than I thought** it would be!"

Annabeth looked up from the antique humidor she was repairing, startled to hear Sophie Osbourne's voice in her shop.

"Sophie! I hadn't heard from you so I thought you weren't coming." Annabeth hurriedly wiped the wood polish off her hands. Sophie hadn't texted or e-mailed in several days, leaving Annabeth to think either the girl hadn't been successful in bringing up her grade or she'd just lost interest. She'd hoped it was the latter, not wanting Hank to be right in his perception of his own daughter.

Annabeth had to catch her breath. Not only because Sophie had launched herself into her arms, but also from the sight of the girl's father standing behind her. Dressed in khaki pants and a Blaze golf shirt, Hank looked more casual then she was used to. More handsome, too. His close-cropped sandy hair was gray at the temples and laugh lines fanned out from his smiling blue eyes, but his body language boasted of youth and vigor. He leaned a hip nonchalantly against one of the glass counters, crossing his arms over a well-muscled chest, a cat-ate-the-canary grin on his face.

"We thought we'd surprise you," he said.

"Guess what?" Sophie stepped out of Annabeth's arms and grabbed her hands. "I got a C-plus in physics!" She skipped gleefully in a circle, pulling Annabeth along with her.

"Oh, Soph, that's wonderful!" Annabeth hugged her again. "I'm so proud of you."

"And guess what else? Dad is taking me to California next week! Isn't that great?"

Annabeth dared a look at Hank. "It's better than great. It's fabulous."

"So I really don't need the job, after all, I guess. I hope you weren't saving it for me?"

Annabeth shook her head. Truthfully, she would have been paying Sophie out of her own pocket. The shop did okay, but not enough to support more than the one employee she already had. "As long as you keep sending me jewelry. You already will have quite a pocketful of spending money for your trip."

Sophie's face lit up. "Ohmigosh! It sold? Really? I brought more, but I didn't think you would have sold any yet. It's in my room at the inn. I'm in the Paisley room. It's sooo cool! We're staying here for a few days. Would it be okay if I hung out here with you while Dad plays golf? Ohmigosh, Dad, can I go get my box for Annabeth?"

She was out the door before either Annabeth or Hank could answer.

"I think you made her day." Hank stepped away from the counter and began exploring the shop.

"I'm just so proud she did it."

"Me, too. I'm giving her a trip to California as an apology for doubting her ability. What boon should I give you?"

She wasn't sure what to say because she really wasn't sure what he was asking. "Me? I don't need anything. I didn't *do* anything."

Hank walked past her, studying the odds and ends lining the counters. He lifted a clock to examine it further. "I wouldn't call fiercely defending a girl you barely know from her nitwit father nothing. Or encouraging her not only to go after her dream, but to put her nose to the grindstone. That wasn't nothing. I told you this before: You have a kind heart, Miss Connelly. At least let me take you to dinner to make up for my error in judgment with my daughter."

"I doubt you've ever made an error in judgment."

"Oh, I've made a few." He moved a step closer. "Have dinner with me, Annabeth."

She wanted to say yes, but she knew it was a bad idea to get involved with Hank.

"No," she forced out before she could change her mind.

Hank didn't flinch. "Golf, then. I'm meeting Greg Norman at his course at Folly Beach. Come with me."

Annabeth shook her head.

"Fine. Parasailing or a ferry ride to Bald Head. Pick one."

"I'm afraid I'm going to have to say no."

Hank reached over and fingered the bracelet she was wearing, one designed by his daughter. The warmth of his finger on her skin sent a shot of desire through her body.

"Are you afraid, Annabeth?" he asked softly. "Because you shouldn't be."

She had to work to swallow the lump in her throat. "I'm afraid that you're offering more than an apology."

He didn't deny it. "And what if you deserve more than an apology?"

"I don't."

His hand moved from her wrist to her jawline. It was all she could do not to lean into his caress.

"I couldn't disagree more, Annabeth. I'll be in town through the holiday weekend if you change your mind."

Annabeth gripped the countertop as he slipped past her. She didn't dare move until she heard the chime of the doorbell indicating he'd left the shop.

"I'm not talking to anyone, Roscoe," Will barked into his cell phone. "I've got nothing to say."

Roscoe sighed on the other end of the line. "We both know that's a lie, Will. And they have ways of compelling you to talk."

"You're my agent, damn it. Can't you do something? I don't want to be involved in this."

"Yeah, I'm guessing no one wants to be involved in this. Look, let me make a few discreet inquiries on your behalf. We need to find out what they've got so we can plan a strategy before this all blows up."

Will paced the wide verandah, the breeze from the ocean ruffling his hair. Roscoe was right, they needed information. "Okay, sure. But *discreet* is the operative word here. I really don't want to get dragged into this."

"Your name's already being mentioned, Will. I think now we're looking at damage control."

He wanted to throw the phone through a wall. It was guilt by association, just as Brody had feared. After seven years in the pros with a sterling reputation, he was going to be tarnished by someone else's mistake.

"How are things going down there?" Roscoe asked. "Are you and your baby mama getting along?"

Will flinched at Roscoe's nickname for Julianne. His agent had been opposed to the marriage, believing it would leave his client more exposed to potential financial claims. Roscoe would blow a gasket if he knew Julianne no longer had an income coming in from her company.

He peered in the kitchen window. Julianne stood on a step stool, reaching into one of the cabinets for something. Her long shirt wrapped around her body, accentuating her fine backside. She was having a conversation with Owen, who was strapped into his swing, seemingly chattering back to her. The kitchen was, not surprisingly, a mess. Julianne was a one-woman wrecking crew who'd in two weeks destroyed his neat, orderly home. She stepped from the stool, her bare feet padding across the room, and began mashing bananas in a bowl. Will licked his lips as her pink tank top showed off her well-toned arms to perfection. Her hair was done up in a messy knot but one strand came loose, forcing her to blow on it to keep it out of her face. The action was so sensual, Will was hard in an instant. Knowing that he was married to the woman but couldn't act on it made him angry.

"She's a mess," he growled into the phone. "And freaking moody. It's like living with a bipolar tropical storm."

Roscoe laughed. "It isn't any easier to live with a woman when you're crazy in love with them, either. It's only temporary. Hurricane Julianne will be out of your house in a couple of months. The separation papers take effect the week before training camp. I should have the custody details worked out by then, too."

Will leaned up against one of the columns and watched as Julianne laughed at Owen, suddenly uncomfortable that this would be over so soon. This morning, in the gym, when she'd touched him, pretending they were a happy family, he'd wanted nothing more than for it to be real. But that meant trusting her and Will wasn't ready to take that leap.

"I don't think it'll be a problem working out custody. Julianne's been reasonable so far."

"*So far* being the key words, Will. Don't forget, her brother is on the committee investigating this whole Bountygate mess. I don't trust her, and neither should you."

"Hey, he promised to keep me out of it if I gave Owen my blood," Will argued. "I did more. I married his little princess of a sister. If I get anything out of this mess, it should be immunity."

"Never trust the word of a politician, Will. And don't think you can hide behind the shield of being family."

Roscoe's words hung ominously in the air even after he'd hung up. Both Will's agent and his brain told him he couldn't trust Julianne. But his gut was telling him something else. She was a flighty artist who rode the crazy bus wherever life took her. Formulating a complicated plot to trap him into marriage was beyond her scope of planning. Roscoe's theory of her being in cahoots with her senator brother seemed even more far-fetched—until he watched through the window and saw Brody stroll into the kitchen and kiss Julianne on the cheek before handing her an envelope. One that looked suspiciously like the one he'd opened in Brody's room the other day. Will bolted for the door.

"Oh, Brody, this one is perfect!" Julianne reached up to hug Brody as Will charged through the door.

"What is going on here?" he shouted.

Owen laughed, his legs and arms flailing at the sight of his father.

"Jeez, dude, will you stop doing that?" Brody stepped away from Julianne, his hands poised to defend himself. "Relax. I'm just giving her a picture."

"A picture of *what*?"

Will saw the moment that realization dawned on Brody's face. His posture immediately went from defensive to aggressor. Will instantly regretted doubting his teammate. If Brody had wanted to out him, he had the means to do so days ago. He didn't need Julianne to make it happen. This whole Bountygate situation had him wound up tight as a drum.

"It's a picture of his sister, for heaven's sake." Julianne waved the photo in front of Will's face. "I need it to work on . . . something."

Will rubbed the back of his neck. He glanced at the picture of Brody's sister in a bridesmaid gown. Suddenly, the situation all made sense. "You're designing?" He wasn't sure why the prospect excited him so much.

Julianne laid the photo on the desk and began pouring the batter into a loaf pan. "Well, I wouldn't call it designing yet. More like doodling. And"—she pointed the spatula at Brody—"no telling your sister until I know I can do this."

"I already promised not to," Brody said, his mouth a tight line. "And I keep my promises."

"Okay, if you two are going to show off your muscles again, save it for the locker room. All this macho posturing is really nauseating." She covered the pan with a lid and stuck it in the fridge, presumably to bake it later, before lifting Owen out of his swing. "Speaking of nauseating, someone needs a diaper change."

The baby cooed at his mother, grabbing for that lone strand of hair as she carried him upstairs. Will looked over at Brody, who stood grim faced, arms crossed over his chest as he rocked back on his heels.

"Sorry, man," Will offered. "This whole thing's got me jumpy."

Brody didn't answer for a minute, silently rocking on his heels. "Yeah," he finally said. "Well, then you're probably not going to like this. Hank Osbourne checked into the inn this morning."

He was right; Will didn't like it. The Blaze front office had been trying to pin him down on his involvement in Bountygate for several weeks now. If what Roscoe said was true and things were heating up, Hank was probably getting anxious about how the scandal would affect the team. If he'd bothered to track Will down in Chances Inlet, the team had to be thinking about its options and where exactly he fit in the future.

Will swore. He loved playing for the Blaze. And he'd never do anything to jeopardize his position or the respect of his teammates. Head coach Matt Richardson was a former NFL player who understood not only the intricacies of the game but a player's mind. A rare find, especially since the man had been a quarterback during his playing days.

Will needed to think. He wandered over to the desk and picked up the picture of Brody's sister. "When did she tell you she would design the gown?"

If Brody knew he was stalling, he was wise enough to let it alone.

"She came into the gym today to tell me. She wanted a picture to help spur her imagination." Brody sat on one of the bar stools. "I already told Tricia it was a no-go, but if Julianne can come up with something, I'm sure she'll be ecstatic."

"They both will," Will muttered.

"Hank invited me to dinner tonight. He's here with his daughter. Something about her selling some handmade jewelry in town this weekend. Anyway, he wanted me to invite your family to join us. Although I think it might be more summons than invitation."

"Not happening."

"Dude, think about it; how much can he grill you with his daughter and your wife and kid at the table?"

"No. Besides, I have the perfect excuse. Owen is too young to be out in public yet. Not after being so sick. You'll just have to tell him we can't make dinner."

"Tell who we can't make dinner?" Julianne asked as she appeared in the doorway. She handed a drooling Owen to Will and went to wash her hands.

"No one." Will replied.

"Hank Osbourne, the GM," Brody said at the same time.

"Oh, the man whose house we were . . . married at?" Julianne began preparing a bottle for Owen. "I thought I saw him in town this morning."

"You what?" Will knew Hank would see that wheedling information out of Julianne was useless. The GM was aware of the circumstances of their marriage, after all. But he didn't want Hank filling her head with all the rumors surrounding the allegations.

Julianne stared at him. "He was out walking in town after I left you two at the gym. He didn't see me, though; he looked like he was on a mission." She smiled to herself, one of those I've-got-a-secret smiles that always made him nervous when he saw one on a woman. "What's so horrible about going out to dinner with him?"

"He wants the three of us to go with him and his daughter. Owen could be exposed to too much in a public restaurant. It's too risky."

"You've got a point." She shook up the bottle.

Will smiled smugly at Brody as if to say, *She bought it hook, line, and sinker.*

"So we should invite them here for dinner. You, too, Brody. And Annabeth, of course."

It was Brody's turn to smile at her words. *Gotcha*, his grin proclaimed.

"No!"

"Why not?" Julianne fisted her hands on her hips. "I'm a very good cook. And I love dinner parties."

"You don't cook for other people, remember?" Will arched an eyebrow at her.

"No," she reminded him. "I clarified this before, I don't cook for *you*. But for tonight, I'm willing to make an exception and let you eat with the grown-ups."

Will shoved Owen into Brody's arms. "Here, keep him busy for a moment." He grabbed Julianne by the wrist and pulled her into the large pantry, slamming the door behind him.

"We are not having a dinner party here, Princess."

Julianne surveyed the shelves. "Well, not with what you have here. I'll need to make you a grocery list. We can have caprese tomatoes, chicken marsala, Caesar salad, and maybe a fruit torte for dessert. You'll have to do the shopping, because I need to give Owen a bath if we're having company."

Will pinched the bridge of his nose. She had to be the most infuriatingly bullheaded woman.

"Will, it's part of the charade. I'm the dutiful wife, we're the happy family. Don't you see?"

He stared at her, totally baffled by her thought process. "Hank knows we're not an actual couple. We don't have to pretend anything in front of him."

Julianne muttered in Italian. "Not for him, for whomever else in this town it was so important you impress. Hank is your boss. He's visiting. They'd think it would be odd if you didn't invite him. People have already noticed him in town."

Will pressed his hands to his head and squeezed. She was right. Likely everyone was already trying to glad-hand it with Hank. They'd assume the two would show up together somewhere. "Look, Julianne, Hank is not in town to socialize. He's here because there's some stuff going on."

"Stuff? That's the best you can come up with using that overloaded brain of yours?"

His jaw was clenched so hard he could barely get the words out. "Football *stuff*. *X*s and *O*s. Stuff you wouldn't be interested in and that doesn't require a dinner party to discuss. I'll have lunch with him tomorrow at the marina. That should be a public enough place to satisfy everyone. You included."

"Huh." Julianne pulled her hair down from her messy knot, shaking her head out to free it. "I didn't get the impression he was in town to discuss football *stuff*."

Will was fixated on the flow of her hair and the shimmy of her breasts as she shook her silky tresses out. It took him a moment to comprehend what she was saying. He crossed his arms in front of his chest. "And you know this, how?"

"Well"—she rolled the hair band between her fingers—"to tell you the truth, he seemed a lot more interested in your mom. They were having a very . . . intimate-looking conversation in her shop when I saw them."

A vein throbbed in his head and Will thought it might detonate any second. "What?" he croaked out.

"See? A dinner party is a wonderful idea. It will give Hank and your mom an opportunity to see each other. They make a really cute couple."

Little specks of red dotted his vision and Will was sure his brain had exploded. *His mother and Hank? Jesus, that could be a disaster!* And the crazy woman in front of him wanted to throw them together.

"This isn't middle school! We aren't having a party so our friends can make out." His stomach rolled at the thought.

She roared right back at him. "We are having the party to reinforce this farce of a marriage you forced me in to, jock brain! Your mom and Hank are just the part that actually makes it worthwhile."

Owen wailed in the background. Julianne moved toward the door. She paused briefly before leaving, her head bowed. "It's lonely here at night, Will. You go to dinner with Gavin and I'm here with Owen," she whispered.

He stopped her as she tried to pass. "That was your choice, Princess."

"None of this was my choice," she said as she slipped out the door.

Will felt her sucker punch all the way to his knees. *Damn it!* He stormed out of the pantry and grabbed Owen from Brody's arms, shoving the bottle into the baby's mouth. "Fine," he bit out. "You've got your damn party."

She was gracious enough not to gloat. "I'll make a list of groceries I'll need from the store."

He pulled the car keys off a rack by the back door and tossed them onto the counter.

"Oh no, Princess. If you want this party, you're doing the shopping." He started up the stairs with Owen.

"But, Will . . ."

"The GPS will get you there." He called down before shutting the door to the nursery.

Sixteen

Julianne gnawed on her lip as she stared at the car keys on the counter. *Crap!* Now what was she supposed to do?

"Hey."

Brody's voice startled her. She'd almost forgotten he was standing beside her.

"You okay?" he asked.

No! "Sure," she lied. Again. "I'm just trying to come up with a grocery list before I head out."

"So how come you look like you're about to pass out?"

She brushed a shaky hand over her now-sweaty brow. *How would she ever pull this off?*

Brody snatched the keys off the counter. "Come on, I'll take you there. I'll teach you how to drive another day."

He was out the back door before she could gather her wits. She shoved her feet into her flip-flops and grabbed the diaper bag that doubled as her purse before following him out the door. The car was already running when she slid into the passenger seat.

"How . . . how did you guess?" she asked as he pulled down the drive.

"Your face said it all." Brody glanced over at her just before pulling out onto the main road. "It's nothing to be ashamed about."

She turned to look out the window. "I'm not ashamed. I actually know how to drive. Carly taught me. I just don't like to do it."

"Hey, I don't need to know your secrets. I'm happy to drive you anywhere you want to go."

"It's not exactly a secret," she told him. "I was in a bad car accident when I was young. I have been a little intimidated by cars ever since."

Brody nodded. "That's a pretty good reason." He was silent for a moment. "Anybody die?"

Julianne rubbed the cross at her neck. "Yes."

He cleared his throat. "Well, there's nothing wrong with not wanting to drive. You shouldn't stress so much about it."

Julianne leaned against the headrest and smiled over at him. "You're a nice guy, Brody Janik. How come a woman hasn't already snatched you up?"

She studied his perfect profile as he drove. His jaw clenched for a moment as his fingers gripped the steering wheel tightly. Just as quickly, his face relaxed into his mega-watt smile.

"I haven't found a woman who's as pretty as me," he joked.

Julianne concluded he'd rehearsed that particular line a thousand times. There was more to Brody than just his good looks and his athletic prowess. She suspected he was waiting for the woman who could see past his charm and interact with the real Brody. Reaching over, she patted him on the shoulder. "You'll find her, don't worry."

"Hey!" He shrugged her hand away. "No distracting the driver!"

An hour later, Julianne was white knuckled as she drove Will's brand-new SUV along the main street through Chances Inlet. "Who knew there'd be traffic in this little town?" Getting behind the wheel of a car had seemed like a good idea after a latte and Brody's relaxed encouragement. But now she wasn't so sure.

"It's Memorial Day weekend. This is the beach. I'd say everyone knew that but you," Brody teased.

She licked her parched lips as she maneuvered the car past a cyclist. A few blocks later she turned onto the side street that led to the driveway, finally relaxing.

"You got this?" Brody asked.

"This is the easy part." Julianne swerved to avoid nearly clipping a tree as she pulled up onto the parking pad.

Brody grabbed the dash as she jerked the car into park. "Yeah, well, I think you're gonna need a few more lessons, Mario, before you go solo, but I'm proud of you for not wimping out. We'll make a soccer mom out of you yet."

Julianne leaned over and kissed him on the cheek. "Thanks, Brody. You're a prince among men."

The smile he gave her wasn't his forced cover-boy mug but a genuine grin. "Everything is going to work out, Julianne. You'll see."

Before she got the chance to ask him what he meant, his car door was yanked open and Will was dragging him out by his shirt collar.

"Will, stop it!" she yelled as she scrambled out of the car and raced to the other side. "What are you doing?" She grabbed onto the back of his shirt and pulled, but it was useless; both men were grappling to get a better hold of one another.

"Damn it, Connelly! Get your hands off me! I'm getting sick and tired of you going all caveman every time I'm around." Brody kneed Will in the thigh and slipped out of his grip, causing Julianne to get tangled up in Will's legs.

"And I'm getting sick and tired of you constantly having your hands on my wife!" Will charged after him again, but Julianne stepped in between them.

"I said stop it!" she yelled. Both men ignored her.

"Dude! If you were a little more sensitive to your wife's needs, I wouldn't have to step in so much!"

Julianne froze at Brody's words. *Did the man have a death wish? And what was he talking about?*

Will's voice was like a whip cutting through the air. "What's that's supposed to mean?"

"It means she doesn't know how to drive a car, you idiot!" Brody shrugged at Julianne's gasp. "My mistake, she does know how to drive. She just doesn't like to. Sorry, Julianne, but he was bound to find out anyway, and I'm getting a little sick of fighting off his ugly mug in my face when I've done nothing wrong. I'm out of here." He stalked off down the drive.

They stood in silence a moment and Julianne worked to regain her equilibrium. Will finally turned toward her, his face stony. "Storms, the ocean, and driving. Are there any more phobias you have that you want to share with me, Princess?"

She swore in Italian before storming around the car, pulling out the bags of groceries, and heading into the kitchen. Tears stung her eyes as she tossed the fresh vegetables on the counter. It was bad enough to live life as a quivering mass of phobias and insecurities, but somehow having Will know all her secrets made her feel totally exposed, raw. It was more than she could handle.

Will carried the remaining groceries in and began unpacking the bags. "It's a fair question. You'll be taking care of my son and I need to know what is going to . . . provoke you."

Julianne turned from the fridge, tears falling freely down her face now. "Provoke me? Besides you, you mean? Should I just give you a list so you can declare me an unfit mother right now?"

His silence told her all she needed to know. As far as he was concerned, she was a flake. Too fragile to take a chance on. Every other man in her life felt the same way: old boyfriends, her brother, her father, even Nicky. Why should her fake husband be any different? Worse, this man could use her insecurities against her to take away her son.

"Well," she choked out, "I believe that's a complete catalog of my phobias, Will. I don't think any of them are hereditary, if that's what you're worried about. He'd have to survive a car accident in a raging thunderstorm that tossed the car into the ocean in order to become as emotionally wrecked as I am. Since all of those things terrify me, Owen should be quite safe when he's in my care."

A sob racked her body as she tried to escape the kitchen, but Will was too fast for her.

"Jesus!" he whispered as he pulled her into his arms.

Julianne tried to pull away, but he was stronger.

"Julianne," he breathed into her hair. "I didn't know. I'm sorry."

His big hand rubbed her back, and her body involuntarily relaxed. There was something about being in Will's arms that called to her. All these years after the accident and she still craved the gentle hugs only her mother had ever bothered to give her. Julianne's father blamed her for the death of her mother, sending her off to boarding school weeks after the accident. Stephen, twelve years older, was a stranger and provided little comfort. Nicky had been the only constant in her life. But his was an emotional comfort, not physical. Until Will, she hadn't known how big that hole was in her life.

"Your mother. Was she driving the car?"

Nodding, she gulped back another sob as she nestled in further against Will's chest.

"I'm sorry, Princess. I'm an ass." He brushed his lips against her forehead. "I didn't mean it."

He leaned down to peer into her eyes. "None of this is your fault," he whispered.

"Except it is," she sobbed. "All of it."

Will lifted her in his arms and carried her to the family room, sitting down in the bulky armchair, tucking Julianne in his lap.

"No, Julianne, it's not. Whatever happened, happened when you were a child. You're not to blame."

He stroked her hair and she snuggled into the haven of his arms. They sat quietly for a few moments with only the sound of the ocean butting up against the seawall and Owen's steady breathing over the baby monitor.

"We were at my mother's studio in San Vincenzo. I wanted to go back to Rome to see my dad. I don't know why, but I was angry at my mom. I've tried for years to remember what provoked me, but I can't. It's weird because I loved my mom. She was my best friend. We never fought, but that day I desperately wanted my dad."

Will said nothing, simply stroking her hair.

"There was a terrible storm. I was in the backseat of the car sleeping, but the thunder woke me. My mom was in the front seat with Nicky."

She felt Will's body stiffen. Julianne sat up and looked into his eyes. "Nicky and I have been friends since we were kids. Our fathers were in the diplomatic corps together. He's like family."

Will slowly nodded. She wasn't sure if he was accepting her defense of Nicky or he just wanted her to go on.

"It's weird, though; my mother and Nicky were arguing, too. I can't remember what about, though. And when I've asked him, he always says it was nothing." She sighed. "Anyway, my mother went to take a sharp turn and the wheels slipped off the road. The next thing I remember, we were in the water, the car submerging. My mom wouldn't move. There was a lot of blood on her forehead." She paused to catch her breath. "Nicky pulled me out of the backseat and pushed me out of the car before it sank all the way. We couldn't get Mama. The car was gone before we could reach her."

"Shh." Will pulled her back against him as tears streamed down her face, his hand once again rubbing her back. "It's okay, Princess. You're safe now. You're with me."

And for the first time in many years, Julianne did feel safe. Safe in the arms of the man who was, but wasn't, her husband.

"No wonder you were such a wreck that night of Chase's wedding." His lips found her forehead again. "I'm sorry. I took advantage of you."

She turned to face him, her finger tracing his jaw. "No.

I needed someone to take care of me that night. And for the first time, someone was there for me . . . you."

He toyed with a strand of her hair. "None of this is your fault. The accident. Your mother's death. Owen. None of it, Julianne."

His face begged her to believe him. Staring into his sparkling green eyes, she felt lighter than she had in many years. More hopeful. She moved her finger to trace his lips, and his eyes clouded with hunger. It would be so easy to lean in and kiss him. To start fresh. The corners of his mouth turned up as if he could read her mind.

"Ahem."

Annabeth stood in the doorway, the baby monitor in her hand. Owen was whining softly.

Julianne jumped from Will's lap. "Annabeth! Hi."

"I'm sorry to interrupt."

"You're not interrupting." Julianne nudged Will, but he didn't get up, a pained expression crossed his face.

"I thought I'd spend a little time with my grandson." Annabeth waved the monitor. "It sounds like he's awake."

Julianne kicked Will in the shin until he stood.

"I was just going to give him a bath, Mom. Why don't you give me a hand?"

His mother eyed them both. "Sure."

"Annabeth." Julianne rushed over to her. "Please, would you join us for dinner?"

Will groaned softly behind her.

"Oh, no. I don't want to impose on your time together."

Julianne shot Will a withering glance. "No, you wouldn't be imposing. We're having a dinner party tonight. You should come. Please. We hardly ever see you. You're always at the shop. It would mean a lot to me."

Will rolled his eyes, and Julianne was tempted to spear him in the side.

Annabeth looked at her son, who just shrugged.

"I'm making chicken marsala." Julianne pasted on a sunny smile.

"In that case, how can I resist?" Annabeth turned to the stairs as Owen's pleas became more insistent. "I'll just go up and rescue the little prince while you get his bath ready, Will."

Will groaned as he followed his mother out of the room. Julianne practically skipped to the kitchen, where she immersed herself in preparing a gourmet meal.

Seventeen

Hank's daughter had pink hair. Will wasn't sure why he found that fact so disconcerting, but he did. The Blaze GM was a taciturn, studious man who managed the team like the former military officer he was. It was hard to reconcile that personality with a father who'd tolerate his teenager dyeing her hair . . . pink.

Yet there Hank stood in Will's great room, a bemused expression on his face as he watched his daughter coo at Owen. The baby was fascinated with her, studying the scene intently from his grandmother's lap. Even more confusing, Sophie with the pink hair seemed very familiar with Will's mother, as if they were long-lost friends. For her part, his mother chatted warmly with the girl but avoided making eye contact with Hank.

Damn it! Will slammed his bottle of beer down on the end table. Could Julianne be right? Was something going on between Hank and his mother? He needed to have a serious talk with the team's GM, and it needed to happen now.

He wandered across the room. "We need to talk."

Hank's cool eyes assessed him. "Yes, we do." He followed Will to his study.

Will wasted no time getting to the point. "What are you doing in Chances Inlet, Hank?"

The GM leaned against an old pie keeper Will's mother had lovingly refurbished, his hand shoved into the pockets of his khakis. "There are some pretty nasty rumors going around, Will. Tales of defensive players being paid to deliberately injure their opponents. Your name keeps coming up as one of a short list of individuals who can corroborate those rumors."

Will stood stone faced, saying nothing. He'd already had this discussion with team management a month ago, and his position hadn't changed.

Hank sighed and sat down in one of the leather chairs. "Look, Will, I know you've never been paid to take out another player while you've been with the Blaze. You're one of the most respected guys on this team, not only for your play, but for your integrity." He pushed his wire-rimmed glasses up on his nose. "But if you know something, for Christ's sake, Will, cooperate with the league. The commissioner is going to come down hard on both players and teams. He won't be so forgiving if you hold out on him."

Will played with an old Hot Wheels car on his desk. It was one of the few toys he'd had as a child. Owen would have mountains of Hot Wheels and trucks and other toys to play with; Will would make sure of it. "I already told you, Hank. I don't know anything."

"Damn it, Will! You need to think about protecting your reputation. If you won't do it for your team, do it for your wife and your son. And your mother," Hank added.

Will spun around. "Ah, yes, my mother! Let's talk about her. What exactly is going on with you two? I didn't even know you were acquainted with her beyond a casual hello at a game. You and your daughter seem pretty cozy with my mom out there, though."

Hank leaned back in the chair and peered at Will over

steepled fingers. "Your mother is a very kind woman. She met Sophie at your wedding and they've become friends."

Will was sure he would have remembered a girl with pink hair at his wedding, but he'd had other things on his mind that day. It also didn't surprise him that his mother would bond with the girl. They were kindred, free spirits. But Hank was giving off a predatory vibe when it came to his mother. And Will didn't like that one bit.

"And you?" Will asked. "Are you and my mother . . . *friends*?" He wasn't sure he wanted to know Hank's answer.

"Whatever is or isn't going on between your mother and me doesn't affect you."

"The hell it doesn't! If you're cozying up to her to get information about me, don't."

Hank rose from the chair. "If I want information about you, Will, I'll ask you directly, as I have been doing over the past month. My advice to you would be to decide where your loyalties lie, before it's too late." He paused in opening the door. "And I'd never insult a beautiful woman like your mother by using her for anything. Not when she deserves a lot more."

Will stood in the center of his study, dumbfounded. It wasn't enough that he had a wife and child he hadn't expected. Or a scandal of epic proportions hanging over his head. Now he had to worry about his mother and whatever Hank Osbourne's interest in her was.

Julianne poked her head around the door. Her smile was radiant as she basked in the excitement of hosting a dinner party. Will would rather stick a hot poker in his eye right now than sit down to dinner with Hank and a petulant Brody. But one look at his wife and he realized he couldn't deny her a thing.

"Dinner's ready." Since her confession earlier this afternoon, she'd seemed happier, more focused. But now, she looked at him shyly as if she were unsure how to deal with him. She held out her hand. "Come on, let's eat."

Will's fingers grasped hers before he could think. Maybe

it was better if he didn't think but just enjoyed the feel of
her hand in his.

Annabeth chewed her dinner without tasting it.
Somehow, she'd assumed Julianne's dinner party would
consist of Gavin and his mother, Patricia. Will was very
selective about who he socialized with and who he let in his
home. It was just another example of her naïveté that she
hadn't suspected Hank, one of her son's bosses, would be
joining them for dinner.

Her entire day seemed to be thrown off balance with
Hank's arrival. He'd made his intentions clear to her in the
shop. She just wasn't sure how she wanted to handle it.
Annabeth had been in relationships before, but not with men
of Hank's caliber. Mostly, she'd been with men who needed
fixing or a rebound after a relationship gone wrong. Nothing
about Hank Osbourne needed to be fixed. He was the most
self-assured man she'd ever encountered—a fact that intimidated her but aroused her at the same time.

Hank raised his wineglass in a silent salute when he
caught her surreptitiously looking at him. She quickly
glanced around to see if the others noticed, but there seemed
to be three separate acts going on at this crazy dinner party.
Brody was doing his best to engage Sophie in conversation,
teasing her about some event at the Blaze holiday party. And
Will and Julianne, seated at opposite ends of the table,
seemed to have eyes only for each other. In and of itself, that
alone was a stunning development.

The scene she'd walked in on earlier this afternoon hadn't
really surprised Annabeth; she'd had an inkling there was
more to this pretend marriage than either spouse believed.
Truthfully, she was glad Will had feelings for his wife. Owen
deserved a shot at the happy family she hadn't been able to
provide for Will. But the marriage wouldn't survive if
neither partner could trust the other, and Annabeth was
nervous that building that kind of trust would take them
longer than the few weeks they'd been married.

"My compliments to the chef." Hank raised his wineglass to toast Julianne. "If you ever decide to give up designing, you could open a restaurant."

Brody choked on his wine.

"Thank you." Julianne shot a look at Brody. "Cooking is as much a passion as designing is. Sophie, I understand you design jewelry?"

Sophie beamed beside Annabeth. "It's nothing fancy. Annabeth is selling it in her store."

Will's eyebrows rose a fraction.

"It's been very popular," Annabeth said.

"She is?" Julianne smiled at Annabeth. "In that case, I'll have to come have a look. I love to wear jewelry that's unique and one of a kind."

"I'm going to work in the shop this weekend, aren't I, Annabeth?" Sophie asked, and Annabeth nodded.

"How long are you planning on staying?" Will directed the question at Hank.

Hank didn't take his eyes off Annabeth as he answered. "Through the weekend."

Annabeth grew warm under both Hank's and her son's gaze.

"Well," Julianne piped in, "that should give me plenty of time to shop at the House of Sophie."

Sophie clapped her hands together. "Oooh. That's my goal, to have my own jewelry design house."

Annabeth didn't hear whatever Sophie said next because the dueling gazes of her son and Hank were making her increasingly uncomfortable. Unable to take it anymore, she excused herself to go check on Owen.

She had no sooner reached the nursery when she heard the echo of a pair of footsteps following her. She prayed it wasn't Hank. Or worse, her son. Instead, it was Julianne who followed her into the room where Owen slept peacefully. She wasn't sure whether she was relieved. Definitely, she was surprised.

"Is everything okay?" Julianne asked as she gently adjusted the blanket covering her son.

"I thought I heard him crying, but he seems fine," Annabeth fibbed.

Julianne glanced at her out of the corner of her eye. "I meant, is everything okay with you?"

Her daughter-in-law was perceptive. Annabeth had tried not to form too much of an attachment with Julianne, knowing that she'd be gone from Chances Inlet in a matter of months and would probably never be back. But it was clear there was something more than just Owen pulling Will and Julianne together. She only hoped they both figured it out before it was too late.

"I don't want to like you," Annabeth blurted out.

Julianne's eyes went from quizzical to sad, but she acknowledged Annabeth's admission with a firm nod. "You don't have to like me," she said, chewing on her bottom lip. "As long as you always love Owen."

Shame brought a flush to Annabeth's face. "That was hateful of me, wasn't it?" she whispered.

"No, it was fair."

"No!" Annabeth shook her head vehemently. "It wasn't. I'm the last person who should be judging any woman. You're Owen's mother, and whether this marriage lasts three months or thirty-three years, that's not going to change. At the very least you deserve my respect. But I think it would be hard not to like you, too."

A slow grin spread over Julianne's face. "I'd really like that."

Owen rustled in his crib. Julianne put a finger to her lips and motioned for Annabeth to follow her into the adjoining bedroom.

"Let's start again," Julianne suggested. "You rushed out of the dining room like you were upset. Is there anything I can do?"

"You could not invite Hank Osbourne to dinner." The words were out of her mouth before she could stop them.

"Aha!" Julianne bounced down on her bed. "At the risk of sounding thirteen again, I think he likes you."

Annabeth picked up a pillow and, under the guise of

fluffing it, gave it a firm punch. "He's made no secret about that."

Julianne sat Indian style on the bed, her chin resting on her hands and a broad grin on her face. "So, what are you going to do about it?"

"Nothing."

"Nothing? Why not?" Julianne protested. "He's a very handsome man. And he's got all his teeth and all his hair."

Annabeth threw the pillow at her.

"Seriously, Annabeth. You're a beautiful, financially independent woman with no one but yourself to answer to. Hank's a pretty good catch, by all accounts. My friend Carly used to work for him. When I talked to her this afternoon, she described him as a very loyal, caring man who'd be devoted to any woman lucky enough to catch his eye."

Annabeth was mortified. "You talked to your friend about this?"

"Well, I didn't name any names, if that's what you mean. But I wasn't going to invite some man over here to leer at my son's grandmother without knowing something about him!"

Annabeth didn't know whether to smack Julianne or hug her. "How did you know there was any interest on his part, anyway?"

Julianne picked at a string on the bedspread. "I might have seen you two in the shop this morning."

Annabeth plopped down on the bed beside her. "Does Will know?"

Julianne snorted. "I mentioned it, but he's a bit obtuse. He believes what he wants to believe."

Annabeth laughed at that. Her son would not be able to steamroll over his wife.

"He's only in town for the weekend, Annabeth. There's no harm in enjoying his company *and* enjoying his attention. You deserve it."

She was right, Annabeth thought. She couldn't get her heart broken in three days. Besides, he wouldn't be able to discover all her faults in that short time.

There was a knock at the door followed by Sophie's voice. "Annabeth?"

Julianne pulled open the door and smiled at Sophie. "Oh gosh, we left you defenseless down there with the NFL's finest, sorry."

Sophie rolled her eyes. "I'm used to it. Hey, Brody says there's a great little ice cream stand a few blocks from the inn. It's called the Patty Wagon. It's named after the inn-keeper. Isn't that cool? Daddy and I are going to go check it out. Do you guys want to come with us?"

Julianne gestured to the nursery. "Owen's down for the night; I need to stay here. How about you, Annabeth?" Her smile held a challenge in it.

Annabeth wasn't sure she was being wise, but there was something about Hank Osbourne that she wanted to explore. Perhaps, if she kept their encounters light, they could be friends. He was Will's employer, after all. And Sophie's father. She enjoyed knowing his daughter and wanted to keep that relationship intact.

"I think that sounds lovely." Decision made, she linked arms with Sophie and headed out the door.

Eighteen

Julianne put her hand on her back and stretched. "That's the one thing about cooking that I don't enjoy: cleaning up."

Will harrumphed as he stacked the frying pan in the cabinet. "Why doesn't that surprise me?"

Their guests had left nearly an hour ago, Brody leading the way to the small ice cream stand that was sure to be packed with holiday weekend tourists. She and Will had just conquered the mountain of dishes left behind.

"You know what they say: A messy kitchen is a happy kitchen."

Will wiped the counters down. "This kitchen was pretty happy the way it was."

"Hey, at least your house looks like somebody lives in it now."

Will glanced around the first floor, a pained look on his face. "Yes, yes it does."

Julianne stuck her tongue out at him. "Tell me the truth. Did you stay around to help me clean up because you really can't stand to have your space out of order? Or was it because you wanted to be able to watch out the window to see when your mom gets home?"

Will draped a dish towel around the back of her neck and pulled her body into contact with his. "Or, option three, I wanted to be with you."

His voice was a low rumble underneath her hands on his chest, and Julianne shivered. They hadn't been alone since this afternoon, when clearly their relationship had hit a turning point.

"Option three works," she whispered.

Will touched his forehead to hers. "We need to talk through a few things, Julianne."

"Yeah."

Will's cell phone vibrated on the counter. Keeping his eyes locked with hers, he picked it up and answered brusquely.

"Roscoe, can't this wait until tomorrow?"

He stepped away from her. Apparently, whatever it was couldn't wait.

Will placed his thumb over the phone's mouthpiece and sighed. "I've got to take this. You should probably get some sleep, anyway, while the baby is sleeping. We can talk tomorrow."

His face looked strained, as if he wanted to do anything else but take this call. Julianne wanted to reach out and offer him comfort, but they weren't there yet in their relationship. She felt they were getting closer, but she didn't want to overstep the invisible boundaries that still kept them apart.

Julianne nodded, and Will disappeared into his study. As she climbed the stairs, she could hear Will's angry voice as he argued with his agent. She checked on Owen before changing into a pair of sleep shorts and a tank top and climbing into bed.

But she was too keyed up to sleep. Instead, she crawled into the big chair under the dormer and pulled out the sketch she'd begun for Brody's sister. Half an hour later, the gown was nearly complete; a few notes on the embellishments still needed to be added, but Julianne was pleased and relieved at the finished product.

A sound from the nursery alerted her to the fact that Will was checking on Owen. She heard his footsteps hesitate in front of the door to her adjoining room, before he left the nursery and moved down the hall to his own room. Julianne knew she wouldn't be able to sleep if they didn't finish what they'd started in the kitchen earlier. She just didn't know if she had the nerve to make the first move. Maybe when Owen woke for his two A.M. feeding, he'd join her in the kitchen and they could have one of their quiet chats.

"Ah, the heck with it!" Julianne couldn't wait another four hours to make her last confession to Will. She needed to do it now while she had the nerve.

His door was closed and she knocked softly, but there was no response. The shower was running in the distance. She debated whether to go in, but she'd come this far, so she forced herself to turn the doorknob and go inside.

Will's bedroom was decorated in much the same style as the room Julianne was occupying, with one exception; the room featured a massive king-sized bed. The bed was situated in front of two sets of French doors leading out to the balcony overlooking the Atlantic. Fortunately, the sound of the shower drowned out most of the roar of the ocean. The door to Will's bathroom was open, and steam wafted into the room.

The shower stopped, and now it was too late for Julianne to change her mind. She sank down on the bed in full view of the bathroom mirror and waited for Will to emerge. When he finally did, the sight of him stole her breath.

Clothed, the man looked like a Viking warrior, but naked, he looked like a Greek god. Droplets of water clung to his broad back, the lucky things making their way over his muscled torso, down from his tapered waist to his dimpled butt and finally to his hard thighs and defined calves dusted with blond hair.

Julianne's nipples were painfully hard and she had to cross her legs to quell the tension between them. Will took a pull from a bottle of beer before grabbing a towel and drying his hair. Using the towel to wipe the condensation from the mirror, his hand suddenly stilled when he spied her reflection. Their eyes met in the mirror, but Will didn't say a word or turn around. Slowly, he wrapped the towel around his waist and grabbed a bottle of ibuprofen. He swallowed two pills with a swig from his beer.

"You shouldn't be in here," he finally said, speaking to her reflection in the mirror.

"You shouldn't be mixing alcohol and pills."

He arched an eyebrow at her as if to say, *Look who's talking*.

Julianne crossed her arms over her chest. "I wasn't drinking that night!" She wasn't sure if he'd heard her because his eyes had glazed over at the site of her aroused nipples. Rising to her feet, she attempted to take a step toward him.

"Don't!" he growled, his back still to her. He closed his eyes and his fingers clung to the vanity. "I can't do this tonight. We need to talk things out, but if you stay here now, we won't be talking."

"I just need to tell you something."

"Not tonight! Please, Julianne, don't you see? We started at this spot and everything got messed up. If we want this to work, we need to start at the beginning. We need to talk, but I've had a pretty shitty evening, and talking is the last thing I want to do with you."

Julianne was beginning to get annoyed. "Well, thanks for the lovely compliment about my dinner. I just came in here to tell you something, but now I don't think I want to."

"Oh, for the love of all that is holy!" Will threw his hands up in the air as he turned and stalked toward her, his towel parting as he walked.

Julianne's legs gave out at the sight of the magnificent body bearing down on her, and she slumped back down on the bed.

"Oh no, Princess." He lifted her by her elbows, his fingers hot against her bare skin. "Say what you came to say, and then you'd better run for your life."

Her hands hovered between them until they finally landed on his chest. He sucked in a breath at the contact. Will was right; she needed to spit out what she wanted to say before things got out of hand.

"I lied," she breathed as his lips found the curve of her neck.

"You don't say."

He was being annoying again, and she dug her fingernails into his chest. He winced before pulling her in closer, his erection nudging against her. Julianne let out a breathy moan before using her lips to soothe the nail marks she'd left on his pectoral muscles.

One of his hands was pushing down her shorts as the other caressed her breast. Julianne needed to tell him before she totally lost her train of thought.

"I lied about the night on Sea Island," she gasped.

Will pulled back to look at her, his eyes cloudy with desire as he sarcastically arched an eyebrow.

"Go on."

She bit her bottom lip and took the coward's way out by avoiding his eyes, instead focusing on his chest.

"That night. I remember it. All of it."

He placed a finger under her chin, raising her eyes to meet his. "Prove it," he challenged.

She'd pushed him beyond reason. Will had tried to warn her, but as usual, Julianne had been stubborn and wouldn't listen. So now he was going to take what she was offering, the hell with talking. Talking was overrated anyway.

They were both naked except for the sexy excuse for a shirt she wore. Julianne slowly pulled it over her head, flinging it to the floor as though she'd practiced the move many times. Will's mouth went dry at the sight. She took a step closer and their bodies were skin to skin, both of them hot and hard. Waiting for her to make a move was killing him.

Snaking her hands up over his shoulders, she cradled his jaw before finally pulling his head down to meet hers.

"You sure you're okay with not talking about this first?" he murmured as his lips hovered above hers.

"Stop being such a girl and kiss me."

It was all the encouragement Will needed. One quick move and he had her sprawled out on the bed. He crawled over her, taking his time, letting his lips get reacquainted with her body, inch by lovely inch.

"Will," she gasped as he pressed tender kisses along the soft belly that had given him his son. She fisted her hands in his hair. "Come here so I can touch you."

But Will wasn't in a hurry. He'd dreamed about having her back in his bed for months now, and he meant to enjoy every moment of it. With his hands, he traced her hips, fuller now after childbirth. She writhed beneath him, her body anxious. He blew a quick breath on her nipples and she groaned, her hand gripping his shoulders.

When he was eventually face to face with her, he could see the desire, and desperation, reflected in her eyes. She didn't waste a minute, pulling his head down to hers and kissing him. Will let her have her way for a moment before taking over, his tongue twining with hers. Julianne wrapped her legs around his waist and thrust her pelvis against his. He was on the verge of losing control, but he didn't want the frenzied coupling they'd had on Sea Island. Tonight, he wanted more.

Pulling out of the kiss, he rested on his forearms and stared down at Julianne's flushed face. She was panting beneath him, and that turned him on even more.

"Somebody's in a hurry." His own breathing wasn't much better than hers.

"Well, that's because one of us has been doing without for a long time," she huffed. "While the other one . . . hasn't."

That was something he refused to feel guilty about, though. Yes, he'd been in a relationship throughout most of Julianne's pregnancy. But had she told him about the baby, things would have been different. Obviously he thought so now, but if he was being honest, he wasn't entirely sure.

He lowered his lips to her shoulder. "This is why we needed to talk first."

"Yeah, probably." A tear rolled down the side of her face.

Will erased its path with his lips. His hand caressed her belly before moving lower.

"It's okay, Princess; I'm going to take pity on you." He eased a finger inside her and her body clenched around it. Will sucked in a breath. "Is this what you wanted?"

She gasped. "It'll do for right now."

Smiling, he eased down to take possession of one of her breasts. They were fuller than he remembered and, as his mouth closed around her nipple, his body jerked in anticipation of what was to come. Julianne's moans of pleasure were driving him wild, the rhythm of his thrusting finger meeting the cadence of her gyrating hips.

She came on a long, deep moan that nearly caused him to climax along with her. Will sank his teeth into her shoulder, then laved the tender spot with his tongue.

"Better?" Will asked when their breathing had returned to near normal.

"Mmm." She smiled slyly before wrapping her hand around him.

Will closed his eyes at her touch. He wasn't going to last long if she kept this up. Reaching over to his nightstand, he withdrew a condom from his wallet. Before he had it open, Julianne snatched it from his hand, pushing Will over onto his back.

"It's my turn." She deftly rolled the condom over his erection.

Will arched an eyebrow at her as she straddled him.

"Do your best, Princess." He tucked his hands behind his head.

Julianne leaned down to kiss the tip of his nose, the move so unexpected it was erotic. The curtain of her hair created a sensual cocoon as she kissed his closed eyes, his jaw, and the corners of his mouth.

"Julianne," he begged, and her tongue was suddenly in

his mouth, this kiss more intimate than the last. He sucked on her lower lip and she reacted by grinding her ass against his erection.

"Julianne!" he nearly shouted.

Humming contentedly, she moved lower to gently suck on his neck. "Now who's in a hurry?" she teased, a fingernail scoring his nipple, causing his body to buck beneath her.

That was the last straw. Will grabbed her by the hips, positioning her over the top of him, and thrust home. She was tighter than he expected, especially after having a baby. He had to catch his breath in order to slow himself down. Julianne's sharp intake of her own breath refocused his attention.

"You okay?" he ground out.

"Oh, God, yes," she breathed. "It's wonderful. You're wonderful." She rose up on her knees before slowly coming back down. "Actually, I think *wonderful* may be an understatement."

Slow wasn't going to cut it for Will. He let her have her way for a few strokes before bringing her head down for a lingering, deep kiss. Grasping her hips, he increased the pace. Julianne threw her head back, and Will was mesmerized by the sway of her breasts. He leaned up to take one in his mouth.

She moaned his name. Pressing him flat against the bed, she adjusted their angle, still meeting him thrust for thrust. Will reached a thumb between them, searching for her sweet spot. She climaxed nearly immediately, a sob escaping her throat.

He wrapped her legs around his hips and flipped them over, driving into her until she came again. Only then did he let himself follow her over the edge. The ocean churned in the darkness as they lay on the bed, their bodies tangled together. It was several minutes before they both slowly came back to earth.

"Hmm," Julianne sighed, a glow of faint contentment spreading over her face. "That was so much better than my dreams." She stroked his calf with the insole of her foot, reawakening his sated nerve endings.

"Not only did you remember, but you dreamed about it, huh?" Will's flagging ego did a little touchdown dance.

He felt her smile against the bare skin on his shoulder. "It's all coming back to me now. I seem to remember there was more." Her husky voice had his body stirring.

"So do I. Much more." Will bent his head and kissed her softly on her swollen lips. She opened her mouth and her arms to him, and the kiss turned fiery in seconds. Needing no more encouragement than Julianne's heated body, he proceeded to reenact the rest of their evening on Sea Island.

Owen's urgent cries woke them several hours later. Will traipsed down to the kitchen to make the bottle, while Julianne changed their son. They fed him sitting against the headboard of Will's bed, her back pressed against his chest as she cradled the baby, Will's arms wrapped protectively around them both.

Nineteen

"You're sure you don't want to go parasailing?" Hank asked as they boarded the ferry to Bald Head Island. It was Saturday afternoon of a holiday weekend, and Annabeth was already feeling guilty about leaving the shop. Hank had arrived an hour earlier carrying a large insulated picnic basket and wearing his devastating smile, making him hard for Annabeth to resist. Her assistant, Lynnette, had taken one look at the man and practically shoved her out the door, insisting Sophie was all the help she needed.

Annabeth was still kicking herself for agreeing to have dinner with Hank, and that was when she thought they'd be in a crowded restaurant with all the holiday beachgoers. A sunset picnic on a secluded island sounded dangerous. And romantic at the same time.

Clearly, she'd had too much wine the other night when she'd agreed to this. But Julianne's words had been reverberating in her head, giving Annabeth a false sense of bravery. Their trek to the Patty Wagon was pleasant enough, with Sophie and Brody taking turns steering the conversation. When it was time for Annabeth to walk home, however,

Brody quickly excused himself to meet a new acquaintance at Pier Pressure, Chances Inlet's night spot, while Sophie claimed to have a program she wanted to watch on cable and disappeared into the inn. Both their exits seemed a bit contrived, but Annabeth didn't resist Hank's escort home.

They walked silently the first few blocks, serenaded by the crash of the surf in the distance and the chorus of tree frogs in the canopy of live oaks above them. Hank asked questions about the town and its history until they'd arrived at Annabeth's front door. She stood there awkwardly, but Hank made no move to touch her as he had earlier that day in her shop.

"Annabeth Connelly, please have dinner with me." He stood beneath her porch light, a moth dive-bombing his head, looking as though the fate of the world hinged on her answer. How could a woman say no to a request like that?

"Okay."

"Are you free Saturday night?"

Lord, did this man think she actually had a social life beyond her book club and her church group? She had to admit to feeling a bit flattered. She couldn't find the words, so she just nodded.

"Great. How about if I just pick you up from the shop?"

She nodded again.

Hank stepped away from her porch, ushering her inside, but Annabeth just stood there like a fool.

"I can't leave until I know you're safely inside, Annabeth."

Right! Embarrassed, she quickly flew into the house, bolting the door behind her. As she leaned against it, she listened to Hank's retreating footsteps down the gravel drive.

And that was how she found herself on the ferry headed for a private dinner for two.

"I have no desire to parasail," she answered Hank. "I leave that to Will and his friends."

He bristled beside her. "Will has a pretty extensive contract that prohibits him from parasailing for the time being, so please don't tell me if he does." He set the picnic basket down on the bench and leaned up against the railing.

Annabeth joined him, watching as the ferrymen untied the boat's moorings. "Will takes his job very seriously; I doubt he's been parasailing in ten years."

"Annabeth, can we maybe forget that you're Will's mother and I'm his boss tonight? I'd prefer we just be Annabeth and Hank, two people who want to enjoy a nice dinner and get to know one another."

The ferry pulled away from the dock, and Annabeth didn't know whether it was the bobbing of the boat or the potent effect of the man beside her, but she needed to sit.

"Okay." She settled on the bench, and Hank sat down beside her. "If we're getting to know each other, tell me about your wife. Elizabeth."

Hank paused in pulling a bottled water out of the picnic basket. "Ex-wife. Elizabeth and I haven't been married for over ten years."

She shook her head when he offered the bottle. "What ended the marriage?"

"Wow, now I see where Will gets it. You pull no punches." He took a swallow of water before capping the bottle and returning it to the basket. "The usual, I guess. I wasn't a very attentive husband, and Elizabeth needed more than I was giving her. So she found it somewhere else."

Annabeth wasn't sure what shocked her more, that Hank would admit to being a neglectful husband or that his wife would cheat on him.

"She cheated on you?"

Hank smiled at her incredulousness. "I wasn't exactly faithful to her, either."

It suddenly felt like a balloon had deflated inside Annabeth. Despite her attempts not to throw her heart into this relationship, she realized that his admission stung. A lot. She pulled her legs up on the bench, resting her chin on her knees to try to keep the disappointment from seeping into her heart.

Hank sighed. "Not in the way you're thinking. It wasn't another woman. Football was my mistress." The boat picked up speed and he had to sit closer to her in order to be heard.

"I played football at West Point. I knew I wouldn't go pro—I wasn't good enough—but that didn't keep me from dreaming of being involved in the game somehow. After I finished my tour in the Army, we'd been married a year and Elizabeth was pregnant with Sophie; the plan was for me to go to Wharton and get my MBA. I'd join the family firm and Elizabeth and I would take up residence in Philadelphia society."

The whipping wind kept blowing a strand of hair in Annabeth's face, and she shoved it aside as she listened to Hank's tale.

"A friend of mine who worked with the Philadelphia Eagles called one day and said they were looking for a scout, someone to travel to college campuses and assess the football talent. The job barely paid anything, but both Elizabeth and I are trust fund babies." He shrugged unapologetically. "I didn't even tell her. Or my dad. I just took the job because I desperately wanted to do something in the NFL."

Hank hung his hands between his knees as the boat jumped across the choppy waters. "The job required a lot of travel. A lot, but I wanted to do it well, so I didn't complain. I nearly missed Sophie's birth and, well, it goes without saying that I missed pretty much all of her firsts."

He glanced out over the ocean, and Annabeth glimpsed the pain in his eyes.

"If she really loved you," she said, "she would have persevered through those years while you pursued a dream."

"If I really loved *her*, I would have found a way to meld my dream and my marriage better. I would have made it work."

His admission stirred something inside Annabeth: empathy, certainly. But jealousy, too. She wanted a man to love her enough to make something, anything, work.

"But thank you, Annabeth. It would have been nice to have someone on my side back then."

"Your family sided with Elizabeth?" She didn't know why that thought hurt her so much, but it did. Hank was a good man. To know that his family turned their backs on him when he needed it pained her greatly.

"They sided with Sophie. Elizabeth is her mother. She and Kevin were discreet in their affair, so nobody but me was the wiser."

"But your family should know she cheated on you!"

"No, Annabeth, they shouldn't. That would only hurt Sophie. She lives with Kevin and Elizabeth and two younger brothers who'd slay dragons for her. Despite her teenage drama, she has a comfortable, stable family life. There's no reason to upset it with something that's in the past."

The boat slowed as it arrived at the island's harbor, giving Annabeth time to study the man seated next to her. He was not what she'd first thought. She'd assumed he'd become less appealing the more she was exposed to him and the more he found out about her. Instead, she discovered that beneath his handsome exterior was a man who had a generous heart. Somehow, her heart beat a few ticks faster just knowing that.

She tilted her head, laying her cheek on her knees. "So football is your first love."

"It was then."

"And now?

His eyes bored into her. "I'm working on developing a different game plan."

The boat bumped the edge of the dock, nearly knocking her from her perch. Hank stood, picking up the picnic basket, and reached down to help Annabeth to her feet. She slid her hand into his, the warm contact feeling right.

They disembarked and headed up the hill.

"You aren't planning on us hiking one of the trails, are you?" She gestured to her sandals with the wedge heel. She'd dressed carefully today in a peach linen blouse and cream capri pants.

Hank leisurely looked her up and down, his face registering his approval. "No. Our chariot awaits us at the surf shack up there."

True to his word, a golf cart with a piece of paper bearing Hank's name taped to the seat was parked outside the shop. He loaded the basket into the back and helped Annabeth in before walking around to start it up. The cart sputtered up the bend through a line of tourists heading for the lighthouse.

"Hey, is that lighthouse actually open to the public?" he asked.

"It is," she laughed.

Hank jockeyed the golf cart up to the small store at the base of the lighthouse. "I've never been in a lighthouse before. Let's go up." His childlike exuberance was hard to ignore.

"It's one hundred and eight steps to the top; do you think you can handle it?' she teased.

"Oh, Annabeth, now you've challenged my manhood and we *have* to go."

He bought them each a ticket, and Annabeth was grateful for her thrice-weekly spin classes as they nearly sprinted to the observation deck. The windows were small and they had to crowd together to see out. The boats in Chances Inlet Harbor bobbed in their slips, the sunlight reflected off them winking back at the lighthouse.

Annabeth peered at her home. "The town looks so small from over here."

"It *is* a small town," Hank said from behind her, his breath fanning her ear. The heat from his body warmed her back. "Do you ever feel like it's too small? Like you want to explore somewhere else?"

Exploring someplace else would be far out of her comfort zone. She knew who she was in Chances Inlet; she didn't have to fake being someone she wasn't. But there were times she wanted to see what else was out in the world. She just didn't think she could face what was out there alone. Not yet, anyway.

"I don't do well with new things and new experiences," she whispered.

Hank braced his hands on either side of the wall beside her head. "Maybe you just need to quit trying new things solo." His words caressed the back of her neck.

She turned her head slightly, her lips an inch from his. "Maybe."

A group of chattering teens stormed up the stairs, and Hank led her back out to the golf cart. They drove across the island to the west side, where a row of spectacular beach houses dotted the dunes bordering the Atlantic. Hank pulled up to a driveway of a large cedar-shake house situated right on the ocean.

"We're eating here?" Annabeth stared at the massive house she was sure she'd seen featured in a magazine somewhere.

"No. Out there." He pointed to a gazebo out on the sand, one side enclosed by a brick wall complete with a fireplace; two of the other three sides were glass to shield it from the wind. Hank parked the golf cart in the small carport. "There's a bathroom at the back there if you want to freshen up." He pointed to a service entrance adjacent to the carport.

After Annabeth made use of the bathroom, she peeled off her sandals and walked out to the gazebo. A table was already set, complete with a linen tablecloth and silverware. Wine chilled in an ice-filled wine bucket.

"Obviously you've been here before."

"Nope." Hank pulled out a chair for her. "It's just my reward for beating a friend of mine at golf yesterday."

"You have some pretty wealthy friends." Most of Annabeth's friends picnicked in the sand.

Hank took the seat across from her. "I have lots of friends, Annabeth. Not all of them wealthy. But I grew up in that world. I won't apologize for that."

His words stung a bit. Had she become such a snob that she faulted him for his birthright?

Hank reached over and grasped her hand on the table. "This is supposed to be the perfect spot to catch the sunset. I brought you here so you could enjoy it."

"Thank you," she whispered, not wanting to ruin the evening.

He poured wine into each of their glasses. "So now it's your turn to tell me your story about your marriage."

She nearly choked as she took a fortifying sip. "I . . . I was never married."

Hank looked at her quizzically.

"Will." Annabeth sighed. "He thinks he has to protect my reputation by telling everyone I was married to his father. I wasn't."

He pulled fried chicken out of the insulated basket, along with a container of Patricia McAlister's homemade potato salad, mixed fruit, and a tray of double fudge brownies.

"All my favorites. You certainly did your research."

"Your friend, Patricia. It only took a passing comment about needing a picnic basket and she took over."

That meant that everyone in Chances Inlet knew she was out on the island with Hank Osbourne. Annabeth wasn't sure how she felt about that, but since the man was leaving in a few days, she figured it didn't matter. Suddenly, though, the thought of Hank being gone by the end of the weekend made her stomach ache. She took another sip of wine as he prepared a plate for each of them.

"So, you weren't married? Ever?"

He'd been forthcoming with his story, so Annabeth didn't feel right not sharing hers. "No. Will's father was a brief fling. My one and only," she added shyly. "He was a young nineteen-year-old Marine, in town with some buddies on their weekend leave from Camp Lejeune. I was the new girl in town. My parents had just died and I'd been here all summer but didn't know a soul my own age. I guess you could say I was ripe for any kind of attention. For someone to tell me they'd love me forever. It was a couple of months before I even realized I was pregnant. By then, he had shipped out to God knows where."

Annabeth took another gulp of wine. "It was the gym teacher who finally figured it out. Unfortunately, she wasn't very discreet about it. She kept trying to coerce my grandmother into forcing me to give the baby up for adoption."

"Why didn't you?" He posed the question gently.

"My reputation was already in tatters. My parents were

dead, and I barely knew my grandmother. I'm ashamed to admit it, but I wanted someone to love. Someone who was all mine and would love me back. I know it's silly, but I've never once regretted my decision."

Hank saluted her with his wineglass. "*Silly* is not a word I'd ever use to describe you, Annabeth. And I commend you for the job you've done with Will. I can't imagine it was easy."

It hadn't been easy. But somehow, against all odds, her son had turned out well. A success.

"Did you ever try to find Will's father? You didn't have to do it all alone financially."

"I did, when I finally discovered I was pregnant. I went to Camp Lejeune but was told he'd died in a friendly fire episode shortly after he deployed. There were no parents to contact because he'd apparently grown up in the foster care system. I'm ashamed to admit it, but I was kind of glad he didn't have any family. That way, I didn't have to share Will with anyone. It was just me and my grandmother, and I couldn't have given my son up." A bemused sigh escaped her lips. "I guess I'm a lot like more like my daughter-in-law than I thought."

She hadn't realized she was crying until Hank reached across the table to wipe away a tear.

"Hey," he said. "Why don't we eat this delicious dinner your friend prepared and enjoy the sunset?"

As they ate their meal, Hank offered up the occasional anecdote from what he termed Sophie's teenage drama. It was obvious he adored his daughter, and Annabeth wondered what it would have been like if Will had had a father who adored him as much.

The sunset was everything Hank promised. By the time they'd packed up their picnic and traversed the dark island back to the ferry, it was a chilly ride back. Still, she huddled on the outdoor deck, Hank's arms around her, watching the lighthouse fade in the distance.

Once in Chances Inlet, Hank deposited the picnic basket back at the inn. Sophie had gone to the movies with

Lynnette's granddaughter and wouldn't be back for another hour. They stopped at the Patty Wagon again for some lemonade before ambling through the back streets to Annabeth's house.

Hank's voice punctuated the darkness. "You know, Annabeth, you are a lot more than just Will's mother. Or a shopkeeper in Chances Inlet. You can be whoever you want to be."

They were fifty yards from Will's house. She could see Julianne silhouetted in the window carrying Owen up the stairs. While Annabeth appreciated Hank's confidence in her, she was comfortable in Chances Inlet. She'd made mistakes in her life, yet the town accepted her anyway. As one of its own. Her business and friends were here and that was enough for her. Reinventing herself somewhere else was just too much for Annabeth to take on. She didn't know why Will, and now Hank, couldn't understand. One thing she did know, she didn't want this magical night to end.

Tugging on the hand he'd wrapped securely around hers, she pulled him deeper into the trees. When they were out of sight of the house, she stood on her toes and kissed him. It was a tentative kiss at first, until he took the reins and began kissing her back.

Hank leaned his back against a tree, pulling her in closer contact to his hard body. Annabeth sighed as she opened her mouth wider to give him better access. Her hands fisted in his shirt before he broke the kiss to push his glasses on top of his head.

She nuzzled his neck as his hands squeezed her backside. Their lips found one another again. One of them moaned, she wasn't sure who.

Suddenly, the yard was flooded with lights.

"Who's out there?" Will shouted from the verandah.

"Ah, hell," Hank whispered. "Please tell me he doesn't own a shotgun."

Annabeth couldn't help it, she laughed. Hank held her closer, but that only made her giggle harder. He chuckled along with her.

"*Mom?* Is that you out here?"

She could hear Will coming down the steps.

"Have dinner with me and Sophie tomorrow." Hank whispered in her ear.

She nodded against his chest. "Go!" she managed to get out between giggles. Hank stood there flattened against the tree, at least the parts of him that could remain flat. Annabeth laughed harder as she stepped out into the yard, now lit up like a Christmas tree lot. Will was advancing toward her.

"Mom! What the hell are you doing out here?"

"None of your business. Go back inside where you belong."

Her son's eyed narrowed to slits. "What's that on your neck?"

"William Anthony Connelly, I respect your privacy. I expect you to show me the same courtesy."

"Oh, for the love of . . ." Will swore. "I'm happy to respect your privacy, but I'd really rather not find you necking in the woods with HANK OSBOURNE!" he roared.

"Will!" Julianne called from the porch. "You'll wake the baby!" She waved at Annabeth. "Hey, Annabeth. We were just going to have dessert. Would you like to join us?"

The last thing Annabeth wanted to do was make small talk with her son right now. "No, thank you, Julianne. I have an early day tomorrow. I'm going home. Thank you, though."

"I'll walk you home." Her behemoth son was being a tad overprotective.

"It's only across the driveway, Will. Your mother isn't in any danger. If it makes you feel better, come up here and stand next to me and we'll both watch her safely to her door." Julianne winked at Annabeth.

Will tried his game face on her, but Annabeth was immune. She strolled inside unaccompanied, making a mental note to offer to watch Owen for Julianne every day for a week.

Twenty

Owen kicked his feet and pumped his arms in his bouncy seat.

"I'm going to have to start calling you Cheerio, little man. You're way too happy in the morning." Will took another swallow of his coffee, reaching over to wipe a spit bubble off his son's chin. "Daddy is not a morning person, so you're gonna have to tone it down a notch."

The baby let out a delighted gurgle at Will's words. Will smiled in spite of himself. Now nearly two months old, Owen was awake for longer spurts of time. Usually Will didn't mind, but this morning he'd hoped to have his son fed and back to sleep before Julianne finished her shower. Unfortunately, Owen had other ideas, meaning there wouldn't be a repeat of yesterday morning's soaping of his wife's back, among other things.

For the past two days, he and Julianne had secluded themselves in the house, taking care of their son and each other. Since her storming of his bedroom, they'd had sex at least a dozen times, and Will still couldn't seem to get enough of her. What they hadn't done was talk. At least not about their relationship. That subject seemed to be the elephant in the room, neither of them wanting to disturb it.

That wasn't the only thing Will had been avoiding. Roscoe had been calling and texting him since their phone conversation the other night, but Will hadn't bothered to answer. The mess with Bountygate was getting uglier, and Hank and Roscoe had been correct: Will's name was right in the center of the storm. He needed to decide what to do, but Paul Zevalos wasn't returning his phone calls, either.

As if all that weren't enough, finding his mother in the woods outside the house making out with his team's GM was proof enough that Will's world was beginning to resemble a busted play. He wasn't naïve enough to think his mother had remained celibate since his birth; she was young and very pretty, after all. But she'd been discerning of her reputation, and his, for many years, keeping her relationships very private. Much as she kept the rest of her life. Hank Osbourne, on the other hand, cut through a swath of rich divorcées like Brody Janik ran through defenses after a catch. His mother wasn't on the same level with the socialites Hank wore on his arm. Will still believed Hank was using his mother to gain information on his relationship with Coach Zevalos, and he worried she'd end up hurt.

Julianne's cell phone buzzed in its charger. Her phone had rung twice already this morning and it was barely nine o'clock. Will handed Owen a mini Blaze football. The baby's hands immediately clamped around it, his long-fingered hold sparking a burst of pride in Will before Owen brought it up to his mouth and began gumming it.

With Owen now occupied, he meandered over to where Julianne's phone sat on the desk. He told himself he wasn't snooping, just curious about whether he should alert her that she had messages. This was the problem with their not having talked. Will was fairly certain he knew all her secrets—surely she couldn't have more—but her brother was still a major player in Bountygate, and Roscoe's warnings about not trusting her played like a highlight reel in the back of his mind.

Two missed calls and one text message from her brother.

His whole body tensed. The shower was still running upstairs. *Damn it!* If he didn't check, Roscoe's voice would poison every interaction he and Julianne had today, including the sexy one he'd been planning for the boathouse later on. If she had something to hide, she'd keep her phone locked or out of sight. With one finger, he slid the keypad open and read the text from her brother.

Call me. You haven't checked in for two days. I need to know what's going on with Will. How's the baby?

A bead of sweat ran down his back. She was checking in with her brother daily? He didn't get the impression they were that close. And she was giving her brother updates? On him? *No!* Will wasn't going to let Roscoe's paranoia get to him. He needed to trust Julianne. And not just because he was beginning to *need* Julianne.

"Dude, are you just gonna let that kid gum that football to death?"

Will jumped at the sound of Brody's voice, nearly flinging Julianne's phone onto the tile floor.

"Jesus, Janik, have you ever heard of knocking?" Will gently placed the phone back in its spot.

"I didn't have to knock. I saw you from the verandah so I knew you were home."

"What are you, a freakin' peeping Tom?" Will needed a punching bag to take out his anger on, and Brody had arrived uninvited. "What if my wife were walking around naked in here?"

A slow grin spread over Brody's face, further stoking Will's anger.

"So it's now that kind of marriage, huh?"

Will still wasn't sure what kind of marriage he had, but he wasn't discussing it with Brody. He lunged across the kitchen at him, but the agile tight end, adept at avoiding linebackers in pursuit, danced out of his way.

"Dude, I brought breakfast!" He shook a white paper sack from the Queen of Hearts Bakery in front of Owen's face. The baby squealed in delight. "Do you want a scone, little dude?"

"Give me that!" Will snatched the bag from Brody, his stomach rumbling as the scent of fresh blueberry scones wafted out of the bag. "You've done your good deed for the day, now get out."

Brody turned one of the kitchen chairs around and straddled it, tickling Owen's bare feet as he sat in front of the baby. "No can do. Roscoe told me I couldn't leave until I physically saw you call him. Seriously, that guy's a pain in the a . . . keester." He winked at Owen. "I may have to look for other representation if he keeps using me as his tool."

Roscoe was getting desperate if he was resorting to forcing his other clients to do his bidding. Not that Brody had to be forced to butt into Will's business. He'd seemed to make a career of it. Will pulled out his cell phone and texted his agent, telling him he'd call him when he was damn well ready.

"Done." He shoved the phone back into the pocket of his shorts. "Now, you can go."

"Jeesh, your daddy is grouchy in the morning," Brody said to the baby.

Will rubbed the back of his neck. "Look, Brody, you were right the other day. This . . . thing could get a little ugly before it gets resolved. While I appreciate your lapdog determination—"

"Hey!"

"—you've got a good career going and I don't want it to get tarnished by a bunch of gossips who want to take down a good coach."

Brody looked him in stony silence.

"Really, Brody. For yourself and the team, you need to distance yourself from me right now. Get out of here. Go back to Baltimore. And please, take Hank Osbourne with you."

Brody chuckled. "Sorry, dude, but the Wizard of Oz is pursuing his own agenda here in town. I have no pull with him. But I *am* leaving today, and it has nothing to do with you bossing me around."

Will was relieved, and not just because Brody was always

underfoot. He'd meant what he said about protecting his teammate's career and the reputation of the Blaze. "When's your flight?"

"You're leaving, Brody?"

Julianne breezed into the kitchen, clean and sweet-smelling in a V-neck T-shirt and jean shorts. Her hair was still damp, pulled back from her face in a big clip. She looked fresh and bright-eyed and Will wanted to throw her over his shoulder, carry her upstairs, and muss her up until her lips were swollen and her scent was musky.

"And look who's still up!" She nuzzled Owen's toes while Will groaned behind her. "Ooo, give me that sloppy, yucky ball, sweetie." The baby shrieked as she tried to take the football from him.

"Hey!" Both men yelled at the same time.

Julianne rolled her eyes, handing the ball back to a screeching Owen. "I hope Carly has a girl," she mumbled.

Will handed her a cup of coffee from the Keurig. "Are you going back to Baltimore?" she asked Brody.

"Cape Cod, actually. My whole family gets together for a three-day party at the beach every Memorial Day weekend."

"Well, by the time you get there, you'll have missed most of it," Julianne pointed out.

Brody shrugged. "They can be a little . . . overbearing en masse like that. My sisters invite all their single friends and I feel like I'm at a cattle auction or something."

Julianne peered over the top of her coffee mug at Brody. "Some guys would love all that attention."

"Yeah, well, it's impossible to make everyone happy, and by the end of the weekend, one or all of my sisters will be gunning for me. It's better to keep my visit as brief as possible."

"Oh! Speaking of your sister . . ." Julianne put down her mug and went to rummage around the desk. Will tensed for a moment, thinking she'd notice her phone wasn't as she left it, but she tossed it aside to pull out a large envelope. The same one that Brody had brought his sister's picture in.

"Here." She handed it to Brody, a shy look on her face. "I finished the design."

Brody's jaw dropped. "You did?"

"I don't know if she'll even like it, but if she does, I know a seamstress in Boston who can make the gown."

He pulled the sketch out of the envelope and a wide grin broke out over his face. "Wow, Julianne, this is perfect. I know she'll love it because it's . . . her. You're a genius."

"Sophie had some ideas for jewelry pieces, too." Julianne lifted a now-whimpering Owen out of the bouncy seat.

"Huh, merging the two businesses already," he muttered low enough for only Will to hear.

Will glared at him.

Brody laughed. "Well, my business here is complete. Connelly, I'm going to kiss your wife now, so you might want to turn your back so you don't go all caveman again."

"Like hell I will."

"Stop it, both of you!" Julianne pulled Brody in for a hug. He kissed her cheek and bussed Owen's head.

"See you both back in Charm City. And Will, don't forget to make that call," he called as he went out the door.

Owen was rubbing his eyes as Julianne turned to him. "What call?" she asked.

Will hesitated. Why was she interested? "I need to call Roscoe, my agent," he finally answered.

"Oh." She smiled at him. "In that case, I'll take this little guy upstairs and put him down for his nap so you can have some privacy."

He felt like an idiot for not trusting her. "No, I'll take him. It's a holiday weekend. I don't need to talk to Roscoe today," he lied.

She handed him the baby and he leaned in and gave her an openmouthed kiss that turned fiery in an instant.

"Come upstairs with me," he whispered.

Her cell phone buzzed just as she turned to follow him up.

"It's been going off all morning." Will hoped he sounded nonchalant.

Julianne checked the screen and turned off the phone.

"Just Stephen." She wrapped her hands around his waist, Owen now dozing on Will's shoulder. "Upstairs, buster."

"Does he call you often?"

"Ugh, every day since I've been here. He's suddenly turned into a doting older brother. It's annoying."

Will laid Owen in his crib, relief coursing through his veins at her words. Roscoe had tainted his common sense with all his warnings about not trusting Julianne. But she wasn't conspiring with her brother. She couldn't be because Will was becoming too dependent on the feel of her beneath his hands, the taste of her on his tongue, and the warmth of her wrapped around his body.

He stalked to his bedroom, where she was already naked on the bed. Will whipped his T-shirt off and stepped out of his shorts, her smile of appreciation arousing him more. If he had any niggling doubts about his wife, he'd bury them now, as he buried himself inside her. When he was alone with her, he forgot all about Paul Zevalos, Bountygate, Hank Osbourne, and Julianne's brother. It was just him and her finding that perfect symbiosis he'd been unable to find with any other woman. For now, that was enough. He'd worry about the world outside Chances Inlet later.

The designs were coming to her fast and furiously now. Only they weren't wedding gowns. Julianne gently swayed on a porch swing in the lush back garden of the Tide Me Over Inn sketching, of all things, baby clothes. Owen slept peacefully in his stroller, Sophie sitting Indian style on a blanket on the lawn next to him, sorting beads from a plastic container.

"Gwen Stefani designs baby clothes." Sophie said around the string she held between her teeth. "And she's cool. Besides, I'll bet most of your former clients are having babies, and they'd probably buy anything you design. You should really try to market those."

Julianne couldn't help but smile at the young girl's exuberance. The idea of creating an entire line of baby clothes had actually begun percolating in her head over the past few days, although she hadn't given much thought to how "cool" her new venture might be. Unlike her elaborate, sophisticated bridal gowns, the baby clothes were bright, simple, and fun. Sebastian would have a fit because they screamed mass market, but Julianne wanted other mothers to be able to afford what she was creating. Not that she'd even mentioned the idea to her business manager. She hadn't even told Will yet.

Glancing across the garden, she spied her husband chatting with Gavin and a few other men she'd seen around Chances Inlet these past few weeks. It was Memorial Day, and Patricia McAlister was hosting her annual picnic for the inn's guests as well as her family and friends. After nearly four days of seclusion, Will and Julianne had ventured out into town again, this time as husband and wife in every sense. True, they hadn't done much talking, at least not about anything involving their relationship. She still had no idea where their marriage would end up, but she felt a deeper connection to Will and a greater sense of optimism that things could work out eventually.

As if he sensed her watching him, Will looked over and their eyes met. Warmth pooled in her belly as her body registered the intense hunger in his eyes. He saluted her with his beer bottle before rejoining his conversation. Blushing, Julianne returned to her sketchpad, the lion on the onesie she drew grinning mischievously back at her as if he, too, could read her thoughts.

Could she share her ideas with Will? Julianne scrunched her eyes closed. She desperately wanted someone to share her life with. *To share her dreams with*. Nicky had been her imaginary partner for so many years. But now she wanted the real thing. She wanted Will. The problem was, she didn't know if he wanted her. For anything more than sex, that is.

"Finished!" Sophie held up a beautiful lapis bracelet.

"Annabeth is going to have to change the sign on her shop to read 'Antiques *and Jewelry*' if you keep this pace up, Soph."

The girl smiled. "This one isn't for the shop. Mrs. McAlister commissioned it."

"Ahh, cutting out the middleman already?"

Sophie's face fell. "Ohmigosh! I didn't mean to cut out Annabeth! Do you think she'll care?"

Julianne doubted her mother-in-law would even notice, much less care. Annabeth's attention was firmly fixed on Sophie's father. She peered beyond the carriage house, down the lane, where the two had disappeared, hand in hand, nearly half an hour before. They'd gone to walk along the beach before dinner. Hank and Sophie were leaving tomorrow, and Julianne sincerely hoped this wouldn't be the end of Annabeth and Hank's blossoming relationship.

"Of course not," she reassured Sophie. "I was just teasing. Annabeth will be thrilled you're making something for her friend."

"Oh, good, because I don't want Annabeth to be mad at me. I really like her." She looked at Julianne slyly. "Do you think she likes my dad?"

A pair of figures moved in the trees behind Sophie. Annabeth and Hank were locked in a serious kiss. Julianne bit back a laugh. "I think she might, actually."

Will and Gavin made their way across the grass toward her. *Uh-oh!* If they come closer, her husband would have a perfect view of his mother and Hank. Will had been staring down the Blaze GM all afternoon, his caveman persona in full force.

Julianne leaped off the swing. "Would you mind watching Owen for a few minutes, Sophie? Will and I are just going to go for a quick walk."

A quick walk in the opposite direction if she moved fast enough.

"Hi!" She tried to make it sound casual as she met them halfway.

"Hi yourself." One of Will's eyebrows inched up, as if he sensed she was up to something. "We were coming over to check on the baby."

"He's still sleeping."

"Uh-huh." Will eyed her warily. "Gavin hasn't seen him in a week. I told him how Owen's changed a lot since then."

Gavin gave the halfhearted shrug of a guy doing whatever it took to appease his best friend.

"Oh, he has, Gavin," she said earnestly. "You should go peek at him. His mustache has completely come in already."

Will scowled at her while Gavin choked back a laugh.

She traced a finger down Will's arm. "You were going to show me that tree with the trunk that grew in the shape of a heart, remember?"

Gavin snorted. "Jeez, Connelly, are you still using that old tree trunk line to lure girls into the woods?"

Will pinned his friend with his death stare.

"Fine." Gavin put his hands up in front of his chest. "I'll go check your son's facial hair. Maybe I'll take him to the barber while you two play in the woods." Gavin ambled over to the stroller.

"So, what's with your sudden interest in dendrology, Princess?"

His overstuffed brain was really obnoxious, especially poised as it was on the body of a virile Viking warrior.

She crossed her arms. "You told me about it, and now I want to see it for myself. Are you going to show me, or do I ask one of your fellow gym rats over there?" She pointed to the men he and Gavin had just separated from.

"If you're gonna ask one of them, you probably shouldn't use the word *dendrology*."

Julianne huffed in frustration as she marched around the massive body that blocked her way and stormed toward the path into the woods. "Never mind. I'll find it myself."

The man was so infuriating! The heck with Annabeth and Hank. She was done protecting them. Let them face the wrath of William the Conqueror on their own.

With his long legs, Will caught up to her in three strides. No sooner had they rounded the corner of the garden shed than he had her pushed against the wall, his big body holding her prisoner. Julianne relaxed immediately into the warmth of his embrace, laying her cheek against his chest.

She let her hands roam the length of his back while he nuzzled her ear.

"What am I going to do with you, Princess?"

"Mmm, I have a few suggestions." She lifted her lips to his jaw.

Will kissed her temples, her eyelids, and the tip of her nose. She moaned, trying to pull his lips in for a kiss.

"Unh-uh." He pulled his mouth away. "I'm trying to think of an appropriate punishment for you for running interference so I wouldn't intercept my mother and Hank."

Busted. Julianne leaned back against the Hardie board wall of the shed, her breathing uneven. "Really, Will. Why does this thing with your mom and Hank upset you so much?"

"Because I don't want to see her hurt!"

"She's a big girl." She stroked a hand over his muscular chest. "And I think Hank must really feel something for her. Or else why would he risk angering his team's star player? He's risking a lot for a relationship with your mom."

Will's eyes shuttered as his giant brain processed her theory, clearly an idea he hadn't considered before.

Julianne arched back into his body, her lips making a beeline for his jaw. "Besides, this part is kind of fun. Sneaking around and all that. Can you blame your mom?"

His big body trembled. "Julianne, that's not the mental picture I want to have of my mother and Hank Osbourne."

She laughed as she slid a finger into the waistband of his shorts, gently tracing the warm, soft skin beneath. Will instantly stiffened, his lips finding that sweet spot where her neck met her shoulder.

"This is what I wanted. I wanted you to drag me back here because you missed me." His breath against her skin made her shiver with need. "Because you want me."

For such a smart man, he was really an idiot sometimes. Did he not see how much she wanted him every moment? How much she needed him? How much power he had over her?

"Oh, God, Will. Don't you get it?" she confessed, giving him the power to destroy her if he wished. "I miss you whenever you leave the room. I miss you as soon as you leave my body. Sometimes . . . sometimes it's so overwhelming that I'm beginning to think I really am bat crazy."

"It's bat-*shit* crazy. And I think we both probably are." And then he finally kissed her.

Twenty-one

"Home sweet home." Will's whole body was tense
as he stood with Julianne just outside the double-wide trailer
in the Seaside Vista Trailer Park, where he'd grown up. The
aluminum exterior had been painted some sort of blue shade
before the sun had had its way with it. His mother's once-
prized rosebushes wilted in the hot afternoon sun, years'
worth of neglect dragging down any buds hearty enough to
attempt to bloom. The wooden sunporch Will had con-
structed with Gavin and Gavin's dad was in dire need of a
fresh coat of paint.

He cringed as he saw his childhood home through Julianne's eyes. When he and his mother had lived there, the
trailer park had been neat and well maintained. Now, the
place just looked . . . tired. The term *vista* was stretching it
twenty years ago. Today, it was laughable.

"Do you think any of your old neighbors still live here?"

Will wandered over to the hive of mailboxes, checking
the names on the slots, but most had worn off. "I doubt it.
It was a pretty transient place. Most of the kids who lived
here ended up in trouble at some point. All the parents, if

they even had one, worked, and there wasn't much supervision for kids outside school. If it weren't for the McAlisters, I would probably have ended up in juvie, too. Having a safe place to go when my mom worked gave me opportunities the kids who lived here never had."

He stood, hands on his hips, and tried to conjure up any good memories of his old home. Sadly, Will couldn't.

"I can't believe my mother lived in this dump for nearly twenty years." He hadn't wanted her to live here alone when he'd been at Yale, but his mother was stubborn. It seemed stubborn women were his lot in life. "The first dollar I got, I bought her a house." Unfortunately, that first dollar he'd earned could destroy a dozen NFL careers, including that of his former coach, if it came out how he'd earned it.

"I doubt it was a dump when you lived here. Annabeth may not have been able to give you much, but I'm sure what she could provide was at least clean and tidy." She lifted Owen out of his stroller and began to point out the birds and the few visible flowers to him.

He wasn't sure why he felt it so important to take Julianne on this trip down memory lane, but he wanted her to see why their son should never want for anything. Once they'd arrived at the trailer park, however, he'd felt extremely uncomfortable. He was revealing more to her than he'd planned .

"This place made you who you are, Will. Living here pushed you to succeed beyond your wildest dreams. You should never be ashamed of that. Especially not with me." She stretched up and kissed the side of his mouth. It wasn't nearly enough for him and he captured her mouth in a hot kiss, tangling his tongue with hers until Owen head-butted him on the jaw.

"Oww!" He rubbed the side of his face. "You've definitely got the head of a linebacker. Come here, Cheerio. Let's take Mommy for a walk to the beach."

Julianne hesitated. She'd been making progress with her driving, but the beach was a different prospect all together.

Will hadn't been able to coax her off the verandah since they'd arrived in Chances Inlet.

He reached for her hand. "It'll be okay. Owen and I will be right there with you."

She slid her small hand into his, trust emanating from her eyes. Since that first night on Sea Island, she'd trusted him. He wasn't sure what he'd done to deserve her faith, but her confidence humbled him.

Pushing the stroller in front, the three of them trod the dirt path through the woods he'd taken hundreds of times before. Except now he wasn't a lonely young boy, but part of a family. A family he hadn't known he'd have over a month ago. Yet the baby in his arms and the woman whose hand he held firmly were now his responsibility. Somehow, that thought didn't seem quite as daunting as it once did.

Annabeth waited patiently as Patricia McAlister stirred sugar into her coffee. The two women sat together as they did every month at the local chamber of commerce meeting. Even after nearly a decade of owning her own business, Annabeth still had to pinch herself each time she attended one of these gatherings, amazed that she was included in Chances Inlet's business community. She'd come a long way from the Seaside Vista Trailer Park, when she drove a school bus and cleaned homes to scratch out a measly living.

Patricia had always been a member of the town's business elite. She and her husband operated McAlister Construction, Chances Inlet's only engineering and construction firm, until Donald's death. Now she'd realized her dream in renovating and operating the Tide Me Over Inn, while her son, Gavin, temporarily ran the construction company.

"So, tell me what's been going on with the handsome Hank Osbourne? It's been nearly two weeks since he left. Have you heard from him?"

Annabeth took a sip of her own coffee before answering.

"He's in California with Sophie, so he really doesn't have a lot of free time to call." Which wasn't exactly true. Hank was in California, but rather than call her, he sent long e-mails to her every day, sometimes more than one. The e-mails weren't flowery or prosaic love letters, but rather detailed descriptions of his day with Sophie, complete with funny anecdotes and exasperated comments about life with a teenager. She replied back, recounting her day in the shop or her time with Owen. As the days flew past, their electronic courtship had taken a more intimate turn and their correspondence now delved into their hopes and desires. Annabeth feared she was falling in love with Hank, and she didn't know what to do about it.

"You mean he hasn't called you?" Patricia stared at her in disbelief.

"Oh, he's called me." In fact, they'd spent nearly an hour on the phone just last night. "It's just that this is his time with Sophie. She's his first priority right now."

Patricia blew out a puff of air. "He was supposed to be spending time with Sophie when they were here, and he made time for you. Don't make excuses for him. Too bad. I really thought he was more interested than it sounds."

"He is," Annabeth whispered. "He wants me to come to Baltimore when he gets back."

Patricia leaned closer, a sly grin on her face. "Now that's what I'm talking about. Stop holding out on me, Annabeth."

"I'm not sure I should go. Or even continue this. It wouldn't be fair to him."

"What are you talking about? He's a fabulous guy." Patricia ticked off on her fingers. "Single, decent job, devoted father, and really good-looking with all his teeth and hair."

Annabeth laughed. "You sound like Julianne."

"How's the sex?"

"Patricia!" Annabeth quickly glanced around the room, but no one was paying attention to their conversation. "We . . . there wasn't . . . Sophie was here with him, for goodness' sakes!"

Her friend rolled her eyes. Annabeth felt awkward even having this conversation. Patricia was almost ten years her senior, with five children and a marriage that had spanned nearly thirty years. The widowed innkeeper was also rumored to be involved with Chances Inlet's newly elected sheriff, a man five years her junior. Clearly, Patricia had no trouble maintaining a relationship with a man, while Annabeth was floundering around in uncharted territory.

Patricia squeezed Annabeth's hand. "I see what the problem is. Sweetie, you're a beautiful woman. Don't be intimidated by those perky little twenty-somethings parading themselves on the beach. If Hank wanted that, well, he could have it. But he wants you!"

Annabeth buried her face in her hands, unsure whether to laugh or cry at Patricia's attempt to buoy her confidence. The fact was, it wasn't Annabeth's body image that bothered her; she knew she was still attractive. Good eating habits and regular exercise kept her in great shape. And Hank's interest had been apparent every time she was in his arms.

It was what would happen after sex that scared her. After he realized she was nothing more than a high school–educated girl from the trailer park. She couldn't compete with the women in his social sphere. Not intellectually, anyway. It was that fear that kept her tethered to Chances Inlet.

"Annabeth." Patricia pried her hand away from her face. "Look at me. I've always admired your resolve and your resiliency. You raised a fabulous son with very little help and even less money. And now you're a successful businesswoman. All my life, I've had the protection of a man to help me. First my father and then Donald. Being alone scared me to death. But you survived it, and since Donald's death, I've looked to you for inspiration."

Annabeth was too flattered by her friend's admission to speak.

"Now, though, you've got a chance at a happiness you can't even fathom. It's really nice to have someone to share things with, Annabeth. Don't shortchange yourself on this opportunity. Take a risk on Hank. If it doesn't work out, you have a safe place to land, right back here in Chances Inlet. This will always be your home."

The mayor called the meeting to order, and Annabeth didn't have a chance to respond to Patricia. She wasn't even sure she could respond. It would be a big risk to take her relationship with Hank to the next level. One that could not only affect her son's career, but her attachment to Sophie if things didn't work out. Unfortunately, the thought of not having Hank in her life frightened her just as much.

Julianne sat on the bench swing located along the perimeter of the small boardwalk in downtown Chances Inlet. Most of the tourists swam at the public beaches located farther out on the island, but a few families with young children strolled along the shoreline eating ice cream and dodging the waves. Will waded up to his ankles, Owen on his shoulder. Julianne gripped the chain on the swing, her knuckles white. She knew her fear was irrational, but that didn't make it any easier. The sea had swept away the mother she loved. It could just as easily do the same with the other two people she loved most in the world: Owen and Will.

Until this morning's trip to the trailer park, she hadn't admitted to herself that she loved Will. She'd desperately tried not to involve her heart in their relationship. But he'd finally started to let her in, sharing a piece of his past with her. Will was a fiercely private man, one who didn't want others to know any of his weaknesses. The shame he felt about his upbringing was totally unfounded in her opinion, but he believed it. Her heart had ached for the boy he once was, convinced the world was against him. It also swelled with pride at how he'd used his brain and his brawn to build a better life for himself and Annabeth.

For now, she'd bide her time, loving him in her heart even if she couldn't bring herself to say the words. She'd already confessed to him how much she needed him. He held all the cards and he could crush her if he wanted to.

Her cell phone buzzed in the diaper bag. Julianne pulled

it out and glanced at the screen. *Stephen*. She'd managed to avoid his phone calls for the past two weeks, instead trading voice mail and text messages. Total avoidance of him seemed silly and petty, though. After all, he was only concerned about Owen's welfare. What harm could there be in letting him know his nephew was fine?

"Hello," she answered.

Stephen hesitated; he was probably stunned she'd finally answered. "You're alive!"

"Don't sound so disappointed," she teased.

He sighed. "Julianne, do we always have to do this?"

She bristled at his tone, feeling chastised. Even worse, her half brother was right. He took his job as older sibling very seriously; there was no reason for her to be churlish. "Sorry. You've got my undivided attention now. What's up?"

"Just checking how everything is going there. You've been thrust into an awkward situation and I worry that you're okay."

"Part of this situation is my fault, Stephen, but I'm taking responsibility for it, trying to correct the wrong decisions I might have made."

"Yes, you are, Julianne, and I'm really proud of the way you handled yourself and this whole crazy situation. You're a wonderful mother."

Unexpected tears stung her eyes. That was twice her brother had complimented her. She wasn't sure how to take it.

"How is Owen doing? Has he completely recovered?"

Julianne proudly regaled him with the latest update from Owen's checkup earlier in the week. "Of course, he's in the hundredth percentile for height and weight. He's going to be big like his daddy."

"I know Faith and the kids would love to see you both. Are you coming up with Will next week?"

She looked across the sand at Will. He hadn't mentioned anything about next week. Of course, they both strategically avoided any discussion of the future.

"Next week?" she asked.

"Blaze mini-camp is next week. Unless, of course, Will is skipping it to avoid all the questions about the bounty issue."

Back to that again. Why was her brother so interested in her husband's supposed involvement in a bounty scheme? Will was headed toward her, a cranky Owen in his hands.

"Umm, I think Carly was actually going to come down here," she fibbed. "But if plans change, I'll let you know, Stephen. I need to feed Owen now. I'll definitely call if we come to town. Bye." She hung up the phone just as Will reached the stroller. For some reason she couldn't explain, she was uncomfortable talking about Will and football with her brother.

Julianne pulled the bottle of water out of the diaper bag and mixed the dry formula in before shaking it up. Will gently sat down on the swing, maneuvering Owen into the crook of his arm.

"Who was that?" he asked, taking the bottle from her and silencing Owen with it.

She wasn't sure why the question put her on the defensive, but it did. It almost felt like her brother and Will were tussling over something and she was caught in the middle. In the end, she decided that given their evolving relationship, she had no reason to hide things from Will.

"It was my brother. Checking up on me again."

If Will had any reaction, she didn't catch it because he was watching Owen drink his bottle.

"He mentioned that you would be going to Baltimore next week. For mini-camp?"

"Yeah."

"Oh." She hadn't meant to sound so disappointed.

They were quiet for a moment; Owen gulped his lunch, punctuating the lull in their conversation.

"You and Owen could come with me."

Julianne's stomach soared at his words. She didn't have a problem being left in Chances Inlet. Annabeth would be there. But the thought of spending several days, and nights, away from Will made her chest ache.

"Where would we stay?"

"I have a loft apartment in Fed Hill. It'll be cozy." He looked up then, his green eyes stormy. "But I think we'll be able to make it work."

She couldn't keep the grin off her face. "I could see Carly!"

"And your brother." He looked at her intently.

Julianne waved a hand. "If there's time. But I'd rather see Carly."

"The team hosts a big family picnic the night before the mini-camp ends. I'm sure Carly will be there."

Her heart was racing. If he was going to introduce her to his teammates, there was a chance he wanted their marriage to last more than just three months. Joy bubbled up inside her. She took a now-sleepy Owen from his arms and gently laid him in the stroller. Together they started back through town, headed home.

"There wouldn't by chance be any shopping near your apartment?"

Will laughed. "I've never really noticed. But"—he sobered—"the place is adjacent to the harbor. Will you be all right with that?"

Julianne thought she'd be all right with any place as long as he was there. "Didn't I just spend forty minutes sitting a hundred yards in front of the Atlantic Ocean?"

He wrapped an arm over her shoulders and kissed the top of her head. "Yes, Princess, you did. I'm very proud of your progress."

It was the second time in less than an hour that one of the men in her life had told her he was proud of her. Julianne felt ten feet tall.

She brought her arm around his waist, sliding her fingers into the back pocket of his shorts. "Of course, all it would take is one nasty storm for me to backslide," she warned.

"Well, Princess, let's pray there aren't any bad storms this summer."

Twenty-two

Will should have realized the futility of trying to pray away a summer storm. All afternoon, the National Weather Service had advised the entire coastline of a brewing tropical thunderstorm forecast to strike the area sometime after dark. As if that weren't enough, Owen had been cranky since their return from the beach earlier, making both Will and Julianne jumpy.

Will sat in his office as Owen fussed in and out of a fitful sleep. He propped the baby on his shoulder and rubbed his back. "Come on, Cheerio. Just close your eyes for a few minutes. You'll feel better. And so will Mommy and Daddy."

He was begging his child to sleep. Next he'd be one of those crazy parents who strapped their kid into his car seat and drove him around the inlet. Will sat up straighter in his chair, digging in his pocket for his car keys. *Why hadn't he thought of that before?* As he was striding out of the room, however, something flickered on the television, catching his attention. He increased the volume.

". . . sources in the commissioner's office confirmed today that the league's investigation of Bountygate has ended in a stalemate. Implicated players and coaches continue to vehemently refute the allegations, leaving the league with its hands tied. However, a Senate committee investigating racketeering charges emanating from this scandal plans to hold its own hearings. Subpoenas are set to be served any day now. The commissioner is said to be hoping that these hearings, along with lawsuits filed by players alleged to be injured under the scheme, will shake loose some tongues, allowing the investigation to move forward to its likely conclusion: fines and/or suspensions against players and coaches."

Will heard thunder in the distance. He wasn't sure if it was real or the pounding of his head. He needed to call Roscoe to make sure he wasn't in the line of fire for subpoenas or anything else. Owen whimpered in his arms.

"Okay, okay. You first, Owen."

Will pulled open his office door to find Julianne standing there, a strange man beside her.

"Oh, hey. Your friend, Chris"—she pointed to the guy next to her—"dropped by. He wanted to say hi before he left town."

Will had never laid eyes on Chris before. The guy had that smarmy look of a tabloid reporter all over him.

"Who the hell are you?" Will growled, handing off Owen to a startled Julianne.

"Chris Masterman of the *Sporting News*. I just want to ask you a few questions."

Julianne gasped as Will maneuvered the weasel reporter through the hallway.

"You came into my house?" Will bellowed. "Are you fucking crazy?"

"Hey, your wife let me in. Congratulations on the marriage, by the way. Cute kid, too. If you could just answer a few ques—"

Will had the dumbass reporter in a choke hold and pushed him up against the wall. "You don't come in my house, Chris. Ever. If you or any of your brethren step a foot on my yard ever again, I will tear you limb from limb."

"Will!" Julianne cried.

Chris was fighting back now. "It's all coming out now, Connelly. You're better off telling your story to someone who can put the right spin on it. I can help you, man, just tell me what you know."

Will pulled the front door open; big drops of rain were pelting the verandah. "Not on your life! Now get the hell off my property before I call the sheriff." He tossed the reporter down the steps.

"You're a maniac, you know that!" Chris yelled. "I've got all this on my iPhone video and when the public sees it, you won't play another down in the NFL!"

Will slammed the door on him, throwing the deadbolt closed. When he turned around, a wide-eyed Julianne stood at the base of the stairs clutching Owen, who was wailing loudly.

"He said he was your friend," she whispered.

"Damn it, Julianne," he yelled at her. "They're gonna say a lot of things to get in front of me. Especially now. You can't be so gullible. If I told you once, I told you twice, you've got to think first! "

He realized his mistake as soon as her eyes narrowed to slits. The last thing he needed to do was take this out on her. Everything was spinning out of control. He thought he could keep the story at bay as long as he remained in Chances Inlet. But if one reporter was ballsy enough to venture to town, others would follow. None of it, though, was her fault. He closed his eyes and counted to ten.

"Julianne." He opened his eyes and reached for her.

She recoiled, gripping Owen closer. "Don't you touch me, Will Connelly." She turned on her heel and scampered up the stairs.

"Julianne!" he bellowed, which accomplished nothing but to make her angrier. The door to the nursery slammed. Will swore. His cell phone buzzed in his pocket.

"Damn it, Roscoe, there was a reporter in my house!" he roared into the phone.

———————

The storm was in full swing, wind and rain battering the windows. Owen had cried himself to sleep, his little head sweaty under Julianne's touch. She covered him with a blanket and dimmed the lamp. Tense and rattled from the events of the afternoon coupled with the relentless thunder shaking the house, she longed for the safety of Will's body.

She settled for a blanket instead, wrapping it around her as she sank into the big chair in her room. Her brother's words echoed around in her head. Stephen had warned her that Will was capable of harm. That he was aggressive by nature. But Julianne hadn't believed him. She still didn't. The stupid reporter had duped her. Will was right, she had been gullible. But Will's reaction had been over-the-top, too. She wasn't frightened of him; she was scared of whatever he was hiding, though. Clearly, her brother knew more than she did. Why else would he call her every day? Julianne sighed. Will knew all her secrets. Why was it taking him so long to share his with her?

The door from the hallway eased open. Will slipped in carrying a glass of wine. She curled up further in the chair, clutching the blanket tighter. He ignored her "keep out" posture and placed the wineglass on the table beside her. Silently, he made his way into the nursery, presumably to check on Owen.

Julianne took a fortifying swallow of the cabernet sauvignon, its rich flavor warming her as it slid down her throat. When she looked up, Will was leaning against the door frame, his hands shoved into his pockets. His Blaze hoodie was dotted with wet spots and his hair was damp as if he'd been wandering out in the storm. He looked tense and unsure of himself, more like the wayward youth he'd once been rather than the composed role model he'd become. Julianne was encouraged by this glimpse of his vulnerability.

"I owe you an apology." His voice was gritty and soft, as

if he were trying to convince himself he wasn't angry anymore.

"No." Julianne's heart went out to him, but she couldn't let him off that easily. "You owe me an explanation."

Will sighed heavily, running a hand through his hair, further mussing it up and making him look way too sexy for the small room. She loosened the grip on the blanket, in need of cooler air. His eyes darted everywhere except her face.

"It's complicated."

"Yeah, well, I might not have gone to an Ivy League school like you, but give me some credit for having survived the school of hard knocks."

He looked at her then, his eyes unreadable. "That wasn't meant to be a put-down."

Julianne nodded. They were about to cross that invisible line—she felt it—and she didn't want to halt their progress by speaking.

Will slumped down on the floor, his back resting against the chair so that he faced away from her. Obviously, he didn't want her to see his eyes as he revealed his tale. An involuntary shiver raced through her body. She wanted to touch him, but that could derail them, too, so she reached for the wine instead.

He was silent for a few minutes, and she began to wonder if he'd ever get the story out when he finally spoke.

"Gavin and the rest of the McAlisters were big athletes. Donald, their dad, played minor league baseball once. I did whatever they did. When we were in high school, Gavin was the one everybody thought would be a pro football player. Our team won the state championship twice. We both dreamed of playing together at NC State, but it turned out I was too small."

Julianne nearly choked on her wine, and Will chuckled.

"I was a late bloomer. I didn't grow until I got to college. Anyway, I was cool with taking out loans to go with my scholarships and heading to State with Gavin, but my high school guidance counselor had other ideas. He had a friend at Yale who was able to get me a tryout with their football team. They liked me, and my GPA, and suddenly there was a lot of merit scholarship money thrown at me. I wouldn't have any debt when I got out of college if I went there. It was really the best choice. And I loved it in New Haven. The professors, the secret societies, a college coach who was my mentor. Everything that makes up life on campus was so different than I imagined. Best of all, no one there knew I was the bastard from the Seaside Vista Trailer Park."

Of its own accord, Julianne's hand found Will's head, her fingers gently massaging his scalp.

"Gavin ended up blowing out his knee after one season. He'd never play in the pros. So the torch was passed to me. Only I didn't get drafted. But Coach Z was hired as the defensive coordinator for the Generals and he managed to work me onto the practice squad. The money wasn't great, five grand a month. I took a second job working nights as a security guard so I could send money to my mother. She needed to move out of that damn trailer park. It just wasn't safe for a woman to live there alone. Times were starting to get tough for everyone, and there were a lot of men in town with way too much time on their hands."

An ominous rumble of thunder shook the house.

"The final preseason game, there were a lot of starters hurt, so Coach Z put me in the lineup. I played my heart out because I didn't want to let Coach Z down, but mostly because I knew it was my last shot." Will hesitated. "It was a clean hit. The quarterback fumbled the ball, I landed on it, and we won the game. The next day, I found out the quarterback was out for the season. I'd separated his shoulder. He ended up never playing again."

He leaned his head onto her lap.

"Even worse, I found an envelope with twenty thousand dollars in cash in my locker that afternoon. When I asked Coach about it, he said it was a bonus for my play. I had no idea they did that in the pros, so I asked a few other players about it. They just slapped me on the back and said it was my reward for delivering a punishing lick to the Broncos' quarterback. I was sick." He let out an explosive sigh. "I'd taken a man out of the game and I was getting paid extra for it. I tried to give the money back, but Coach told me to keep my mouth shut and enjoy the cash. The next day, I was cut from the team. I'd like to believe Coach was doing me a favor by cutting me, you know, looking out for me. But now . . . I don't know."

Julianne didn't know what to say, so she just stroked his cheek.

"The Blaze called a few days later. Apparently, they liked the hit, too. I wasn't sure what to think when I got to Baltimore. I've never gotten any more cash in envelopes, though, thank God."

"What did you do with the money?" she asked.

"You're living in it. A college friend of mine invested it in a hedge fund and I made a killing in six months."

She looked around the cozy house, the only thing standing between her and the raging storm outside.

"I feel guilty every time I walk in here," he whispered.

"No, Will!" She crawled onto the floor beside him, taking his face between her hands. "You shouldn't feel guilty. You didn't do anything wrong. It was your job to hit the quarterback. You didn't know about the bonus. If you did, you wouldn't have hit him. Will, you would never intentionally hurt someone. I know you wouldn't!"

"I almost strangled that reporter today."

"*Almost!* And that's different. The jerk lied and misrepresented himself to get in the house." She ran her fingers through his hair. "But he does have a point. If you tell your story, people will know you're innocent. That you didn't do anything wrong. And then they'll leave you alone."

Lightning cracked outside and Will jumped to his feet.

"I can't, Julianne! Don't you see? I'm the one who can bring it all down. I'm the missing puzzle piece. The players who willingly took the money aren't going to talk."

Julianne stood, too. "But, Will, what they're doing is wrong. They have to be stopped, and you're the only one who can stop them."

"It's too late. I've already condoned the practice with my silence these past eight years. Besides, the man they're trying to name as the ringleader, Coach Z, is dying. I wouldn't be here today if it weren't for him. No matter how I feel about his practices, I don't want his last days to be a witch hunt." He sat on the edge of the bed, his hands hanging between his knees. "If they dig deep enough, they'll probably dredge up something minor that happened while he was coaching at Yale that could inadvertently damage the program. There are a lot of good kids with backgrounds like mine who are getting a shot at a better life through that football program. Whether or not they turn pro, doors will be opened for them. I can't sabotage that, Julianne, I can't."

She sat down beside him on the bed and laid her cheek on his shoulder. The thunder boomed again and he wrapped his arm around her.

"Now do you see why I can't talk about it?" he whispered.

Julianne nodded. His dilemma was real, but he hadn't actually done anything wrong. The demons in the scenario were his former coach and the players who took money to injure their opponents. Hopefully, all the talk about a bounty scheme would deter other players from instituting one in their own locker rooms. For now, though, she just wanted to reassure Will.

She reached up a finger to trace his jaw. "Whatever you decide to do, Will, I'll still love you."

The words were out there and she couldn't take them back. Wide-eyed, he answered her by pushing her back on the bed and claiming her mouth in a deep, soulful kiss. She reached under his sweatshirt to touch his warm skin as she wrapped a leg around his hips. Lightning cracked above them and they both jumped. Will listened for a moment to hear if Owen had woken, before pulling her off the bed.

"Come on." He grabbed the monitor and towed her toward the door.

"Where are we going?" Panic gripped her at the thought of going out in the storm.

"We're going to exorcise your fear of storms, Princess."

Her feet were rooted to the floor and she shook her head from side to side. No way was she moving from the safety of this room. And she'd prefer Will stay with her, thank you very much.

He pulled her in closer, leaning his forehead against hers. The heat of his body began to relax her tense limbs.

"I just trusted you with a secret only my agent knows. Trust me on this, will you, Julianne? I promise you'll enjoy it. Every. Single. Moment," he breathed.

Like a lamb to slaughter, she followed him out of the relative safety of her bedroom toward the front of the house, where the surf bombarded the coast and the storm waged war over their heads. His bedroom door was ajar and she dragged her feet as the sounds outside became louder.

"It's okay," he reassured her. "I'm right here."

He led her into his bedroom, where the drapes were wide open, revealing the ocean as lightning lit up the night sky. She trembled.

"Shh." He kissed her temple. "It's just a storm. You can do this. You've done it before. *We've* done it before."

Stepping back, he peeled the sweatshirt over his head, revealing his bare chest. As always, the sight made her mouth go dry. He lifted her hand and gently placed it over his heart, the pectoral muscle jumping when her fingers made contact. She swayed on her feet and he pulled her in closer.

"That's right." He urged her nearer. "Forget the storm and lose yourself in me. Just like that night on Sea Island."

Her lips found the warm skin of his chest and she dragged her tongue over his flat nipple. He ground his hips into hers as he unzipped her sundress and slid it down to her hips.

"Last time you needed me." His breath fanned her ear. "Tonight I need you, Princess." Her knees buckled as he pressed an openmouthed kiss just below her ear.

She let her lips wander lower as her hands found the snap to his shorts. Unzipping them, she pushed his boxers and the shorts down over his hips. Her mouth stopped at his happy trail before her hands followed his shorts to his knees. Wearing only her bra and panties, she sat back on her heels before him as he stepped out of his shorts and underwear. His eyes blazed down at her as she took her time enjoying the view.

Rising to her knees, she trailed her fingers along his hard thighs before taking him in her mouth. With a hiss, he arched his back and fisted his fingers in her hair. Her name fell reverently from his lips as she pleasured him.

Suddenly, she was on her back on the big bed, her legs dangling off the side. Will towered over her, a sheen of perspiration glistening on his chest. Julianne crooked a finger at him, but he shook his head.

"Unh-uh." He nudged her legs open wider and settled his hips between them before leaning down to capture one of her breasts in his mouth. Her body bucked off the mattress.

"Hold on, Princess." He moved to the other nipple and she moaned his name. She felt him smile against her skin as he rained kisses down her belly.

Kneeling before her, he hooked her legs over his shoulders and Julianne whimpered. This time he laughed as his tongue trailed along her inner thigh. He blew a breath over her sensitive skin and she squirmed again.

"Stubborn woman, I told you to hold on." And then his mouth found her sweet spot and Julianne fisted her hands in the sheets to keep from flying off the bed. Will tortured her, bringing her to the edge twice before finally letting her fall free, her climax a blinding display of bright lights. She let out a silent scream before she went limp.

On his feet again, Will rolled her over and pushed her onto her knees. He entered her in one hard thrust, nearly causing her to climax again. Wrapping his arms around her body, he leaned over her, his breath sawing in her ear as he pumped into her.

"The next time you're in a storm, Princess," he panted, "think of this. Think of how good this feels. I guarantee you'll never be frightened again."

He reached a finger around to play with the sensitive nub,

and she squeezed him tighter inside her. She came in a rush. With a harsh cry, Will was right behind her.

They lay on the bed trying to catch their breath for several moments, his body still cocooning hers. The storm outside seemed to have subsided long before the one in the bedroom. A soft rain now fell in the night, nearly muting the sounds of the sea. Will gently slid Julianne beneath the covers before turning out the lights and joining her. She snuggled against his warm body as he wrapped his arms around her.

"Thank you," she whispered.

"Mmm," was all he said.

She trailed a finger over his shoulder. "As exorcisms go, that one was pretty good. But it may take a couple more attempts to make sure I'm fully recovered."

Julianne heard the smile in his voice. "You think? Well then, you keep checking the weather forecast because I'm your man."

She burrowed in closer, satisfied that Will was exactly that.

Twenty-three

"You've got a little over ninety thousand left after the sale. Nigel and I are good for at least another hundred. That means you need only to raise another sixty or so more to cover the start-up costs. Several of your creditors from JV Designs would be interested, despite the fact you're going to manufacture over *there*."

Julianne chuckled at Sebastian's words. He was excited about the prospect of helping create a new design company, but the thought of having to relocate to the United States was killing him.

"Suck it up, Sebastian. It's only temporary. If this takes off, you and Nigel can hop back across the pond and handle the European end of things. But right now, I need to keep things close to home."

"Home, is it?" Sebastian's voice on the other end of the phone dripped with sarcasm. "And here I thought Italy was home."

She peered out the bay window in the kitchen, searching the shoreline for Will. He'd taken Owen out with him on his daily jog along the beach. Despite his attempts to acclimate her to the ocean and exorcise her fears, Julianne still suffered tremors at the thought of them both being swept away. She wouldn't be able to draw a thing until they got back. So she'd called Sebastian instead to discuss financing her latest venture.

"Home is wherever Owen is." *And Will*, she added silently.

He hadn't told her he loved her, not in words at least. But she felt his constant protectiveness, since the first night they'd met. And his trust. Each day, he was sharing more and more about his past. Whether it was visiting his childhood haunts or taking her to meet Mrs. Elderhaus, his first-grade teacher, this morning, Will was opening up. He didn't trust many people with his innermost thoughts, but he was sharing them with her. She knew that by letting her in, he was showing her he loved her, even if he couldn't say it yet.

"And I really don't want you and Nigel investing everything you have in this. I can borrow against my grandmother's trust fund again. I just need to get Stephen's approval since he's the trustee."

"Jules," Sebastian drawled. "Nigel and I *want* to be partners with you. You're the bomb. Mums all over the world will be clamoring for your baby knickers. And you needn't worry about our finances. Nigel and I have money tucked away for our retirement. Now if you're really worried about us, you'd reconsider setting up shop in rustic North Carolina."

Julianne spread her notes out on the kitchen table. "No way. It's perfect here. There are four closed textile mills within a fifty-mile radius and scores of people looking for work. The company would give the local economy a big boost. Annabeth and her friend Patricia are virtual goddesses at all the ins and outs of owning a small business. We're going to look at potential sites tomorrow."

"Good God! Women on a mission! Heaven help the men of that little hamlet. What does your muscle man say about all of this?"

She checked outside again. Still no sign of Will. "I

haven't told him yet. He seems to have the impression that I fly by the seat of my pants."

Sebastian snorted.

"I want to prove to him that I don't." She ignored him. "I've successfully run a business in the past, and I can do it again. This past year has just been a cosmic glitch, a pregnant pause, pun intended. But I'm back now."

"That's our girl. You can bring home the bacon and fry it up in the pan."

They agreed to talk again after she'd toured the mill sites. Sebastian and Nigel planned to arrive in the States the following week so they could meet with potential suppliers. Julianne danced across the kitchen, exuberant about how everything was coming together. In a few weeks, she'd have her career back. Owen was healthy and thriving. And there was Will. Her body heated at the thought of him.

She picked up her phone to call Stephen when the red jog stroller appeared on the horizon, a shirtless Will running behind it: muscles rippling, his nylon gym shorts blowing with each stride he took. The wind whipped his hair. The sight was magnificent.

Best of all, he was jogging toward the house. Toward her. Julianne ended the call mid-dial and tossed her phone on the desk. Ignoring the tremors, she stepped out onto the verandah and took a few tentative steps across the lawn toward the dunes that separated the house from the shore.

Will pushed the stroller along the pier leading over the dunes. He stopped in the middle and turned the stroller around so Owen faced her. The baby chortled when he saw Julianne, his chubby legs pumping up and down. Will knelt beside him.

"That's right, Owen. Tell Mommy she can do it. Tell her we'll protect her." He was speaking to the baby, but his eyes never left her face.

Will pushed his sunglasses up on his head, and she could see the encouragement beaming within those eyes.

Julianne pondered the quiet ocean at Will's back as she chewed her bottom lip. The shore was still twenty yards or more beyond the dunes. If she joined them on the deck, the ocean couldn't exactly reach out and grab her. She was being ridiculous just standing there on the grass. Before she could think about it further, she sprinted across the lawn and up onto the pier. Will greeted her with open arms, twirling her around by the waist, before pulling her in for a lusty kiss. Owen squealed in delight, his fisted hands punching the air.

"Soon, Cheerio, we'll take Mommy swimming with us," Will promised.

Julianne bit her lip as she buried her face in Will's bare neck to avoid looking at the ocean behind them. In Will's arms she felt invincible, but for now, this was as brave as she wanted to be. She'd think about swimming later. *Much later.*

Julianne was seated at the small desk in the kitchen sketching when Will sneaked up behind her, bending down to kiss her neck. She shoved the drawings into her folder. "You'd better be careful, Brody, my husband is upstairs and he might hear us. Oww!" She yelped as he bit the tender skin.

"What are you drawing?" he asked as he made his way over to the fridge and pulled out a bottled water.

She hesitated a moment, unsure whether to reveal her plans now or wait until everything was finalized. Deciding to stick to her original plan, she turned to face him. Will leaned against the counter, his hair still damp from his shower. He was dressed in shorts and a Yale T-shirt, ready to help Gavin coach a Little League game.

"Just some ideas I have for Owen's clothes," she hedged. "What time is the game?"

Will looked at her quizzically for a moment, as if he knew there was more she wasn't telling him. She held his gaze.

"I need to be at the field in a few minutes," he finally answered.

Julianne ambled over to where he stood and wrapped her

arms around his waist. "Well, as much as I hate to let you wander around town alone looking so fine, I have to wait until your mom gets off work to babysit Owen before I can join you. Don't forget, you promised me a beer at Pier Pressure after the game. I'm a lightweight, so you'll definitely get lucky later." She stretched up on her toes and kissed the side of his mouth, running her tongue along his lower lip.

He pulled back slightly to better study her. "Julianne, you sure everything's okay?"

With both hands, she cupped his chin. "Better than okay. I'm drawing again, but things are still evolving. Please don't take it personally. Please?"

Their eyes held for a moment before he nodded. He kissed her on the forehead.

"Owen's asleep, so you should have some quiet time to work before my mother gets here. I'll see you at the ball field later." He grabbed his gym bag and headed out the door.

Julianne wrapped her arms around herself. It wasn't like she was hiding anything from Will. She just didn't feel comfortable involving him in this part of the process because it meant raising money. Their relationship was still tenuous and they were still establishing trust with each other. She didn't want him to get the wrong idea and think she was only with him for his money. With a sigh, she looked at the clock: four forty. If she hurried, she could still catch Stephen before he left his office.

After nearly ten minutes on hold, her brother picked up the phone. "Julianne, how are you? Is the baby okay?"

She sighed. "Owen's fine, Stephen. I didn't mean to panic you by calling. I just thought I'd save you the trouble of calling me today."

"I thought we'd gotten past this."

"We have. Look, Stephen, I called because I'm putting together a business plan for a new line I'm designing. You were concerned when I sold JV Designs, so I just wanted to give you a heads-up that I am thinking about my future."

Stephen was silent on the other end of the phone.

"I'm launching a line of baby clothes," she blurted out. "We'll start out as an online or catalog company first, but Sebastian has a lead on potential retailers who might be interested."

"Well, Julianne, that sounds great. I hadn't realized you were ready to get back into the business so soon. Just a month ago you sounded as though you didn't know what you would do. This is certainly a vast improvement. How are you going to pay for it?"

It was just like her brother to cut directly to the chase.

"I have money left from the sale, and Sebastian and Nigel are investing. But I need to borrow from Grandmother Marchione's trust again."

Their paternal grandmother had left money for each of her grandchildren to do with what they chose. With the exception of Julianne. It seemed her grandmother had not approved of her son's second wife, Julianne's artist mother. So she'd insisted that Julianne not receive her funds until she was thirty—still two years away—in hopes that by that time she would be less inclined to waste the money on the bohemian artist's lifestyle her mother had pursued. Ironically, Julianne's career in fashion would not have been possible had her brother not suggested she borrow against the trust in the first place. She'd paid the fund back, with interest. Her grandmother had likely somersaulted in her grave.

"The fund wouldn't be as big today were it not for the interest I contributed, Stephen."

"I realize that. And of course you can borrow the money. I'll never understand why Grandmother chose to punish you for how your hippie mother lived her life. She shouldn't have put such severe stipulations on your trust fund. I certainly don't need to be the gatekeeper to your inheritance."

Julianne sank down in the chair at her little desk in the kitchen, relief and agitation rolling through her at the same time. It was no use arguing with her brother about her mother. Like their grandmother, Stephen had never been fond of his stepmother. Fortunately, he never took it out on

Julianne. He had made her jump through hoops to borrow the money originally, but she'd proved herself a competent businesswoman, so she hoped he'd be more lenient this time.

She began doodling Stephen's name with devil horns on her folder. "So can we just use the same terms we did eight years ago? I'd like to get the cash as soon as possible."

"How much do you need?"

"The whole seventy-five thousand if possible." She drew a star with *$75,000* written inside it.

Stephen blew out a breath. "I'll see what I can do. But it may be next week before I can get it to you. And the terms will be adjusted to reflect today's rates. You'll need to sign your agreement to that."

Julianne finally relaxed in the chair. She knew he could make it more difficult for her, but it still irked her to have to ask her brother for the money. It was hers, after all. "Next week will be fine. Thank you, Stephen."

"Too bad your marriage isn't real. Will is a rich man who could loan you the money. Although, given what he's facing right now, you're probably better off that the marriage is going to end in a few weeks," her brother added.

She shot to her feet. "Ohmigod, Stephen! Be serious! This whole Bountygate scandal is ridiculous! Will hasn't done anything wrong. He didn't even know why they gave him the money!"

Silence greeted her on the other end of the phone line. Julianne's heart leaped to her throat. She shouldn't be discussing this with her brother. Granted, he wasn't a sports reporter, but Stephen didn't need to know Will's secrets.

"Julianne . . ."

She cut her brother off before he could say more. "Stephen, please don't ask me any more about this. The sports media has blown this all up, but it's really nothing. Will is a good man. He's Owen's father. We need to stand behind him in this. He's part of the family now. If you could just take care of the trust fund for me, I'd appreciate it."

The sound of Stephen furiously tapping his pen on the

desk traveled over the phone. "Sure. I'll have the money to you next week."

It wasn't until after they'd hung up that she realized Stephen hadn't said anything about supporting Will. She doodled on her folder again. If the truth ever came out, her brother was going to owe her a huge apology for doubting Will. She was looking forward to that day.

"Hi there!" Annabeth strolled through the kitchen door, setting her bag down on the table.

"You're early." Julianne jumped to her feet and clapped her hands. "Perfect! I have news."

Annabeth laughed. "I hope it involves food, because I'm starving."

Julianne pulled a salad out of the fridge and began adding grilled chicken to it. "It was too hot to cook anything heavy," she explained. "There's fruit here, too."

"Mmm." Annabeth poured herself a glass of wine. "Will isn't the best at expressing his appreciation, but I am." She saluted Julianne with her wineglass. "Thank you for pampering the babysitter."

Julianne blushed. If Will's mother only knew her son had been appreciating her against the island in the kitchen just hours before, she'd be shocked. Placing the salad on the table, she ushered Annabeth to sit down and pulled out a chair to sit beside her.

"I have news about the new company." Julianne had shared her plans with Annabeth last week when her mother-in-law and her friend Patricia discovered her sketches. Both women persuaded her to proceed with the line and to locate her company in their economically depressed hometown. "I have the start-up funds, so we can move to the next phase."

Annabeth's face lit up. "That was fast. How did you manage it so quickly?"

"I had money left after paying Owen's medical bills, and my business manager is investing. I also have money in a trust that my brother is allowing me to borrow against."

Annabeth arched an eyebrow at her. "Your brother?"

Julianne waved a hand. "Long story. But after selling my soul to the devil, my brother has agreed get me the money. I should have all the funds by next week."

Annabeth had offered to loan her the money, but that would be like taking Will's money, and Julianne still felt the need to do this on her own. She needed to prove to Will that her career wasn't some flight of fancy, that she did have some direction to her life despite her screwups of the last year.

"So tomorrow we check out the mills?" Annabeth asked before taking a bite of her salad.

"If you and Patricia can still make it, I'd love to. We're headed up to Baltimore next week, and I want to have some ideas to present to Sebastian by then."

"She and I are planning on it. The only new business we've had in two years is an orthopedic rehab hospital. While it's great for the community, the only ones who've been able to find a job there are those with technical skills. We need jobs for the less skilled employees who are out of work in town. In the past five years, this town has lost a blue jeans manufacturer and a linen company. A small company manufacturing clothing will provide jobs to those who stuck around and are scrimping by on the wages they earn during the tourism season."

Julianne stood, brushing out her skirt. "Great. Owen is asleep upstairs. There's a bottle made in the fridge. I should hurry over to the ball field to catch up with Will." She hesitated. "You're okay with not telling Will about this yet, right?"

Annabeth snorted. "If you know what's good for you, you won't tell him yet. Most men are domineering when it comes to business, but Will is over-the-top. He went ballistic when he found out I bought my grandmother's shop in town. It didn't fit with his idea of what he wanted me to do with my life. As if I were going to follow his plans."

"Where'd you get the money to buy the store?"

"His rookie season, he gave me money for a down payment on a house. I used it to buy the store instead. I lived in the trailer for another nine months, saving up what was eventually the down payment for this house."

Julianne stilled. "Does Will know this?"

"Heavens, no! I like to let him think he got his way." Annabeth eyed her sternly. "Don't you tell him, either, Julianne. That one's our secret."

Julianne smiled and held up her pinkie. "Pinkie swear!" Instinctively she leaned in and hugged Annabeth. Her mother-in-law paused a moment but then hugged her back.

Owen's eyes rolled back in his head in complete contentment as Annabeth slipped the finished bottle from his lips. A small smile formed on his face as he dozed off to sleep. She brushed her thumb over his soft, wispy hair.

Had Will ever been this content as a baby? Her son had come out of the womb with a chip on his shoulder, it seemed. He was a colicky, cranky baby. Nothing like the adoring, devoted child she'd envisioned. Everything went so fast back then. She was just a child herself trying to figure out how to be a mom. It had been a lot of work.

But eventually they'd made it through, and Will became her protector, a little mini-man who was in a sense devoted to her. It seemed at times that Will was growing up faster than she was. He'd been smart as a whip and determined to make a name for himself and make everyone in Chances Inlet respect him. All that had done was isolate him further. Today he had teammates, but he wasn't close to them. Will was their leader, and he liked maintaining that distance.

Then along came Julianne. Annabeth couldn't condone her daughter-in-law's action with regard to withholding Owen's paternity, but things had ultimately worked out. While neither Julianne nor Will would admit it, Annabeth knew the two of them were more involved than they claimed.

"Unless that's you putting all those love bites on your mama's neck, little one," she whispered to the sleeping baby before reluctantly putting him in his crib. "For your sake, I hope they aren't playing games and are serious about this relationship."

She had the feeling Julianne had already committed her heart to the marriage; from what Annabeth could tell she wasn't one to love halfway. Her son, on the other hand, kept his emotions locked deeply inside, believing they were a sign of weakness. For all she knew, Julianne could just be a convenient sexual partner for him; he was a man, after all.

Closing the nursery door, Annabeth prayed she was wrong about Will. He needed Julianne and Owen as much as they needed him. Will just didn't know it yet.

Her cell phone was ringing when she reached the kitchen. Hank's number popped up on the screen. Annabeth took a deep breath. She couldn't keep holding him off, yet she didn't want to end their relationship. Hank would do it eventually, she was sure of that, and Annabeth would rather save herself the heartache. Except she found herself looking forward to his e-mails and his calls every day, and she'd miss him when they stopped coming.

"Hi," she answered as she slid down onto the sofa overlooking the sea.

"Oh, good, you answered. I was beginning to think I'd missed you." The deep timbre of Hank's voice reverberated in her belly and parts farther south.

"I was up putting Owen to bed."

"How's the little guy doing?"

"He's wonderful. Perfect, actually."

"So is his grandmother." The reverence in his voice made her quiver.

Annabeth needed to change the subject. "How's Sophie?"

Hank's resigned sigh echoed over the phone. "She's on her way to Alaska. Elizabeth and Kevin have been planning this cruise for a couple of years. Despite her whining about sharing a cabin with the twins, I think Sophie will enjoy it."

"I've always wanted to see Alaska." She was unsuccessful at keeping the wistful tone out of her voice.

"Why haven't you?"

His question made her both angry and sad at the same time. It was another example of why they could never be a couple. Once the sizzle of the sex appeal died down, he'd be stuck with a small-town girl whose education was made up of what life threw at her in a small corner of the world. He'd end up hating her or worse, pitying her. Either alternative made her stomach seize up.

"I'm trying to fit it in between my trips to Switzerland and Bora Bora." She didn't bother concealing her sarcasm.

"Stop it, Annabeth! My question was a valid one. You have the money and certainly the free time to go. Why don't you?" He was testy now, too.

"I have a business to run, Hank. It may not be as important as a football team, but it is my livelihood."

"Bullshit."

Annabeth felt the force of the word through the phone, like a slap in the face.

"You wanna know what I think?" he asked.

"No!"

He ignored her. "I think you like using that shop, that town, as a shield. A place to hide so you don't have to go out in the world and make another mistake or take another chance. That's no way to live your life, Annabeth. You can't be afraid of being the woman you're meant to be or of how others will perceive you. Damn it, you're so much more than you think you are. You just need to prove it to yourself first."

"Well, I hadn't realized you had a psychology degree hanging on the wall with all your other college degrees, Hank. Thank you for explaining my problems so the girl with the GED could easily understand them."

"And that's another thing, Annabeth," Hank's voice boomed over the phone. "The only one who gives a damn about your supposed lack of education is you! No one else is holding it against you or judging you. Everyone looks at you and sees a smart, savvy, beautiful businesswoman."

"And what happens when I'm not so beautiful anymore, Hank?" she snapped. "When I actually have to hold a conversation with you or your friends and I don't measure up?"

"What?" Hank's exasperated voice shouted in her ear. "What are you talking about? We've spent the last two weeks talking. Have I ever given you the impression that you didn't . . . *measure up*? That I haven't *enjoyed* our conversations? Or that they've somehow been lacking?"

Annabeth could feel his anger biting through the phone. She felt a little ashamed, but she had no other way to explain herself.

"Tell me, Annabeth, did you think these past two weeks of e-mails and phone calls were just a prelude to sex?" His voice had gone very quiet. "Do you honestly think I'm that shallow?"

No, she wanted to shout. She knew he wasn't shallow, that his interest went beyond just a physical relationship. The problem was, she wasn't sure she could keep him satisfied beyond a physical relationship, and she didn't want to see his face when he came to that realization. Annabeth cared about him too much to endure that kind of pain.

When she didn't answer, he spoke. "Well, I'd hoped for more, Annabeth. A lot more. I know you're capable of that, but until you realize it too, there's nothing more I can say." He swallowed. "I hope one day you find the courage to see who you really are. Have a nice life, Annabeth," he said softly before hanging up the phone.

Numb, she slumped back into the sofa and let the tears fall.

Twenty-four

Will Connelly was in love with his wife. He wasn't sure when or how it happened, but somehow he'd fallen head over heels in love with Julianne. Flighty, messy, neurotic, sexy Julianne. Maybe he'd fallen for her that first night on Sea Island, where the connection between them had sparked to life. Or perhaps it was watching her fight for their son, sacrificing so much so he would live a happy life.

However it had happened, Will was glad she'd weaseled her way into his heart. He sat on the bench in the locker room of the Ship's Iron Gym studying the wedding band on his left hand in wonder. It actually looked good on him.

"Damn, Will. You could warn a guy first before you blind him with that," Gavin teased.

Will knew his friend was happy for him, but there was an edge in Gavin's voice, too. His own fiancée had called off their wedding last summer, just days before the ceremony. While Gavin played down her desertion, Will sensed it still stung.

"Sorry." Will didn't need to say any more. They'd been friends long enough that Gavin knew he meant it in a variety of ways.

Gavin shrugged it off. "I'm just a little miffed I didn't get to toast the bride and groom at their wedding. You married so quickly, we never got a chance to celebrate."

Will paused in packing his workout clothes in his bag. He and Julianne had married quickly, but it wasn't supposed to be a marriage based on love, so he hadn't cared. Now, though, their marriage meant something more. Something to be celebrated. He pictured Julianne in one of her sexy wedding gowns. Every woman wanted a wedding, didn't they? Perhaps he should suggest they have a more traditional ceremony and reception. One with music and flowers and cake. All the things he'd denied her the first go-around.

He glanced at the gold band again. Will hadn't been able to bring himself to say the words back to her the other night. Instead, he'd gone out and bought a wedding ring. Hopefully, by wearing it, she'd know he loved her.

"Maybe we'll have another ceremony. With a reception this time." The more Will thought about it, the more he liked the idea. They could start over, actually meaning the vows they spoke to one another.

"Ah, now you're just trolling for wedding gifts, Will. I'm not buying you any china."

"Funny." Will zipped his gym bag closed. "We bought china for a wedding gift for Chase last year."

"Yeah, that's because we listened to Amanda, who was filling my place with crystal and place settings for sixteen. Seriously, who needs sixteen sets of dishes? If I'm having that many people over for dinner, I'm ordering pizza." Gavin slammed his locker shut. "I still say we should have gone with our guts and gotten that vintage pinball machine. Chase would have loved it."

"It *was* an awesome game," Will agreed. At the same time, he could picture Julianne easily entertaining sixteen for dinner with a meal she'd prepared. And it wouldn't be pizza. His kitchen would end up looking like a war zone, but it would be worth it.

"Jeez, Will, are you gonna wear that shit-eating grin on your face all day?"

Unaware that he was smiling, Will glanced at his friend. "Sorry, I was just thinking about—"

"Whoa!" Gavin held his hands up. "TMI. I really don't need the details, bro."

They stood in awkward silence for a moment.

"I'm really happy for you, man." Gavin finally said. "Everything worked out, and I'm glad. You deserve it."

Will rubbed the back of his neck. "I wish things had worked out for you and Amanda."

"They did work out, just not the way everyone thought they would. But she's happy and that's all that matters."

Will eyed his friend, wondering if he would be so magnanimous if Julianne suddenly changed her mind about him. Probably not. He stepped toward to Gavin.

"Connelly, if you're gonna hug me in the men's locker room," Gavin protested, "I'm gonna have to take you down. Which, by the way, I can still do. Come on, you can buy me lunch instead."

"Fine," Will laughed. It had been many years since Gavin had bested him, but he'd let that ride for now.

"And a cigar," Gavin said as they headed out the door. "I never got a cigar when your son was born."

Another thing Will would have to remedy. He needed to organize a wedding and a proper celebration of Owen's birth. They headed to Pier Pressure while he contemplated both.

An hour later, Will walked back to his house. He was eager to see Julianne and get her reaction to the ring he wore. Hell, he was looking forward to the things she'd do to him in appreciation, and him to her. His body hardened in anticipation and he widened his stride.

Damn! As he turned onto the sandy drive, he remembered that his wife had disappeared with his mother and Patricia earlier, a happy Owen in tow. They were going shopping, they'd said, all three of them looking like the cat that had eaten the canary. Will was glad his mother and

Julianne were getting along. His own relationship with his mother was often fragile. He loved her, that was irrefutable, but he didn't understand her choices. Her life could be so much more, yet she was content to remain here in Chances Inlet. Perhaps now she'd venture out more, if nothing else but to visit her grandson during the season.

Rounding the curve, he spotted an unfamiliar car in the driveway. Curious, he picked up his pace but nearly stopped in his tracks when he noticed his agent, Roscoe, sitting on the verandah. Will's breathing ratcheted up a couple of notches. The two hadn't spoken in two days, when Roscoe had assured him there wasn't enough evidence for the Senate committee to subpoena him. With luck, Bountygate would fade away. The fact that his agent hadn't called but instead was here in person didn't bode well.

Roscoe looked haggard where he sat in the shade, an empty water bottle in his hands. Will climbed the stairs, his own body now tense.

"Your phone broken?" he asked Roscoe.

"Nope." Roscoe stood, his suit rumpled from the heat. "This conversation needed to take place in person."

Will muttered a few choice words under his breath as he entered the key code unlocking the kitchen door. Roscoe followed him in and Will headed directly for the refrigerator and pulled out a bottled water. He handed it to Roscoe, who shook his head.

"Got anything stronger?"

Will's whole body went on alert. He handed Roscoe a beer while taking a swig of the water for himself.

Roscoe took a long swallow. "Where's your family?" he asked.

"Out."

Roscoe nodded before taking another pull on the beer bottle.

Will couldn't take it anymore. "Do you want to tell me what this is all about, or are you waiting for me to get out the chips and salsa?"

Sliding onto a stool at the island, Roscoe ran a hand

through his hair. "According to my sources, you're going to get served. They'd prefer you be in Baltimore to do it, but they'll come here if you force it."

Will gripped the countertop, trying to neutralize his shock. "You told me it was all over."

"That's what I was told. But last night, the Senate committee got some new information. They think it's enough to subpoena you."

"I don't understand." Will's hands were shaking. They couldn't force him to testify.

"Neither do I. Zevalos certainly didn't give you up. Neither would anyone else involved. Especially since it would only implicate them. The only other people who know about this are you and I. And I certainly didn't say anything."

A roaring sound commenced in Will's head. His fingers were tingling where they gripped the countertop and his breath was sawing through his chest.

"Jesus, Will."

He could hear the panic in Roscoe's voice, but his eyes wouldn't focus any longer.

"Tell me you didn't tell anyone else. Tell me you didn't tell *her*!" Roscoe demanded.

Will didn't need his agent to clarify who he meant by *her*. The only person he had told was Julianne. But she wouldn't tell her brother. Not that. She'd said she loved Will. Certainly, she wouldn't betray him.

Roscoe's voice sounded like it was coming through a tunnel now. "Damn it, Will! I told you not to trust her. Her brother is on the freaking Senate committee, for crying out loud!"

Will tried to swallow around the lump in his throat. Could she have broken his trust? He refused to believe she had. Unclenching his fingers from the countertop, he staggered over to the small desk she'd been using. Yesterday, she'd been awfully secretive about what she was working on. He pulled a folder from the desk, stunned by the doodling he saw on the outside. Her brother's name was there, with a pair of devil horns along with a star surrounding the notation of seventy-five thousand dollars. The folder dropped from his hand as if it burned him. Sketches of babies rained down on the kitchen floor.

Roscoe crouched down to sort through the papers. "It looks like she's starting another company." He whistled through his teeth. "And guess who's providing the financing?"

The question was rhetorical because Will already knew the answer.

"She sold you out to her brother to get herself back in the design world. Looks like she plans to use Owen, too."

"No!" Will roared, slamming his hand against the stainless steel fridge.

"How much more evidence do you need, Will? Jesus! She tried to steal your son from you. The woman must be a sexual sorceress in the bedroom if you can overlook all that."

Will lunged at him, but Roscoe was adept at avoiding his clients' punches after all these years.

"Settle down!" Roscoe yelled at him. "I've only let one of my clients actually deck me and only because I owed it to him." Roscoe pulled a kitchen chair between them. "You pay me to watch out for you and to tell it like it is, but you don't get to shoot the messenger."

Will felt a great weight settle in his chest as he slumped into the desk chair. He wanted to wail. Had her love been a lie, too? His gut rolled just thinking it. All of his life, he'd been the kid looking in the window from the outside. Watching his friends love and be loved. His mother loved him, but she'd been too busy making sure they both survived to notice those painful moments when all the other boys played catch with their fathers or went on father-son campouts together. Or the dads who wouldn't let their daughters date him because of where he lived or his parentage. The kids in school who'd cozied up to him to get help with their homework but made fun of his Goodwill clothing behind his back. Even in college, he'd stood apart from the rest, the poor scholarship kid whose mother could barely afford even a bus ticket for him to go home for the holidays while they were jetting off to tropical destinations.

But finally, he'd thought he'd found true happiness with Julianne. She and Owen would be his family. They would belong to him and he would belong to them. Could it all have been just a lie?

"Will." Roscoe's voice permeated the fog. "We need to get back to Baltimore. Ron can fly us back as soon as we can get over to the airport."

"Not until Julianne and Owen get back."

Roscoe sighed. "Okay, yeah. You need to say good-bye to your son. We can go over custody scenarios on the flight back."

Will didn't want to think about how this was going to impact his son. He just knew he needed to speak with Julianne. To ask her directly if she'd done what Roscoe thought or if it was just a big misunderstanding.

"Maybe you could throw some things in a bag while we wait," Roscoe prodded him.

"Yeah." Will slowly stood. "They can't compel me to testify, can they?"

Roscoe didn't respond immediately. "No. But the league has made it clear you'll be suspended if you don't."

Will's legs felt like wood as he climbed the stairs to his bedroom.

Julianne sang along to the U2 song on the satellite radio. It had been a beautiful day. They'd found two potential mill sites, both well within the price range Sebastian had specified. Patricia had been a pit bull, hammering the owners with construction questions Julianne wouldn't have thought of. Annabeth had been a bit subdued all day, but she'd kept Owen occupied and happy. She'd left the two of them at the inn with Patricia while she'd come home to find Will. Although she'd only been gone for the day, she missed him.

The purpose of their fake marriage was so Will could bond with his son. But the real bonding had been between Will and Julianne. The potent attraction that had pulled them together on Sea Island was now a fierce connection. She'd told him she loved him the other night, and he hadn't run screaming into the ocean, which she took as a positive sign. They still hadn't talked about their future, however. It was as if neither one of them wanted to broach the subject, choosing to live in the moment instead, enjoying what they could of each other. Julianne hoped they could sustain whatever it was between them, because she now knew she couldn't live without Will.

She cautiously steered the SUV up the drive when she noticed another car parked near the house. There was a rental car sticker on the bumper, but nothing else to identify its owner. Pulling her car beside it, Julianne turned off the ignition and hopped out, quickly striding up the steps.

"Will!" she called as she entered the kitchen. His large form sitting stonily at the kitchen table startled her.

"Hi," she said warily as she placed her purse on the counter. She took a couple of steps toward him, but something stopped her. He was back to being formidable and unflappable in his business suit and tie. His face was the same stoic one that had greeted her in the hospital over a month before.

"Where's the baby?" he asked. Something about his tone made her stomach drop.

"Umm . . . he's with your mom. She's going to walk him back in the stroller. The ladies in the yarn shop like to pinch his cheeks." She sashayed her hips a little and smiled at him, but he didn't see the joy in little old ladies cooing over their son. Her smile vanished as unease began to grip her.

"Will, what is it? What's wrong?" Her voice shook slightly.

A movement out of the corner of her eye captured her attention. Will's agent emerged from the shadows.

Julianne's gaze darted from one man to the other. "Hello."

Roscoe acknowledged her with the briefest of nods before turning to Will. "I'll wait outside."

Her palms were sweating now. "Will?" she pleaded.

He stood from his chair and closed the gap between them.

She wanted to reach up and wrap her arms around him, but there seemed to be an invisible force field in place keeping them apart.

"I have to go to Baltimore tonight."

Julianne shook her head in confusion. "I thought we were together this weekend. Is something wrong?"

His eyes were full of anguished fury. "I'm going to be subpoenaed to testify."

Her hand shot to her mouth. "No!" she cried. "You said"—she pointed toward the door where Roscoe had slipped out—"*he said* it was finished. You wouldn't have to testify. Everything was going to blow over."

Her heart ached for him. This had to be devastating for Will. She reached a hand to his face, but he recoiled slightly. Julianne's chest constricted and the breath caught in her throat as her hand hung there in the air. Unshed tears burned behind her eyelids.

"It's not over. I'm being yanked in front of a Senate committee investigating racketeering charges." His words were like hard blows to her stomach.

"Se—Senate committee?" Black dots swam before her eyes. This was the point where Will had always stepped in, his big hands holding her, comforting her. But he made no move to help her now, and her heart nearly shattered. With weak knees, she backed up against one of the bar stools and leaned against it.

"Yes, Princess. You've heard of those, haven't you? I'm sure you must have, since your brother is on the committee that subpoenaed me." His voice was cold and her body shivered involuntarily. "I have to know, Julianne. Why did you do it?"

Oh, God! What had she done? She'd ruined everything. "I didn't," she cried. Except she had. A gasping sob escaped and she placed both hands over her mouth.

"All this time, you've been here collecting information for your brother. Was it fun, talking to him every day sharing my secrets, Princess?" The look on his face was savage now.

"It wasn't like that! I didn't mean it, Will! I didn't!"

"Save it." Will's words cracked like a whip. Then he slammed her file folder down on the counter. "How much did he pay you? Was that what this was all about, Princess? Money?"

She shook her head, the words lost in the sobs. Everything was a tangled mess and she couldn't find the right words to fix it.

"You used me to get money so you can go back to your glamorous life as a designer."

"It isn't like that," she insisted. "I was going to tell you about the new company next week. It's not what you think." She was pleading now. "Will, I would never betray you. I love you. Please, believe me."

He grabbed both her arms and pulled her in closer. She nearly sobbed in relief as his body drew near, her own body arching toward his. But he didn't gather her in or kiss her. Instead, his fingers tightened around her flesh.

"Why should I believe you," he snarled, "when all you've ever done is try to deceive me. And don't you dare mock me by saying you love me." He shook her. "Not ever again, Princess, because I'm not buying it."

"William Anthony Connelly!" Annabeth shouted over Julianne's choking sobs and Owen's wails. "What is going on here?"

Mercifully, his fingers loosened on her arms, and that was when she saw it: the wedding band on Will's left hand. A ferocious sob escaped her now-shaking body. Will's eyes followed hers to the ring. He tore his hands away and stripped the band off his finger, waving it in front of her face.

"I'm all done with your foolish games." He stormed out the door toward the pier.

"No!" Julianne cried, running out onto the verandah behind him. "Please, Will!"

But her cry was whipped away by the rising wind. It was too late; his long strides had already carried him to the dunes. She wept along with her son as Will tossed the ring into the high tide. Julianne's knees buckled at the sight and her body landed in a heap on the wood decking.

She wasn't sure how she got to her room. Several hours had passed since the confrontation with Will, and darkness had settled like a shroud over the house. Switching on the bedside lamp, Julianne had vague recollections of Will stepping around her crumpled form earlier and kissing a tearful Owen on the head. He'd told their son he'd be back in a few days, but he hadn't bothered speaking to her. Then he drove off in the rental car with his agent.

Julianne's eyes were heavy and they burned. Her legs wobbled as she made her way to the nursery. Owen was sleeping fitfully in his crib. As she gently rubbed a hand over his back, he instantly calmed to a deeper sleep. The wind whipped beyond the windows and the ocean roared. How foolish she'd been, always worried the sea would sweep away the ones she loved. The ocean hadn't taken Will away; Julianne had accomplished that with one misspoken sentence. And the pain was like a knife wound to her belly.

Voices rose from the kitchen. It sounded like Annabeth and Patricia below. Julianne crept toward the stairs.

"I don't know what happened, Patricia. I've seen him look at her like that before, but those other times, he had pure lust in his eyes. Today . . . today it looked like he actually hated her." It sounded as if Annabeth choked out the last words.

Julianne swallowed around the lump in her throat. Will did hate her. And she couldn't blame him. He'd trusted her with his secret when he hadn't trusted anyone before. And look what she'd done with his trust. She silently trod down the stairs.

"Oh, come on Annabeth, it can't be all that bad." Patricia handed her friend a cup of tea.

"I'm afraid it is that bad," Julianne said softly from the doorway.

Annabeth sprang from her seat at the table. "Julianne, will you please tell me what's going on?"

"I wish I could, but I've already unintentionally divulged one of Will's secrets. You're going to have to go to him for this one."

"For heaven's sake! You're just as cryptic as he is. Will isn't talking. He won't answer his cell or return my texts. One of you needs to tell me what's happened."

"Umm, I don't think we need either of them to explain it to us anymore." Patricia pointed to the television screen in the great room. She grabbed the remote to turn up the volume as the ten o'clock news began and an image of Will disembarking from a small plane filled the screen.

"Baltimore Blaze All-Pro linebacker Will Connelly is the first NFL player to be served with a subpoena to appear before the Senate committee investigating racketeering in the National Football League, stemming from allegations surrounding Bountygate."

The three women watched in silence as a man handed Will an envelope, a disgusted Roscoe looking on.

"According to sources within the senate, Connelly has information that can substantiate the rumors of an alleged bounty scheme. Connelly's testimony could make or break several lawsuits filed by players claiming to have been injured as a result of the scheme."

Annabeth gasped.

"Sources close to Connelly say he will invoke his Fifth Amendment rights, a move that will ensure him an indefinite suspension from football, according to the league office. The hearing is scheduled for next week. No word yet from the Blaze as to whether Connelly will participate in the team's mandatory mini-camp also scheduled for next week."

The tears were running again down Julianne's cheeks, their salt stinging her raw skin.

Annabeth whirled on her. "Dear God, Julianne, what did you do? When you said you sold your soul to your brother yesterday, did that include selling my son's as well?"

Julianne had gone numb hours ago, so Annabeth's words didn't inflict the pain they might have. Wrapping her arms around her midsection, she stood there and let Will's mother attack her, happy that he had someone in his corner.

"This is all a bunch of lies! How could you tell your brother lies about Will?" Annabeth demanded.

"I have to agree, Julianne," Patricia chimed in. "Will and the Blaze are known throughout the league for their integrity and fair play. What would even make you think such a thing about Will?"

Julianne locked eyes with Annabeth. "He wasn't with the Blaze when it happened."

It only took a few seconds for the realization to dawn on Annabeth. With a sharply drawn breath, she plopped down on the sofa. "Oh no." Patricia sat down beside her, taking her hand.

Julianne knelt on the floor at Annabeth's feet, telling Will's mother and Patricia the tale of his unintentional involvement in Bountygate. Resting her head on her mother-in-law's lap, she tearfully recounted her phone conversation with Stephen.

"I didn't do it on purpose. I was defending Will. I never would have said anything had I known what my brother would do with it. Stephen used me," she cried bitterly.

"Hush, Julianne," Annabeth soothed, gently stroking Julianne's hair. "None of this is your fault." She gave Julianne a sad smile. "I'm sorry that I even doubted you. You're an impulsive woman, but only because you want to protect the people you care about. Your brother is the guilty one here."

Julianne gave a heaving sigh of relief just as the thunder rumbled overhead. She *was* impulsive—and gullible—but it was comforting to know her mother-in-law understood. Too bad Will hadn't trusted her enough to stick around and allow Julianne to defend herself. It seemed to Julianne that her husband was just as impulsive. Annabeth patted the couch beside her. Julianne climbed off the floor into her mother-in-law's arms.

"Well, this is quite a mess," Annabeth said as she wrapped a blanket around a now-shivering Julianne. As lightning crackled outside, Julianne snuggled against her. For once, she was too preoccupied to muster the strength to be frightened of the weather. Will would be so proud of her. If only he didn't hate her.

Twenty-five

Owen had been cranky all morning, jarring Julianne's already frazzled nerves. She pushed him along the main street in Chances Inlet, one of the wheels of the stroller squeaking as it rolled along. A strong breeze blew off the ocean, the remnants of the previous night's storm that had kept most of the tourists indoors. The isolated sidewalk perfectly matched her mood.

Most of the town's residents had already heard about Will's subpoena. The sports networks quickly connecting the dots had surmised Julianne was the culprit, shredding her brother's carefully crafted wedding story of her and Will's reconciled love. Now she was painted as the woman who'd stop at nothing to wrangle out of a marriage of convenience and return to partying in Europe with her son.

The people of Chances Inlet had been giving her the cold shoulder all morning. Mrs. Elderhaus, Will's first-grade teacher, however, went one step further, haranguing Julianne on her walk through town. "Shame on you!" she railed at her. "That boy is as honest as the day is long and always has been. You've done nothing but cause trouble in his life. If he's smart, and he is, he'll dump you like a sack of hot potatoes!" Chin high, she'd stormed off to catch up to the rest of her walking club.

It was ironic, actually. Will thought the people of his hometown pitied him, mocked him, or considered him less than they were because he didn't have a father. She wished he could be here today to see how wrong he was. He was one of them whether he'd grown up in the Seaside Vista Trailer Park or in one of the stately houses on the inter-coastal waterway. Too bad he'd never understand that.

As she pushed the stroller into Annabeth's shop, she nearly ran over Gavin. He blocked her path, his arms crossed over his chest. Gavin wasn't quite as massive as Will, but he was well muscled and nearly as tall. Whereas Will's face was chiseled and hard, Gavin's was more rugged, with laugh lines bracketing his twinkling eyes and a pair of devastating dimples. His wavy hair was always in some disarray from where he'd pulled his fingers through it. Of the two men, Gavin always looked the most approachable.

Except for today. The hard line of his mouth warned Julianne that Patricia's son was clearly in Will's camp. Not that it surprised her. Once again, she was relieved that his friends were still loyal to him.

"What is it with you women?" Gavin stood there as if he expected an answer.

"I just don't get it," he continued. "You think it's okay to just sucker punch a guy like that. To ruin his name. His career. The sad part about it is the dumbass would have given you anything. *Anything.*"

Julianne had to look away because she felt the tears threatening again. Owen whimpered, stretching to try to reach his foot. Gavin crouched down on his haunches as he reached into the stroller to let Owen play with his finger.

"He loved you, you know. I didn't think it was possible he'd ever find anyone to love, he's such a stubborn asshole. But he did." Gavin's voice was gravelly, as if he were wres-tling with his own emotions. "It hurts when you women rip a guy's heart out and stomp on it. Some guys don't ever get over it. Unfortunately, I think Will is going to be one of those guys."

She forced the lump in her throat down as Gavin kissed Owen on the head. He didn't bother to look at her when he stood and walked out the door. Shoulders slumped, she pushed the stroller deeper into the store. Lynnette, Annabeth's assistant, swooped from across the room to pull a now-fussy Owen out of the stroller.

"I think he might want a bottle," Julianne said, handing her one from the diaper bag. "He's really out of sorts today, so don't take it personally if he doesn't drink too much."

"Likely the boy misses his daddy." Lynnette gave her the evil eye before disappearing into the back office with the baby.

Annabeth sat at her computer eyeing Julianne over her reading glasses. "Has he called you?" she asked.

There was no point asking who *he* was. Neither woman had heard from Will in nearly twenty-four hours. Julianne shook her head.

With a resigned sigh, Annabeth removed her reading glasses. "So what's your plan, Julianne?"

"My plan?"

"Yes, Julianne, your plan. Surely you have one?"

She didn't, actually. Not a single one. All her life, she'd never needed a plan, simply moving from one thing to the next. She'd started designing on a whim when a wealthy friend from boarding school fell in love with one of Julianne's sketches and just had to have it as her wedding gown. From there, her business had spread by word of mouth. When Sebastian had come along and taken her under his wing, she'd left all the planning to him, enjoying life as it came.

"Flying by the seat of your pants." She cringed as Will's description of her echoed through her mind.

Her pregnancy had altered her lifestyle. Now she was responsible for another human being. But she hadn't planned that well, either. She skirted around the truth, keeping secrets from those around her. And look where that landed her. She'd acted brashly selling JV Designs, not thinking how she'd support herself in the future. Regrettably, she hadn't planned, and the results were stupid choices. The one decision she didn't regret, though, was marrying Will.

"Do you love him, Julianne?" Annabeth's delicate voice interrupted her thoughts. "Do you love my son?"

Julianne nodded through her tears. "Yes. Yes I do."

"Then you have to have a plan."

The antique Hepplewhite chair creaked as Julianne sat down on it. "I don't even know where to begin. Will won't answer my calls or respond to my texts. He doesn't care about listening to my side of things. He just assumes the worst."

"Can you blame him?"

Annabeth's words stung, but she spoke the truth. Their relationship didn't have much of a basis in trust. And it was Julianne's fault.

"One thing is for certain, you're not going to get to talk to him by hiding down here in Chances Inlet." Annabeth stood and walked out from behind the counter. "I, for one, am done with hiding."

"You think I should go to Baltimore?"

"Well, the mountain isn't going to come to you, Muhammad. Believe me when I say no one does stubborn martyr better than my son. He'd just as soon think the whole world is against him than admit he might have made a mistake. And believe me, he shares in the blame for this mess. A lot of people do," she said with quiet certainty.

Julianne ran her hand along the smooth mahogany arm of the refurbished chair. "How do I get him to listen to me? To really trust me?"

"It's too bad your Slytherin brother can't be persuaded to tell the truth to Will," Annabeth mused.

"Not unless there's something in it for him."

Julianne had left a caustic voice mail on Stephen's phone the previous evening, Annabeth and Patricia cheering her on. She'd told her brother to take the money from their grandmother's trust fund and shove it. She wanted no part of the Marchione money. And, she'd added for good measure, she wanted no part of their family anymore. After all, had her grandmother loved her enough, she would have left her the money outright. She'd told Stephen she'd never forgive him for what he'd done to Will and subsequently to their marriage. He'd tried to call her repeatedly since then, but she'd let the calls go unanswered.

It had been liberating to tell her brother off, but the pain of his deception still cut deeply. It hurt to know her family loved and respected her so little. Her father had essentially written her out of his life shortly after her mother died, leaving her brother as her guardian. The two were never close, but she enjoyed being an aunt to his children. She'd miss that. Annabeth had stayed by her side during last night's storm, reassuring Julianne that she and Owen were her family regardless of what happened with Will. The thought was both comforting and tragic.

"You should have let me invest the money when I offered it." Annabeth interrupted her thoughts. "If I give it to you now, Will would certainly misinterpret both of our intentions. It's too bad because that company was just what this town needed. And I think Will would have been proud of what you were going to do with the profits in his name."

Julianne contemplated her mother-in-law as her inner Scarlett O'Hara took control. "Who says we have to shelve the idea?" A germ of a plan was formulating in her mind.

Annabeth chuckled. "I guess we don't. You know what? Who cares if Will gets mad if I invest with you? It's my money."

"That might not be necessary." Julianne paced the small store. "The last thing I want to do is drive a wedge between you two. But I may have another strategy for financing that I hadn't considered before."

"Like I said a few minutes ago, it's always good to have a plan, girl."

Julianne hugged her mother-in-law. She still wasn't sure if she had a plan to get Will back, but at least she was going ahead with cementing his legacy in this town, whether he wanted it or not.

"It's settled then," Annabeth said as she pulled out of their embrace. "We're going to Baltimore. But first, I have to look up some old neighbors from Seaside Vista."

"And I have to call a priest."

For a second night, Will couldn't sleep. His body was sluggish and tired, but his brain wouldn't give in to the numbness that slumber would provide. He couldn't stop thinking of her. Julianne had never been in his loft or in this bed, but he swore he could smell her on the sheets. Everywhere he turned in the bed, her scent was there.

He was going mad. Bat-shit crazy like his wife. *His fake wife.* Make that soon-to-be-ex-fake wife. Somewhere along the way, he'd forgotten about the fake part. And that was how he'd gotten screwed.

Yanking off the tangle of sheets, Will jumped out of the bed in frustration. The sounds from the city blared beyond the windows. It was just the noise. Will always had trouble adjusting to the traffic sounds when he returned to Baltimore. He turned on the white noise machine and set it to play ocean sounds. Soon the room was filled with the sound of Chances Inlet and the sea lapping at the beach.

But when he turned back to the bed, he was once again reminded of Julianne. The tousled sheets brought back memories of rolling around on the mattress with his wife beneath him. She was a whirling dervish, leaving chaos in her wake. He was glad to be rid of her. Except his body was hard just thinking about what she could do to him.

Damn it!

Will gave up on the idea of sleep and trudged down to the kitchen. A half-eaten pizza sat in its box on the counter, surrounded by three empty beer bottles and two dirty plates. Hell, even his kitchen looked like Julianne had been in it. He grabbed a slice of cold pizza out of the box, not bothering with a plate this time. Padding over to the refrigerator to get a beer, he heard his cell phone beep. He'd purposely left it downstairs to avoid the incoming calls, mostly from his mother and Julianne.

Settling on the sofa, Will took a bite of the pizza before tossing it onto the coffee table as the phone beeped again. He ripped the phone out of the docking station and glanced at the screen. Just as he suspected, a voice mail from Julianne. Hadn't she gotten the message? He didn't want to talk to her. *He couldn't bear to talk to her.*

The voice mail had been left just after midnight. *Good, she couldn't sleep, either*, Will thought with satisfaction. But then he immediately considered Owen. What if the baby was sick? Or worse? Panic clenched at his gut as he put the phone on speaker and clicked on the message before thinking better of it. Julianne's husky voice filled the loft.

"Hi." Just that one word was enough to rip the breath from Will's lungs, his body heating up instantly. He hated how much power she had over him. Even in disgust, he still craved her, ached for her.

"Um," she continued. "Since it looks like you plan on being in Baltimore for the next few days, I've decided to bring Owen up there so you can spend time with him."

No! Seeing Owen meant seeing the boy's mother, and Will wasn't ready for that yet.

"The whole point of this . . . marriage was so you could bond with him, and that's not going to happen if you're seven hours away. He misses you," she added tenderly.

Her words nearly ripped Will's heart out of his chest.

"We'll be there tomorrow afternoon. I guess I'll just text you when we arrive. Unless you want to be a grown-up and talk directly." There was an exasperated pause. "Good night, Will."

He chucked the phone onto the coffee table, barely missing the slice of pizza. She wasn't just crazy, she was the queen of manipulation. Julianne would definitely use their son to get back into Will's life. Fortunately, he saw right through her. He didn't need the distraction of her in Baltimore this week, but the fact of the matter was, he did miss

Owen. Something would have to be worked out. Something that didn't involve him having to interact with Julianne.

Grabbing his phone again, Will scrolled through the photos of Owen he had taken. His throat constricted as he perused the pictures. He missed the feel of Owen sleeping against his chest and the sweet smell of clean baby after his bath. Will hadn't realized how much of his life revolved around the little guy. After the hearing, the two of them would probably be spending a lot more of the season together than Will had originally imagined. It was the one consolation of the decision he'd made.

He laid the phone back on the table, which was littered with documents. The subpoena sat next to the custody agreement Roscoe had drafted up earlier. His agent had not been happy with either of the decisions Will had made over pizza and beer a few hours before.

"I know if I look hard enough," Roscoe had advised him. "I can find something on her that will ensure you full custody."

"No," Will had replied. "That would only hurt Owen. Besides, you're going to need to spend your time trying to get my suspension lifted so I can play football this fall."

Roscoe had heaved a sigh. "Or you could just tell the committee and the league what they want to know, thus avoiding suspension altogether."

"I'm not snitching."

"The man is guilty, Will," Roscoe had argued.

"Probably. But it's not my story to tell, Roscoe. I have no proof where that money came from. Neither does the committee. It's all conjecture. There are likely dozens of guilty players who know a hell of a lot more than I do. Let the committee target them."

"The whole world will presume you're guilty if you don't talk."

That part wasn't as easy to swallow, but Will figured it was the price he had to pay for keeping quiet these past eight years. Back then, he'd been a fledgling player without a home in the league, his only evidence coming from his gut. Now he would play the waiting game, hoping Coach Zevalos developed a conscience before he died. Hoping the man wasn't as diabolical as the media made him out to be. That would mean Will's loyalty those early years was totally misguided.

"And your son? What will you tell him when he's old enough to ask?"

Will had taken a long swallow of beer before he was able to answer Roscoe. "Let's hope it's cleared up before then."

Roscoe had muttered a few choice words about not getting paid enough, but then he'd let it go. "At least you were smart enough to have Julianne sign all the separation papers before the marriage. It will move the process along that much more quickly. I want to file right away, so people will know she sold you out. We don't want her to have any sympathy with the public. You'll need it all on your side."

Will wished he'd felt a little more comfortable with Roscoe's plan than he actually did. But he couldn't overlook the fact that Julianne had shared his secret with her brother. She was guilty and she deserved what was coming. It was her fault their separation would be linked to his testimony.

"You have to wait a full year for the divorce, so that's another key reason to get the papers filed as soon as possible," Roscoe had added.

"Great, now I really feel like a famous celebrity. My separation is going to last longer than the marriage," Will had said wryly, before taking another sip of his beer.

"Don't feel bad, you've still got Britney Spears beat."

Will had scrubbed his hand down his face. "Hell, I'm not sure I want to ever hear my name and Britney Spears's in the same sentence."

That had made Roscoe chuckle. "Seriously, we're not done talking about Owen's custody." He held his hands up. "After the hearing. For now, I'm just glad I have the kid's birth certificate in my safe. She can't get him out of the country without it."

"She won't take Owen out of the country."

"Yeah? This is the same woman who sold you out to a

Senate committee, dumbass. Stop thinking with your dick and use your brain. She's capable of anything."

Will's temple had begun to throb. He let out an explosive sigh. The Julianne he'd spent the last month with wouldn't take Owen back to Italy. Not without asking. But apparently, the woman with whom he'd shared his body and his soul these past few weeks didn't exist.

He and Roscoe had agreed to meet again tomorrow to discuss the strategy for the hearing. As far as Will was concerned, the plan was simple; he'd plead the fifth. End of story. Everyone would have to leave him alone because he had nothing to say.

The lights of the Inner Harbor shimmered through the tall windows in the loft. Will lay down on the sofa, pulling the cashmere blanket that the decorator insisted he buy with it over his body. He'd just sleep here tonight. As he stared up at the high ceilings of his loft, listening to the city rumble on outside, Will realized just how alone he was. It was a feeling that used to never bother him. Until now.

Twenty-six

It was seven A.M. on Monday when Annabeth dialed Hank's cell phone. They hadn't spoken since the night she'd babysat Owen, and she prayed he'd at least answer her call. The Senate committee's hearing was the next day, and she desperately needed Hank's help to make things right.

"Annabeth." As usual, Hank's gravelly voice made her internal body temperature spike. "Is everything okay? "

"Yes. I mean no. Of course it isn't." She was dissembling when she needed to focus. "I didn't wake you, did I?" *Not exactly the smartest question.*

"No, I just got out of the shower."

An image of a naked Hank popped into her head, and Annabeth had to gather her scattered wits. "Oh, well, good."

Hank sighed. "Look, Annabeth, I'm sure you're upset about this whole thing with Will, but he could have prevented it from coming to this. Obviously, the team wishes he'd cooperate because we'd prefer not to lose him to an indefinite suspension. But he's being stubborn."

Annabeth snorted. "Tell me about it. But that's not why I'm calling you. Well, not exactly, anyway." She heard rustling in the background, as if he were toweling himself dry. Annabeth fanned herself with the printed directions she had in her hand. "Remember when you said you'd like to take me places? To travel with me?"

The rustling stopped, and only Hank's breathing could be heard through the phone.

"Well," she continued, "I'd like you to take me somewhere. Today."

"Today?"

"Yes, today." She swallowed. "It has to be today."

"Today," he stated again, sounding a little as if he were trying to decipher something Sophie had said to him.

"It's work related, if that helps." She reminded herself that this was an ambush and to not take his impatience personally.

"Uh-huh." He chuckled softly. "And what exotic destination do you have planned for us, Annabeth?"

She sat down on the flagstone porch, relieved he was taking her seriously. At least she hoped he was. "It's not really all that exotic. Although it *is* called the Garden State."

"New Jersey?" Hank choked out. "You want to go to New Jersey?"

She sighed. "I don't *want* to go to New Jersey, Hank. I *have* to go."

Hank slipped into military mode. "Annabeth, I think you'd better tell me what this is all about."

"In the car. I'll tell you everything when we're on our way. Just hurry up and get dressed."

Hank was silent for a long moment. "Where are you?" he finally asked, his voice a harsh whisper.

Annabeth crossed her fingers. "Outside. On your front porch."

She heard the sound of feet clamoring down the stairs, and suddenly one of the ornate oak doors was being pulled open. Turning to face Hank, Annabeth had to bite her bottom lip to keep her mouth from falling open as her gaze traveled up a pair of bare feet and well-defined legs, to slim hips wrapped in nothing but a black towel. Hank's sculpted abs and chest were bare, his fifty-year-old muscles rivaling anything she'd seen at the Ship's Iron Gym. His hair was still damp; a dab of shaving cream lingered behind his left ear. He hadn't even bothered to put his glasses on.

"Hi," she managed to push out as her entire body sang with joy at the sight of him.

"Get in here," Hank hissed.

Easier said than done—Annabeth's knees had turned to Jell-O—but she managed to scramble off the porch and into his foyer. She placed her purse on the beautiful Chippendale table in the entryway, quickly calculating the amount of weight it could bear before sharply reminding herself that they needed to get to New Jersey right away. Spinning on her heel, she turned to find Hank leaning against the massive front doors, arms over his chest and his feet crossed at the ankles. Apparently, he was not as affected by his near-nudity as she was.

"Look, Annabeth, if you came here about Will, I can't help you . . ."

"I didn't come here about Will." She took two steps toward him. "New Jersey is about Will. I came here, *to you*, because you were right. Because I want to be more," she whispered as she tentatively placed a hand on his heart. Immediately, his hand covered hers, cocooning it in the warmth of his skin. "I came here because I'm done hiding."

Moving her body closer to his, she stretched up on her toes and kissed him. It was a sweet kiss, one in which she tried to apologize for the way she'd hurt him the other day. But Hank would have none of it. His hands went to her hair as he delved deeper into her mouth, their tongues sliding against one another. She moaned as his mouth left hers, finding its way to her sensitive neck.

"God, Annabeth, I thought I'd never see you again," he murmured against her skin. "I've missed you."

She pulled his mouth back to hers and kissed him with a slow hunger that threatened to completely obliterate her plans. Somehow, the backs of her thighs had come in contact with the Chippendale table and her dress was now bunched up at her waist. Hank's hands squeezed her bottom as he lifted her onto the table. When she wrapped a leg around him, her calf came in contact with his bare ass. Annabeth drew her hands over his sides, and then his back, reveling in the muscles bunched beneath her fingertips.

With a soft moan, she pulled out of the kiss. Hank rested his forehead on her shoulder as both of them struggled for breath.

"We can't do this right now." She traced her finger down his rib cage. "We have to go to New Jersey first."

"The Jersey Turnpike will be a parking lot at this hour." He stroked a thumb over her pebbled nipple.

"We have to. For Will."

Hank let out a long-suffering groan in protest. She felt his erection jump between their bodies. He took a step back, reaching down to the floor to retrieve his towel.

"I'm not going to New Jersey for Will." He tied the towel around his waist as Annabeth's heart stopped in panic. "I'm going for you."

She sucked in a relieved breath. "Thank you," she whispered. "And if you still want me after what I have to do there . . ."

Hank closed the space between them, bracketing her face in his hands. "Annabeth, I've wanted you since long before the morning I saw you standing in my library." He placed a tender kiss on one side of her mouth. "I've adored you since you first stuck up for Sophie." Gently his lips brushed her mouth's other corner. "I fell in love with you on a ferryboat. Nothing you can do could make me want you, adore you, or love you less." He kissed her fully this time with the promise of wicked things to come later, while totally annihilating any brain cell activity Annabeth had left. When his mouth reluctantly left hers, her lips nearly whimpered in protest.

"But we'll do it your way. We'll go to New Jersey." He pinned her with an arresting glance. "But afterward, you're mine."

Annabeth was grateful to be still sitting on the small

table as she met Hank's azure eyes, now blazing with passion. She gnawed on her bruised lip before nodding.

"Coffee's in the kitchen. You'll find the travel mugs in
the cabinet. I'll be ready to go in five minutes."

Annabeth watched him disappear up the long staircase
as she tried to calm her thundering heart. Her body felt
slightly bereft and a little agitated that they hadn't finished
what they started. But she was still grappling with the heady
concept that he loved her. Adjusting her dress as she slid off
the table, she had trouble holding back her grin. *Hank
Osbourne loved her. Her. Annabeth Connelly.* The thought
made her giddy. She wandered to the kitchen for the promised coffee, thinking her day was starting off better than
she hoped. Now all she needed was for the rest of it to go
as well.

"Okay." Hank slipped his cell phone into its
charger. "The two NFL attorneys are going to meet us there.
Since you've asked for witnesses, I assume you aren't taking
me to a mafia hit. Or are you, Annabeth?"

She laughed at him. They'd ended up taking Hank's car,
a sleek little Audi that slipped easily through the rush hour
traffic. Hank drove like he did everything else, with author-
ity. Annabeth curled up on the leather seat, her legs tucked
beneath her, her torso turned to face Hank's profile.

"Nothing that nefarious. Although I can't rule anything out."

"Just tell me this, are we expected?"

"No. I'm counting on the element of surprise."

Hank took Exit 18W toward Fort Lee. They traveled
through the center of town before finally entering a suburban
neighborhood of tree-lined streets and quaint Craftsman
houses. He parked along the curb across from their destination, the car purring to a halt as he killed the engine. Leaning his head against the headrest, Hank took a swallow of
his coffee.

"This is Coach Zevalos's house," he said without preamble.

Annabeth tried to hide her surprise. "You've been here?"

Hank turned his head to face her. "Of course I have. When the whispers started to include Will's name, I came here to try to make sense of all of it. Will wouldn't talk to me, so I tried to get Zevalos to tell me. Obviously, I wasn't successful."

"Well, maybe you didn't have the right incentive to make him talk." She undid a button on the bodice of her sundress.

Hank sat up in his seat. "What the hell are you planning on doing here, Annabeth?"

She made note of the fact that the tops of Hank's ears got red when he was angry. Or jealous, whichever the case might be. Annabeth pressed a hand to his chest. "Relax. He wouldn't talk to you because you wear pants. Trust me. He'll talk to me." She leaned across the console and kissed the corner of his mouth. "You'll see."

A blue American-made sedan pulled up and parked behind them.

"Ah, the cavalry has arrived," Annabeth said as she grabbed her purse and hopped out of the car.

Standing on the sidewalk outside Coach Zevalos's house, Hank made the introductions, but Annabeth wasn't paying attention. There wasn't time to waste if she was going to preserve her son's name. Smoothing down the skirt to her dress, she marched past the pots of carefully planted zinnias and geraniums up the concrete steps. The door opened before she knocked, startling her.

"Mrs. Connelly?"

Annabeth had met Marie Zevalos several times during the years Will had played at Yale. In her late sixties, the woman was a throwback to the housewives of the mid-1900s, treating her husband with deference, acquiescing to his every whim. With her big, overbleached hair and round body, she was the perfect foil to the arrogant, macho coach whose ego knew no bounds.

"It's Miss Connelly," Hank clarified from where he stood beside her.

Annabeth brought her elbow back, slightly making contact with his ribs. He took the hint and stepped back, the message received that she was running the show.

"Mrs. Zevalos, how nice to see you again," Annabeth began. "I believe you've already met Mr. Osbourne?"

Marie broke out into a bright smile at the sight of Hank before her face registered her confusion. "Yes, he came to visit Paul a few weeks ago. But Paul told him not to come back."

"We're actually here to see you, Mrs. Zevalos." Annabeth answered with a grin of her own, hoping that behind her, Hank was treating the woman to one of his more charming smiles.

"Oh . . . well . . . I can't imagine what you want with me." Flustered, Marie stepped back from the doorway.

Not wasting the opportunity, Annabeth stepped across the threshold. "I wanted to speak with you, woman-to-woman," she said, letting her voice carry throughout the small house.

"Oh!" Marie wrung her hands as the three men behind Annabeth crowded into the foyer.

"This will only take a minute," Annabeth reassured her. The last thing she needed was a panicked Marie Zevalos. Her plan wouldn't work if the woman collapsed on the floor. Gently taking the woman's elbow, she steered her toward the airy kitchen at the back of the house. "We have so much to catch up on," she said loudly.

A spasm of coughing from a nearby room grabbed Marie's attention.

"Marie!"

Annabeth's knees nearly buckled with relief at the sound of the raspy bellow. Coach Zevalos had heard her, just as she'd planned.

"Oh!" Marie reached for a tray with a can of ginger ale and an empty glass on it. "Just let me give this to Paul and we can have some tea."

"Tea would be lovely. And please tell Coach Zevalos I said hello." Annabeth poured on the saccharin.

As soon as Marie disappeared with the tray, Hank gestured for the two league representatives to sit on the sofa in the living room. He turned to Annabeth, a sly smile on his face. "Well played," he mouthed.

She beamed under his praise but silently worried what he'd think of her after the second act. Marie shuffled back to the kitchen, flustered once again.

"Paul said he'd like to see you. Right now. Before we have tea." The poor woman clearly didn't like the idea of anyone upsetting her ill husband, and Annabeth wondered what it was like to love someone so blindly.

"Sure, but I'll only keep him a minute. Then we girls can chat." She patted Marie's shoulder. "Mr. Osbourne is going to go with me to apologize for upsetting Coach during his last visit."

Before Marie could protest, Annabeth grabbed Hank's hand, towing him behind her as she made her way into the small sitting room where Coach Zevalos was holed up. The sight before her nearly stole the wind from her sails. The man in the oversized recliner looked nothing like the one she'd met thirteen years ago. Coach Zevalos was now a haggard shell of himself, lung cancer from his pack-a-day habit diminishing what had been a tall, robust, athletically built man. His ashen skin sagged at his jowls and his once-haughty dark eyes were now just angry; whether it was from the sight of her or the fact that his time on this earth was short, she wasn't sure. Nor did she care.

When he spied Hank, his eyes grew wide and he grabbed the mask from the portable oxygen tank beside him. "Get out!" he gasped, pointing at Hank.

"He stays."

Annabeth's tone forced the coach to pull several puffs on his oxygen.

"What do you want?" he asked around the mask.

She clasped her hands in front of her. "For you to do the right thing."

He wheezed into the mask. A television droned quietly behind her and the cloying smell of sickness teased her nostrils. Annabeth felt a swell of nausea roll through her stomach, but she willed it down. This had to be done.

"I told him," he gasped, leveling a finger at Hank. "I've got nothing to say."

"Fine." Annabeth held her ground. "If you won't talk, I will."

The coach struggled in the chair, but it was no use. He no longer had the strength to stand and intimidate her with his dominance. He took another frustrated pull of oxygen.

"I'll tell your wife about the day you came to the trailer park to discuss Will's college potential *privately* with me. And when I refused your disgusting requirements for the advancement of my son's career, you found another willing participant in the trailer next door."

Her hands were trembling. She felt Hank's body draw up to full alertness beside her.

"I took what she offered!" he spat out. "I had no idea how old she was."

"She was fifteen!" Annabeth cried. "With the body of a twenty-five-year-old and the morals of an alley cat. But that didn't mean you were allowed to touch her. "

"Jesus," she heard Hank whisper.

"Someone should have been watching her," the coach wheezed before a coughing spasm overtook him.

He was right; someone should have been watching over Bethany, but her mother worked two jobs and her father had been a long-haul truck driver. The teen was left on her own more than she should have been, wandering the trailer park looking for anyone who'd pay attention to her. She probably thought a man like Paul Zevalos was her ticket out.

Annabeth's knees were shaking now. She felt Hank take a step closer, his warm hand settling on the small of her back. He was breathing forcefully beside her as if it were taking all the strength he had to contain himself.

His coughing subsided, the coach narrowed his eyes at

her. "Why bring this up now? Will got his scholarship. I even hooked him up in the pros."

She swayed slightly in shock, but Hank's steady hand propped her up. Annabeth had long suspected that her rebuff of the coach all those years ago might have cost her son his scholarship had she not caught the man coming out of Bethany's trailer later that day. But to hear him confirm that made her sick to her stomach.

"Except now you're letting him take the fall for you," she said, amazed her voice sounded so steady.

"I'm a dying man. He owes me."

"You're not worth him destroying his good name."

"He took the money."

"He didn't know what it was for and he tried to return it!" she shot back.

He coughed again before taking another puff of oxygen. "It's too late to erase the past."

Annabeth stiffened her spine. "Yes, and it's too late to erase your past." She pulled a photo out of her purse, flipping it onto the coach's blanketed lap.

He wheezed uncontrollably, sucking on the oxygen mask as he caught sight of the picture.

"Imagine my surprise when the Taylors moved in the dead of the night two months later. Or when I encountered Bethany in a shopping mall in Wilmington a few months after that, her belly swollen with pregnancy."

Hank let out a hiss beside her, his fingertips curling into her back as he fought for self-restraint.

"Tell me this, Coach," Annabeth asked. "Does your wife know about your son? I met him the other day. He's quite a boy, as you can see by the photo."

The coach was gasping heavily now, dragging air through the mask in deep draughts.

"Of course she doesn't know," Hank said from behind her. "He'd just as soon wait until he dies for her to find out. Because he's a coward. An honest man, a real man, would own up to his sins before he goes. But this man doesn't have the guts to deal with the mess he's made."

A gurgling sound came through the oxygen mask, where the coach's tears mixed with the air his body so desperately needed.

"I didn't know she was a child," he croaked out. "I made amends to that family and to the boy. I never laid a hand on a woman other than my wife again."

She snorted at his confession. Whether she believed him or not was irrelevant. The damage was already done.

"What more do you want from me?" he pleaded.

"I told you. For you to do the right thing," she repeated.

The three were silent for several moments as the coach used the oxygen to regulate his breathing.

Coach Zevalos broke the silence. "Fine. If you'll leave the boy out of this, I'll call my lawyers and make a statement."

"We conveniently have two NFL counsel here with us," Hank told him in a matter-of-fact tone.

Another coughing fit followed. "You . . . you don't expect me to do it today?" he gasped.

Annabeth lunged at him. "Yes! You'll do it now! Today!"

"Annabeth!" Hank grabbed her arm, but she shook him off.

"For thirteen years, I've lived with the guilt of what you did. *I* was the reason you came to Seaside Vista in the first place. *I* was the reason a lecherous man had sex with an underage girl. How do you think that's felt all these years? God! I should have spoken up sooner, but I didn't. This isn't going on one day longer. You're going to tell them the truth about your stupid bounty scheme before more people get hurt."

She felt Hank's arm wrapped around her waist, gently pulling her back as the coach dissolved into another round of wheezing.

"Shh," Hank whispered to her. "It's over now."

Annabeth gulped in a few deep breaths of her own as she pulled out of Hank's restraint. She anxiously smoothed down her skirt and swiped at her tears. Hank patiently stood by her side, giving her space as she regained her composure.

"Okay?" he asked, his gentle voice restoring her courage.

Gnawing on her bottom lip, she gave him a quick nod. He winked at her, nearly making her come undone.

"I'll go get our friends." He eyed the coach directly before striding from the room.

The coach's eyes brimmed with tears, but he sat in his chair belligerently silent.

"You know what the worst part is?" Annabeth wrapped her arms around herself. "Will worshipped you. And I let him."

Tears streamed down her face again as the league representatives sheepishly entered the room, one of them setting up a video camera.

"Come on." Hank quietly ushered her down the hall and out into the backyard. Annabeth took fortifying breaths of fresh air as she brushed the tears off her face. Coming up behind her, Hank wrapped his arms around her waist, pulling her back against his body.

"Shh." His warm breath was comforting on her neck. "It's over. You did it."

She turned in his arms, burying her face in his chest. "Yeah, it only took me thirteen years."

"Whoa, whoa!" Hank put his hands on her shoulders, putting an arm's-length distance between them. "This was *not* your fault. The man in there would have found someone else to prey on if he hadn't found that girl. Trust me on this, Annabeth, you didn't do anything wrong."

"But I didn't tell anyone. I didn't report it."

"From the looks of it, the girl's family didn't report it, either. Obviously, they found out who the father was. If they wanted to charge him, they could have."

"They took his money instead." Annabeth had been disgusted when she met with Bethany's parents the other day. Coach Zevalos had been a gravy train for the struggling family. Marie Zevalos would likely not see the money she expected when her husband died. Sadly, she'd probably never know why.

"Annabeth, look at me," Hank commanded.

She lifted her gaze to meet his concerned one.

"From this moment on, you are not to blame yourself for this. Do you hear me?"

She wanted to, but she still carried so much guilt. "I let Will go play for him," she whispered through her tears. "He was so excited to go to Yale and take advantage of all the opportunities it would provide. I couldn't tell him. I let my son go off with that creep so he'd have a chance at his dream. A career. A life outside of Chances Inlet. He looked up to the man. He was always so distrusting of people, men in particular. I didn't want to shatter his illusions. I'm a terrible mother. "

Hank pulled her in against his body, holding her while she cried. "You did what you had to do. The best you could. No one is blaming you." She felt his lips brush the top of her head.

"I'm sorry for all this." Her words were smothered against his chest.

Reaching a finger beneath her chin, he tipped her damp face up. "We already covered this back in Baltimore. Don't apologize for being a good mother to your son."

"But I dragged you to this horrible interview . . ."

Hank stepped out of their embrace and her body nearly went limp without his warmth. He pointed to the house.

"That? Are you kidding, Annabeth? I wouldn't have missed that performance for all the money in the world. You were brilliant! My God, generals on the battlefield would weep at the magnificence of your strategy." He wrapped her in his arms again, pulling her body flush with his. "And, if I'm being honest here, I've never been more turned on in my life."

Laughing through her tears, she tossed her head back, giving Hank better access to her neck.

"And now." He kissed his way along her collarbone. "Per our agreement earlier this morning, you're mine. Prepare yourself, Annabeth Connelly, because we may not make it back to Baltimore. In fact, I know a place in Atlantic City that has big, comfy beds and an amazing shower."

His mouth found hers in a searing kiss. Annabeth

wrapped her arms around his neck, letting herself relax into his body. She could not have gotten through today without Hank. Thankfully, she wouldn't have to go through any more days without him.

His cell phone vibrated at his waist. He muttered a few choice words as he pulled the phone out. "It could be the office," he explained as he checked the screen. "Nope, just Sophie." He began to return the phone to his belt.

"Sophie!" she squealed, grapping the phone and hitting the talk button. "Hi, Soph!"

"Annabeth? Hi," Sophie gushed over the phone. "Ohmigosh, it's so good to talk to you. We just boarded the cruise ship and it's soooo cool. Well, except for the twins jumping from their bunks. Be quiet, guys!"

Annabeth could hear the joyous shouts of the two boys in the background.

"Arghhh," Sophie groaned. "Hey, so why are you answering my dad's phone? Everything's okay, right? Is he there? Ohmigosh, are you guys together somewhere?" Sophie's voice rose an octave as she began to put two and two together. Thankfully, she couldn't see her father's hand kneading Annabeth's bottom while his mouth made a beeline for her breasts.

"He's right here," Annabeth breathed, her pulse ricocheting.

The look Hank gave her promised retribution in the near future, and her body throbbed happily with anticipation.

"Hey, Soph."

"Wow, Dad!" In her excitement, Sophie spoke loud enough for Annabeth to hear. "What's happening between you and Annabeth?"

"Nothing if you keep interrupting us." Hank winked at her.

"Hank!" Annabeth mouthed.

"Wow, Dad, this is so cool. I was gonna tell you all about the ship, but this is so much better."

"I'll call you tonight and you can tell us both all about your trip."

"Ohmigosh, I've got to tell Mom!"

"Sophie Claire, do not share my personal life with your mother!"

"Sure thing, Dad. You two have a nice day! Bye!"

They both could hear her screaming for her mother as she hung up the phone.

Hank swore. "Now we'll have the two of them badgering us all day."

Annabeth grabbed the lapels of his suit and pulled him flush against her body. "Tell me more about this amazing shower. I'm pretty sure we won't be able to hear the phone in there."

He framed her face with both hands. "Annabeth Connelly, have I told you lately how smart you are?" He didn't wait for an answer, instead kissing her with all the promise of an exciting life ahead.

Twenty-seven

"I was serious when I told you that you and Owen are welcome to stay at our house," Carly said with a huff as she snapped one side of the portable crib into place.

Owen dozed in his bouncy seat, his face puffy from the tears he'd been crying off and on all day. Seven hours confined to a car seat had been too much for the baby who'd passed the last month in the arms of one person or another. He'd spent most of the trip either indignant or annoyed that he wasn't being held, letting everyone between coastal North Carolina and Baltimore know about it.

Her son's distress had only added to Julianne's agitation. Will hadn't bothered to call or text in nearly three days. She'd resorted to bullying Brody to find out if her husband was still alive. Brody's affirmation that Will was in fact working out at the training facility had only infuriated her more.

"I told you, we'd just get in the way. Owen still doesn't sleep through the night. Besides, I don't want to put Shane in an awkward position with his teammate." Julianne pulled out the crib sheets from the travel bag.

Originally, she'd hoped to take Carly up on her offer, longing for the familiarity and understanding her best friend would provide. But when her friend had first offered, Julianne could hear the hesitation in her voice. It wasn't hard to see where Carly's loyalty now lay. Fortunately, Sebastian had already rented a fully furnished house for him and Nigel. When she'd told Carly she and Owen were staying there, the relief in her friend's voice had been palpable. Worse, her friend hadn't brooked any argument.

This arrangement was the best for everyone. But that didn't mean Carly's defection didn't hurt. Perhaps most painful of all, Julianne sensed that her friend accepted the story that she had deliberately told Stephen about Will.

Julianne's only confidante, Annabeth, had made her own way up to Baltimore, citing an appointment she had early today. Patricia had volunteered to drive with Julianne and a howling Owen, claiming to want to check out the competition, a bed-and-breakfast in Annapolis. It seemed they'd made the trip for nothing, however, because Will hadn't bothered to contact Julianne about seeing his son.

"Besides," Julianne said as she unpacked Owen's clothes and piled them in the dresser drawers, "I'm not even sure how long we'll be in town. I hope to get back to Chances Inlet as soon as possible."

Carly looked up from what she was doing with a speculative pause. "You'd stay there even without Will?"

Julianne tried not to bristle at her friend's question. "It's Owen's home now, too. And it's where my new designs will be manufactured."

"When you mentioned you were designing again, I didn't think you'd progressed so far as to begin manufacturing." Carly's statement was more of a question.

Julianne shrugged. "There's no sense in waiting. People need jobs, and I've got the means to employ them. It will be a huge boon to the town."

"That's good, I guess," Carly said. "It'll certainly keep you busy. But how will you handle starting a new company and taking care of the baby?"

"Will's mother is going to help. And I have Sebastian to take care of the business end of things."

Carly totally ignored the second half of her statement. "Will's mother? I'd think she'd be on his side. I mean . . ." Her voice trailed off.

"She's on Owen's side." Julianne struggled to keep her voice steady. Clearly, her friend thought the worst of her. "It's best if Owen puts down roots in one place so that he's not shuffled around constantly. Locating the company in Chances Inlet will allow him to have a more stable life."

"Wow, you've really thought this through." The surprise in Carly's voice burned through Julianne. Once again, she was reminded of irresponsible decisions she'd made this past year, but she didn't think that qualified her for being a total nitwit.

"Try not to sound so shocked," Julianne said, unable to keep the bitterness from her own voice.

Sorrow and regret shimmered in Carly's eyes, forcing Julianne to look away. Fortunately, she was saved from continuing their conversation by the sound of the doorbell. Julianne's heart leaped instantly.

Will had come at last.

She raced to the front door, checking her frazzled appearance in a mirror as she passed by. Smoothing down her wild hair, she pasted a bright smile on her face as she pulled open the front door. Her smile vanished quickly, though, when she caught sight of the man standing on the front step.

"Roscoe?" Carly said from behind her.

Disappointment surged through Julianne, forcing her to tightly grip the doorknob so she wouldn't collapse onto the tile floor. She glanced past Will's agent, but he was alone. Will wasn't coming, after all. Her throat constricted and she was glad Carly was asking questions because she wasn't able to speak at all.

"What are you doing here?" Carly asked.

Roscoe lifted the baby seat he held in his hand. "I've come to get Owen for a visit with his father."

Julianne rocked back on her heels, her fingers whiteknuckled around the doorknob as she tried to process

Roscoe's statement. Not only was Will not coming, but he'd sent his obnoxious agent to fetch their son. Was this how their life was going to play out from now on?

"Don't look so surprised, Julianne." Roscoe set the carrier down on the floor and assumed his belligerent lawyer stance. "Your text said Owen would be available this afternoon for a visit, so here I am. Obviously, Will would prefer to have as little contact with you as possible, so I'll be the go-between until we can set up a more formal procedure."

If Roscoe intended his words to wound, he was definitely on target. But Julianne would die before she let this man see that. "I'll pack some things," she said as she stiffly turned away from the door.

"Not necessary. Will has already bought everything he'll need. Today's visit will only be for a few hours, anyway. He and I still have some legal prep work to get through before the hearing tomorrow."

This time, Roscoe hit the bull's-eye. Guilt swept through Julianne's limbs and she sank down on the small bench in the entryway. This mess was all her doing. If only she had kept her mouth shut.

"Why don't I go get Owen?" Carly's offer saved Julianne from having to negotiate with her protesting body to stand.

Roscoe handed over the new baby carrier and Carly disappeared into the house to get Owen. No doubt Will had an entire nursery decorated and ready at his loft. Obviously, he'd thought of everything. Including a strategy to never see her again.

"I'm surprised he didn't send you with Bubble Wrap," she quipped.

One corner of his mouth twitched before he apparently remembered she was the enemy. He pulled an envelope from the pocket of his suit jacket. "Your copy of the separation papers. I filed them this morning."

He held the envelope out for her, but Julianne was having trouble making her arms move. Roscoe finally tossed it down onto the bench beside her. "The divorce will be final one year from today. For now, you share joint custody. But we'll revisit that after we finish with the hearing tomorrow."

Julianne's hand flinched as the envelope grazed her fingers. The rest of her body was numb. "How annoyingly efficient you are, Roscoe. I hope Will pays you well."

If he answered, she didn't hear him because Owen had begun crying again. His forlorn wails filled the foyer as an anguished Carly handed the baby, now strapped in his carrier, to Roscoe.

"Shh." Roscoe gently swung the car carrier as he brushed a thumb over Owen's temple. Owen calmed measurably as his mouth settled around the pacifier Roscoe offered him.

Julianne wrapped her arms around her midsection in order to keep from grabbing her son back. If she touched Owen, even kissed him good-bye, she'd never be able to let Roscoe leave with him. "Please," she pleaded. "Be careful with him."

Empathy touched his eyes. "I have twin boys. They've made it almost three years with me as a parent. Owen will be just fine. I'll have him back, safe and sound, by eight o'clock."

He whispered something to Carly as he walked back out the open door.

"Roscoe!" Julianne called, springing to her feet.

He turned to face her, his bland expression returned to his face.

"Will," she stammered. "Is . . . is he okay?"

She wrung her hands, chewing on her bottom lip as he seemed to take ages to answer her. It was as if he were trying to come up with the words that could hurt the most. And he did.

"No."

Julianne watched as he walked down the sidewalk, a whimpering Owen swaying by his side. Mercifully, Carly closed the door just as Julianne landed in a pile of devastation on the floor, sobs wracking her body.

"My God," Carly said as she crouched down and wrapped her arms around Julianne. "You love him. *You're in love with Will.*"

Julianne would have laughed at Carly's incredulousness

except she felt as if her body had broken and she'd never feel joy again.

"You don't know how happy I am to know this," Carly was saying as she stroked Julianne's back. "Shane swore you'd told your brother about Will to get back at him for forcing you to marry. But I told him you'd never, ever do that. No matter how mad you were at Will, you'd never sell him out like that. It's just not in you. It was actually our first big fight."

Her words propelled Julianne to sob harder. Not only had she torpedoed her own marriage, but she'd caused tension in Carly and Shane's as well.

"Oh, Jules, I don't know how this happened, but we're going to make this right. We have to make Will believe you didn't do this."

Julianne shook her head violently. "But I did do it, Carly. I did!"

Carly's face was incredulous again. Her hand stopped mid-stroke on Julianne's back. "I don't understand."

"It was an accident. I told Stephen, but I didn't mean to. Honest, I didn't do it on purpose."

"Does Will know this?

"I tried to tell him," Julianne croaked out. "But he wouldn't listen. He and his cretin agent found my notes on the new company. It was supposed to be a surprise. For Will."

"Jules, I'm still not following you. What does one have to do with the other?"

Julianne brushed the tears off her face and wiped her nose with the back of her hand. "My new clothing line. It's for infants. I want to manufacture them in Chances Inlet. I was . . . *am* going to give the company to Will. He thinks everyone in that town looks down on him because of his circumstances as a kid. It's his hometown and he feels like he doesn't belong. This will give him that chance to feel a part of Chances Inlet. Not only will he be giving people an opportunity to work, he'll get something back: pride in his hometown."

"Go on. Where does Stephen come into all this?" Carly asked.

"I needed to borrow against my grandmother's trust. I asked Stephen to facilitate it. While I had him on the phone, he started going off about Will and this Bountygate mess. He played me like a violin, Carly. I defended Will, of course." She gulped around a sob. "I had no idea he was heading up the Senate hearings. Until it was too late."

Carly smoothed the hair back from Julianne's face. "Of course you defended him. Because you love him." She gave Julianne a knowing smile. "Now we just have to make him see how much you love him."

"Right now, I'd just be happy if he didn't hate me," Julianne whispered.

"Not good enough," Carly said. "I was almost killed last year before I could tell Shane I couldn't live without him. If you love Will, Jules, you have to be all in with my plan."

"You have a plan?"

"Yep. And we have to hurry if we want to get to the media before the hearing tomorrow."

"Media?" Julianne was stunned at her friend's enthusiasm for dealing with anyone wielding a press badge. "You avoid the paparazzi. They've stalked you most of your life."

"Mmmm. I know, but I've forced myself to swim with the sharks a few times this past year to help the people I love the very most. Don't worry. It'll work. I promise. The first step, though, is to get you off the floor. My legs are all tingly."

The bourbon no longer burned when it went down. Will wasn't sure if that meant he was suitably inebriated or the alcohol had eroded the lining of his throat. He was going for mind-numbing drunk, but the fact that he was still sitting upright probably meant he had a few more glasses to go.

A key turned in the lock and Will let out a string of curse words. He tried to get off the sofa to intercept Brody, but his head swam as soon as he stood. *Hmm. Drunker than he thought. Good sign.* Will slouched back down in a satisfied stupor and attempted to pour the amber liquid into the glass in front of him, but the stupid thing kept moving.

"Dude."

Brody's voice startled him and Will swore as half the bourbon ended up on the coffee table. Slamming down the bottle, he wiped up the spill with the T-shirt Owen had spit up on earlier. "Get out," he growled at Brody.

Brody ignored him, sliding into the leather recliner across the room. "Love what you've done with the place." He glanced around. Owen's baby paraphernalia was strewn about the loft, along with an assortment of take-out containers and dirty clothes. "Early preschool fits you somehow."

"Fuck off."

The annoying tight end perched his sneaker-clad feet on the coffee table, a move guaranteed to annoy Will, who swatted at the bright yellow shoes but missed, nearly falling off the sofa instead. Will unleashed another string of locker room prose.

"Somebody needs a Snickers bar."

"I mean it, Brody." Will's lips weren't working as well as he'd have liked because the words were slurred. "I don't want you here. Go home."

"No can do."

"I don't need a babysitter!" Will roared.

Brody just raised an eyebrow, gesturing to the stuffed Elmo doll Will clutched in his hand. He heaved it across the room, which in turn caused the entire loft to spin.

"Dude." Brody employed his most solicitous tone, the same one he probably used to get half the women on the East Coast to slip off their panties for him. "You should probably eat something. Get something in your belly to soak up all that liquor. Let me call for take-out." He reached for the bottle, but Will snatched it away, gripping it tightly on the sofa beside him.

Rubbing his hands through his hair, Brody placed both feet on the floor and leaned toward Will. If Will wanted to, he could have the pest by the throat in an instant. Only his hands weren't working so well right now.

"Look, Will," Brody said. "I came tonight because the guys want you to know we all stand behind you. No matter what you did or what you do tomorrow. We've got your back."

Will snorted. "They didn't need to send you over here to annoy me. They could have just told me at the training facility rather than talking behind my back."

With an exasperated sigh, Brody shot to his feet. "Easier said than done when you're acting like a surly shit all the time. No one wants to talk to you in person. I actually drew the short straw, asshole, and was rewarded with the honor of wasting my evening watching you slobber in your bourbon. But I'm out of here."

He stepped around Owen's swing, brushing over a stack of papers on top of the coffee table. Will's reflexes were too slow and the separation agreement floated to the floor right in front of Brody's obnoxious sneakers. He plucked it off the rug before Will could get to it.

"That was fast," Brody said as he scanned the document.

"Mind your damn business." Will reached for the paper, but Brody took a step back.

"I just thought the way things were going in that hometown of yours, you wouldn't let her go without a fight."

"I told you, Brody, it wasn't that kind of marriage."

"Could have fooled me." Brody flicked the paper back toward Will. "Well, I guess now she's fair game for the rest of us."

Will wasn't sure how he got across the room so quickly, but he had Brody pinned against the wall, his forearm to the little twerp's throat, poised to crush his windpipe. Unfortunately, Brody wasn't fighting back. Instead his eyes were bright with mischief.

"So I wasn't wrong," Brody taunted him. "You do love her."

"Give me a reason to kill you," Will hissed. "You've been a pain in my ass for too long, Brody Janik."

Brody ignored him, enduring whatever pain Will inflicted and still managing to piss him off. "I picked up some pretty strong vibes that she was hot for you, too. So what did you do to screw it up?"

Will increased the pressure to Brody's throat, but the idiot didn't even flinch. "I didn't do anything," Will grunted. "She sold me out to her brother, *the senator.*"

"Are you sure about that?"

Will felt as if his head were going to explode, his skull was throbbing so hard. "Yes, I'm sure, you asshole. She admitted it."

"Huh."

That was it. He was going to strangle the little prick. Except the harder he pressed, the more relaxed Brody became.

"Did you ask her why?"

Did he ask her why? Will stepped back in aggravation, nearly tripping over a giant metal maze he'd bought for Owen to play with. Brody didn't even reach for his neck, simply crossing his arms in front of his chest, tucking his long hands between his armpits. Will leaned his hips against the recliner to keep himself upright.

"I didn't have to ask her," he shouted. "She sold me out for money so she could start a new design company."

"Nah." Brody shook his head in disbelief. "She didn't need money that badly. The gown she designed for my sister was worth an easy fifty grand. I tried to pay her several times and she wouldn't take my money. It's gotta be something else."

The burning sensation had returned to Will's throat, as well as every other part of his body. Brody was talking nonsense. Will really wanted to hit him, but the room was spinning again.

"Dude, maybe you should ask her why she did it. She could have a perfectly logical explanation."

"I told you why she did it," Will bit out.

"Your theory doesn't make sense." Brody stepped away from the wall. "But I forgot. You're William the Conqueror. You have ice water running through your veins. You'd rather live your life thinking the whole world is against you. Or keep your teammates at arm's length. Hell, you'd even rather believe the worst of the only woman who, besides your mother, probably *actually loves* you. Suit yourself, Connelly. It's your life."

He headed for the door.

"Brody," Will managed to croak out.

Brody stopped in his tracks but didn't bother to turn around.

"Leave the key," Will commanded.

"No way, dude. If you pickle yourself silly and die tonight, I want to be able to get your behemoth ass out of here before the stink sets in."

He closed and locked the door behind him as he left.

Twenty-eight

The small anteroom where Roscoe and Will waited was blessedly quiet. After running the gauntlet of reporters and video cameras staked out in the rotunda and along the marble halls of the Russell Senate Office Building, Will was glad to be able to have a few minutes to catch his breath before the hearing. He leaned his pounding head back against the wall and closed his eyes, while Roscoe stared out the large window overlooking the garden courtyard below them.

"I could get used to working in a place like this," Roscoe mused. "The history and the architecture of this building can be a little awe-inspiring." There was a touch of reverence in his voice.

"You're starting to sound like Gavin." Will didn't bother opening his eyes; they still burned from the assault of the strobe flashes on the video cameras. Or maybe it was the aftereffects of the bourbon. Both, most likely. "He's always waxing on about cornices and fluting and masonry and porticos. Sounds like a woman half the time."

The chair next to Will creaked as Roscoe eased into it. "I'll be sure to tell your best friend you called him a girl."

Will grunted.

"Are you gonna be able to make it through this thing?" Roscoe asked, his tone equal parts concern and annoyance.

"I only have to repeat one line the entire time. A monkey could do it."

"Yeah, but most monkeys aren't fighting a colossal hangover. Stupid move on your part."

"It felt good at the time."

Roscoe snorted. "It always does."

The sounds of Roscoe clicking through his messages stirred the quiet of the room. "Uh-oh."

Will cracked an eyelid. Roscoe was scanning his iPhone.

"Shit! I cannot believe she did this."

"Your wife posting compromising videos of you on You-Tube again?" Will teased.

"Not my wife. Yours."

That got both of Will's eyes open. "What?"

Roscoe was scrolling through his phone. "She just released a statement to the press."

What remained of the previous night's bourbon rolled through his stomach, cresting in a wave that threatened to spew out of him. What bombshell had she dropped now? Was there any more damage that woman could do to him?

"About?" Will managed to grind out.

"Huh," Roscoe said as he continued to scroll. "About her new company. Apparently she's designing baby clothes now."

Will had to admit the concept made sense. Julianne's priorities had shifted, and this way she could focus her talents on something that allowed her to include Owen. He quickly snuffed out the burst of pride he felt knowing she'd begun drawing again, though.

"Well, I'll be damned," Roscoe mumbled.

"What?"

"She's manufacturing the clothes in a textile factory located just outside Chances Inlet."

Will felt his weary muscles tense along his spine. "Great. Now I've got another reason to avoid that place." It was ironic that his fake wife had found more acceptance in his hometown than Will ever had.

"That won't be so easy." Roscoe looked up from his phone, his eyes shining with what looked like admiration. "She's named you as the president of the company."

What? "Can she do that?" Clearly Will had killed a few too many brain cells last night because nothing Roscoe said was making sense.

"Sure she can. It's her company. She can do whatever she wants." Roscoe paused, a bemused look on his face. "Only, now it's your company, so I guess you can give it back to her."

Why would Julianne do such a thing? Brody's words filtered back through the haze of the previous evening.

She didn't need money that badly. She could have a perfectly logical explanation. Did you ask her why?

"Give me that." He ripped the phone from his agent's hands and began scrolling through the screen. The mayor of Chances Inlet was singing Will's praises for being a visionary, persuading Julianne to locate her company in their town. She'd named both his mother and Patricia McAlister as members of the board of directors. And Mrs. Elderhaus! What did his first-grade teacher know about running a company?

"She's crazy," Will muttered. "Bat-shit crazy."

"Skip down to the part about the profits. You're gonna love that." Roscoe was definitely amused now.

According to the press release, the profits earned from the company would be used to establish a sports and activities club for youth in Chances Inlet where kids could hang out after school. The Second Chances Center, as Julianne had dubbed it, would also provide academic assistance and job training to the area's most needy kids. It was visionary, all right. A freaking brilliant way to get back in Will's good graces. The problem was, he wasn't buying it. If this was her way of apologizing, it was too little, too late.

"I seriously underestimated your wife's manipulative skills, Will. I've gotta hand it to her, this move trumps our attempt to get public opinion on your side. Not only that, but she's just proved that she doesn't need your money. It's all over the Internet that stores are clamoring for her designs."

Will wanted to howl with frustration, but the door to the large hearing room opened and his attention immediately focused on Senator Marchione. The buzz from the assembled media reached a crescendo before Julianne's brother closed the door behind him.

"I'm sorry to keep you waiting, gentlemen."

Will didn't think he looked sorry at all.

"We've had a change in plans for today . . ."

Roscoe shot to his feet, his game face firmly back in place. "Wait just a minute! You can't change things up without consulting with us. My client is not at your beck and call."

The senator perched one of his hips on a corner of the desk under the window. "I beg to differ. As a subpoenaed witness, he *is* at the mercy of the committee's schedule." He held a hand out, thwarting Roscoe from interjecting. "But that's neither here nor there. The fact is the hearing has been canceled. We have no need for your testimony."

A trace of unease traveled down Will's spine.

"So all this was for what, then?" Roscoe was working himself into indignant fury.

"To get at the truth, Mr. Mathis. And we've done that."

Will nearly snapped off the wooden arms of the chair in which he sat. He was close behind Roscoe in the anger department. And confused. Where did this all leave him?

The senator made a show of adjusting the sleeves of his suit jacket, prolonging the suspense. "It seems Coach Zevalos has decided to clear his conscience in his last days. He made a full confession to the NFL yesterday."

"Yesterday?" Roscoe nearly shouted as he grabbed for his briefcase. "How come we heard nothing about it?"

Will stood to follow his agent out the door.

"Because it doesn't impact you or your client."

That stopped both men in their tracks. Will focused a measuring glare at the senator.

"That's right." The senator locked eyes with him. "Coach

Zevalos named quite a list of names, but yours wasn't on it. It seems we were in error in subpoenaing you."

Roscoe didn't waste a breath. "I want that in writing," he demanded. "Today."

The tension crackled in the room as the three men stared at one another for a moment. Finally, the senator gave the briefest of nods. Will squeezed out a breath through lungs he hadn't realized he was constricting.

"In that case, we're out of here." Roscoe headed for the door, Will at his heels.

"Just one minute," the senator called after them. "Will, can I have a word with you?"

Roscoe stopped, his hand poised on the doorknob. Curious, Will figured it was worth a few minutes of his time to hear the senator's excuse as to why he and his sister had used him. Hell, yeah, he wanted answers. If for no other reason than so no woman would be able to dupe him again like Julianne had.

They both turned back to face the senator, who was still seated on the corner of the desk.

"Alone, if you don't mind." He phrased it as if it were a question, but all three men knew it wasn't.

Roscoe shot a sideways glance at Will, an eyebrow raised in question. Will nodded.

"Don't do anything stupid," Roscoe mumbled as he slid past. "We're almost home free."

A roar went up in the other room as Roscoe slipped out. Will remained where he was. Propping a shoulder up against the doorjamb, he tucked his arms across his chest. He tried to give the impression that he couldn't care less about what the senator had to say, when in fact apprehension coursed through his veins.

The senator heaved a sigh. "It seems I owe you an apology."

"Yeah, I believe that's what the written statement is for."

"No, a personal apology. It's because of me you're in this mess."

Will arched an eyebrow at him, wishing somehow one

of the hundreds of media piranhas outside could record this.

"You and your sister, you mean."

He brushed Will's comment aside with a hand through the air. "Julianne was tangential to my reasons for giving the information to the committee. I honestly thought I was doing the right thing."

"If you consider ruining a man's career the right thing," Will said tersely.

"Obviously I misjudged the whole situation. I thought I was doing her a favor."

"By having her spy on me and seducing my secrets out of me so you could drag me in front of your committee and totally unman me?"

"That wasn't how it was," the senator argued. "Julianne wasn't spying on you. I could barely get her to tell me how the baby was, much less answer questions about you."

"Really, so I'm supposed to believe those cozy phone calls and texts every day were innocent?"

"Yes!" The senator yelled. He leaped off the desk and began pacing the room. "When I dragged you up here that first day, it was to help the baby. For Julianne. She was sick with worry over the possibility of losing her son. I certainly never intended to force her to marry you."

Will tried not to cringe. Apparently, even the duplicitous sister of a con-man senator wasn't good enough for a boy from the Seaside Vista Trailer Park.

"She was out of her mind, selling her business to pay his medical bills. Too proud to ask for help. So yes, I called her every day because I was worried about her and Owen. I was full of guilt for pushing her down a path she might not have otherwise chosen."

"You've made the point quite clear that I'm not the first choice either of you would have made."

The senator snorted. "Yeah, well, I was wrong. Very wrong."

The breath in Will's lungs began to seize up again.

The senator pinched the bridge of his nose. "Apparently,

she was blissfully happy being married to you. Until I screwed it up."

Will's body went rigid, his heart slowing to a near-stop as he contemplated the senator's words.

"I should have guessed that she was in love with you by the way she so vehemently defended you that day on the phone. She never intended to tell me your secret, but it was out before she could stop it. You have to know she had no inkling of anyone in the Senate investigating you. It would never be on Julianne's radar."

He let the senator's words sink in. Julianne had been telling the truth. She hadn't told her brother on purpose. And Will hadn't believed her.

"She's let me know in no uncertain terms how she feels about you since then, though." He sat down lethargically in the chair Roscoe had occupied earlier. "Not to mention how she feels about me. Definitely not the same feelings, in case you were wondering." His smile was rueful. "So please, don't blame her for my actions. I was simply playing big brother. I saw an opportunity to get her out of the marriage before the agreed-upon time frame, and I exercised it. She would never believe this, but I would use anything at my disposal to make her happy. Even if it meant making an enemy out of you."

Will was stunned. He was afraid to move a muscle in case this was all some sort of dream. First he'd been exonerated from Bountygate. Now he was hit with the truth about Julianne: She did love him. *And she hadn't sold him out.* His heartbeat was more rapid now and his body burned to take action. He only hoped it wasn't too late. Unfortunately, the senator was in a mood to commiserate.

"The truth is I don't know my sister as well as a brother should. Julianne's mother, Daria, was my father's second wife. My dad never really loved my own mother. Theirs was one of those society marriages, the kind good for a diplomat's career." He looked at Will as if he expected him to agree. "Dad worshipped Daria, though. When she died, he

was devastated. He couldn't bear to look at Julianne anymore because every time he did, he saw Daria. Our father
didn't care that the poor girl had just lost her mother; he sent
her off to boarding school almost immediately. I was in the
States, in law school with a life of my own by then."

The senator dragged his fingers through his hair. "She
grew up without anyone to protect and guide her. I'm a father
myself now and I now know how lonely Julianne's life must
have been. I let her down. I guess I just thought . . ." He shook
his head in disgust, not bothering to finish his thought, before
standing to face Will. "Anyway, for what's it's worth, I apologize. To both of you, for all the trouble this has caused. Please,
tell her I was only doing what I thought was best for her and
Owen. It may have been misguided, but it was out of love."

Will shifted to his full height, amazed his body could
still move. He felt like he'd taken a pounding from an entire
offensive line.

"I'm sure she'd rather hear it from you." Will had his own
groveling to do.

"She hasn't returned a text or phone call." The senator
shoved his hands into his pockets, a melancholy expression
on his face. "The only message she left was to tell me she
never wanted to see me or anyone with the last name Marchione again. She even refused the money from our grandmother's trust she'd asked me to secure for her."

"Then what did she use to finance her new company?"

"You knew about that? She gave me the impression that
was supposed to be a surprise."

Chagrined, Will shifted his weight from one foot to the
other. Her plan hadn't been a preemptive strike, after all,
but a well-thought-out business proposal. "It was a surprise,"
he admitted. "Julianne released the details to the public
today."

Her brother was caught off guard also. "Did she, now? I
must have missed it with all the hullabaloo in there," he said,
gesturing to the hearing room. He rubbed the back of his
neck contemplatively. "Julianne has a lot of wealthy friends
whom she could have asked for financing, but she's careful

about combining her business with her friendships. There
are only two other people she trusts, who she'd turn to in
order to help her out of a jam: Carly or Nicky. Your guess is
as good as mine as to which one."

The senator held out his hand to Will. "I understand if
you can't forgive me, but I do appreciate you listening."

Will was still for a moment, staring at the outstretched
hand of the man who'd tried to ruin not only his career, but
his one chance at happiness with the woman he knew he
couldn't live without. He hesitated before finally shaking
the senator's hand. Trust was a perilous thing, Will was
learning. Something he needed to give as well as receive.

"Nicky," Julianne crooned as she buried her face
in the priest's neck. His arms wrapped around her in a familiar embrace she always found to be comforting. She'd been
on pins and needles all morning, worried about how the
hearing was going for Will. ESPN was televising it live, but
she and Carly had decided against watching it. Nicky's
arrival provided a welcome diversion.

And yet things were so different now. For most of her
life, she'd had a crush on the man holding her close. But in
a moment of absolute clarity, she realized that what she
thought had been love was nothing more than genuine affec-
tion and admiration. Not the deep soul-wrenching love she
felt for Will. No man in Julianne's life had ever measured
up to Nicky. Until Will. In a way, her epiphany was freeing,
but it also made her sad. If Nicky were to be suddenly gone
from her life, she'd miss him, but she'd survive. Julianne
wasn't sure how she'd survive if Will refused to forgive her.

"I told you that you didn't have to come," she said. "You
could have just wired the money after you found a buyer."

"The Vatican has diplomatic business here in Washington. I was able to combine business and pleasure this trip."
He pulled away from her, holding her at arm's length. "You
look marginally better. Still not as happy as I would like to
see you."

Julianne forced a bright smile onto her face. It was the least she could do for her oldest friend. He was doing her a huge favor, after all.

Carly entered the spacious screen porch of the house Sebastian had rented. "Owen is sound asleep." She placed the monitor on the rattan table and took a seat. "I want to go on the record as saying that I think it's a terrible idea to sell your mother's paintings, Julianne. They are all you have left of her. If you don't want me to invest, than at least let me loan the money to you."

"Actually, the paintings have already been sold." Nicky wrung his hands as he looked between both women.

"They have?" Julianne had trouble controlling her emotions. She needed the money their sale would generate, but she thought she'd have a little more time to adjust to the loss of her mother's heirlooms. Carly was right, the paintings were the last link to her mother, and Julianne suddenly felt a little sick to her stomach at the thought of never admiring them again, and of Owen never seeing them. "Will they go to a private collector?" she managed to choke out.

"Yes, but he's allowed for them to be displayed indefinitely at a small gallery in Milan."

Hope burned in her chest once more. "So Owen might be able to see them when he grows up?"

Nicky looked sheepish. "Actually, he'll be able to do more than that. The paintings now belong to Owen."

"What?" Julianne leaned forward in her chair. "Owen doesn't have any money, Nicky. Who bought those paintings?" She glanced sharply at Carly, figuring it would be just like her friend to find a covert way to lend her the money, but Carly's face showed as much bewilderment as Julianne felt. She shrugged her shoulders at Julianne's questioning glare.

"They were bought by the person who gifted you the paintings in the first place." Nicky reached out to take her hands between his. "Your father."

Shock reverberated through Julianne's body as Carly released a surprised gasp.

"I don't understand." And really, she didn't. Her father had barely been able to look at her much less speak to her since the accident that took her mother from them so many years ago. He'd washed his hands of any reminders of her mother—both her artwork and Julianne—immediately after the funeral and moved on with his life. The scars left from his rejection still stung. Will's rebuff had stirred up all the insecurities her father's banishment had caused, and Nicky's words weren't helping. Julianne was suddenly light-headed and unable to manage coherent speech.

Nicky gently squeezed her hands as Carly left her chair to kneel at Julianne's feet.

"Breathe," Carly prodded. Julianne's chest squeezed and tears pooled in her eyes as her body ached for the feel of Will's big hand comforting her, admonishing her to breathe. *How could this be happening?*

"Why? My father doesn't care about my mother's paintings," she managed to sputter out. "Or me."

"That's not true," Nicky said.

Anger pulsed through Julianne, rapid and hot. She yanked her hands out of Nicky's as if her skin was burned by his betrayal. "Don't you dare take his side!"

"I'm not taking his side." Nicky reached for her hands again, but Carly had gathered them up in her own, throwing a menacing glare at the priest. He pressed on anyway. "You know I disagree with how your father treated you. But grief is a weighty emotion. It does things to people. Changes them. Believe me, in my profession you see what type of damage grief can do, how it can destroy a person. Or, worse, a relationship."

Julianne choked back a sob. Her father had rejected her. Now Will had, too. Was she destined to be rejected by everyone she loved?

"I'm not defending his behavior, Julianne. Just explaining it. He was wrong to push you away. But I refuse to believe he did it out of hatred. At least not hatred toward you."

"Of course he did," Julianne cried. "He blames me for the accident and he hates me for it!"

Carly wrapped an arm around Julianne's shoulder and pulled her into a hug. "Shh, it's all right."

"The accident wasn't your fault, Julianne. If anything, your father blames himself for it, for demanding that your mother return home before she wanted to and for using you to make sure she did."

Julianne's head was swimming. Her memories of that night and the days preceding it had always been a jumble. The doctors and counselors told her it was better that way; it was the brain's way of protecting her. The little snippets she did recall never made sense. But Nicky had been with them. It was time he filled in the blanks.

"Tell me," she demanded.

Nicky sighed. "There really isn't much to tell. Nothing sordid or dramatic. Your mother wanted to stay at the villa a few days longer than she'd planned so she could finish a painting. My parents weren't returning to Rome for another week, so I didn't mind. Plus, there were some teenagers in the villa next door who'd I'd been hanging out with. You were a little annoyed that I wasn't paying attention to you and your father used that to his advantage. He never could stand to be apart from Daria for too long. I think he bribed you with a kitten if you'd beg your mother to go back to Rome."

Julianne almost smiled at the memory. Once, her father had been a doting parent, but he'd slipped away just as quickly as her mother had slid into the Mediterranean Sea.

"Daria finally gave in. Neither of your parents could refuse you anything." Nicky pierced her with his gaze but Julianne refused to feel guilty for being loved by her parents at one point in her life.

"The weather wasn't cooperating, though, and I tried to persuade your mom to pull over and wait out the storm, but by that time, she was just as eager to see your father. When she wasn't wrapped up creating her art, she was just as lovesick as he was." The corners of his mouth turned up in a slow grin.

Julianne wrapped her arms around herself. She wanted that kind of relationship. And she wanted it with Will.

"The rest of that night was fate, Julianne. It was nobody's fault. Not yours. Not your mother's. Not your father's." Nicky's tone was unyielding. "You can't continue to blame yourself. Your father doesn't blame you."

"I still don't know how you can be so certain. Or why you involved my father in the first place."

"Because as Carly said, the paintings are all you have left of your mother. They should remain in the family. For you and for Owen." Nicky's voice softened. "It's not that your father doesn't want them—or you. He just didn't know how to get past his grief. Perhaps this is his way of making amends."

A tear slipped from Julianne's eyes. She didn't dare hope that her father would ever be a part of her life again. That ship had sailed long ago. But she would do anything for her son's sake. Hadn't that had been her mantra since discovering she was pregnant? She could take her father's guilt money and rebuild her company. Then she would figure out how to get Will back because that was one ship she wasn't going to let sail away.

"My mother would be delighted that her grandson owned her paintings," she said through her tears.

"That settles it," Carly said as she wiped her eyes. "You're taking your father's money whether you like it or not. The paintings stay in the family for Owen."

"What happened to the reserved, well-mannered girl who used to be your best friend?" Nicky asked Julianne, a teasing glint in his eye.

"She married the devil of the NFL and now he's gotten her with child. You might want to stick around in case we need an exorcism."

Will sat in his car, his hands firmly gripping the wheel. He was sawing ragged breaths in and out in hopes of getting some control over his bruised heart. The senator said Julianne hadn't snitched on Will. That she loved him. He'd raced over to the house she was staying in to have the talk they should have had weeks ago. Before the sex messed things up. To work on cultivating that seed of trust before everything was ruined for good. To salvage a marriage that she'd only agreed to for the sake of their son.

When no one had answered the door, he'd walked around the back of the house. Staring into the screened porch, he'd seen her with her friends, locked in an embrace. *There are only two people she trusts*, the senator had said.

These past months, Julianne had been forced down a path not of her own choosing. Starting with the night in Sea Island when he'd taken her to his bed. The consequences of that night were just as much his fault as they were hers. He could no longer blame her for trying to shield him from those consequences by keeping Owen a secret.

Julianne didn't need a bastard from the Seaside Vista Trailer Park to complete her. She had her talent and her friends—*who she'd turn to in a jam*. Friends she obviously trusted more than him, not that he could blame her. If Will loved her, and he did, he couldn't stand in her way any longer. She wouldn't keep Owen from him. And Will wouldn't trap her in a marriage she never wanted. Sure, she'd said she loved him, but he knew she'd say and do anything to protect her son.

He forced his hand to turn the key in the ignition and drove away.

Twenty-nine

"Julianne! Julianne!" Annabeth clamored through the house shouting.

Julianne, Carly, and Nicky rushed into the kitchen to find her gasping, tears running down her face.

"Annabeth, where have you been?" Julianne raced toward her mother-in-law, panicked by her distress. "I've been trying to call you since I got here yesterday."

Carly pulled out a chair and Annabeth sat down, her face a mixture of smiles and tears.

"Well, we've been trying to call the two of you for the past hour," Annabeth said.

Carly grabbed her purse off the table and pulled out her cell phone. "Ohmigosh! She's right. Shane, too." She yelped as she read the text message on the screen. "It's over, Jules. The hearing never took place!"

Julianne looked from her friend to her mother-in-law. "Is this true? Will didn't have to testify?"

Annabeth shook her head as her smile beamed. "Nope. He wasn't even named by Coach Zevalos as one of the offenders. Will is totally cleared."

Shaking with relief and joy, Julianne retrieved her own cell phone, desperately hoping for a message from Will. Her body sagged as she scanned the screen and saw only missed calls from Annabeth.

"Give him time," Annabeth whispered as she came up beside her, draping an arm over her shoulder. "He needs to process everything first."

Leaning a head on the older woman's shoulder, Julianne pushed out a breath. She'd never been a very patient person, and giving Will time was killing her. Hopefully, though, when Will *processed* everything, he'd see she hadn't meant to hurt him.

"You did something to make this happen, didn't you?" Julianne asked.

"Nothing that I shouldn't have done years ago," Annabeth confessed. "But the less you know the better."

Julianne smiled at her. "I'm just glad it worked out."

"The rest of it is going to work out, too," she reassured Julianne. "You'll see."

"You still haven't answered my question, though. Where have you been?"

Annabeth's face flushed beneath her broad smile.

Julianne actually laughed. "Never mind. Your face just told me everything I need to know." She hugged her mother-in-law. "Good for you. At least one of us is happy."

"Hey!" Carly clicked off her cell phone. "Shane says they're having a big party at the training facility. Roscoe and Will are supposed to get there soon. Jules, let's get Owen and bring him."

A spasm of misery clenched in Julianne's stomach. "I don't think that's a good idea. At least not for me to go." She turned to Annabeth. "You should take Owen, though. Will would want to show his son off to his teammates."

"Oh, no you don't, Julianne." Annabeth's hands were on her hips. "There's no chickening out anymore. You two are going to resolve this if I have to lock you both in a room together."

"Oooo," Carly chimed in. "I know the perfect room, too.

Shane and I had a nice little talk in there once. It was very productive." Her grin and rosy cheeks told Julianne that a lot more than talking went on between Carly and Shane in that room.

Annabeth rolled her eyes. "Carly, get the baby."

Nicky excused himself, saying he had business in Washington. The two women somehow managed to get Owen packed up quickly, bundling him and Julianne into the car before she could protest. When they arrived at the facility, the celebration was in full swing. All that was missing was the guest of honor.

Shane greeted them at the door, hugging both Annabeth and Julianne before wrapping his wife up in his arms. "Hey there, Dorothy," he murmured, using his favorite pet name for Carly before kissing her soundly. He pulled away a little reluctantly, their gazes still locked in a form of nonverbal communication that hinted of something more to come later.

Julianne bit her lip to keep from weeping out of sheer jealousy. She and Will had briefly had that.

Hank slipped an arm around Annabeth, and Julianne's anguish gnawed a little harder in her belly. Everywhere she looked she saw happy people, happy couples. Coming here was a ridiculously bad idea. She turned to make her escape, but Brody blocked her way.

"Little dude," he said, holding his arms out for Owen. "Come to Uncle Brody and I'll introduce you to the guys."

He had the baby out of her arms before she could stop him. Owen squealed with delight. Tears stung her eyes as she realized even her infant son was having a better time than she was.

"Julianne."

She whipped around, and her heart leaped as she once again found herself peering past Roscoe in search of Will. But he was nowhere to be found. She pulled in a deep, calming breath, forcing her gaze back to Will's agent.

"I owe you an apology," Roscoe said, sheepishly. "It seems I jumped to some very wrong conclusions about you."

Julianne was too stunned to reply.

"Your brother set Will straight today, though. And he, in turn, set me straight. The assumptions I made were totally off base. Even under the defense of protecting a client and friend. I sincerely apologize."

Julianne hadn't heard a word past the part about Stephen setting Will straight. "Stephen spoke to Will today?" she repeated.

"Thank goodness for miracles," Annabeth said from somewhere behind Roscoe.

"Yeah." Roscoe stepped back to include Annabeth, Hank, Carly, and Shane in the conversation. "Right after the hearing was canceled. He explained that you didn't know anything about the hearing. You were simply defending Will, and your brother took advantage." He looked around, confused. "Will didn't tell you your brother spoke to him?"

"I haven't seen Will."

Julianne's heart was pounding as if she'd raced up ten flights of stairs. Will knew the truth. Could this possibly mean they could start again? Her knees began to shake and she reached out a hand to steady herself on something. Brody appeared at her side, propping her up.

"Whoa. Are you okay?" he asked.

She was definitely not okay. Instead, she was a quivering mass of nerves as she searched the crowded room for any sign of her husband.

"Will didn't bring you here?" Roscoe asked, a touch of concern in his voice.

"No," Annabeth answered for her. "Carly and I brought her."

"I don't understand. I dropped Will off at his car an hour ago. He was on his way to talk to you."

The bottom fell out of Julianne's stomach, and she gripped more tightly onto Brody's arm.

"We just left there," Annabeth said, reaching for her cell phone. "Maybe we crossed paths."

"No. Like I said, he would have been there almost an hour ago." Roscoe pulled out his own phone.

But Will hadn't come to the house. And suddenly, Julianne

saw the situation through his eyes. Will was giving up without a fight, most likely figuring he wasn't worthy of a relationship. She was familiar with his game plan because it had been her own rationale right up until a few weeks ago. Now, she realized true love was messy and worth fighting for. Fury replaced her anguish and Julianne ripped her arm off Brody's, her weak legs suddenly strengthened by anger. The idiot Neanderthal was jumping to conclusions—again. This time, though, she wasn't going to let him get away with it.

Annabeth and Roscoe were dialing their cell phones to no avail. Will was off playing the martyr somewhere. Most likely at his loft.

She turned to Brody. "Take me to him. Now."

Brody flinched minutely at her words, but then his mouth curled in a devilish smile. "Your wish is my command."

Julianne stalked out of the room. Brody took a few steps before turning back and grabbing Roscoe and Shane's cell phones out of their hands. "No way am I gonna let you boys warn him. I'd hate to spoil William the Conqueror's ass-wuppin'."

Will tossed the pizza boxes and take-out containers into the large trash bag. His loft was a mess. Thirty years as a neat freak and in one week it had all gone to hell. Time to right the ship. Still dressed in his suit, minus the torturous tie, Will had immediately set out to clean the place up once he arrived home. At the very least, it would keep his mind off Julianne.

As he loaded dishes into the dishwasher, he heard the key turn in the front door lock. *Shit!* He huffed out an exasperated sigh.

"Dammit, Brody, I should have broken every one of your million-dollar fingers last night and taken my key back."

When Brody didn't respond with his typical sarcastic retort, Will turned around. His lungs seized. It wasn't Brody standing on the other side of his kitchen counter, but Julianne. The rest of his body heated up at the sight of her.

Wearing a dress that looked like it untied with the pull of a string, she wobbled slightly on her wedge heels before purposely striding toward him. Silently she placed the key on the counter. Then she slid off her wedding band and dropped it down beside the key. The ping of the gold hitting granite reverberated throughout Will's nerve endings.

He stood frozen as she maneuvered through the living area, littered with Owen's baby items and a week's worth of laundry. She glanced at the sofa he'd been using as a bed, piled high with a pillow and blankets. Reaching down, she pulled out the Elmo doll Owen had been gumming the day before.

Owen!

"Where's Owen?" The words came out raspy because he was still struggling to catch his breath.

She looked over her shoulder at him, and something flared in her amber eyes. He thought it looked a little like seduction, but he figured that was just wishful thinking on his part.

Her full lips curved slightly. "He's at the party. The one your friends and teammates threw for you."

Nope, definitely not seduction. Will flinched from the bite of her sarcasm. His teammates would take his absence as another affront, but he hadn't felt in the mood for a party after realizing he couldn't hold her in their marriage.

"He was happily ensconced in the heavily tattooed arms of someone named Mongo, who was introducing your son to his first beer." She tucked the Elmo doll to her breast and moved toward the windows.

She was goading him. Will wasn't sure if that was good or bad.

He decided to play along. "You shouldn't have left him with Mongo. He's an offensive player."

Julianne tsked. "Just because he has a few tattoos doesn't make him offensive."

Will stifled a groan as he rubbed the back of his neck with a hand that was less steady than it had been before she arrived. "I assume my mother was there."

"Yep." She kept her back to him. "But she's too busy playing kissy-face with Hank to watch over Owen. Mongo will have to do."

Ah hell, he should have gone to the party. But he didn't want to go because he'd been certain that his mother would ensure Julianne would be there. And he'd made up his mind about giving her her freedom. From now on, the choices would be up to Julianne. Seeing her again would just tempt fate.

Except she'd left the party and was standing in his loft. The wedding band on the counter indicated she'd made a choice. His body ached to take her in his arms and persuade her to change her mind, but that was how this whole mess started. They needed to talk.

"Julianne . . ."

"You said there was a view of the harbor here." She quickly turned from the window. "I don't see the harbor."

He'd misread her eyes. They weren't seductive, they were anxious and maybe a little angry. Her chest was moving up and down rapidly as she drew in quick short breaths. Elmo was clutched in a death grip to her breast. Will wanted to soothe her, but he didn't dare touch her.

"Um." His mind tried to wrap itself around her question. "Upstairs. The view is from the bedroom."

She pointed to the stairs at the side of the room. "Up there?"

No! He couldn't sleep up there as it was. If he let Julianne up into his bedroom, he'd have to freaking move out. Instead he nodded, like an idiot. "Uh-huh."

His body throbbed as he watched her sashay up the stairs to his bedroom. Clearly still in idiot mode, he followed her. When he got to the landing, she was standing with her back to him, the glory of the Inner Harbor silhouetting her. He leaned a shoulder against one of the pillars supporting the ceiling, shoving his hands into his pockets to keep from hauling her to the bed.

"I'd like you to explain something to me." She didn't bother turning to face him. Her ramrod-straight spine and tense shoulders were his only indication that this was difficult for her. "How is it that you can be so fierce on the football field, never stopping until the play is dead, but you run away from a relationship at the first opportunity?"

An abashed sigh escaped his lips. "It's not like that, Julianne."

"Really? It seems that way to me. But then this marriage wasn't exactly a relationship, was it? Just an arrangement to benefit our son." He watched her struggle to swallow. "So I guess it really doesn't matter, does it?"

"It may have started out that way, but it quickly changed to something more for me." His voice was hoarse as he tried to work around the lump in his own throat. "Hell, maybe deep down I always felt that way and that's why I pushed for the marriage."

Slowly, she turned from the window, her eyes shimmering. Will wanted to close the distance between them, but he knew that wasn't the best course of action.

"So," she hesitated. "It came down to you not trusting me."

Will rubbed a hand over the back of his neck. He was ashamed to admit he was guilty of that infraction. "I didn't want to believe you'd sold me out. But I guess I was trying to sabotage the relationship just like you said."

Julianne nodded resolutely. "And today?"

His gaze connected with hers. Obviously she'd figured out he'd been by her place earlier. Honesty was the cornerstone to trust, so he led with the truth.

"Today I figured I'd let you make your own decisions."

Her face was baffled as she continued to stare at him.

Will sighed. "It was something your brother said this morning."

"Stephen?" she choked out. "You're suddenly listening to my mercenary brother?"

"No! I mean, yes." He held his hands up. "Let me explain. Your brother's rationale makes sense. He felt guilty that he'd allowed me to force you into a marriage. So he used the information against me to help get you out of it."

"What?" Her eyes got all squinty as she crossed her arms beneath her breasts. Will stifled a groan.

"Okay, the flaw in his plan was that he didn't ask you how you felt about the marriage. Don't you see? Neither of us asked you how *you* felt. We just took your choices away from you." Will blew out a breath. "Today, when I saw you with your friends, I realized that if I hadn't gotten you pregnant, then forced you to marry me, you might have been happy with someone else. And I didn't want to force you again."

She muttered something in Italian that sounded if not illegal, at least obscene. "That has to be the stupidest thing I've ever heard!" She was furious. Gorgeously angry. On the one hand, Will was grateful they were having this conversation upstairs, away from the kitchen and its ready supply of knives. On the other hand, her heaving breasts and flushed cheeks were really starting to turn him on.

"First of all"—she stalked across the room, ticking points off on her fingers—"there isn't anyone else. Yes, I blurted out Nicky's name that night, but not because we were in a relationship. It was because of some stupid crush I had on him for years. He'd been my fantasy lover for years. Until you."

Will's body went rigid as she drew to within six inches of him. "Second, no one forced me to do anything I didn't want to do. It took both of us to have a baby. And I didn't have to marry you. I could have contested you. But I didn't." Her voice softened to a near-whisper. "I felt a connection to you that first night on Sea Island. One that goes deeper than just our son. Something spiritual. Owen was created out of that connection." A tear leaked out of her eye. "But I can't risk my heart if you won't fight for me. For us. You can't just hide and ignore the hard stuff. You have to tell me what you want."

Tentatively, he reached across with the tip of his finger and wiped her tear away. "All I want is for you to be happy, Julianne."

"Prove it."

It was all the invitation Will needed. Cupping her face in his hands, he pulled her closer for a kiss, his mouth feasting on hers as she arched her body to meet his. It wasn't enough. He needed to be skin to skin with her. Without breaking the kiss, he reached between their bodies and tugged at the tie holding her dress on. Julianne pushed his jacket off his shoulders.

Will swore as he broke off the kiss and tore at the clothes on his body. Julianne seductively shed her dress, making him pant as she paraded toward the bed in her high-heeled sandals, bra, and panties. "If you want to be able to put those on again afterward, you'd better take them off before I rip them off," he threatened as he stalked toward the bed. Her eyes went wide as she did as she was told with a renewed sense of urgency.

Once she was naked, Will tossed her on the mattress, a seductive smile alighting on her face as she landed. He collapsed on top of her, supporting himself on his forearms, bringing his nose down to rest gently on hers.

She traced a finger along his biceps. "You haven't been sleeping here?"

"I couldn't. It seems I can't sleep without you in my bed."

"Hmm. That's going to make those away games awfully difficult."

"Yeah, but I can't think about that now. I need to tell you something before I totally lose my mind here." His body was on fire pressed against hers. He needed to get the words out. "I love you, Julianne. I was going to tell you that day when I screwed everything up. But you have to know how deeply I love you."

Her eyes glistened with unshed tears. "Like I said before, prove it."

Will kissed her then, reveling in her hot, silky mouth as his hands found all his favorite places on her body. He took his time pressing his lips to her temple, her ears, her cheeks, her jaw, her neck before exploring the rest of her body. Julianne murmured words of love in a multitude of languages, her hands stroking his skin. A sheen of exertion covered both their bodies by the time he finally entered her. She tilted her hips to better accommodate him and they both

abandoned themselves to the fevered lovemaking that was
and had always been the foundation of trust for them. Only
now, Will understood it.

They spent long, tender moments afterward lying inter-
twined, whispering to one another about their desires and
dreams. Will texted his mother, making sure Owen was
being taken care of. He got a smiley face texted back to him.

Julianne chuckled as she nestled in the crook of his arm,
her naked body arousing him again. "You see, second
chances aren't so hokey, after all."

"Speaking of second chances, Julianne, you don't have
to give me your design company."

She crawled onto his chest, bringing her face to face with
him. They needed to have this conversation, but the position
was doing crazy things to his body.

"For someone so smart, you can really be obtuse sometimes. I'm not giving it to you. I'm giving it to the town.
For you."

He tried to speak, but she pressed her fingers to his lips.

"You don't feel a part of the town because you don't have
a stake there. Despite the fact you grew up in Chances Inlet.
I understand that. So I'm giving you a stake. Use it or don't,
but it's there if you want it. You can have as little or as large
a role as you choose. Whatever is going to make you comfortable living there."

Will still didn't understand her logic. Maybe he never
would. The idea of a center for kids was intriguing, though.
And if it made Julianne happy to make Chances Inlet their
home, he wasn't going to argue.

He pushed a lock of hair off her face. Unease dimmed
her bright eyes.

"I'm going to have to trust you on this, Julianne," he said
gruffly.

Her face glowed as she leaned down to kiss the corners
of his mouth. "You won't regret it. You'll see." And she
proceeded to show him just how magnificent trust can be.

Epilogue

"You look amazing, Julianne. Like an actual princess," Sophie said reverently from where she sat at Julianne's feet, the skirt of her own dove-gray bridesmaid gown flared out around her on the floor.

They were in the large Glasgow suite of the Tide Me Over Inn, dressing for Julianne's wedding to Will. He had been adamant there be a real wedding, one with all the trimmings, including a wedding dress of her creation. This time, when they said their vows to one another, it would be for keeps.

Julianne stared at her own reflection in the floor-length mirror. The woman gazing back at her did resemble a princess, a look of faint wonder on her face. The gown had come to her one night, her fingers numbly sketching what would be her wedding dress, her mother's voice in her ear adding the subtle, artistic details of ruching and delicate beading. The result was so stunning, Julianne was very nearly transfixed by her own reflection.

Smoothing her hands down the skirt, she inhaled a deep, cleansing breath to calm her nerves. She couldn't figure out why she would be anxious. They were already married, after all. Nicky had even performed a private marriage mass the night before. Today was for show. A day to celebrate with their family and friends.

"And the necklace looks magnificent with it, if I do say so myself," Sophie added.

Sophie was at that awkward stage in life where she couldn't decide whether to be an artsy girl or a sophisticated socialite. Today, the teenager was all glamour. The pink highlights long gone, her cinnamon hair was curled loosely around her face, her apple-green eyes shimmering with delight. Her flair with jewelry was uncanny, and Julianne was looking forward to watching Sophie flourish as an artist. If only because the teenager reminded her a little of herself a decade ago.

"It is a lovely piece. Thank you for making it for me." Julianne smiled at Sophie's reflection in the mirror.

"Hey, I'm just glad you're having a real wedding this time. Unlike *some* people who get married on the beach, forcing me to make their jewelry out of pukka shells." Sophie scoffed with indignity.

"Really, Sophie, your father and I could have just hauled off to Las Vegas and gotten married. But we wanted to include you. So sorry you had to suffer through a week in Aruba. But you have to admit, your tan does complement the dress beautifully," Annabeth teased as she reached a hand down to her new stepdaughter, helping her to her feet. She wrapped an arm around both Sophie and Julianne. "What an incredibly lucky woman I am today. Two new daughters in one week." The last was said in a whisper as Annabeth's eyes misted over.

"No crying!" Julianne and Sophie chorused.

The three women stood arm in arm facing the mirror, with smiles ranging from bemusement to rapture adorning their faces.

"The flowers are here," Carly, dressed in a gown similar to Sophie's, called as she entered the room. "And the flower girl, too."

Julianne's four-year-old niece, Ariel, danced into the suite, a wreath of roses wrapped precariously around her blond curls, dipping below one eye. Her miniature dress was adorned with the same beadwork as Julianne's, making her look like a fairy princess, too. She gave her aunt an impish smile.

"Daddy says to hurry up because his tummy is rumbly."

Smiling fondly, Julianne reached down to adjust the wreath on her niece's dainty head. The young girl's cheeks were already flushed with excitement.

"Well, we can't have the senator's stomach rumbling throughout the ceremony, can we?" Gathering up her skirt and bouquet with one hand and Ariel's tiny hand in the other, she led the way down the grand staircase toward the garden where the wedding would take place.

Reconciling with her brother was also something Will had been adamant about. He'd insisted Julianne give Stephen a second chance. Considering the man had almost ruined Will's career, Julianne figured if he could cut Stephen some slack, she could, too. In the end, she realized Will and her brother were determined to protect her like the domineering alpha males they both were, and it was better to just accept it rather than fight it.

Stephen bent and chucked his daughter under her chin as they arrived at the vine-covered arbor leading to the garden. His eyes sparkled as they met Julianne's.

"That gown is stunning, Julianne."

"Daddy," Ariel singsonged, hopping on her toes. "Aunt Jules said I get to wear it when I get married."

A look of severe angst gripped Stephen's face. "That's great, sweetheart, but let Daddy get used to you going to preschool before you start talking about getting married, okay?"

Julianne laughed at her brother's discomfort. He wrapped her hand around his arm, elegantly clad in a gray morning coat.

"I guess it's never too early for me to start practicing walking the bride down the aisle," Stephen said with a grin.

Brody came through the arbor looking devastatingly handsome in his own morning coat. Catching sight of Julianne, he immediately clutched a hand to his chest. He looked back up the aisle toward the gazebo where Will presumably stood waiting for her. When he turned his head back, bright mischief burned in his eyes.

"I've come for the mother of the groom, but Julianne, it's not too late. Run away with me. Now. You're too good for that big ugly caveman."

Sophie giggled as Carly let out a long-suffering groan.

"She's marrying Will!" Ariel stomped her foot. "He's Owen's daddy and they love each other."

Annabeth grinned as she laced her arm through Brody's. "You heard the child, Brody. You're stuck with me."

Brody winked at Julianne before leaning over to gently kiss her cheek. "He's one lucky guy," he whispered.

Before he could step back, Julianne pulled him in for a tight hug. "There's some lucky girl out there who gets you, Brody," she murmured next to his ear. "The real you. Just be patient."

She squeezed his hand just as the harp began to play. Ariel gave a little squeal of excitement.

"That's our cue." Annabeth blew a kiss to Julianne as she took Brody's arm and headed through the arbor and down the aisle.

Sophie was next, her face radiant as she turned the corner and glided toward the gazebo.

"Okay, Ariel," Carly instructed as she handed Ariel her basket of flower petals. "Your turn. Carefully drop the petals just like we practiced."

A chorus of *ahhs* greeted Ariel's appearance through the arbor.

"Air kiss," Carly whispered as she hugged Julianne before taking her turn down the aisle.

The harpist began the wedding march and Stephen stiffened beside her.

"Last chance," he said. "You're sure about this? This is truly what you want?"

Julianne yanked on her brother's arm. "Yes, Stephen. I'm positive."

He grinned. "Brody's right. Will's a lucky guy."

She kissed her brother on the cheek, leaving a lipstick mark that she didn't bother to wipe off.

As they turned the corner, Julianne caught a glimpse of Will, superbly outfitted in his gray morning coat, standing stoically at the gazebo, Gavin and Brody beside him. He swayed slightly as she came into view and their gazes connected. A hint of a smile formed on his lips as his heated emerald eyes followed her path down the aisle.

Julianne barely noticed Will's teammates and the townspeople seated in the white folding chairs. She passed by Sebastian, Nigel, and Nicky without so much as a glance, her eyes fixed on those of her husband, the hum of desire burning deep within her. Her face nearly ached from the widespread grin she couldn't hold back.

The music stopped once she and Stephen reached the gazebo.

"Definitely a princess," Will said softly.

Julianne's knees nearly buckled at the heat of his stare. It was ironic, she thought; around the league it was believed that Will had ice running through his veins. One look into his eyes and Julianne saw only hot passion there.

"Your very own crazy princess," she whispered back.

The minister cleared his throat.

"Who gives this woman to be wed?" he asked in a booming voice.

There was a speculative pause as Stephen looked from the minister to Julianne. She held her breath, wondering what her brother was up to now.

"No one," Stephen stated, deviating from what they'd rehearsed the night before. "This woman comes of her own free will out of love for this man. And with the support and love of her family."

A tear rolled down Julianne's cheek. Stephen wiped it away before kissing her forehead and taking his seat beside his wife in the front row.

Owen chortled in delight as Julianne and Will said their vows for real this time, signifying their love for one another with matching wedding bands and sealing their promise with a kiss.

Turn the page for a preview of
Tracy Solheim's next novel

RISKY GAME

Coming in May 2014
from Berkley Sensation!

Prologue

THE GIRLFRIEND'S GUIDE TO THE NFL

It's that time again, girlfriends! Kickoff weekend in the NFL. Men in tight pants fighting over a ball. Yum. And while those macho talking heads on cable are breaking down the plays, we'll be giving you all the stats you really want to know: the inside scoop on your fantasy players. Ladies, forget about the games, because we all know the real scoring takes place *off* the field. So let's get right to it.

Rumor has it Miami running back Al Stephens and his estranged wife are reuniting—in court that is. According to sources, Stephens will spend his day off next Tuesday in a Dade County courtroom answering to his wife's claims of infidelity. Prepare yourselves, ladies, because it's about to get nastier than an episode of *The Real Housewives*. My spies tell me Stephens's wife, Jackie, will be naming the girlfriend of one of his Miami teammates as the *other woman.* Wouldn't you just *looove* to be in that locker room next week?

Speaking of *other women*, a little bear told me that Chicago head coach Ray Clooney has not one, but two new ladies in his life—besides his wife, of course. Clooney is apparently the secret father of a daughter with a certain Chicago-area restaurant hostess. No word on Clooney's wife's reaction, but I think it's a safe bet he'll be dining out for the foreseeable future.

Finally, the return of the pigskin brings back the fine tight end of Baltimore's Brody Janik, every girlfriend's favorite fantasy player. Brody and his sexy baby-blues have been laying low this off-season. Apparently, he's lost interest in a certain flavor of Candi. One has to wonder how—and with whom—he's been spending his free time.

Got some football fantasies to share? Maybe a photo of our favorite guys of the gridiron doing something naughty? Send it to us at TGFGTNFL@TWITTER.

One

Shannon "Shay" Everett had been in some compromising positions in her life. Many of them even of her
own doing. Growing up in a small town in Texas as the
daughter of a down-and-out rodeo rider and a beauty salon
owner, the rebellious tomboy had gotten into more embarrassing scrapes than she could reckon. That being said, she
never envisioned herself stuffed into a cubby inside an NFL
locker room late at night. A locker room that was supposed
to be empty. Only it wasn't.

Hell's bells.

Shay would have kicked her own butt for this little esca-
pade if it wouldn't call attention to her presence. The guilt
she felt over her task had already swayed her to abort the
whole thing the minute she'd entered the players' domain.
Not to mention that she was risking her internship with the
team and her scholarship along with it. She'd just have to
keep riding her bike to work and the bus downtown to campus because the money to replace her car's muffler wouldn't
be coming from some mystery Internet blogger who paid
handsomely for personal information on professional

football players. Shay was ashamed for even attempting it, but desperate times called for desperate measures.

Now she just needed to quickly extricate herself from her perch in a dark corner of the Baltimore Blaze's state-of-the-art locker room. Unfortunately, her punishment was to endure painful pins and needles in her legs and feet as she waited out the room's other two occupants, both of whom seemingly had all the time in the world. Not that any woman would complain, given the view. Standing twenty feet in front of Shay was Blaze tight end and all-American heart-throb Brody Janik.

A deliciously naked Brody Janik.

Shay willed her stomach not to growl at the sight before her, but Brody was a spectacular example of Grade-A Prime athlete in all his physical glory. Her mouth watered as she took in six-foot-three inches, two-hundred-ten pounds of perfectly sculpted muscle standing beneath a single shaft of light, the scene reminiscent of a statue of a Greek god on display in a museum somewhere. All that was missing was the pedestal for him to stand on.

Not that she hadn't seen nearly this much of his perfect body before. The whole world had. As the spokesman for an international designer's line of men's underwear, pictures of Brody wearing nothing but his sparkling blue eyes and his skivvies had been plastered all over billboards and buses for months now. Except tonight, those skivvies were notice-ably absent.

She licked her lips as he scrubbed his neatly trimmed brown hair with a towel, the muscles in his broad back rip-pling. Her eyes drifted lower to the two fine dimples on his backside—a backside that saw a lot of sun based on the lack of a discernible tan line. She slammed her eyelids shut as he turned to reach for something out of his locker. Surely this was an invasion of his privacy and she ought not to be look-ing. Except when would she get another chance like this one?

She blinked one eye open. *Dang!* He'd already pulled on a pair of skin-tight gray boxers, a noticeably abundant bulge hidden beneath the Egyptian cotton.

"It's going to be hard to keep this under wraps," a heavily accented male voice said from the shadows, a few lockers over.

Ain't that the truth, Shay thought. She mentally shook herself in an effort to refocus her attention from the sexy scene in front of her and tried to make sense of the conversation. The other voice in the room wasn't hard to recognize; the distinct accent belonged to Mr. pomegranate-smoothie-with-extra-flax-seed, Brody's personal trainer whose last name was something Scandinavian and unpronounceable. Shay only knew him by what he ordered in the Blaze commissary each time he visited.

"It won't be that hard, Erik." Brody tugged on a pair of jeans over his well-defined, long legs as Shay stifled a sigh. He sat down on the folding chair in front of his locker and pulled on his socks and sneakers. "The Piss Man only checks for banned substances. He's not checking my blood sugar."

Pardon? She tore her eyes away from Brody's still nude torso to concentrate on the words coming out of his wicked mouth. She'd heard the phrase "Piss Man" before; it was the players' nickname for the league representative who tested their urine for illegal steroid use. It was the second part of Brody's sentence that sent Shay's brain scrambling. *Was something up with his blood sugar?*

"That's not the point." The fair-haired Dane moved out from the shadows to stand beside Brody's chair. "What if you get disoriented on the field again and miss a route or a pass? It was only practice today, but it could happen during a game if you can't keep your sugar regulated."

Brody stood up from the chair, his chiseled body elegant and assured as he peered down at the stocky trainer. Good looks, superior athleticism, and an affluent upbringing gave him the confidence to believe he could beat anything. Even, apparently, a problem with his blood sugar.

"Not gonna happen." He pulled a black Lacoste polo over his head.

"You can't beat it by mainlining Pop-Tarts like you did

before your training camp physical," his trainer persisted. "That ended with you nearly comatose two hours later."

Shay worried her bottom lip as she considered the implications of Brody's predicament. As a PhD candidate in nutrition, she knew full well how the tight end's fluctuating blood sugar could spell doom for his career. She also didn't want to contemplate the scenario of him trying to regulate it by himself.

Brody shoved his sweaty clothes into his gym bag. "You worry too much. I'll take precautions before and during games. Whatever I need, I can have on the sidelines or in the locker room during halftime. My plan worked fine during the opening game last week."

His friend shook his head. "I'd feel better if you told the training staff. That way, someone could keep an eye on you during the game. You aren't always aware that your sugar's dropping until it's too late."

"No. Nobody knows. Not even my family." The vehemence in Brody's voice echoed throughout the empty locker room. "I'm in the last year of my contract and my mom is a diabetic. If the team finds out my blood sugar is a little schizophrenic, the negotiations for a new deal will spin out of control. Besides, Nate the Narcissist is a pain in the ass. The guy's got a real Napoleon complex. He'd lord it over me and take over my life. No thank you, dude." Brody shuddered as he zipped up his bag.

Shay sucked in a breath. Nate, the team's head trainer, was her boss, and she had to agree with Brody's assessment of him. As her mama would say, Nate was "all hat and no cattle." It was a relief to know she wasn't the only one who suffered under the man's delusions of grandeur.

When she'd accepted the internship, Shay was told she'd be working with the training staff on the day-to-day nutritional coaching for the players. The information she obtained would be useful in the compilation of her dissertation, an examination of carbohydrates used during peak athletic performance. Instead, Nate had banished her to the team's cafeteria, telling her he needed the extra hands to help the catering staff during training camp. Now the season was in its second week and he showed no intention of allowing her to move up from food service. By the time Shay realized she wouldn't get the experience she wanted, all the other internships had been taken. She needed the credits to fulfill a requirement to receive her degree at the end of the semester. Worse still, she wasn't even getting paid for the work she did.

"I don't like the risk you're taking, Brody."

"It's not a risk. I'll be fine as long as I make sure to eat a balanced diet every day. I wasn't diligent during the off-season and I'm paying for it now, that's all."

His trainer let out a harrumph of displeasure.

Brody's whole body tensed, his cover-boy jaw firm as he spoke. "I assume this is something we can keep between us. Or do I have to specifically invoke client-trainer confidentiality?"

The trainer bristled at Brody's tone. Normally laid-back and carefree, Brody was all business now, forcing his trainer to take a step back.

"Whoa." he held his hands up. "I'm on your side, Brody. Of course this stays between us. But you pay me to train and advise you. I'm just giving you my opinion, that's all."

Brody's face was cool and calculated for a brief moment before relaxing into the boyish charm he was famous for. "Duly noted, Erik." He slapped the trainer on the back, leading him toward the exit. "Tell you what. You can *advise* me on what to order for dinner tonight to keep my blood sugar from taking a nosedive."

"Are you buying?"

Brody's laugh sounded hollow. "Aren't I always?"

The room went dark and Shay waited a few minutes before letting out a pained breath as she eased her numb legs out from under her. She sat still for another moment, allowing her eyes to adjust to the darkness and her mind to adjust to everything she'd heard. Her heart skipped a beat as her cell phone buzzed in her pocket, its noise loud in the now ghostly locker room.

"Holy shitake!" she whispered, nearly jumping out of her

skin. "Good thing that didn't go off five minutes ago." She hadn't thought to silence her cell phone, innocently assuming the locker room would be empty. Her hand shook as she checked the bright screen to scan her text message. It was from Ken Daly, the manager of Celtic Charm, one of Baltimore's newest night clubs.

I need a bartender tomorrow night. R U interested?

Shay exhaled a slow, cleansing breath. She'd entered the locker room earlier to do something nefarious, only to have her conscience remind her that the ends don't justify the means. Now the answer to her financial woes had just landed in her lap—or on her cell phone, to be precise. Her mama would call it providence. Shay just called it dumb luck. Whatever it was, she needed to get out of there before someone else wandered in and spotted her where she shouldn't be.

She stood up slowly, her legs still tingling. Using the flashlight app on her cell phone, she carefully traversed the dark room toward the exit, happy that she didn't have to betray any of the team's players. The Blaze organization was known around the league for its professionalism and values. Aside from Nate, everyone Shay came in contact with at the training facility was friendly and she actually enjoyed the work—even if it wasn't what she'd expected.

Of course, the author of the blog *The Girlfriend's Guide to the NFL* would probably pay big money for Brody Janik's secret. But a Friday night tending bar at the hugely popular Celtic Charm could bring in a couple hundred dollars in tips—more if she dressed in a tight blouse and the kilt the waitresses wore. That kind of money would buy a new muffler and a month's worth of cell phone service, if she was careful. She didn't need to sell anyone's secrets.

Shay made it to the door and listened carefully to make sure no one was lingering in the hallway. The building was supposed to be empty, but Brody and his trainer friend could still be wandering around. Leaning against the doorjamb, she thought about the Blaze tight end.

Brody Janik was the epitome of a superstar jock; talented, rich, and gorgeous. Men wanted to *be* him and women wanted to be *with* him. Even more appealing, arrogance hadn't tainted his persona. Brody used his slow, wicked smile to charm everyone he met. He doled that smile out to everyone else like it was candy. Everyone except her. Instead, he treated Shay with his innate politeness. Almost as if he didn't put her in the same category as other women. And that stung. *A lot.*

Just like every other woman between the age of two and one hundred and two, Shay had a big-time crush on Brody. Of course, she knew it would never amount to anything. After all, she was the tall, awkward brainiac with frizzy hair and a wide mouth who was used to being the last one chosen to dance. At twenty-four, she'd had a lifetime of experience being ignored by men like Brody as they scoured the room for the attractive, self-assured women.

A more callous woman, bent on revenge, might sell Brody's story. But Shay Everett wasn't that woman. Brody was just like every other man who'd looked through her at some point in her life. She really couldn't single him out for it. It wouldn't be fair to all the rest of the men who'd ignored her.

Slipping out the door into the deserted hallway, Shay resolved to forget everything she'd heard while hiding in the locker room. Brody Janik wasn't her problem. It's not like they'd exchange more than a *please-and-thank-you* in the cafeteria as she slopped his meal on a plate each day. And she *wouldn't* worry about his blood sugar, either. At least that's what she kept telling herself as she crept out of the Blaze training facility.

Grabbing her bike, she donned her reflective vest and headed out for the ten-minute trek to her apartment, her conscience clear. She'd do some research for an hour or so before grabbing some sleep. She had swim practice to coach in the morning before arriving at the training facility at eight thirty. If she happened across information on hypoglycemia while she was scanning articles for her dissertation, so be it. As she pedaled along, she told herself it was professional interest making her curious. *Not* anything special about Brody Janik.

*She thinks she knows this player—but he
has a few surprise moves.*

From *New York Times* Bestselling Author

JACI BURTON

THROWN
by a
CURVE

A PLAY-BY-PLAY NOVEL

For Alicia Riley, her job as a sports therapist for the St. Louis Rivers baseball team is a home run—until she becomes the primary therapist for star pitcher, Garrett Scott. Out of the lineup with an injury, he's short-tempered, hard to handle, and every solid inch a man.

Right now, the only demand he's making on Alicia is that she get him ready to pitch in time for opening day. Except the sexual chemistry between them is so charged, Alicia's tempted to oblige Garrett just about anything. Garrett also feels the hot sparks between them, and the way he figures it, what better therapy is there than sex?

Now all he has to do is convince the woman with the power to make the call.

"Jaci Burton's stories are full of heat and heart."

—Maya Banks, *New York Times* bestselling author

jaciburton.com
facebook.com/AuthorJaciBurton
facebook.com/LoveAlwaysBooks
penguin.com

M1299T0413

If you want to score, you have to get in the game...

FROM *NEW YORK TIMES* BESTSELLING AUTHOR

Jaci Burton
TAKING A SHOT

A PLAY-BY-PLAY NOVEL

The last thing Jenna Riley needs is more sports in her life. While her brothers are off being athletic superstars, she's stuck running the family's sports bar, whether she likes it or not. Then in walks pro-hockey stud Tyler Anderson. As much as Jenna would like to go to the boards with him, she's vowed to never fall for a jock—even one as hot as Ty.

Ty, intrigued by the beautiful bar owner, becomes a regular. He senses that Jenna wants to do something more with her life. And as he gains her trust, the passion between them grows, as does Ty's insistence that Jenna should start living for herself. With his encouragement, Jenna starts to believe it, too...

"A wild ride."

—Lora Leigh, #1 *New York Times* bestselling author

"Jaci Burton's stories are full of heat and heart."

—Maya Banks, *New York Times* bestselling author

jaciburton.com
penguin.com
facebook.com/AuthorJaciBurton
facebook.com/LoveAlwaysBooks

"She is a rebel, a rule-breaker,
and above all, a romantic."
—Lisa Kleypas

FROM

SHERRY THOMAS
Author of *Private Arrangements*

Beguiling the Beauty

❧❧❧

When the Duke of Lexington meets the mysterious
Baroness von Seidlitz-Hardenberg on a transatlantic
liner, he is fascinated. She's exactly what he's been
searching for—a beautiful woman who interests and
entices him. He falls hard and fast—and soon proposes
marriage.

And then she disappears without a trace . . .

For in reality, the "baroness" is Venetia Easterbrook—
a proper young widow who had her own vengeful reasons for instigating an affair with the duke. But the
plan has backfired. Venetia has fallen in love with the
man she despised—and there's no telling what might
happen when she is finally unmasked . . .

penguin.com

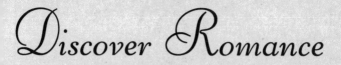